CATRIONA MCPHERSON

Dandy Gilver and a
Deadly Measure
of Brimstone

HODDER

First published in Great Britain in 2013 by Hodder & Stoughton
An Hachette UK company

First published in paperback in 2014

1

A CIP catalogue record for this title is available from the British Library

B format PB ISBN 978 1 444 73190 3
eBook 978 1 444 73189 7

Typeset in Plantin by Palimpsest Book Production Ltd, Falkirk, Stirlingshire

Printed and bound by Clays Ltd, St Ives plc

Hodder & Stoughton policy is to use papers that are natural,
renewable and recyclable products and made from wood
grown in sustainable forests. The logging and manufacturing
processes are expected to conform to the environmental regulations
of the country of origin.

Hodder & Stoughton Ltd
338 Euston Road
London NW1 3BH

www.hodder.co.uk

For Nancy and Jeff Balfour,
with love

I would like to thank:

Editrix 'Suzie Dooré' Lestrange, Francine Toon, Poppy North and everyone at Hodder & Stoughton in London.

Marcia Markland, Kat Brzozowski, Hector Dejean and everyone at Minotaur in New York.

Imogen Olsen for the copy-edit, Jessica Hische for the beautiful jacket design and Bronwen Salter-Murison once again for the Dandy Gilver website.

My wonderful agent, Lisa Moylett.

My family and friends in Scotland for their stupendous welcome when I returned to research this book.

My friends (who feel like family) in America for their stupendous welcome back again.

I certainly have fallen in with some good crowds.

And thanks, of course, to the smallest and best crowd of all: Neil McRoberts.

Prologue

Every time it was the same: almost midnight and the only light a quarter moon, bleary as a lamp on the last of its oil through the clouded glass of the window far above. Even that dimmed as the vapours shifted, stirred by movement, but was still enough to see by for someone who knew the way.

The thick steam muffled breathing and footsteps so there was near perfect silence, nothing but the occasional plink as a drop of water formed and fell, rippled and slowly calmed again. In the dream just as in waking life, to enter the water when it was still was a ritual. To shed clothes and shoes and slip under without a sound was a sacred thing.

Then came the perfect moment, floating in silence, in moonlight and cold still water. But in the dream something was wrong. The water should have been silken but felt sluggish, sucking and clinging instead of parting clean and clear. How could water be heavy?

Before the thought was fully formed, the touch came. Slow and bumping, far below the surface, a heavy object, rolling now, turning, until a cold soft arm and the trail of caressing fingers could not be denied. It was open-mouthed, tangle-haired, its limbs waving, dirt lifting off the skin. There was not the faintest gleam in its milky eyes, but in the morning and all through the day, when the rest of the dream had faded, those eyes kept staring.

I

Thursday, 26th September 1929

Dante believed, and has had some success dragging public opinion after him, that the ninth circle of hell, the last and lowest, the blackest and bleakest, the icy innards of Lucifer's mouth itself, would be the worst one. After recent events, I am unconvinced. Once having been besieged by foul weather with the gluttons, and sunk in ordure with the flatterers, could one really raise a shriek about a serpent or two? One would be numb, surely, long before one were bound in chains with those giants down there – poor giants, anyway: hardly their fault – and long past caring.

So it was with me by late September of 1929. Hugh and the boys had been ill with influenza for more than a month. Or rather, they had all started off with flu but had soon parted company: Hugh to a rumbling bronchial cough, Teddy to the sharp hack of pleurisy and Donald, always so much more trouble than his brother, to a full-blown case of putrid pneumonia which melted the flesh from his frame like candle wax and left him tottering.

I resisted all infection but not, more's the pity, because I had swept off to an hotel at the first sniffle (as had been my unmaternal and unconjugal impulse). No indeed, I had remained, mopping fevered brows, holding cups of broth to trembling lips and even removing noxious handkerchiefs with laundry tongs to carry them out to the boiler, but my eyes were as bright and my cheeks as rosy as ever. Which is to say, rather sallow, but rouge is a wonderful thing.

Not everyone was so stalwart. A few weeks in, maids and footmen were dropping like grouse on the Twelfth and even

3

village women began refusing to come in and do the rough lest they succumb to our pestilence.

'Good thing,' croaked my husband when I told him. 'This accursed germ must have come from the village in the first place. Let them keep it there.'

I set down the cup of broth smartly enough to make a little of it slop onto his bedclothes and then hurriedly dipped the corner of his napkin in his water jug to dab it away, for washing blankets was far beyond the current skeleton crew.

'Honestly, Hugh,' I said. 'You spent eight hours out-of-doors on the filthiest day of the year and refused to wear mackintoshes. You have no one to blame but yourselves.'

'Mackintoshes on a grouse moor!' said Hugh. 'Why not umbrellas?'

'Why *not* umbrellas?' I snapped back. 'I put Donald on the bathroom scales this morning and he weighed nine stone three.'

'What bathroom scales?' replied Hugh, shamelessly changing the subject.

'Nine stone three at six foot one,' I said. 'Which—'

'News to me we had such an article,' he went on. 'Mind you—'

I did not like the glance he cast at my frame as he said this and, although I knew very well he was baiting me, I rose.

'They are Grant's. I borrowed them.'

Hugh said nothing, but settled back against his pillows with both hands cupped around the broth and a look on his face that one could only call mischievous. My husband cannot hide his views of Grant, my maid, and my dealings with her: he thinks her above herself and me under her thumb; he deplores her taste in modish clothes and despises me for wearing them; he thrills to remember the many times in our early married life when he instructed me on the dangers of getting chummy with the servants. He imagines (*I* imagine) that I regret not listening and obeying and that I try to hide my regret to lessen his triumph. Marriage would be so exhausting if I really gave it my all but I rather let things wash over me, from maid and husband both, and find life easier that way.

Besides, Grant was another who had remained in peak form through the plague and I was feeling very kindly disposed towards her just then. She had taken on all manner of unseemly duties and the previous afternoon I had actually seen her carry a bucket of coal.

By such means had the household limped along for a month – soup at luncheon and the like – until without warning lightning struck us. Pallister, the butler, Gilverton's lynchpin, was seen to be red-faced and glassy-eyed one night at dinner and was heard at breakfast the next morning to issue four or five great whumphing sneezes. By tea he was in his pantry, wrapped in a shawl and shivering.

I went to the kitchen to tell Mrs Tilling and there found that the lightning had struck twice. She was blowing her nose into a linen square big enough to line a picnic basket, and was coughing carefully with a hand pressed against her bosom, a pleuritic cough if ever I heard one (and by then I had cause to know).

'My dear Mrs Tilling!' I cried, sweeping across the floor and pressing her into the Windsor chair by the range. 'You must— Gosh!' I had put the back of my hand against her forehead – the household had become a sort of Russian commune in the last few weeks, where such liberties were taken and no one to blink at them – and was rattled to feel the waves of heat and the high drumming pulse in her temple. 'Off with you!' I commanded. 'Straight to bed with a hot bottle.'

'Dinner . . .' she said in the weak voice of high fever.

'Rarebit for the invalids, and I shall go to Mr Osborne's,' I replied. 'Now not another word out of you.'

She filled a bottle and one for Pallister and took herself off towards the servants' staircase and the steep climb to her bedroom, leaving me standing in the silent kitchen meeting the huge startled eyes of the scullery maid with, I suspect, a huge startled look of my own.

'Yes,' I said. 'Now then. Go and see that Mrs Tilling has a fire in her room, please, Norah, and then send Becky to see me in my sitting room.' Becky, the head parlourmaid, was unbowed.

I had moved the other two maids out of the room they shared with her as soon as temperatures started climbing, had instituted, in fact, a ruthless quarantine all round. There were all manner of bunk-ups going on in the attics now – that Russian commune again – and pride was going to have to be restored by a perfect flurry of extra wages and little gifts when we were on our collective feet again, but the segregation was working.

At least, I thought with a groan, sinking down into Mrs Tilling's chair, it had been. Without her and Pallister, we might as well be rats in a sewer.

Upstairs in my sitting room, therefore, I tried to make myself ring the agency in Edinburgh again, to beg a cook, a housekeeper, even an extra maid or two, but I held out no great hopes of success. The gorgon in charge of the telephone knew how things stood at Gilverton and appeared to view the girls on her books as orchids to be tended, not as labour for hire at all. It was too disheartening to be borne and in the end I rang the doctor instead, to arrange what was beginning to feel like a standing order.

It was then, at that moment, that the ninth circle of hell was unleashed upon me and, as I say, benumbed by misfortune, I took it calmly.

'He's no' in, Mrs Gilver,' said his housekeeper. 'Have you no' heard?'

'Heard what? I don't think so,' I said, suspecting misfortune.

'It's all over Dunkeld. Scarlet fever. Thirteen cases and that was this morning.'

'Thirteen?'

'It was a birthday party. And one poor wee soul has been carried away.'

'Dreadful.'

'But she'd been bad with the flu already. Laid low, you know. And it's a terrible fearsome strain of it, I'm thinking.'

Whether she meant the fever or the flu I could not say for sure, but I withdrew my appeal for the doctor's attention – pressed it hard upon her that he was not required – and rang off. Neither Donald nor Teddy had had scarlet fever and, while I would not ordinarily worry about great lumps of eighteen and sixteen, I could not get the picture out of my mind of Donald shivering in his pyjamas as he stood on those bathroom scales.

'Come on then, my darling girl,' I said to Bunty. 'Let's walk down and shut the gates, eh?' She was fourteen now, a tremendous age for a Dalmatian, and the loss of her daily romp while I was nursing had not been the privation it should have been to her even a year ago. Still, she got to her feet, stretched, shook her ears and came to lean against my legs with her tail waving. I put a hand down and felt the jut of her pelvis under her warm fur, the slight scrape of bone against bone where all other tissue was gone. As Alec had said, 'if you boiled her for stock these days, she wouldn't set to jelly'. Just the sort of remark that the owner of a five-year-old dog will let drop unthinking. I had stored it up meanly deep inside and planned to use it on him when Millie, his spaniel, was toothless and threadbare, that way that spaniels go.

'Not like you, my love,' I said, letting her step ahead of me into the breakfast room, off which my sitting room opens. 'You are as beautiful as ever. Aren't you, my darling? Hm?'

'Oh, madam!' Becky had entered the breakfast room by the other door. 'She is that but she's awful stiff in the mornings. And when you think!'

She referred to an incident early in Bunty's life when she had just grown from a fat bundle of puppy to a lolloping, seemingly boneless creature with easily eight enormous paws, three tails and half a dozen affectionate tongues. Becky had opened the garden door at dawn one day and Bunty had jumped clean over her head to escape, knocking Becky flat on her back and out cold when her head hit the flagstones. This was better than the garden, of course, and Bunty wheeled round to make the most of it – a human who lay there obligingly to be trampled over and saluted with the moistest kisses a dog could muster. When Becky came round she was bruised but giggling.

'I can't bear to contemplate it,' I said. 'Well, Becky, it looks as though you're in charge. I won't be in for dinner, so eggs on trays or whatever seems best, and no visitors, I'm afraid. There's scarlet fever in the village.'

'I've had it,' said Becky.

'Good. I'll cancel all deliveries and perhaps you could go down in the dogcart and collect them instead.'

'It's just the fish tomorrow,' said Becky. 'Will I tell Miss Grant you're away a walk then, madam? She was getting ready to come up to you.'

'I shan't be dressing,' I said. 'Tell Grant she's free.'

Alec Osborne rarely uses his dining room. It's a miserable crypt of a place (even as dining rooms go, and they are, to my mind, the least inviting chamber of any house) with dark oak panels to its ceiling, mossy green wallpaper all round, and only two small windows facing due east on its short side. Add to that the usual measure of ancestors in oils and sideboards like mastodons, and a party would be stone dead before it had half begun. For that reason, Alec times what few dinners he cannot escape hosting for the summertime and spreads his board in a little temple by a pond with room to seat twelve in comfort and a fireplace which throws out heat like a steam engine. (I wish the mason who built that summerhouse chimney had built a few of ours, is all I can say.) Out of season he restricts himself to cocktails in his drawing room and on ordinary evenings Barrow, his valet, sets a table for one or two in the library as cosy as cosy can be.

'Still,' Alec said, as Barrow withdrew and left us with the soup, 'I usually manage to wriggle out of my tweeds, Dandy. Are you making a point?' He raised his eyebrows at my coat and skirt and then at his own smoking jacket.

'Of course not,' I said. 'When did I ever do anything so mealy-mouthed as that? I've just crossed some kind of Rubicon. Be glad I crossed it after tea or I might be here in my bedroom slippers and nightgown.'

'Better than poor Miss Havisham at least,' Alec said. 'She'd have been much more comfortable over the years if the clock had stopped when she was in her nightie. What's shoved *you* over the line then?'

'Scarlet fever,' I said. 'The boys haven't had it and it's all over the village, so the butcher and baker are forbidden the gates and I'm going to have to go shopping for pounds of tea and legs of lamb like a housewife.'

'Is every maid down?' said Alec.

'Not quite but they always make such a jaunt of it whenever they get away and Pallister and Mrs Tilling have got the flu.'

He dropped his spoon, but it was a plum-coloured smoker and Alec's valet-cum-cook doesn't allow so much as a sprig of parsley into the consommé so no harm came to him.

'Remus and Romulus have crumbled?' he said. 'You seem remarkably calm.'

'Yes. Good soup.'

'You can take it home in a jar if they haven't finished it up in the kitchen.'

'That's about the size of it,' I agreed. 'The kindness of my neighbours is all that stands between me and destitution now. I only hope the range doesn't go out because no one left standing knows how to relight it.'

'Mrs Tilling won't be off her feet for long,' said Alec. 'She's an ox. And Pallister . . .'

'Exactly,' I said. 'Pallister ill is so far outside human understanding that no one could hazard a guess as to *how* it might go. Like those tiny objects the physicists keep falling over that are never doing what they ought to be. My worry is that as soon as they're better the winter will set in and you know what that house is like in winter.'

'Bracing,' said Alec.

'Bracing to the hale and hearty,' I said. 'Flattening to the convalescent.'

'Are you thinking of going away?' Alec had an odd tone in his voice, hopeful-seeming in a rather unflattering way. 'Taking them off to the seaside and building them up with salt air and beef jelly?'

'It's a thought,' I replied. 'It would get us away from the scarlet fever and actually it might go along very well with what I was intending.'

'Which was?'

'Although we'd have to go a long way south to find seaside that wasn't a trial in October. France, perhaps? The mountains? But I'd spend all the money I'm hoping to use for my grand idea.'

'Which is?'

'Central heating,' I proclaimed. 'A boiler and pipes and radiators and every room in the house like a fireside nook from wall to wall and floor to ceiling.'

'Hugh *must* be ill,' said Alec.

'Hugh doesn't know,' I told him. 'So you see, getting him out of the house would be pretty handy.'

'Can you afford it?'

'Well,' I said, 'the thing is, you see, that Hugh has just offloaded some shares.'

'Really?' Alec cocked his head. 'He's selling? Everyone's buying.'

'That's what Hugh says too, but he won't tell me what. What are *you* buying?'

'Oh Dandy, join the modern age,' Alec said. 'One doesn't buy shares in *things* any more. One buys securities on margin with a broker's loan.'

'What does that mean?' I asked.

'I don't know,' said Alec. 'I think it's an American invention.'

'Aha! Then you *are* both at the same game. Hugh offloaded these shares, as I said – ancient old things he's been holding for sentimental reasons more than anything; I think his father first bought them – and he offloaded his London broker too and got one in New York.'

'Sounds like it then,' said Alec. 'Good for Hugh.'

'So we're sloshing in actual cash for a change, until he spends it on these New York securities. Only with the flu and bronchitis it's been the last thing on his mind. Or maybe he thinks I've done it for him. I couldn't say.'

Alec's face betrayed a not uncommon mix of emotions; he is my friend – mine, not ours – and his loyalties lie properly with me, but every so often when it comes to such things as farming, shooting and evidently money too some deep masculine chord begins to thrum in harmony with Hugh.

'You can't possibly be serious, Dan,' he said. 'Hugh thinks you've stepped in and carried out his business for him whilst he was ill – as he has every right to expect you to, by the way – and instead you're planning to fritter away shares in a gold mine just so you can waft about in backless frocks and not get gooseflesh?'

'I don't see it that way at all,' I said. 'I think if I choose to spend money wisely on solid goods instead of gambling on ticker-tape fairy tales Hugh should be thankful for my sound sense.'

'Sound sense?' Alec cried. 'Dandy, this is the biggest year the stock market's ever seen!'

'Why?' I asked.

'I haven't a clue,' said Alec. 'But the brokers and bankers do. That's good enough for me.'

'Well,' I said, 'I hope your trust in them is warranted.'

We tore bread, drank soup and glared for a minute. Alec gave in first.

'The mountains? The Alps, you mean? For the air?'

'The mountain air does the same job as ozone, doesn't it? Not to mention all the clinics and tonics and what have you.' I hoped he would not notice the inconsistency of my advocating cold mountain breezes while I was plotting to banish the fresh air of a thousand draughts from Gilverton for ever.

'And I'd take over Gilver and Osborne, would I?' said Alec. 'While you're away.'

'If a case comes in,' I said. 'It's been rather quiet.'

'Only . . .' He drank soup, then sherry, then a mouthful of water. 'I might be busy.'

'I can always have my post forwarded,' I said. 'If I go at all, darling. It was only a thought.'

'The thing is,' said Alec, 'I'm thinking of taking a wife.'

To my great satisfaction I did not drop my spoon, inhale a

crumb or utter a gasp. With perfect honesty, however, that was because my thought when I heard him was 'Whose wife? Take her where?' and by the time I had properly parsed his odd phrasing I was past the danger.

'Well, let me be the first to offer my congratulations,' I said.

'And so I'm going to have to put a bit of effort into finding one.'

'You— You mean— You're planning to marry someone but—'

'I need a wife,' he said, like someone telling a waiter he needed a fork. 'I need an heir. I'd quite like a daughter or two. A family, I suppose you'd say.'

'You've picked a funny time to start the auditions,' I said and my tone of amusement, my air of calm interest, was quite a feat, even though I myself say so. 'Why not wait until next season? You'd not get in the door of the first ball before one of the mammas picked you off.'

Alec shuddered.

'I can't face a season and the mammas,' he said. 'Not to mention some drip of a girl making eyes at me. I'd like to marry a woman who wants a home and a family of her own and won't pester me with a lot of silly nonsense beforehand.'

'You want to marry Hugh,' I said. 'If only he had a sister. Or a niece, I suppose.'

'Sister,' said Alec. 'Someone over thirty and past all the lovey-dovey stuff would be ideal.'

'Well,' I said briskly, 'I shouldn't have thought you'd have any trouble. A personable young man under forty, good family, nice estate, reasonable income.'

'Would you like to tap my ribs with a rubber hammer, Dan?' he said. 'I told you I couldn't face the mammas and you instantly become one.'

I laughed and he laughed with me and Barrow came in for the soup plates and the evening passed away on teasing and stock market gossip. It wasn't until I was in my little motorcar driving home that I let the mask fall and plunged into mourning. It was over then, Gilver and Osborne, Alec and me. Whatever he said about a sensible girl and life going on as usual except punctuated by babies, there was not the faintest chance that our pleasant round would survive the advent of a wife. I could picture her already and, try as I might, I did not care for her.

So I stopped in on Hugh, instead of making straight for my sitting room.

'How would you like to go away for a bit?' I said. 'A change of air, build you up again.'

'Bournemouth kind of thing?' said Hugh. 'Rather late in the year, isn't it? Last thing Donald needs is a sea fog seeping in at his bedroom window. I just paid him a visit and I see what you mean.'

'How about mountain air?' I said. 'Some crisp mountain air and those clever doctors?'

'Germans?'

'Swiss, I was thinking.'

'Same thing,' said Hugh. 'Can't say I could face the journey anyway.'

'Then put it out of your mind,' I said, bending to peck his cheek. 'Goodnight, dear.'

'Are you all right, Dandy?' he said, understandably startled. 'I didn't mean to shoot the idea out of the sky, you know. I'm with you as far as the clever doctors anyway. Marvellous what they can do with salts and hot towels and electrical currents these days.'

By which I took it that Hugh had been reading the back pages of old *Blackwood's Magazine*s again. I left him to his amusements and retired to mine, and to my daily duties too.

It was a good thing that Gilver and Osborne *had* been enjoying a peaceful spell because this evening, when I did not even open my correspondence until bedtime, was typical. We had caught a thief in March, unmasked a poison pen in June and then apart from Alec tracking down a bad debtor in August – this being quite a speciality of his these days, much less sordid to have someone like him tap the shoulder and 'old man' and 'dear chap' his way to a settlement than to have bailiffs calling – our little operation had been in dry dock. That was about to change.

'Dear Messrs Gilver and Osborne,' the letter began. 'We would like to engage you to solve a murder which has been grossly mishandled by the Dumfriesshire Constabulary and scandalously hushed up by the Dumfries Procurator, leaving our dear departed mother without justice and letting a brutal killer go free.'

I turned up the lamp and put my feet back down on the floor; I had tucked them under me, but this letter needed a straight back.

'Our mother was a guest at Laidlaw's Hydropathic Establishment in Moffat during the late summer, there to take the waters for a recurring back complaint. She was recovering nicely and was otherwise in excellent health, being a sensible lady of quiet habits. Her heart was perfectly sound. The doctor's diagnosis of acute heart failure was nonsense and the Fiscal's capitulation is an outrage. We await notice of your terms and remain, sincerely yours, Herbert Addie and Mrs Jas. Bowie (née Addie), "Fairways", Braid Road, Edinburgh.'

Well.

On the one hand, murder is the gold standard for a detective and any of that ilk who says otherwise is afraid of sounding callous and so is lying. On the other hand, these Addies – or rather this Addie and Bowie née – sounded like the very worst sort of client. They had already made up their minds and looked to Gilver and Osborne for corroboration; I would be forced to warn them, along with sending our terms, that we were servants of truth and that our fee only paid for us finding out *whether*, finding out *what*. No treasures on earth could buy our agreement to finding out *that*, dear dead mother or no.

However, the Addies were only part of the picture here. Fate, or coincidence as she is known in these rational days, had painted rather more, in the form of a hydropathic hotel with, one assumed, salts and hot towels and electrical currents, whither a loving wife and mother could remove her convalescing household while the plumbers were in. So long as she did not mention the brutal killer still at large, anyway.

2

Of course, I did not mean actually to deposit Hugh and the boys in the Hydro itself to take their chances; I am far from the doting domestic angel of popular imagining but there are limits. Besides, Hugh would not stand for it. He detests hotels and since I guessed that a hydropathic one would also be devoted to the doctrine of temperance there was not a chance of getting him to stay there. Surely though, I told myself, there would be a house somewhere in the environs that we could have on a short let. If Moffat were anything like Crieff and Peebles, or indeed Harrogate or Buxton or Bath, or *any* town where sulphurous waters bubbled up and Victorian merchants got rich from them, there would be any number of sandstone villas left over from the heyday. I would set Gilchrist, Hugh's factor, on it in the morning.

Before retiring, I composed a letter to Mr Addie, stipulating terms as he had asked but also requesting a meeting, for his to me had been as short on useful detail as it was long on epithets. At the beginning of the third paragraph I hesitated long enough to make a blot and then plunged on. It was easier in writing than face-to-face and if I offended him it would save me the trip on the train.

'Mr Osborne and I will carry out our investigations with the utmost rigour and attention,' I wrote. 'If we find cause to question the Fiscal's findings we shall report to you with all possible haste and shall stand by our conclusions as far as testifying in a court of law or at a second inquiry. Furthermore, in this case as in any, if we discover evidence of a crime we shall turn it over to the proper authorities as any responsible citizen would.'

Nice and pompous. My hope was that he would be so impressed

with the rectitude of my expression that he would miss the veiled rebuke. I signed myself D.D. Gilver, thinking that there was no point in meeting trouble at the gate, and took myself off to bed, walking at Bunty's pace and listening outside all three bedroom doors on the way. Pages were turning in Teddy's room but his breathing was too quiet to be heard through mahogany; Donald was wheezing a bit in his sleep but it was nothing to the dreadful gurgling and rattling one might have heard even a week ago, and Hugh was snoring with rampant abandon. No one who was not well on the mend could snore that way without coughing, surely.

In my room, I dragged the low stool from my dressing table over to the side of my bed and Bunty ascended in her new stately way, like a dowager clambering into her carriage. I banished from my mind the memory of her taking the width of the room in three bounds and sailing through the air to land in the middle of my counterpane with feet splayed and tail whipping strongly enough to flutter the curtains.

It took over a fortnight, in the end, to arrange our removal to Moffat but the delay was propitious in a number of ways. First, it gave me plenty of time to commune with plumbers by letter and on the telephone. Also, Hugh and the boys were at the perfect pitch of convalescence, rallied enough to be ready for a change of scene after weeks of their bedroom walls and the west terrace on warm afternoons with many blankets, but not so far recovered as to impose their masculine wills and drag the party off northwards to a moor or river to start the whole exercise again. What is more, the short wait for quarters meant that we could take Pallister and Mrs Tilling with us. They could hardly have come along in their dressing gowns when they were utterly bedridden and they would have baulked at missing out on the joys of Gilverton sans Gilvers in the ordinary way of things, but when I floated the notion of the healing waters and the sitz baths they each got a wistful, yearning sort of look in their eyes, never mind that neither they nor I knew what a sitz bath might be. (I have since learned that it is a fussy arrangement of large and small tubs filled with hot and cold water, between which one hops about, feet in the hot, seat in the cold, then seat in the hot, feet in the cold, until the doctor declares the process complete. It seems designed to frustrate the very reasonable hopes one might have that a bath will provide relaxation and comfort and it is one of the many aspects of hydropathy which led me to conclude that the doctors, despite the white coats and multisyllabic descriptions, are sadists and jokers and that their patients are credulous chumps.)

But all of that came later. On the day when Pallister and Mrs Tilling agreed to form part of our expedition to the southern hills and Grant got down my trunk and started packing, I had high hopes of killing two plump birds with one well-aimed stone.

After all, we had come through that tricky visit to the Addies without being stripped of our commission.

They were exactly as thrilled as I had foreseen upon discovering that Gilver was a scandalous female and not a respectable retired police inspector, a northern Holmes with an air of genius, or whatever they had been expecting when they rolled my name around and decided they trusted it.

Alec made up for me a little, as far as I could tell, when we were shown into Fairways' parlour three days after receiving the Addies' letter. I had decided that toughing it out was my best hope and, accordingly, I strode forward and thrust my hand out to the female of the pair.

'Mrs Bowie? Mrs Gilver,' I said. 'And this is Mr Osborne.'

'Mrs Bowie,' said Alec, with a little bow. 'How d'you do? And you, sir.'

'*Mrs* Gilver?' said the brother in a dazed sort of way.

'Mr Addie,' I concluded. 'And that's the lot.' I beamed at him and then adjusted my expression in accordance with the remarks to follow. 'First of all, let us offer you both our condolences.' This observance of convention seemed to soothe them; Mrs Bowie lowered her eyes and nodded and Mr Addie twisted up his face into a look of masculine stoicism. It was very similar to the look one would have if standing on a headland facing into a biting wind and, as they would have there, his eyes watered.

'And be assured,' said Alec, taking up the baton, 'that we will do our utmost to assuage your concerns about the manner of your dear mother's passing.' It was his 'endeavour to give satisfaction' speech, tinged with a little undertaker's mummery as this occasion demanded. I cannot deliver it with a straight face, but Alec is a marvel.

'I shall take you at your word, Mr Osborne,' said Mr Addie. He looked rather sharply at me and then back at Alec. 'As one gentleman always can for another.'

'Mrs Gilver,' said Mrs Bowie, as one lady to another perhaps, hoping to smooth the slight away. 'Do sit down and I'll ring for tea.'

Before the pot was empty we were well acquainted with the late Mrs Addie. She had been a widow of the sort that always makes me imagine she viewed the marriage itself as an irksome hors d'oeuvre. She had sewn hassocks, bred Sealyhams, terrorised troupes of little girls through their Brownie badges and generally kept a good slice of the world around her bowling along in proper order. When she had put her back out pitching tents at a Brownie camp in the Pentland Hills she had, according to her practical nature, taken to bed with unguents and embrocations to spare; and when these had failed her, she had rung up that nice Dr Laidlaw at Moffat and booked her usual room.

'For she was subject to it,' said Mrs Bowie, 'but Dr Laidlaw always cured her before.' She rose and came to stand behind my chair to look at the portrait photograph which had been fetched for us. Mrs Addie had been a solid woman of strong features and very smooth skin. These attributes, along with her little dark eyes, lent her what can only be described as a porcine countenance. Her children had inherited her looks, as is always the way when a parent is as plain as pudding, and Mrs Bowie had, besides, come in for her mother's scant and colourless hair. (Mr Addie had got himself a head of thick dark locks, but had let most of them go.)

'So your mother knew and trusted this doctor?' I said.

'She did,' said Mr Addie, darkly. 'She was quite taken in by it all. Always running off there.' He caught himself just before he absolutely started speaking ill of the dead. 'However,' he went on, 'Dr Laidlaw is gone.'

'And the place came under new management?' asked Alec.

'His children,' said Mrs Bowie. 'They inherited it. His daughter . . .'

'Oh, he *died*,' I said and, although there is no shame in dying, for it happens repeatedly in the best of families, one could not help seeing a little unflattering light cast on the spa.

'And they're . . . what? Attempting to run the place without his medical know-how?' Alec said. 'That should have caused questions to be asked, surely.'

'From what my mother said,' Mrs Bowie volunteered, 'it seems to be going along the same as before. After a little initial . . . They had opposing views on whether to sell up but their father's will split everything two ways and so they carried on. Some of the treatments had changed, but that's progress, I suppose.' She lifted her chin and gave her brother a defiant look as she spoke. I noticed it and Alec did too.

'They still have a hydropathic doctor on the premises then?' he said. 'Overseeing the . . . what have you . . . that goes on.'

'They do,' said Mrs Bowie.

'Of sorts,' said Mr Addie.

'What do you mean, sir?' I asked. 'Do you have reason to doubt the man's credentials?'

He stared at me, breathing out and in as if it cost him some effort.

'I couldn't say,' he said. 'Besides, it was a local man, a Moffat GP, who signed the certificate. Then the police, as we said. And the Fiscal. Passed the buck all the way. And now, sir,' he turned to Alec again, 'it falls to you.'

'And stops here,' Alec assured him. Then he added firmly, 'With Mrs Gilver and me.'

'Now, Mrs Bowie,' I said, 'you mentioned just now that your mother reported continued satisfaction with the Hydro. Did she write to you? Might I see the letter if you've kept it? Or the relevant portions if there are private matters therein?'

'She rang me,' Mrs Bowie said. 'On the Sunday. A very quick word, after her supper and before her bath.'

'Did she now?' I said, sitting forward and readying myself to take notes. Alec is wont to smile at my little block of paper and my pencil, but my notes have helped us many times. 'On the very last evening? What – to the best of your remembering, Mrs Bowie – did she say?'

The poor woman tried her best but, having retrod the ground countless times in the weeks of mourning, she remembered it only too well: the portents unleashed by the very ringing of the telephone bell; the darkening tone in her mother's voice; the sudden chill as they said goodbye. I managed to glean that Mrs Addie had reported a comfortable journey down in the train, had been pleased to be shown to her favourite room and happy that it had not been redecorated since her last visit. She had detected a falling off of quality in the cooking, with a greater emphasis on grated raw vegetables and lemon juice than she could greet with enthusiasm, but overall she was home-from-home again and her back was aching a little less even before the first splash of magical water was felt upon it. By that Sunday bath-time she was already anticipating putting on her outdoor shoes and taking a stroll into town for a cup of tea in the near future. Not on the Monday, because of her 'treatment', but very soon; and she would buy a picture postcard of the well or the bath house and send it to her daughter with her love.

'And she said she would post me off a box of tablet,' said Mrs Bowie. 'From the toffee shop.'

'What treatment would that have been?' I asked, with my pencil poised.

Mrs Bowie stared at her brother with wide eyes.

'Oh, I'm not an educated woman,' she said. 'I couldn't tell you all the fancy names and what they mean.'

'But nothing, one assumes, that would have put her heart under strain,' I said. 'Surely the Fiscal must have considered that.'

'We shall ask him,' said Alec, rather grandly. I resented a little the air of him sweeping in and summing up after his secretary had fussed on with her questions and her pencil. On the other hand, it was a competent way to bring matters to a close and one should be glad, I daresay, whenever Gilver and Osborne or either of its parts looks competent. Lord knows, we display other qualities often enough.

Our decampment to the Moffat hills was not as orderly as one might have hoped. My packing caused Grant no trouble, for she is an old hand, and with almost a whole motorcar at her disposal – since Hugh was neither hunting nor dancing and needed only tweeds, flannels and something for dinner – she did not need to pare her selections down. Indeed, I noticed three hatboxes being carried downstairs but said nothing. Donald and Teddy, along with Bunty, were going by train; Donald because he had never grown out of his childhood's carsickness and Teddy to keep him company. They were recovered enough to pack their own trunks with Becky's help and I kept them on their honour by requiring them to tick items off a list and sign it at the end. It had worked while they were at school and continued to work now; they are good boys really. The problem arose with Pallister and Mrs Tilling, for he could no more imagine serving us dinner without his silver spoons, wine without his decanters or tea without his pot than she could envision a distant kitchen having its own sharp knives, fish kettle and marble pastry board. When I saw her wrapping a rolling pin in brown paper, though, I had to protest.

'I like my own pin, madam,' she said. 'That there pin might be wood. There might be weevils.'

I declined to point out that weevils do not bore into wood and set up home there.

'We could run to a new one if so,' I said. 'Or – the cook at home when I was a child used a wine bottle filled with crushed ice. I used to help fill it. You really can't take everything, you know.'

Mrs Tilling gave a smirk of triumph whose source I could not immediately locate and unwrapped a corner of the rolling pin from its paper covering.

'There,' she said. 'That's a rubber stopper, madam, for the ice water to go in.'

I left her to it. Pallister and she were following with Drysdale in my motorcar and, although they outranked him, in this one respect he had final authority. He alone was responsible for the Cowley and he was quite firm enough to throw Pallister's wooden boxes or Mrs Tilling's rush baskets out onto the gravel if he felt the suspension was in danger.

Auchenlea House, where we were bound, was a whitewashed villa with red sandstone round its windows, sitting on an east slope with a view over the valley towards the Moffat hills. It was only two miles from the town and its bath house by road, less than that on the footpath, and from its drawing-room window the chimneys of the Hydro could just be seen above the tops of a pine and larch wood. It occurred to me, gazing across on that first afternoon, that looking due west towards trees was not the prospect I should have chosen for a healthful place such as I imagined hydros to be. A cliff top, I should have thought, or at least rolling downs, with morning sun to get the invalids in the mood for the new day. But then I was forgetting that the spas grow up around the springs and the springs bubble up where they please. I turned from the window and surveyed my lodging. It was commodious enough as a drawing room, well served with sofas and chairs, these in turn well served with tables and lamps. The fireplace was a good size too and there were radiators besides, but when I considered that this was it for sitting rooms – no library, no morning room, no billiards room even – I rather quailed. Hugh, Donald, Teddy and I would be in here all day every day when we were not actually eating or over at the Hydro, and I could not imagine it. I foresaw a lot of walks and tearooms if Alec and I were to discuss this case the way that we usually do.

For Alec had abandoned the planned hunt the minute he heard

the word 'murder' and was even now on a train, taking his hastily concocted bad back and tingling legs to a private suite with bath at the Hydropathic to see what they could do for him.

'Are you sure?' I had said. 'You're not worried that it might really have *been* a murder then?'

'Nice try, Dandy,' he had replied. 'But there's no way I'm letting this pass me by.' He referred, cynically in my view, to the fact that our last few cases had put me – by no efforts of my own – squarely in the middle of the action and had left him rather clinging to the side. That business at Portpatrick had merely been the last and worst of it. Even Alec had conceded that if one of us were to infiltrate a girls' school it would have to be me, but before that I had forged my way deep into a ladies' dress department in a High Street emporium and before *that* we had had to choose which one would sleep in a client's bedroom with her, pretending to be a maid. It was Alec's turn now without a doubt, and I was happy for him. He would worm his way into the heart of the Hydro and find the truth there and I would trail about the offices of the town officials checking their statements and putting their backs up. It was a sorely overdue rebalancing of the scales.

'Are you quite well?' said Grant, coming into the drawing room. 'Madam. You're frowning like anything. No point spending all that money on vanishing cream if you're going to scowl, you know. There isn't a cream invented that could smooth *that* out.'

'I've been looking into the sun,' I told her, flustered. Grant glanced out of the window, where thick banks of grey cloud filled the sky, but said nothing. 'Did you want something?'

'Oh yes!' she said. 'The master wants you. He's in a right old—'

I quelled her with a look; Hugh is quite wrong about the disposition of power between us.

'He has something he would like to discuss upstairs,' she went on, then bobbed, turned and left. 'Before he bursts,' she said as she passed through the door and her footsteps quickened as she hurried away.

Thinking that I might as well get it over with right away, I followed her. The hallway of Auchenlea House was square and imposing with a stone fireplace and a suit of armour at the bottom of the stairs. The dining room was across it on the other side of the front door, a mirror image of the drawing room, and the stairs went up the back with soaring stone-mullioned windows at each landing. It was a perfectly pleasant, solid, comfortable house. I squared my shoulders and went to find Hugh.

He was standing in the middle of my bedroom, with Pallister at his side. I blinked, but I suppose it was not actually my bedroom just yet. It was still, strictly speaking, one of the rooms in a house we had let, albeit the best one which was why Grant had ordered my trunk to be deposited there and had put all three of my hatboxes on the bed.

'Thank you, Pallister,' said Hugh.

Pallister bowed his head and left, no parting shot from him on his way out, I noticed.

'Dandy,' said Hugh. 'Pallister is displeased.'

'Pallister is always displeased,' I said. 'The last thing that pleased him was the Jubilee.'

'I too am a little surprised,' said Hugh. 'This house doesn't seem at all up to scratch.' I blinked again and looked around me. The bedroom had windows on two sides, four in all, looking out to the hills, and was big enough to hold a dance in. In fact, I glanced around it, it must have been the same size as the drawing room beneath it. It had a pale Aubusson carpet and pale green wallpaper. The hangings were green and white stripes and what with the dark mahogany furniture, the whole room reminded me of nothing so much as a chocolate peppermint cream.

'I think it's lovely,' I said. 'Much prettier than I dared to anticipate.'

'Four bedrooms,' said Hugh. I nodded. This one, its opposite number above the dining room and another two on top of these. And in between, on each landing, what had been dressing rooms were now beautifully cosy bathrooms, with gleaming pipes and the untold luxury of sheepskin rugs on the floor. I was already imagining stepping out of my bath onto sheepskin and was planning to buy some for Gilverton when we returned home to enter into the new era of luxury. On the other hand, this house with its radiators and bathrooms was supposed to be softening Hugh up for the unannounced changes. He looked about as soft as flint just now.

'Four of us, four bedrooms,' I said. 'What's the problem?'

'Pallister,' said Hugh. 'There is no basement, Dandy, beyond a sort of cellar. No butler's pantry. Just three servants' rooms above the kitchen wing.'

'Have you been scampering up stairs and down, Hugh?' I interrupted. 'You must be feeling better.'

'All very well for Grant and Mrs Tilling and the girl,' Hugh went on. 'But is Pallister to doss down with Drysdale in the stable loft?'

'Well, Grant doesn't mind sharing with the local girl,' I said. 'It won't be the—'

'*Interlocking* rooms, Dandy,' said Hugh. 'Three in a row.'

'Ah,' I said. I thought about it for a moment, wondering if there was some way to work it. If Pallister was in the outermost room then the women would be trapped until he was up in the morning. That would never do. If, on the other hand, he was in the innermost room, he would have three slumbering females to get past if he should need to. Worse and worse. 'I don't suppose there's an outside door?'

'To the roof?'

'Or Pallister could have one of the rooms upstairs and Donald and Teddy can share.'

'One bed in each,' said Hugh.

'Well, then there's only one thing for it,' I said. I felt my colour rising and I attempted a light laugh. 'It'll be quite a second honeymoon.' Hugh did not return my smile. In fact, his mouth formed a grim line as we both heard the sound of Bunty's toenails on the stairs. She appeared around the edge of the door, wagged her tail at me, gave Hugh a cold look and then made her way to the bed. It was lower than my bed at home and she managed without any difficulty to clamber onto it. She pawed at the counterpane, turned around twice and lay down, heaving a sigh and stretching.

'I shall inform Pallister that the matter is resolved,' Hugh said and stalked out.

I should have liked to avoid him for a few hours but if Bunty was here that meant the boys were too and I was anxious to see how Donald fared after his journey. I changed my shoes and hurried downstairs. They were in the drawing room, to where Mrs Tilling had already brought in the tea-things, having somehow managed to conjure bread-and-butter, scones and sugary cakes from somewhere. I subsided into the chair nearest the teapot and beamed at all three of my menfolk.

'You look all right,' I told Donald. 'Not too tired?'

'I fell asleep,' Donald said, causing me a pang. An eighteen-year-old boy should not fall asleep on a two-hours train journey during the day.

'Which made it pretty dull for me,' Teddy said. 'I had brought a pack of cards.'

'One doesn't play at cards on a train, Teddy,' I said. 'Who put that idea into your head?'

'You did,' he said, his eyes wide. He looked cherubic; it has always been a talent of his to be able to look that way. 'Going to Granny's. Snap.'

'Oh!' I said. 'Snap. I see.'

'You live in a very different world from us now, don't you, Dandy?' said Hugh. 'It would never have occurred to me to suspect my sons of setting up a poker school on a railway train.' For all the world as though gambling at poker – indeed, at anything – were not his favourite indoor pursuit in the world.

'Speaking of your world, Mother,' said Donald, 'guess who we saw.' He rolled a slice of buttered bread into a cigar-shape and bit the end off it.

'I can't imagine,' I said. I *could* imagine, of course, even if I lamented the rotten luck that put him on the very same train with the boys.

'Mr Osborne,' said Donald. I frowned at his cigar, offered the scones to Teddy and handed Hugh his cup.

'Hah,' I said. 'He must be on his way to London.'

'On this line?' said Hugh. Railways and their efficient use were an interest of his.

'No, he got off,' said Teddy. 'Of course he might have been stretching his legs,' he added helpfully. 'The train did stop for ages.'

'Although,' I said, 'I seem to remember we had a letter from Moffat recently. Perhaps he's decided to look into the case.'

'What was it?' asked Teddy, swallowing a huge mouthful of scone to allow himself to speak. He was twelve before we broke his habit of speaking with his mouth full and his new habit of half choking himself so that he got a share of the conversation was not much of an improvement. 'Burglary, blackmail, kidnap, murder?'

Hugh regarded me over the rim of his teacup. He did not frown or scowl, but just looked at me very smoothly. Grant would have been delighted with him.

'My dear Teddy,' I said. 'Most of my work is straightening out very dull grown-up misunderstandings. Sad and painful for those concerned, of course, but nothing to gloat over.'

'I wouldn't say dull, Mother,' said Donald. 'Not when you look back over all of them.' He put his cup down and sticking out the index finger of one hand and the little finger of the other he drew breath to begin to recall them.

'Or perhaps he's making a visit to someone in the vicinity,' I said. 'I do have a piece of news of the kind it's quite all right to pore over, you know. Mr Osborne is seeking a wife.' That arrested all of them. 'Perhaps he's visiting Moffat with matrimonial intent.'

Donald and Teddy were, as boys always are, mortified by this turn of the conversation. Teddy turned crimson to the tips of his ears and Donald simply rolled his eyes. He had had a terrible habit of chasing little girls, all through the pigtail-pulling years and well into the years of more dangerous attentions, but he had been cured of it by a hard-bitten Frenchwoman who had unveiled the mysteries of love and broken his tender heart. Teddy, at sixteen, was entering the eleventh year of finding girls and talk of girls quite simply ghastly.

Hugh loaded a plate with two scones and a cake, refilled his teacup, and made it to the door before he remembered that there was nowhere for him to go. He plumped down into a chair by the front window.

'Nice view,' he said. 'Too hot over there with that enormous fire. Think we were roasting an ox.'

'It *is* very warm, Mummy,' said Teddy. 'Sort of stuffy.'

'It's the hot pipes blasting away,' said Hugh. 'I'll investigate the boiler and try to temper the heat before we're all ill again.'

Yet another part of my plan, so neat on paper, seemed to be unravelling in messy reality. If Hugh and the boys did not glory in the warmth of Auchenlea House, I was in for some trouble when they got home to Gilverton and saw what had happened there. With relief, I turned my thoughts away from such domestic trivia and towards the case. Mrs Enid Addie and her heart attack (alleged) were what I had to pay attention to now.

3

I had jotted down the details from Mrs Addie's death certificate, with her grieving offspring watching me closely lest I make a mark upon it, and my first unenviable task was to track down the doctor who signed it. (I counted myself lucky that I had come this far in my detecting career without ever before having been pitched into this particular nest of vipers, for I could not see how a doctor could take such an enquiry as anything but a slur. I only hoped I could escape from his surgery without a threat of slander chasing after me.)

Escaping him, however, was not my only difficulty. Effecting an excuse to visit him was giving me some trouble too. Hugh and the boys awoke on the morning after our first night at Auchenlea House eager to plunge into their watery new pastime and appeared to take it for granted that I would be their hand-maiden for the duration.

'I'd like to go to the well itself,' said Teddy. 'It's only a bit up into the hills and there's a path.' He was making a good breakfast, despite the extra solidity that had come of Mrs Tilling attempting porridge on an electric stove whose efficiency had clearly caught her unawares. I grimaced to see him hack off a mouthful with the edge of his spoon and literally chew it before swallowing. 'But Donald's being a ninny.'

Donald did not throw anything, raise his voice, call Teddy worse or badger me to punish him and I glanced with real concern at him.

'Don't be rotten, Teddy,' I said. 'Neither of you is tramping the hills and sharing water with sheep when there is a perfectly good bath house in the town, where the water is served in glasses. In fact, I would imagine that the Hydro has its own supply of the water and there's no need to go to the public room at all.'

'Might be fun at the pump room,' said Donald. 'Might meet people there.'

Had I not been sure that my elder son was a stranger to the novels of Miss Austen, and had his heart not still been bruised by its recent travails, I would have worried that he expected an Isabella Thorpe to be promenading the pump room in a bonnet and waiting only for Donald Gilver to make her morning perfect. As it was, I took it as a good sign for him to be showing interest in society at all, even if he was not well enough to have taken up his lifelong war with his little brother again.

'There will be lots of people at the Hydro too,' I said.

'Ancient invalids,' said Donald.

'In bath chairs,' added Teddy, giggling.

'Interestingly enough,' I said, 'if there are, that's because the bath chair gets its name from the city of Bath where the hot springs drew the very invalids you dread, Teddy.'

'Gosh, let's get up there,' Teddy said. This was outrageously rude but, seeing Donald smirk at it, I let it pass.

'Hugh?' I said. 'Pump room, Hydro or hillside for you?'

Hugh was behind his newspaper. I held out no substantial hope that he would be impressed by there being a newspaper for him to be behind on this first morning. He spoke without lowering it.

'I don't intend to drink the local brew,' he said. 'I'm here for science, not magic.'

A devoted wife would have believed him. I, on the other hand, suspected that he knew what to expect from a glass of healing spring water and hoped to dodge it. In contrast, I am sure that my sons had in their minds something delicious; a kind of icy, sparkling cordial. Well, they would soon see.

'Let's stop off at the pump room,' I said. 'Just to see what it's like and then on to the Hydro for luncheon. You all have consultations booked with the doctor this afternoon and your treatments begin tomorrow. Back here for an early dinner and a quiet evening, I think.'

'What do you think the treatments will be, Mummy?' said Teddy.

'Oh, tremendous fun,' I said. 'Lots of splashing about. No mixtures, I assure you.'

For Teddy was the ninny when it came to anything in a brown bottle to be taken off a spoon. I had once seen Nanny and two nursemaids beaten when trying to get him to swallow castor oil. He wriggled out of the arms of the nurses and sent the bottle flying out of Nanny's hand before running off to hide in an attic. All I could say was that given the mess castor oil makes of carpets and polished wood I was not at all sure he was wrong in feeling it had no business in his insides.

The card propped up by the counter in the bath-house refreshment room – 'First glass 6d. Later glasses free.' – did not augur well for the stuff (no one would ever offer ginger beer on those terms) but the boys did not have enough experience of disappointment to be warned by it. The first sign that they were in for a nasty time came when the glasses were placed in their hands and they felt the warmth and saw the cloudy swirling. I took mine and glared at Hugh, standing there with his hands clasped behind his back and a smile on his face, then said a rousing 'Cheers' and toasted the boys' health.

No one else in the place seemed to be making a fuss about it. In fact, looking around at the other people settled at tables, sipping slowly, I thought that the Gilvers were probably the only newcomers. One old woman in long skirts and a shawl had come in, paid her sixpence, swallowed her measure and left with a promise to 'be back the morra'. She had not so much as glanced at her surroundings and I guessed that she had been coming here for all of her considerable years. If it was good stuff perhaps she was ninety-nine and past counting, had stopped looking round at the place decades ago. It was diverting enough for me, though. A grand room on a miniature scale, making me think of those gatehouses which mimic the splendours of the palaces they serve. Partly, it was the fact that the bath house was built in stone for even after all these years in Scotland, far from the softness of Northamptonshire, it still surprises me sometimes to see the lowly structures which are made of great square lumps of the stuff. Banks, charity schools, bowling clubhouses, public facilities of the very humblest kind, are all set to stand a thousand years as though they were castles for kings. It is very worthy, I suppose, but I still yearn for the ochre lime, horsehair plaster and crumbling ginger brick of home.

Inside was a miniature replica of the assembly rooms at Bath itself: a large chamber for promenading and doubtless for dancing too, a reading room, a discreet door to the closets where one might actually bathe, and all decked out in Adam plaster and sugared-almond paint from ceiling to floor. The decoration of the ceiling was particularly welcome: something distracting for when one tipped one's head back and took a good deep swallow.

Sulphur is a very necessary element, I am sure, for God would not have gone to the bother of it otherwise, but between the taste, the smell and the yellow tinge, it takes a worshipful frame of mind to thank Him for it when one is drinking a lukewarm quarter-pint of the stuff. I drained my glass and set it down.

'Goodness,' said Donald. 'It must be awfully beneficial.' I smiled at his composure.

'Ugh,' said Teddy. 'That's disgusting! Mummy, that's absolutely disgusting. Why didn't you tell me?' The other tables of patrons tittered softly at his ringing tone and look of outrage. 'This is mixture of the worst sort. And a whole cup of it too, instead of a spoon.' He put his half-full glass down on the counter and went to stand beside his father. The lines, I could see, were drawn.

'I'll have another glass, please,' Donald said to the grey-coated attendant who plied the ladle. He flicked the merest glance at Teddy and went on. 'It's a curious thing, isn't it, Mother, how late in one's maturity one gets a taste for such things as olives and whisky?' These were high-scoring cards, close to trumping his brother, for Teddy had felt the two years between them like a thorn his whole life through.

Donald accepted his second glass and sipped it as though it were nectar. He had, however, goose pimples of disgust all over his neck and I was sure he was paling.

'Sit down at a table and take your time, Donald,' I said. 'I have a little errand on the High Street but I'll be back directly. Hugh? Don't let him drown in the stuff, will you?'

My first enquiry, of a drayman stopped at the Star Hotel, furnished me with directions to the surgery of Dr Ramsay, which was a short stroll along the High Street and another up a narrow street running off it. I set off still with a sense of foreboding and turning the corner caused an extra jolt, for while Moffat High Street is wide, pleasant and Georgian, Well Street is a perfect microcosm of that sort of Dickensian city which puts one in mind of gin shops and pie shops and blue-legged urchins. To go along with this impression, Dr Ramsay's brass plate was on a narrow door beside a bowed shop front and his surgery was up a steep staircase in what I assumed was a converted tenement flat.

The doctor of my imagining was out on his rounds in a pony and trap and I would need an appointment to see him, an appointment I would make with a fierce secretary who guarded him like Cerberus at the jetty. Dr Ramsay, in reality, answered his door himself and waved me right in to his consulting room, seeming glad of the custom, almost of the company.

He settled himself back down in his chair, a leather affair on wheels, allowing him to whizz about between desk, patient and medicine chest (doctors these days are in thrall to the machines), and I took the chance to study him. He was a thin young man but with an air of repose which would have suited an older, larger person. He certainly had none of that nervous energy which might have explained his gaunt frame.

'Now then,' he said. 'And what can I do for you?'

'Yes,' I began. 'Well, my name is Gilver. I don't live here; I have my own doctor at home in Perthshire, but I'm staying here a while.' Dr Ramsay nodded.

'At the Hydro,' he said, which I supposed would be the usual thing.

33

'Actually, we've taken a house, but *for* the Hydro, certainly.'
He kept nodding. 'And I have a question to put to you. I believe you are . . . connected to the place?'

'Not . . . no,' he said. 'Not officially, no. Although I know the Laidlaws, of course. Now, what can I tell you? I am anxious to set your mind at ease.'

There was no real reason not to forge ahead with my questions; they were few and they were straightforward enough, but something about his manner arrested me. 'Set my mind at ease'? What made him think my mind was *un*easy?

'Are you the attending doctor for the Hydro?' I asked. 'If that is the correct expression.'

'They have no need of one,' he replied. 'Hydropathy is . . .' He drew a deep breath and opened his eyes very wide. '. . . a specialism beyond the norm, but Dr Laidlaw is a medical doctor.'

'But Dr Laidlaw is dead, isn't he?' I said.

'Dr Laidlaw Jr, I should say,' he replied.

'Ah!' I said. 'The King is dead, long live the King.'

'Almost,' said Dr Ramsay with a slight smile.

'But then,' I began, for this was puzzling, 'if Dr Laidlaw is a real doctor and was in attendance . . .'

Dr Ramsay had been reclining as far as his chair would let him, as though to take a long view of me, but now he sat up straight.

'Attending whom, Mrs Gilver?' he said.

'A friend of mine,' I lied in response. 'She was staying there recently.'

'What a remarkable coincidence,' he said.

I did not see what made it so, since I had sought him out. Different if we were in London and had bumped elbows at a party. My sense was growing that something was amiss here.

'Yes,' I said, making sure that none of that sense showed on my face or in my voice. 'A Mrs Addie, you might remember.'
He sat up even straighter and became even more remarkably still. 'And her daughter is so very distraught. It often happens, doesn't it, with a sudden death when the loved one is far from home. I

34

said I would have a word while I was down here, just to be able to reassure her that there was no need to worry.'

'And you are able to do so,' he said, sitting back again. 'There isn't. You have my word.'

'But why yours?' I asked him, innocent tone and expression going strong. 'Why didn't Dr Laidlaw sign the death certificate, Dr Ramsay? I always thought it was preferred for a doctor who knew the patient to take care of these things.'

'It is, it certainly is,' said Dr Ramsay. 'In this case, Dr Laidlaw chose not to.'

'But why?' I said.

'You would have to ask Dr Laidlaw that,' he said. I was surprised to see that there was a glint of amusement in his eyes. He put his foot up on the bar of his desk and leaned further backwards than ever.

'It didn't worry you to be asked?' I said. 'You didn't hesitate?'

'Clearly not,' said Dr Ramsay, with a smile. 'I was happy to help.'

'Of course,' I said, smiling back and hoping he would not see past it. Dr Laidlaw could not *possibly* have any innocent reason for refusing to sign a death certificate of a patient actually living at the Hydro. Far from Dr Ramsay's word being an assurance, the very fact that he was dragged into the business was extremely fishy. 'Well, acute heart failure is probably something you cover in chapter one,' I went on breezily. He frowned. 'Of your big red book of medicine.'

'Mrs Gilver,' he said. 'What laymen such as yourself often seem to forget is that everyone dies of heart failure in the end. That's the only cause of death there is, really, when you strip away all the secondary considerations.'

I nodded slowly for a bit as though digesting this. In truth, my thoughts were rattling about like those Mexican jumping beans one sees in the little snippets between the newsreel and the main feature.

'You are right, of course,' I said at last. 'I think my friend, Mrs Addie's daughter, would have preferred one of these secondary considerations, that's all. She was sure that her mother's heart was fine.'

'If her heart had been fine she would still be with us,' said the doctor. He spoke kindly as though to an imbecile. 'Healthy hearts don't just stop beating, you know.'

I could barely contain my astonishment. Healthy hearts stop beating all the time. They stop when someone jumps off a cliff, for instance, or drinks a bedtime cup of strychnine. Contain it I did, though, and forged on.

'I suppose – forgive me for this – there's no chance that you missed something, is there?'

'None,' said the doctor. 'She bore all the signs of having suffered a severe heart attack. And do you know what the chief of these is?' He was truly patronising me now. Had I been twelve and in cotton socks and had he been sixty and grizzled I might have been able to stomach it. As it was, it took all my effort not to draw myself up and squash him. With difficulty, I kept the annoyance off my face and simply shook my head.

'Being dead,' he said, very proud of the sound of it. 'It's a sad fact that dying of a heart attack is often the first clue that your heart wasn't healthy. And the last one.'

I nodded and even managed another smile, in acknowledgement of the clever points he was making, but inside I was reeling. Nonsense that a woman who had just been carefully attended through a bout of crippling back pain would not have had her heartbeat listened to! Nonsense that it would not, under the strain of illness, show signs of the weakness which was going to overcome it only weeks in the future! I could not understand why no one had thought it except me. He was speaking again and I snapped my attention back to him.

'I'm sure if you go to the Hydro,' he was saying, 'you'll soon be able to fill in any troubling little details. Beyond the medical facts, I mean.'

'Troubling little details'? Had the man any idea how suspicious he seemed? I supposed not or he would surely have shut up, and yet he was still talking.

'What she'd been up to,' he was saying. 'How she spent her last hours. All that – very soothing to the family that'll be.'

'I'm sure you're right, Dr Ramsay,' I said. 'Thank you for speaking to me.'

'Happy to help,' he said. It appeared to be his response to anything. A fellow doctor asking for his signature after a death with no visible cause? Happy to help! A perfect stranger asking questions about it? Happy to help her too. The man was a fool.

So I took my leave, descended the narrow stairs, hurried down the narrow street and emerged into the blustery morning again, just in time to see Hugh and the boys coming out of the bath house and beginning to look around for me. I waved and picked my way across the road between carts and bicycles and a motorbus which was wheezing away from the stop. I could not wait to get to the Hydro now. I had half thought the Addies were simply baulking at unwelcome reality, setting their faces against a natural death because they would rather it was not so. Dr Ramsay had changed everything.

It was with some initial difficulty that I put it out of my mind and tried to concentrate on my family as we drove from the High Street up out of the town towards the Hydro, but we were all impressed with our first sight of the place. Even Donald, who had been rather white and preoccupied-looking on the journey, as might be expected of someone who suddenly found himself two pints of sulphurous warm water the better just after breakfast one day, was distracted from his suffering. It was quite simply huge, much bigger than the place in Crieff and dwarfing Peebles' effort, more like a Russian palace than something Swiss-trained doctors would dream up to plant on a Scottish hillside, and as ornate as a Russian palace too. It was missing the onion domes and stained glass, but more than fully compensated with turrets, moulding, escutcheons, and the like.

The drive led along the hillside and behind the building, meeting it halfway up, and I assumed that there would be garden floors below with windows opening onto the terraces the brochure had promised. I had been right about the situation, though. It might be pleasant later if the clouds cleared before the sun went down but on a typical autumn morning it was gloomy beyond belief and, looking up at the forbidding bulk of it, counting the windows and considering how unlikely it was that any boiler known to man could heat so many rooms well enough to call them cosy, I was suddenly glad of my fox fur and drew it closer around me.

There were Turkish baths in there too, I thought, and steam rooms, unless they were the same things, and the famous sitz baths of which the brochure barely shut up for a single page and, all in all, I did not see how so much steam and hot water could be contained in a Scottish house without the whole of it being beset by seeping damp.

As we entered, I was half looking to see if the wallpapers were curling away from the plaster beneath and if the grain on the wood was rising.

As is so often the case, I was quite wrong and all was well inside the Moffat Hydro. The vestibule, entrance and hall were warm, dry, sweet-smelling – I saw a towering container of lilies on each of the side tables as we passed – and hushed. Hugh looked around himself with interest, evidently finding the place gratifyingly un-hotel-like. I saw Donald's expression clear as he relinquished his quiet foreboding that it would be some sort of hospital in all but name. He loathes hospitals even more than the generality and no one, let us face it, ever wants to go on a picnic there. Teddy's attention was caught by one feature only and that was the two-storey-high, coiling, gleaming, unbroken banister rail which, to judge by the way he was gazing, clearly sang to him.

'No,' I said.

'No what?' said Donald. Teddy did not turn from the siren song.

'No?' said Hugh. 'I like the look of it so far. Beats me why you took that so-called house if this is what's on offer.' I shook my head and said nothing, although I dearly wanted to know how Hugh slept at night with tenants living in cottages of three rooms in total, if Auchenlea with its seven bedrooms and three bathrooms was a 'so-called house', for Grant had regaled me that morning with news of the servants' facilities: hot and cold taps and a snake with a rose on the end for rinsing one's hair with jets of clean water.

'Think what your hair could look like,' she said, 'rinsed in pure clean cold water.'

'Cold?' I said.

'Good for the scalp,' said Grant.

'In fact . . .' Hugh was walking about the hall with a very proprietorial air, a few steps this way and then a few steps that, looking up the stairwell and all but testing the floor under his feet with little stamps as though to see if it was sprung for dancing. 'Well, we shall see.'

I could not pursue the hints because we were being borne down upon by a magnificent figure. She was quite six feet tall in her flat shoes and tremendously ill served as to *ligne* by her plain white dress, poor thing. On her head was a confection of starched linen, twisted and folded into a fantastical shape. (I only knew it had started as a linen square because I had seen the nurses in the convalescent home during the war constructing these sculpted enormities with my own eyes. They made them up seven at a time, deft and distracted, while smoking and laughing with their friends, and I had always thought they should do it out on the street corners for sixpences.)

'Matron?' I said, guessing.

'Well,' said the impressive individual, 'I suppose so, but I don't insist on it. Mrs Cronin will do nicely. And you must be the Gilvers.'

We admitted as much and before Mrs Cronin could do more than gather breath to begin her welcome, we were hallooed from above by a voice as loud as it was fruity.

'Welcome one, welcome all. Welcome to Laidlaw's House of Potions,' it said, and then a trousered bottom appeared hanging over the banister rail and shot downwards towards us. The owner of voice and bottom jumped clear of the finial, garnering Teddy's instant admiration (the dismount of a finialled banister is what separates the real daredevils from the pretenders), and bent himself double in a bow.

When he rose, it was with an extravagant gesture, flicking back his butter-coloured hair into perfect place. He smoothed it once with a hand, shot his cuff deftly and stepped forward to shake hands.

'Thomas Laidlaw,' he said. 'How d'you do.'

'How d'you do,' said Hugh, baffled.

As was I. The banister trick and low bow were at one with the man's costume: black tie before luncheon, like a conjuror. But the easy smile upon his sleek, pink face, his confident manner, almost over-confident for one who surely could not yet be thirty-five, and that fruity voice said otherwise. His greeting of me was impeccable too, a nod and a handshake in place of the kiss and smirk for which I had steeled myself. The boys shook hands and murmured their 'sir's and Laidlaw turned and presented his sister to me. I had not noticed her joining us; who would have while the brother whizzed down and vaulted clear?

'Dorothea Laidlaw, Mrs Gilver,' he said to me. The female half of the operation was not decked out in matching form, no evening gown nor spangles here. Instead she was dressed in rather plain tweeds and one of those very soft felt hats which look as though a limp lettuce leaf has been laid on one's head and left to wilt there. She resembled her brother in the usual way – the same nose (a family nose is hard to escape; when bemoaning my inheritance of straight hair and sallow skin I try to be thankful that the Lestons do not have one), the same lean figure, although hers looked set to remain lean whereas his was softening, the same hazel eyes except that hers were wide and clear and gazed at one with an engaging frankness while his were crinkled up at the edges in merriment or mischief.

'Shall we divide and conquer, Dot?' he went on. I saw her wince and did not blame her. 'Oops!' he said, without any attempt to make it convincing. 'We were Dot and Tot as children and these things do tend to stick, don't they?'

'Yes, Mrs Gilver,' said Miss Laidlaw. 'Let me show you around the hotel and—'

'Tut, tut, Dorothea,' her brother said. 'Hotel? Laidlaw's Hydropathic Establishment is not a hotel.'

'—my brother can take care of the rest of the party,' she went on, ignoring his interjection absolutely. 'Is it too late for coffee? Let's say coffee in the drawing room in twenty minutes then, Mrs Cronin, shall we?' She had a pleasant voice and an easy way with herself and, as I followed her out of the grand entrance hall into a passageway, I was forced to smile at the thought which had popped unbidden into my mind: to wit, that she was a lady. I suppose it was possible, for some doctors are gentlemen and her father had been a proper doctor and not a mere salesman of patent cures and odd contraptions, but somehow one put hydropathists, or hydropathologists, or whatever they were called, into the same drawer as lay-preachers and prison visitors, nonconformists all and not likely to come from the highest tier, whose members are usually, for obvious reasons, quite content with the status quo. Perhaps her father had used his money to buy his children into society, but then what of the dinner jacket and black tie at half past eleven on a Monday morning? What of Tot altogether?

Miss Laidlaw was pointing out 'treatment rooms' on either side of the passageway and I peered into one or two to be polite. In each there was a bier or couch arrangement covered in snowy bath towels and a smaller handcart, two-tiered like an hotel pudding trolley, upon which bottles and jars were laid as though to hand for operations at whose nature I could not guess. In one room there were contraptions, equally unguessable, drawn up on either side of the couch and in another, sturdy lamps mounted on tripods were trained on the empty bed. It all looked rather gruesome.

'You seem very well fitted-up,' I said, withdrawing my head again. 'It really is rather more than an hotel.' Rotten of me to return to the unpleasant moment, but I was interested in any sort of trouble here at the Hydro, sibling quarrels and all.

Miss Laidlaw, in reply, trailed a hand along the dado rail of the corridor, a fancy in ceramic, which formed rolling green waves, one after another, like pin curls, stretching all the way to double glass doors at the end.

'And rather less too,' she said. 'My father was a great deal more interested in the therapeutic side than in the question of bed and board. Tot was aghast when he saw the spartan state of the bedrooms. He was ready to give up before we even started. And I suppose, you do have to offer some comforts and entertainments as well as the actual . . . that's very true.' Then she gathered herself with a slight sniff and a rise of the chin. 'Father would be entranced to see the modern improvements in electric heat particularly, but through here, it's all as he envisioned it. Exactly as he laid it out.' She opened one of the double doors and ushered me into Equatorial Africa.

It was the changing room for the Turkish and Russian baths, I discovered, a short corridor lined on both sides with cubicles, wooden shelves and lockers at the near end. At the far end was another doorway covered over by a curtain and there were no words for the heat which rolled out as we passed through.

'Phew,' I said, letting my fur slip down to my elbows.

'This is the cool room,' said Miss Laidlaw. 'One hundred and twenty degrees.'

I sank down onto one of the beds arranged about the walls of the 'cool' room and looked around while I waited to become accustomed to it. The place was beautifully appointed: mosaic underfoot and colourful china tiles depicting Roman scenes on all the walls. At the far end, more of the heavy velvet curtains were drawn across a second doorway.

'The warm room,' said Miss Laidlaw. 'One hundred and thirty-five. Let's walk through quite quickly, since you're dressed in outdoor things.' She held one of the curtains aside and I followed her into the warm room, across it into the hot room – an unspeakable hundred and seventy – and across that, at a trot, but still sure my hair was dropping out of set and my face-powder caking, through the last set of velvet curtains and into the delicious coolth of a marble chamber like a little temple, with niches all around and beyond it, steps leading down into a long bathing pond surrounded by silk ferns and soft lamplight.

'The plunging pool,' said Miss Laidlaw. 'Dip your wrists, Mrs Gilver, and you will be refreshed.'

I shrugged off my gloves, pushed back my sleeves and sitting on the lip of the pool reached my hands down into the water.

'Oh!' I could not help exclaiming. It was icy cold, as cold as the burn water in Perthshire. 'Gosh, how do you keep it like this?'

'It's from the upper spring,' said Miss Laidlaw. 'It comes straight to us, beautifully cool.'

'Well,' I said, 'I suppose it's healthier freezing cold than warm, anyway. Dirt and all that, I mean.'

'Dirt?' said Miss Laidlaw, looking rather startled.

'Not to say dirt, exactly. But don't germs at least do rather better in warm water?' I gabbled on, making it worse than ever. 'And I'm sure you're never done draining it and cleaning.'

Her face now was quite frozen, as well it might be at this blatant and clumsy meddling in her business. She said no more on the subject but only offered me a small towel to dry my hands and went on. 'Through there is the Turkish bath or steam room.' She indicated an etched glass door with a chromium handle. 'And just here you see the beds for salt rubs and oil rubs.' She had waved a hand back at the little temple and I thought to myself that she might call them beds but in fact they were marble slabs with water sprays looming above them. I felt quite sure too that it would be 'cool' spring water which would come spouting out of these sprays to finish one off after the pummelling.

'Wonderful,' I said, thanking God in His Heaven that I was well and needed none of it. 'And do you advise the patients on how long to stay in and what have you?'

'No, no,' said Miss Laidlaw, 'the Turkish and Russian baths are open to all our guests at their discretion.'

'Ah,' I said. 'They're . . . closed just now?' I looked around the empty beds and still water.

'Um, no,' said Miss Laidlaw. 'I expect everyone is having treatments.' There was a pause while she and I both remembered the

43

long passageway with empty treatment rooms on either side. 'Or getting ready for luncheon.'

I gave her a bright smile and then, to help the moment pass away, I strolled over to a second door leading out of the spray-bath temple and put my hand on its chromium handle.

'And what—?' I began, but stopped as I met resistance.

'We don't use all the facilities any more,' she said. She glanced at the door and her face clouded briefly. 'There's a great deal of research being done all the time on hydropathy and physiology. Some of the earlier treatments have been superseded by others. And to be honest, fresh air and exercise are a lot more use than some of the more . . .'

'I see,' I said. I noticed that as I let go of the handle and moved away, the little bit of tension which had hitched her shoulders up left her and she smiled again. 'Do you have trouble persuading your regular guests to move with the times?' I asked. I was inching my way towards Mrs Addie. She frowned politely, not under-standing me. Perhaps I needed to inch a little more boldly. 'I would imagine that any of your father's patients who had always enjoyed "the old ways" would be hard to dissuade of their benefits.'

She threw another look at the locked door, her eyes showing a lot of white like those of a nervous horse.

'People can grow very attached to ideas,' she said quietly. Then with a valiant lift of her chin, she went on in quite a different tone. 'So, these are the medical facilities. I'll just take you up the ladies' stair and show you the private rooms.' She was off. 'You'll see the ladies' drawing room when we rejoin the rest of your party. As well as that we have a gentlemen's billiards room, a gentlemen's smoking room, the winter gardens and the dining room. But we encourage all our guests to be outdoors all day if the weather is even slightly cooperative.'

She had galloped up a staircase as she spoke, with me puffing along behind her, still feeling the effects of the stultifying heat, and now we found ourselves on a bedroom corridor, with carpeted floor and satiny papered walls covered with pictures of roses and fat children in aprons.

'I did a little redecorating,' said Miss Laidlaw. 'Not that that's my particular . . . but as I said, my father . . . And I did so want to be able to keep it going after he died.' She threw open a door.

I stepped forward to see what she meant and found myself in yet another world, far from carpets and watercolours. The walls, curtains and linens were blinding white, the floor stained almost black and the furniture – the high narrow bed, the bare dressing table, the small hanging cupboard and the inevitable towel-draped couch – were made of plain oak without the slightest adornment. It was a wonder Miss Laidlaw's father had managed to find such stuff: the Victorians were not known for their love of clean lines and the kind of beds one could sweep under with a broad broom.

'How delightful,' I said. 'And how amusing that what must have seemed very peculiar when your father chose it is now slap bang in the fashion.' I told the truth about being amused; I was not, however, delighted for I *am* a Victorian – I have given up pretending otherwise – and to sleep in such a room would make me feel either as though I had taken the veil or had been found guilty and was serving it out in solitary confinement.

One thing which did strike me as we made our way down the main – shared, one assumes – staircase was that Hugh would love it. He prefers his quarters barrack-like and added to the fact that the billiards room was for gentlemen alone at the Hydro (and the smoking room too), and that the ladies could be hounded out into their own drawing room with glares and snubs, he would have been as happy as a sandboy here.

When we arrived in the drawing room, which was an unre-markable enough apartment, only a good deal larger than normal and with more pillows strewn in the chairs and chaises (one assumed for the comfort of rheumatic guests), Hugh, the boys and the other Laidlaw were already there. As well as, I was happy finally to see, a few other residents, perhaps as many as five – and this in a room which could hold fifty without it showing.

'Dandy,' said Hugh, rising. 'I've made a decision.' I managed to contain my amazement as he laid out the many sound reasons for it. 'Right on the spot,' he said. 'And you'll be much more comfortable too. And Laidlaw here tells me that he's a great believer in port wine and stout as tools of convalescence.' Laidlaw, looking more like a waiter than ever, gave a short bow and clicked his heels. I wondered if he had a medical excuse to serve whisky too, for Hugh could not survive an evening without at least one glass of the filthy stuff. 'In fact, perhaps the boys could join me.'

I did not answer at once because, looking around following Hugh's gesturing wave, my attention had been caught by one of the other few guests present in the drawing room. I could see nothing more than a pair of crossed ankles and a pair of brown brogues, the rest being hidden behind a *Scotsman* (held in a grip rather tighter than its customary editorial style could explain). But I knew those ankles well and recognised the easy way one was slung across the other.

'Not the boys,' I said. The Laidlaws took my pronouncement without any show of emotion beyond a faint smile on her part and a sentimental dip of the head on his. 'Mother love', his face seemed to say. And 'typical female' was what I took from hers. The boys themselves, with the perfect self-absorption of the young, accepted their parents' clamouring for the honour of their company without turning a hair. It was Hugh who skewered me with one of his best looks. No chance of getting 'mother love' past *him* unexamined.

'Let's not discuss it now,' he said, loath to pitch into a domestic dispute in public, although I foresaw that there would be no avoiding one in private later. 'Now we three fellows all have medical examinations this afternoon, I believe? In the meantime, I think I'll take a stroll down the path you mentioned, Laidlaw, and have a look at the river. Ash path, Dandy, perfectly dry underfoot, in case you're worried. Donald? Teddy?' They rose; a river, even one which could only offer a lowly trout, and that to three gentlemen without a rod amongst them, was still a draw. Hugh would inspect the banks and plantings, scrutinise the water for gravel clarity or peaty opacity, scramble down and tug out scraps of the very water weeds to determine whether and how well this river was managed and discover exactly how short its management fell of his own of the rivers at home. Donald would listen and offer thoughts about the rivers of Benachally. Teddy would throw pebbles and, if there was an overhanging tree-limb, might climb out along it and dangle there.

'I shall see you at luncheon,' I said, waving them off, and then wandered over to sink into an armchair beside the brogues and wait for the newspaper guard to be lowered. Alec gave me his most impish smile but did not mention the awkwardness.

The first thing he did say to me was as much a surprise as a disappointment.

'Pretty clear why Ramsay got in on things then. Poor Dr Laidlaw couldn't even sign the death certificate, much less get a fool like Addie to face simple facts head-on.'

'Why couldn't he?' I said.

'Blind prejudice,' said Alec. 'Although I've always wondered how prejudice can be blind if justice is too. Blind to different things perhaps? Funny sort of blindness, though.'

'Alec,' I said. 'You're wittering. Why couldn't he?'

'I'm musing,' said Alec. 'Perhaps even philosophising. I don't, my dear Dandy, witter. She, by the way.'

'Ahhh,' I said. 'Dr *Dorothea* Laidlaw. I see. I didn't *think* that peculiar man looked much like one. What does he mean by such a get-up in the middle of the day?'

'He hasn't been to bed yet,' Alec said. 'The get-up's left over from last evening.'

'Why on earth—' I began and then Alec's bombshell, which had rolled across the carpet intact, burst at last. 'Medical examinations!' I said. 'Dr Laidlaw's going to examine Hugh? He'll curl up and die!'

'Only his chest,' said Alec. 'When I found out the doctor was a female I made sure my back trouble was in the shoulder blades – I had been tending towards the lumbar region; that's where I always feel it after a day's hunting – and only my shirt was disarranged. My trousers—'

'He'll die,' I said.

'—passed through the exam without a glance from her.'

47

'The boys are used to Matron, but Hugh will climb out of the window and down a drainpipe to get away.'

'Didn't he have a Matron of his own in his day?'

'A retired sergeant!' I said. 'Sergeant Black. Poor little boys of eight and suddenly only Sergeant Black instead of Mummy.' We spent a moment thinking – I was anyway – what a lot that explained if you went in for such things and then got down, at long last, to business.

'If Mr Addie's mistrust of a lady doctor is all that's afoot here,' I said, 'then you could melt away before Hugh sees you.'

'Would that it were, would that I could,' Alec said, sounding like someone translating Latin verb tables.

'You said Dr Ramsay got wheeled on out of blind—'

'Exactly!' said Alec. 'The Laidlaws must have thought the Addies would swallow his certificate with less of a gulp than they'd take to swallow hers. But don't you see? They'd only care about having the death cert. spat out if they had something to hide. And they do have something to hide. I know it.'

'Yes,' I said. 'I got a strong whiff of something fishy during my tour with Miss— Dr Laidlaw. I couldn't say what exactly. What about you?'

'I couldn't say what at all,' Alec answered. 'Not even a fishy whiff. I just . . .'

'Hah!' I said. 'Don't tell me you've had a hunch. After all the sneering you've done about hunches to me over the years.'

'I don't sneer, Dandy,' Alec said. 'I tease. And it's not a hunch. It's a proper hydropathic clue.'

'Oh?' I said, sitting forward. Of course, he had been here overnight and might well have uncovered something already. 'What do you mean?'

Alec grinned. 'I mean,' he said, 'I feel it in me water.'

I told myself that they would have all sorts of salves and mechanicals here with which to treat bruises and so I kicked him.

4

Luncheon was, on several counts, a revelation. Remembering what Mrs Bowie née Addie had reported I had expected clear soup and rye wafers, but when I joined Hugh and the boys at one of the many tables in the vaulted and pillared dining room, the menu card announced potted shrimps, brown bread, cold ham, baked potatoes, egg mayonnaise, tomato chutney, apple charlotte and custard, and lest one faint from starvation before teatime there was the further option of biscuits, radishes, celery and cheese. Far from such fare driving one down to Moffat to the Toffee Shop for tuck, I wondered how one could rise from one's armchair even to start the journey. That was the first surprise: the menu.

The second was the crowd. After the empty treatment suite, the deserted baths and the hollow, echoing drawing room, I had expected the four of us to be marooned in a vastness (Alec had volunteered to take a tray in his room until I could break the news of his presence and hence the reason for ours to Hugh).

The dining room was certainly vast. It was designed after the fashion of a winter garden – indeed I was later to learn, when I got to know the layout of the Hydro properly, that it matched the winter gardens in the other wing – except that only the ceiling was glass, the walls between the mock pillars being plaster painted with outdoor scenes. The painter, very sensibly, had decided to depict rather better weather than was often to be viewed through the glass walls of the winter gardens proper, and there were palm trees, bougainvilleas, stretches of white sand and the straw roofs of distant village huts besides. Inside these exotic walls, tables were set for couples, fours and sixes, with good white linen and glittering Sheffield plate and, as I say, there was a trickle, a steady trickle, of guests entering, taking seats and unfolding napkins. I could not help noticing, as I glanced around, that there was not a Mrs Addie amongst the lot of them.

To be sure, I had never met the woman, but I had seen her photographic portrait, her children and her house and could have told an inquisitor everything about her from her felt hat to her rubber galoshes, from her morning paper to her evening prayer. None of the characters filing into the Hydro dining room that day were the sort to wear felt and galoshes, nor yet to say prayers, and the few who had newspapers under their arms, as though it were breakfast and not luncheon, had them turned to the sporting pages and society columns.

I was now, frankly, staring as they sat themselves down, lit cigarettes and started up desultory conversations with their neighbours. I could not get the idea of breakfast to leave my mind, for most of them had a dishevelled look, some yawning, some coughing as they lit what looked to be the first smoke of the day, and a few positively hungover. I recognised the careful movements and the yellow-tinged pallor from my unmarried days when I would have to go down to breakfast at house parties and face the bloodshot eyes of some young man as uninteresting now, in his headache and stomach troubles, as he had been in his wine and stories the evening before. One of the several benefits of giving up girlhood for husband and home was breakfast in bed at house parties and never having to look at a hangover again. Hugh, thank goodness, does not go in for them.

'Funny lot,' he said now, looking around. This was a wild excursion into gossip for him; usually he affects complete oblivion of anyone in the surroundings to whom he has not had an introduction. Before my detecting days I used to too. I wondered at the comment and turned to regard him. I found him staring back out of wide, unblinking eyes. Odder and odder.

'Invalids, I daresay,' I murmured. 'Here for their livers, by the looks of them.'

Hugh nodded and turned to address a speech to Donald.

Rivers was the topic and I stopped listening, but I did not stop watching and I am sure that I did not imagine the look in Hugh's eye. Amusement. Satisfaction. One of those looks that gleams, anyway.

As I worked my way through my potted shrimps, which were delicious and would make an ideal luncheon followed by the cheese and biscuits, if one could sidestep all the ham and custard in between, I watched the dishevelled masses come slowly to life. Glasses of warm water and lemon were served, brown bread was nibbled, shrimps ignored, and eventually conversation began to ripple and swoop amongst the tables. Someone laughed. Someone else called across half the room to arrange a tennis match. Someone groaned, but it was the groan with which a silly joke was answered, not a groan of suffering.

And as I watched I began to notice that here and there, like big black crows in a cage full of budgerigars, there *were* parties of Addies after all. Whatever their names were they were Addies at heart, sitting bolt upright like nannies at a party, eating their way stolidly through the courses and ignoring the twittering and plumage around them.

Mr Laidlaw appeared as the coffee was being served and took a cup with him as he walked about the room. He had ditched his dinner jacket at last, into a normal suit although rather light for the country, but looked no less of a head waiter as he made his circuit, stopping to chat, beaming, evidently entertaining since gales of laughter met his every word. He did not neglect the tables of Addies, but here he modified his demeanour, bowing, murmuring, cocking his head and spreading a look of grave concern over his face as one dowager seemed to issue a complaint. Indeed, he went as far as to set down his coffee cup, extract a small notebook from his breast pocket and jot something down in it with a pencil. The dowager did not crack a smile but she nodded firmly and with a word he was on his way again. He was making his way towards our table and he caught me watching him. I was facing him head-on, no chance to dissemble.

'Hello again,' he said. 'Hello, hello. Now, how are you settling in? Everything running smoothly? Feeling better already, are we?'

He was just the sort of man – hail fellow, well met – that Hugh normally cannot stand but there was no look of scorn or detestation here today although he did not go as far as to answer such inanity.

'Jolly good fodder,' said Teddy. 'I don't wonder people get better, sir, if you feed them like this every day.'

'Hear, hear,' said Donald. And I was torn between feeling fond pride at their manners for once and smarting at the sideswipe to Gilverton's kitchens.

'And your medical chores will all be over by tea,' said Laidlaw. 'Ginger snaps and cherry cake, I believe. But I did just want to warn you of the fire drill.'

'When is it?' asked Hugh, getting out his watch and flipping it open.

'Over the course of the next few days,' said Laidlaw. 'A better drill if we don't know exactly when, eh? But it'll be in the night, save anyone clambering out of a bath and shivering on the terrace in a towel.'

Hugh looked understandably disgruntled at this news but I knew he would not lament to me. He had been so pleased at besting me and escaping Auchenlea House that he would not for a pension admit he had let himself in for inconvenience and that I, tucked up alone in the room he had spurned, might have the better of it.

'Very sensible,' I said. 'What's a fire drill if everyone knows it's coming?'

'But you're not actually staying in the Hydro, madam?' said Laidlaw. 'Nor the young men?' He was giving me a sharper look than I had yet seen upon his face. I offered a faint smile in return. 'And your husband tells me you made quite a recent booking. I see, I see. Well, welcome one, welcome all.' He tipped me a salute and moved away.

I roundly hoped that he did *not* see and I did not think that he could, for neither Alec nor I had done a single thing to raise suspicion of our intent. Still, I worried because his words were puzzling.

'What a peculiar person,' I said, falling back on my grand-mother's way of dealing with puzzlement: stake a claim to sense and normalcy and blame the other party for any troubled feelings or confusion they might have caused. 'Finished, boys? What shall we do?'

'I'm awfully tired,' said Donald. 'Like a pit pony at dusk.'

'Like a python who's just eaten an antelope,' I corrected, looking at the crumbs on his cheese plate. 'I'm not surprised. Why don't all three of you tuck up on some of those nice deckchairs out on the terrace and I'll tell the doctor where to find you.'

'There's a croquet lawn,' said Teddy, hopefully.

'Rest first,' I said. Even Hugh agreed, to my surprise, and so I accompanied them out there, a deep terrace facing the lawns where the afternoon sun warmed the stones and released billows of scent from the stands of jasmine which stood like sentries outside all of the french windows. The deckchairs were filling fast, with the bright young things – not so young, all of them, but very bright – from the dining room, and I was forced to walk at an unseemly pace to secure three together from under the nose of another party.

'Hmph,' said one of these, a woman in her forties with the naked look of one who normally wears a great deal of paint but is currently doing without any. Perhaps such a look could not possibly be; it might come down to the over-plucking of eyebrows or the sheen of the wrinkle cream such women trowel on out of the same vanity that leads to the painting.

'Awfully sorry,' I said. 'Were these yours?'

'Come on, Pegs,' said one of the men who was with her. 'Let's go and float in the swimming bath and call that our day's treatment.'

'Pegs' giggled and turned with a swish of her pleats to follow the men back along the terrace.

'We're going to float,' she called, waving at some swaddled nappers she was passing. 'No contraptions for us today. Yah-boo! Sucks to you!'

53

There was a wave of laughter at this wit. We four Gilvers pretended not to hear her and instead made ourselves busy with pillows and rugs and cranking the backrests up and down until the angles were agreeable.

'I'll tell someone to let Dr Laidlaw know where you are,' I said. 'And I'll see you later. Now, be brave boys when the time comes, won't you?' I was looking at my sons but thinking of Hugh, naturally.

'Brave?' said Teddy. 'There won't be needles, will there?'

'Not a one,' I said. 'I'm sure the doctor will be as gentle as gentle can be.' I might have given Hugh a gleaming look of my own, something for him to ponder. Then I kissed all three of them on their foreheads and withdrew.

I told a passing maid – she might have been a nurse-orderly; the uniform made it hard to say – that Dr Laidlaw's afternoon's patients were on the terrace and then set about the task of finding Alec. There was no reception desk or lobby as in a normal hotel and there did not appear to be an internal telephone system either. I was loitering with no firm intent near the door which led to the men's treatment rooms when I heard heels clip-clopping rapidly across the parquet and caught sight of the matron-like figure from the morning whisking across the end of a passageway dressed in outdoor clothes. I shot after her.

'Mrs Cronin?' I said.

She stopped and turned. 'Mrs Gilver?'

'I was just wondering,' I said. 'Is there a . . . well, on a cruise it would be a passenger list. One of my sons thinks he spotted a neighbour.'

'Very possibly,' she said, and I was at a loss to explain the dryness of her tone. 'Name?'

'Oh, but with the Hydro so full, you couldn't surely . . . ?'

'Let's see,' she said. 'It depends if he's one of Doctor's or one of Master's.'

'I understand,' I lied, hoping that my face betrayed nothing. 'It's a Mr Osborne. A young chap. Bad back.'

'Ah, yes,' she said. 'I put him down as Master's but I was wrong. He's one of the doctor's after all.'

'And how would I find out where his room is?' I asked. She blinked. 'So I can slip a little note under the door.'

'I could deliver a note,' she said. 'Or you could pop it in the bag in the entrance hall.'

'Of course,' I said.

'But as it happens, there's no need. I'm glad you hailed me, Mrs Gilver.' There was a dramatic pause. 'I was looking for you to give you this.' With quite a flourish she produced an envelope she had been holding behind her back. My name was written on it, in Alec's hand. 'He thinks he spotted you too,' she said with a smile which lifted one side of her mouth, but left the other and both of her eyes unchanged.

'Ha!' I said. 'Gosh, what a— How—' I cleared my throat. 'Thank you.' I took the envelope.

'Don't mention it,' she said. 'We don't get many folk from Perthshire, what with all the hydros up there, right to hand. Two at once is very remarkable.' The rat-a-tat-tat of her heels on the polished floor began again and she was gone before I could shut my mouth, much less open it again to answer.

'Matron's onto us,' I said, slipping into Alec's room a few minutes later. It was another of the white chambers, with a metal bed-frame and an enormous bare window taking up most of one wall, but the view was across the valley and so the room was flooded with afternoon light. It was so warm, with the sun beating in, that the paint, distemper and wood varnish, the very soap which had been used to wash the floor, were releasing their pungencies to mix in the stifling air. Alec sat in the room's only armchair, a wicker one, looking stupefied.

'I have a hearty appetite, Dandy, as you know,' he said. 'But that luncheon and this sunshine have almost done for me. Could we take a turn about the gardens?'

'Hugh and the boys are on the terrace,' I said. 'Did you hear me?'

'I did, but all my blood's in my middle dealing with the apple charlotte. None left in my brain. Onto us how?'

'How disgustingly detailed,' I said. I crossed the room and after a moment's wrestling with the unfamiliar catch I threw open the window. 'I'm not sure, but she certainly hasn't swallowed the notion of our just happening to meet here.'

'Oh.' Alec was taking deep gulps of fresh air but was still not exactly sparking.

'I hope she hasn't twigged that we're detectives. If she's neck deep in Mrs Addie, anyway.' I turned away from the breeze to light a cigarette. 'Odd about the food, after what Mrs Bowie said, isn't it?'

'We haven't started detecting yet,' said Alec. He hauled himself to his feet and joined me, looking down over the grounds, and farther out across the valley. 'With any luck she only suspects us of an assignation.'

I coughed out a puff of smoke.

'In any case, we need to box shy of her,' I said. 'Pity. Because she gave an interesting little view of the Laidlaws just now. There's a split down the middle of this place as far as Mrs Cronin's concerned. There's them as is here for the doctor and there's them as is here for the master.'

'So Mrs Cronin might only be neck-deep in factional loyalties – remember the Addies told us that one of the Laidlaws wants to sell up and one of them wants to carry on?'

'But on the other hand she *might* know something about how Mrs Addie died,' I supplied.

'So Mrs Cronin's card is duly moved to the front of the box with one corner turned down,' Alec said.

'And actually, I don't know if you noticed it yourself but there do seem to be two distinct *sorts* of Hydro inmates. I thought so myself at luncheon.'

'But which sort is Matron all for?' Alec asked. I shrugged. 'Master is the more respectful term. And don't nurses tend to loathe lady doctors?'

'But she's a woman as well as a nurse,' I said. 'And Laidlaw is a bounder.'

Alec was lighting his pipe and he snorted and choked a little.

'A bounder, begad?' he said. 'And a cad and a rotter?'

'Oh all right then, a creep,' I said. 'As Donald and Teddy would say. Don't you think so?'

'Despite the fact that he's latched on to me in a rather mysterious way,' said Alec, striking another match and taking a second run at it, 'I took his act to be tailored to ladies.'

'Ugh.'

'I went as far as to think it a shame that all the charm and frivolity came to him and none to the poor dear doctor when it was she who got the actual looks.'

I thought back to Dr Laidlaw, her floppy hat and drab dress, and could just about see what he meant. She had very large soft brown eyes, like a Labrador retriever, and good cheekbones. An elegant jaw too, whereas her brother had the pudgy cheeks and double chin of a bon viveur.

'How do you mean, latched on?' I asked.

Alec shrugged. 'Seems to want to find something out without asking. Veiled remarks and all that, very tiresome. But probably irrelevant. Right,' he went on, after one of the long series of puffings with which he gets his pipe going. I always want to make choo-choo noises as he does so. 'Where do we start?'

'We need to piece together Mrs Addie's last day,' I said. 'See if we can find out where she was, what she did, try to fall in with the staff she'd have been seeing. You could cultivate any other long-term guests too.'

'And you?' said Alec, not exactly trustingly.

'I shall have to go and talk to the police, I suppose. I don't much care for them, you know.'

'You care for Inspector Hutchinson.'

This was true. Inspector Hutchinson had treated Alec and me to an unrelieved diet of sharp questions, scornful remarks and deflating summations during the case we had worked together, but had somehow earned our undying devotion that way.

'Not much chance of meeting his equal.'

'What are you going to say?'

'I have no idea. I'm hoping to hear more than I tell.'

'I wouldn't have thought so,' said Alec. 'Still, you have to keep busy somehow.'

I did not intend to steal his thunder. Nothing was further from my mind. Alec was here in the heart of things and, for once, I was not. It was no more than a redressing of the balance between us and at that it was long overdue. Nevertheless, when I left him, I found myself neither descending to the town nor returning to the terrace to see how my menfolk fared. Instead, I made my way back to the corridor of treatment rooms and to the Turkish baths at its end.

It was a very different place from the one Dr Laidlaw and I had walked through that morning. Almost all of the lounging couches in the resting room were occupied now, the occupants swaddled in robes and fanning themselves with paddles. I took no more than a couple of steps before I was accosted.

'Here, miss!' I turned. 'Oh, madam, I beg your pardon.' It was a nurse of some sort, a round little person in a blue uniform dress anyway, with the sleeves rolled high up on her reddened arms. She pushed a bale of white towelling cloth into my arms and propelled me towards one of the cubicles. 'You'll melt away if you come in here like that,' she said. 'Never mind ruin your fur. Lovely fur, madam, if you don't mind me. Just you ring the bell when you're changed and I'll come and take your things.' She banged the door shut on me and left me inside the tiny cubicle. There was a hook to hang one's clothes on, a net to pull on over one's hair lest it be disarranged upon undressing, and a bench with a velvet cushion to sit on while one unfastened one's shoes. I ignored the net, blessing my shingle, but sat down and started unfastening. How far was one to go? How many of one's things should one remove and how many retain? I unrolled the bale of towelling and found inside it a very fine lawn shift, armless and only a slit for a neckline like a partly unpicked pillow-case. It seemed to suggest that complete divestment was the order of the day, so after shrugging out of my tweeds and shirt, I peeled off my underthings too. I took off my earrings and wristwatch, my pearls and my bracelet and then wriggled into the shift, bound the robe tightly about me, and rang the bell.

The round little person reappeared like a jack-in-the-box. She held out a velvet bag, somewhat bigger than a boxing glove to look at and much bigger on the inside, having no padding, with a hinged wooden half-moon clasp, like a broken embroidery ring. 'For your jewels and things, madam,' she said. I scooped them up along with my bag and dropped them in. She snapped the half-moon closed, turned a little key and held it out to me. It was a silly little thing on a silk ribbon and I could not see the point of it when the velvet bag could be cut through with a pair of nail scissors anyway, but I dutifully held out my hand and allowed her to put the key around my wrist.

'I know what you're thinking,' she said, 'but feel it.' I took the bag out of her hands and had to tighten my grip before it fell.

'What on earth?' I said. 'Why is it so heavy?'

'It's lead-lined,' she replied. 'Safe as houses. Some of our guests use these instead of the hotel strongroom. And the key locks the cubby hole too.'

I followed her to the end of the cubicles where she deposited my clothes on a shelf and I locked the boxing glove into a tiny cupboard above.

'Now, on you go, madam, and have a lovely bath.'

'I've never . . .'

'Slowly does it,' she said. 'Cool to warm to hot, steam if you like, and into the pool to refresh again. Just ring a bell if you feel like a rub-down. It's Mrs Cronin's afternoon off but we're quiet enough.'

I wanted to tip her but my bag was under lock and key so I determined to learn her name and leave an envelope for her later.

'Thank you . . .'

'Regina,' she said.

'Gosh,' I said, unable to stop myself.

'That's being polite about it, madam,' she said. 'On you go.'

The cool room was about half full, the slatted cedar chaises covered over with towels and on the towels, a mixture of solid matrons and daughters swathed in their lawn shifts, heads wrapped in turbans, and brighter younger things swathed in . . . I took a closer look . . . nothing at all! Like one of the Old Masters come to life, they lounged singly, in pairs and threesomes: Susannah without the elders, the rising and the setting sun together, Venus, Minerva and Juno awaiting Paris, all set for the judging.

I sank down onto the nearest couch, loosened the cord of my robe and stared steadily ahead, unsure whether I was blushing or whether the flood of heat into my head was the beginning of this ridiculous process by which I would boil myself, like a lobster, gradually, avoiding any pain.

Conversations were all around me as they often seem to be when one is alone – desultory remarks batted back and forth at full volume and other, more hushed and hurried exchanges, the sort where illicit knowledge changes hands. Usually it is an effort not to eavesdrop, today I was engaged in the slightly different effort of listening to all of them whilst appearing not to listen to any.

'Dear Tot, but what a stickler he is!'

'You should have had a pummel instead, my love.'

'My second daughter, now, she had ever such a bad' – whisper – 'but she's through it now.'

'—*had* heard that the' – whisper – 'were called in, but it came right in the end.'

'Fiend! That woman terrifies me. Pummelling indeed.'

'—carries on like this, we might have to make other arrangements. I mean to say' – whisper – 'even if she didn't understand what it meant.'

'—wouldn't like to upset the poor dear. I was always so very fond' – whisper – 'but it's only common decency.'

'That's enough for me! My hair will never be the same again and my face will still be red at midnight.'

'Tot doesn't count the cool room.'

'Tot needn't know. I'm going to have a bath and a rest, darling. Knock on your way down, won't you?'

This last speaker rose from her chaise and walked, as naked as the day she was born, trailing her shift and robe behind her along the floor as though she were laying a scent to train a pack of puppies. I caught the eye of the swaddled and be-turbanned woman opposite me and could not keep my eyebrows in place. She took this as a cue for speech.

'If this is your first time, dear, you'll doubtless be surprised at the sights you're seeing. It's changed days, I can tell you.'

'You know the place well?' I asked.

'Been coming here for years with my chest.'

'Ah, just like my dear friend Mrs Addie,' I said. 'Mrs Enid Addie? Have you ever bumped into her?'

'Is it her chest, dear?'

'Her back.'

'It's my chest, see.'

Could the clientele possibly be organised by body parts as well as being split into two teams under Doctor and Master? Judging by the way the chest woman's attention had strayed when I said back, it appeared so.

I gave her a meaningless smile and stood up to move away. Of course, the only place to go was the warm room. I parted the velvet curtain and slipped through.

There were even fewer shifts in here, and those that were worn were useless, transparent with perspiration and leaving their wearers looking more like Old Masters than ever, given the way that the clothes of the ancients, at least as rendered in oils, are always diaphanous and slipping off at one shoulder. It was undoubtedly warm too; even the tiled floor was hot under my bare feet and, while there was a smell of fresh linen rising from the towels, the base note was of humanity, only just mild enough not to be troubling.

I arranged myself for rest and felt my scalp prickle as my hair gave up and lay down on my head like a dead thing. Grant's spray bath would have its work cut out making me presentable again, I could see.

'God, it's hot,' said a voice, with considerable redundancy. 'What's this supposed to do?'

'It's a treatment,' said another, making no great contribution in my view. 'It counts.'

'If you'll excuse me,' came a third. It was a youngish woman, with long black wavy hair hanging down her back, sticking to her shift in fact in the most uncomfortable-looking way. Indeed, her shift was sticking to her, neck to ankle, twisting as it clung to her legs. I surreptitiously peeled mine away from my moistening skin and tented it over my knees. 'I couldn't help hearing,' she said. She leaned towards the two naked women who were lying like seals on rocks, heads lolling, feet flopped inwards in a fashion which would have had Nanny Palmer trembling for their knee joints. (Nanny Palmer always did seem to think that little girls' legs were put together like the less expensive kind of French dolls, meant to bend one way and one way only, calamitous agony in store if one misused them.)

'The dry heat of the Russian bath relaxes muscles, eases joints, softens cartilage, lifts impurities from the skin, exercises and cleanses the lungs and blends the blood.'

'Softens *what*?' said the younger of the naked women, lifting her head to squint.

'If only my impurities were skin deep!' said the other and they both snorted with laughter.

The speaker made a great show of twisting her hair into a rope over one shoulder and lay back again. The few hairs she had missed, still snaking over her arms and shoulders, looked more ticklish than ever. Just looking at her made me itch.

'Thank you,' I said. 'That was most informative.' The two lolling heads twitched up again and regarded me. 'My dear friend Mrs Enid Addie told me the baths were wonderful but she didn't explain why.' There was no spark of recognition in any of them and so I closed my eyes and concentrated on exercising and cleansing my lungs, trying not to think about what my blood might be being blended with. Re-blended with itself perhaps, the red corpuscles and the white corpuscles reassembling in a healthful rosy pink, like a salad dressing which had been left standing and must be shaken up again. No chance of that here.

The boiled red bodies and the slim white shifts might be side-by-side but they would never emulsify.

Perhaps my brain was cooked and the appearance of good sense was mistaken, but I felt I had made a tremendous discovery. One of the doctor's or one of the master's, Mrs Cronin had said. Tot's ladies were the naked yellers; Dr Laidlaw's the swaddled whisperers. Whether it had anything to do with the case (if there was a case) was another question, but perhaps the air of scientific rigour was rubbing off on me, for no sooner had I formed the hypothesis than I longed to test it. I eyed the further set of velvet curtains covering the entrance to the hot room. In there would be naked women, drawling and giggling, and women in shifts talking about cartilage and decency. I gathered myself, swung my legs, sat up and prepared to stand. My head was pulsing, my feet too and they made the most repulsive wet slapping noises as I walked along the tiles between the rows of couches.

'You're moving rather fast,' said the dark-haired woman.

'Probably right,' murmured one of the others. 'Like ripping off a sticking plaster.'

I blundered on. Through the velvet curtains, in the hot room, there were no more chaises, just marble benches lining the walls and softened – a little – with folded towels. There were three women in here, all naked, and within a moment I made a fourth. The joy of removing that sodden shift and feeling a little air move over my sweltering skin cannot be described. As to what my companions made of me, I could not have cared if the three strange women had been bishops' wives or Bloomsbury poetesses; they could damn my soul or feast their eyes, I was too hot to mind them.

It was almost mesmerising, the baking heat; I could taste it. I thought I could feel myself shrivelling too, as moisture left my body and ran down my skin to soak into the towel beneath me. Were there impurities in that moisture, being carried away? Was I going to emerge shrunken but serene, muscles like rubber, cartilage like jelly, blood like mayonnaise?

'I think I'm still squiffy,' was the first remark which intruded onto my budding serenity. 'That nasty big excrescence on the ceiling up there looks just like my dancing master.'

'Of course you are! You drank enough to float a navy last night. I can smell it from here.'

'Don't be foul! How dare you say you can smell me, you beast. It was therapeutic. Guinness, don't you know. Tot counts that, so really I'm in oodles of credit, chumming along with you in here today.'

The third member of the party piped up then.

'Guinness might well be medicinal,' she said. 'But what's your excuse for mixing it in with champagne?'

'Oh well, you know,' said the first woman. 'Guinness! Ugh!'

And although they were almost talking about medicine, I felt that my experiment was successfully complete. Three naked women and not a whisper among them.

I hauled myself to my feet, put my robe around my shoulders – the shift was not fit to mop the floor with, really – and exited in a kind of helpless stiff-legged hurtle, feeling as though I might burst like a sausage from the heat roiling inside me, not so shrunken after all.

The steam room had not even entered my mind; it had sounded like a cruel joke when Dr Laidlaw had shown it to me that morning: hotter than ever and muggy too, but just as I reeled along towards the resting room where I thought, with enough tea and cool cloths, I might be returned to my usual self in a day or so, three robed ladies of great age and girth opened the frosted glass door and went in. I could not resist. My hypothesis had only been half tested. Here was the rest of the . . . I believe the word is cohort; Hugh taught it to me when he was testing soil amendments in his barley fields and it left an impression on me which has never faded.

I slipped my arms into the sleeves of the robe, belted it, and pulled open the door onto a great engulfing billow of scented steam which rolled out and enveloped me. It was like taking the lid off a steaming kettle and putting one's head in and it seemed impossible to me that one could enter and survive, impossible that one could draw down such boiling fog into one's lungs without drowning.

My view was not that of the majority. As I stood there, a sharp voice accosted me.

'Here, shut that door. You're letting the heat out.' For all the world as though I had introduced a chilly draught to a parlour.

'So sorry,' I muttered and stepped inside, to the strange, ghostly, pungent embrace of the Turkish bath. I could not see a thing. I tripped over a pair of feet, uttering another apology, and felt my way to a marble shelf, dripping and slippery, where I sat down and shrugged my robe off again, letting my head fall backwards and my mouth drop open. This could not possibly be good for the human frame! It smelled rather pleasant, of eucalyptus or some such, and since it was impossible to say whether the moisture now streaming down me like rain down a window in a storm had its source without or within, I might even have said I felt less pricklingly uncomfortable than I had before, but it was like trying to breathe wet cotton wool through a sieve; I laboured and sighed and sounded, I am sure, like every variety of farm animal, only saved from mortification because I could hear breathing just as stertorous, just as vile, from all around. I blew upwards into my hair. I didn't manage to shift a single sopping strand of it, naturally, but at least the draught made me need to blink. I was quite sure I had not blinked once, had not needed to, since I had pulled open the door.

I was just summoning my reserves to leave when a curious thing happened. The three ladies, I am sure of it, simply forgot that I was there. Even though I had just trodden quite hard on one of their bunions, the pall of steam had cloaked me and perhaps my breathing was softer than theirs after all, but I am sure that the words which filled that muffled air were not meant for the ears of a stranger.

'And you're sure, are you, Mrs Riddle?'

'Absolutely positive, Mrs Davies. My lady in Glasgow was perfectly clear that we'd not find them here. Not for a minute.'

'They, Mrs Riddle? Is there more than one? That nice young man mentioned one only.'

'Who's to say, Mrs Scott? I'd be very surprised if, after everything that's happened here in seventy-five years, it's only been that one single time. That "nice young man" was out of his depth completely.'

'Feeling his way.'

'By pure faith.'

'So unusual to find it in a youngster, never mind in a man.'

'But we're safe in here?'

'As houses.'

'But you shouldn't be thinking of safety and danger, Mrs Davies. There's no need to worry.'

'I'm sure I don't need to be lectured on that, Mrs Riddle. I've been active in my circle for twenty-odd years, a founder member, as you're very well aware. And I have no fear of what we know. But this is something else again. All these . . . poisons, all these . . . ill humours.'

I was, as can fairly be imagined, electrified with interest about it all. As lost as a blind lamb on a moonless night, certainly, but fascinated all the same. I was breathing as quietly as I could, sitting stock still lest my feet make another of those slapping noises should I move them and only wondering if I could possibly stay without melting.

'Actually,' it was the voice belonging to Mrs Scott, 'I've done a thorough check on my bed-sitting room and I'm convinced that we'd be fine there.'

'Your bed-sitting room?' Mrs Riddle's voice could not ring out in that soft enfolding dampness but she gave it a good try. 'Then what in the name of all that's holy are we doing in here?' There was a sucking noise as she peeled herself off the marble. I tucked my feet up and tried to disappear against the wall behind me. Either I managed it or, despite the swirling caused by their movement, they did not notice me, but in any case the door opened, once more drawing a great draught of the steam out into the clear air on the other side, and then it shut behind them, leaving me alone, in a state of perplexity edging into utter bafflement.

When my attention at last returned from my eavesdropping to my own comfort, I realised that besides being sopping wet, my head itched like a plague, my breath rasped in my throat and my cheeks and temples and my very eyeballs heaved in time to my pounding pulse. In short, it was long past time for me to draw my life's association with Turkish bathing to a close. I stood, waited until I was sure I would not swoon, and then slipped out of the steam room.

Regina, the round little person in the blue uniform, was outside, almost as though waiting to pounce upon me.

'Mighty!' she said, taking a look at my face. 'You've maybes overdone it, madam. Now, quick about you and cool off then I'll give you a nice salt rub-down.'

'Cool off?' I echoed, hopefully. It sounded lovely but I needed details.

'Plunge pool or cold sprays?' she said, leading me through an archway towards the wet marble temple with the slabs. I could see a woman standing rigid with horror in one of the niches as jets of water assaulted her from every angle and a downpour from a rose contraption, such as one would find on a giant's watering can, drenched her head and plastered her hair to her face.

'The pool,' I said firmly. Regina led me through a second archway from the temple to the long room where the pool lay waiting. I shivered. Even the air was cold in here, but I could still see vapours rising off the surface of the water and I had not forgotten the feeling as I dipped my wrists in. I moved to the edge and looked down.

'Should one use the steps?' I asked. 'It is called a plunge pool after all.'

'It's up to you, madam,' said Regina. 'Do you knock back castor oil or sip it with milk? Not that pool's not lovely.' This last part was rather late and did not convince me.

'Down in one,' I said. I sat on the marble wall, swung my legs over the water, shoved myself off and dropped.

The one good thing that could be said about the water in the plunge pool was that it was less sulphurous than that in the pump room. This I knew because I swallowed a good half-pint of it, opening my mouth and gasping, helpless not to. It was like needles, like a hundred hedgehogs rolling over me, pressing hard, and as well there was an ache, instant and profound, deep inside my body, and another in my head and yet another in my teeth. I rose, thrashing like a salmon, and coughing until my eyes streamed and I could feel the tears as they rolled down my cheeks, could tell them apart from the rest of the water coursing off me, because they were warm. Shuddering, almost whimpering, I galumphed my way towards the steps in an ungainly paddle.

'Quite cold,' said Regina. 'Quite a surprise the first time, I daresay. But if you can just stay under till you're settled it would do you a power of good.'

'Settled?' I said. I was perturbed to hear how loud my voice was, ringing round the room. I even thought I heard a titter from through the archway at the far end that led to the resting room. 'I'll be st-stone d-dead if I don't get out of here. I'll be d-dead of . . . what is it that they keep dying of on p-p-polar expeditions?'

'Hypothermia,' said Regina. 'But this water wouldn't give you hypothermia unless you stayed in twenty minutes or more. And so long as your heart's strong there's no chance of palpitations.'

'My heart?' I said. I must have looked alarmed.

'You don't have a weak heart, madam, do you?' Regina had rushed forward, eyes wide, and was down a couple of steps, with her rubber-soled shoes in danger of spoiling. 'Please come out, madam, do.'

'I d-don't have a weak heart,' I told her. 'Although I have to say it f-f-feels rather shaky right now. So the st-steam and p-plunge is not for everyone? Dr Laidlaw told me to help mys-s-self.'

'Just . . .' Regina attempted a smile. 'Just me being daft, madam. Nothing at all to trouble you. And please don't say to Dr Laidlaw that I caused you alarm, for she has enough on her pl— Anyway, all's well, madam. All's well.'

But I had seen where she had looked, a flicked glance she could not help before her smile widened, and unless I was greatly mistaken (and I could well be, for I am able to get lost inside houses I have visited dozens of times), nevertheless, I was quite sure her eyes had turned to where Dr Laidlaw's eyes had turned. In short, to that same locked door.

5

Like a peg on one's nose for profile, like a book on one's head for posture, like all of those minor tortures we girls went through, it was worth it in the end. I felt, once out, dried and dressed again, as though I could have lifted off from the stones of the terrace and floated over the valley floor on waves of . . . who knows what exactly. My woollen underthings felt like the softest silk against my skin; my lisle stockings too, and from the inside my face felt dewy and rosy and beautiful. I could have stretched backwards to grab my own heels and turned myself into a hoop, so limber did I fancy myself after my sojourn in the baths.

It was spoiled rather when Hugh caught sight of me.

'Good God, Dandy,' he said. 'What's happened to you?'

'Mother, really,' said Donald, opening a sleepy eye.

'Never mind, Mummy,' said Teddy. Then he ruined it: 'No one knows us here.'

True enough, there had been no looking glasses in that little changing cubicle and when I put my hand up to my hair what I felt there was far from usual, but the wonders of the steam bath were more than skin deep and my serenity, though dented, was not cracked and sprang back as I smiled down at them.

'How did you get on with the doctor?' I asked, sitting on the edge of Teddy's deckchair and nudging his feet out of the way.

'Never saw hide nor hair of him,' said Hugh, his choice of pronoun confirming as much. 'Suits me.' He stretched his arms and put his hands behind his head. 'I'm perfectly capable of deciding what I fancy from the brochure.' He patted his breast pocket, from which I could see a folded catalogue peeping out.

'But I must insist when it comes to the boys,' I said, thinking

70

again of Regina's look of alarm as I thrashed in the icy water of the plunge pool. 'They are not to be electrified or . . . pummelled unless the doctor says so.'

Hugh nodded absently.

'Hot salt bath, galvanic wrap, dab of mud, spot of ultraviolet heat,' he said. 'And a quiet game of cards in the evening.'

'Starting tomorrow,' I said. 'Have dinner with us tonight, dear, and then come back before bedtime.' Of course, I needed a little time with him to finesse the Alec problem. 'And now I must just go and see what's kept the doctor.'

'Oh, don't make us see him, Mummy,' said Teddy. 'I'm not going to do all that salty, muddy nonsense anyway.'

'Don't be impertinent,' I said, for I had noticed Hugh's brows twitch down at the word 'nonsense'. 'I shall remake your appointments for tomorrow morning. Meet me in the hall in ten minutes, please, and we shall drive back in time for tea.'

'Mr Laidlaw said there was cherry cake here,' said Teddy.

'Cinnamon toast and maids of honour at home,' I said. 'Donald?' Donald opened his eyes which had fallen shut again.

'I'm not hungry,' he said, so languidly that Hugh caught my eye.

'I'll speak to the doctor,' I repeated. 'Ten minutes, please.' And I hurried away.

Dr Laidlaw's office was on the ground floor at the drive side of the house, unspeakably gloomy, but I supposed it was inevitable that all the west-facing rooms were reserved for guests. There was a little ante-room lined with those tall wooden cabinets for holding files of papers and in the middle of the floor one of the four-sided settees I had seen in the drawing room, a very practical way for four strangers to await their consultations without having to look one another in the eye or breathe one another's germ-ridden air. At the moment, all four seats were empty. Nor was there anyone at the little desk with the telephone and type-writing machine. I passed to the inner door and knocked.

'Oh! Who—? Come in.' Dr Laidlaw's voice came in a series

of chirps and, when I entered, it was to find her peering up from behind a fortress of papers on her desk, with a startled look on her face, like a baby bird in the nest when it hears its parents' wings.

'Mrs . . . ah,' she said.

'Gilver. You arranged to see my husband and sons this afternoon, Dr Laidlaw. I wonder if it would be convenient for us to leave it until the morning?'

The baby bird appeared to realise that the wing beat was that of a marauding hawk, not its parent at all. She ducked slightly and almost disappeared behind the wall of articles, books and files she had built around her. I walked closer to the desk, not to seize her in my talons, but from the look of her one would not know.

'I am so, so, so very sorry,' she said. I moved another pile of dusty paper, made up into bundles with pink tape, and sat down. The furniture in the room comprised the desk and chairs, the bookcases lining the walls, an examination couch with a curtained screen half pulled around it and upwards of a dozen wooden crates, all packed with books, all standing open, all thick with dust. In fact, the whole office was lavishly untidy, its good glass-fronted bookcases stuffed to bursting with books not only in rows but jammed in horizontally on top of the rows too. I saw that the doors of one case, particularly under strain from its contents, were held together by more of the same pink tape threaded through the handles and tied in a bow. Buff-coloured files with carbon papers frothing out of them like coxcombs were stacked along the windowsill, bunching and pulling the grey-yellow lace curtain which looked as though it had not been washed since it was first hung there many years ago. On the chimneypiece there was a perfectly conventional clock flanked by two perfectly conventional vases, but behind the clock, numerous bills and chits threatened to push it forward to smash in the grate, and more of them bloomed in the vases instead of posies. A bunch of keys and a couple of syringes, still with their needles attached, threatened to crack a delicate Staffordshire bon-bon dish with their weight, or at least scratch its beautiful pattern with their sharp edges.

I turned my attention away from the disorder and back to Dr Laidlaw again, thinking that although my impression had been that she was dowdy, seeing her in her lair like this she seemed a daisy on a dung heap. She had noticed me looking around and apologised again.

'Not to worry,' I said. 'They've been wrapped up and snoozing in deckchairs all afternoon. I'm sure it's done them a world of good to rest without interruptions.'

'I— You are very gracious,' she said. 'But it won't do. I could see them now. My consultation hours are over, but to make it up to you – a shocking lapse. That is to say, there was an emergency. But I should have sent a message. I could see them right now.'

I considered it. Specifically, I considered Donald's lungs breathing in the dust and dirt of this frowsy chamber and, although I truly did think she was making a fuss over nothing, I decided to turn it to account.

'What would make up for it,' I said, 'would be if you could manage a house call instead. Might I trouble you to examine the boys at home in the morning? Come and have coffee,' I finished lamely. I can sometimes manage to be grand, but not often.

'Most gladly,' she said. 'Thank you.'

'I see that the emergency ended well,' I said. I am not naturally Machiavellian, never was, but detecting has changed me.

'It did,' said Dr Laidlaw. 'Thankfully, yes it did. But how did you guess?'

'Just that surely you would not be back in your study absorbed in reading had it not,' I replied with a smile.

'Of course, I see, yes of course,' she said. 'Yes, my work is absorbing. Not that the patients are not my work. What I mean to say is that when a paper comes under review and the reviewer . . .'

'Gosh, so you are a researcher, Dr Laidlaw, are you?'

'I am,' she said, gesturing around the piles of books and scribbled-on papers.

'Do you then not *do* house calls?' I said. 'I mean to say, you *are* a doctor, aren't you? Hydropathy being your specialism?'

'My poor father would turn in his grave to hear it,' she said, 'but no. Hydropathy is not exactly . . . that is to say . . . on the Continent . .' She cleared her throat. 'I have an MD from Edinburgh, Mrs Gilver. In short, yes, I certainly am a doctor and as for your house call I certainly shall do it. Happy to.'

'Excellent,' I replied. 'It's good to know that there is someone right here on the premises should anything go wrong. Moffat is a step away and – between you and me, my dear – I've heard some things about one of the *local* doctors, from a friend, you know.'

Her face, blanching to the colour of putty, told me that she did indeed know. I felt a heel but I did not let that stop me.

'A friend who used to come here. Before she died.' Dr Laidlaw considered this, as one would consider a rattlesnake in one's bed with one.

'Can you give me any idea as to what ails your sons?' she said, in a wavering voice, as I stood and brushed the dust from my coat. 'So I know what to bring, you know. I don't travel with a Gladstone bag every day like Dr Ramsay.'

'Pleurisy and pneumonia after flu,' I said. 'Nothing serious like weak hearts or anything. In fact, let's not pander to them with a house call after all. What was I thinking? I, like you, Dr Laidlaw, believe in fresh air and exercise. And yes, it *was* Dr Ramsay. How did you know?'

The putty had faded to chalk, leaving her lips blue – rather prettily bowed lips, dimpling in at the corners; I had not noticed them before, unpainted as they were – and her eyes dark and enormous, with purple smudges around them. I felt a familiar thrill as I let myself out and made my way to the front hall to meet the others. It was becoming clearer and clearer that the Addies were not imagining things. Their dear dead mother had been wronged in some way, I was sure of it, and we would avenge her.

* * *

Naturally, Hugh and the boys were nowhere to be seen when I got there, Hugh's stringent punctuality being reserved for beaters, chauffeurs, ministers of the kirk and fellow officers, not for the likes of me. Whenever he saunters in late to some rendezvous we have arranged, he looks at his watch and says, 'Good, good. Let's make an early start then since you're here in nice time,' as though I have come up to scratch for once in a blue moon and surprised him. Today I was glad of it, because an opportune meeting came my way. There was an inopportune one first, though.

As I waited, installed in one of those throne-like chairs with which hallways come equipped, seat-cushions stuffed with something which gives them that stodgy and unyielding consistency, like fudge, I was far from delighted to hear whistling and see a silhouette sauntering towards me along the passageway with its hands in its trouser pockets. Thomas Laidlaw; I could not take to the man.

'Well, well, well,' he said, when he reached me. He took his hands out of his pockets but only to rub them together as though with vast relish of unknown source, hardly more civil than if he had left them there. 'Off already, Mrs Gilver?'

'For the evening, Mr Laidlaw,' I said. 'In the morning I shall return.'

'Once the sun is safely up, eh?' he said, giving me a solemn look. 'I think you'll have to summon more courage than that, Mrs Gilver, if your trip's not to be a wasted one.'

I stared and summoned, not courage, but my haughtiest voice and my most disdainful expression.

'I do not have the pleasure of understanding you, Mr Laidlaw,' I said. 'You speak in riddles.'

'Can I ask who recommended us to you?' he said. 'A family who hails from Perthshire needn't by any means come as far as Moffat to a hydro.' They were almost the words Mrs Cronin had spoken to me. 'Any particular reason we took your fancy?'

'Your sister – such a scholar – has no equal in Crieff,' I said and I was intrigued to see him lift his chin up and away to the side to give me a narrow look from the corner of his eye. He

75

reminded me of an archer sighting prey along his drawn bow. Then, at a sound from outside on the drive, he spun around on the balls of his feet to face the door.

'Reinforcements,' he said. 'Who do you suppose this will be?'

It was only to be expected that the owner of such a large hotel in such a dull spot would be charmed by arriving guests, but I found myself paying more attention than Nanny Palmer would have called polite as the door opened and the newcomers entered. I was agog to see if these would be more of the solid but sickly bourgeoisie I took to be the doctor's lot or more of the vacuous crew I had filed under her brother's name.

I had momentarily forgotten my overhearings, but as soon as I saw the little caravan which hove through the baronial doors of the Hydro with bags and boxes aplenty as though planning to stay for a month I thought to myself: Aha! Class 3. For if Mrs Scott, Mrs Davies and Mrs Riddle – those odd, earnest ladies in the steam room – had had clothes on I was sure the clothes would be these.

They were five in number, two men and three women all somewhere in the sixties or beyond. The men were dressed with outlandish – one might almost say Dickensian – extravagance in their tall hats, velvet facings, satin pipings and brocade upon any garment that brocade could applied to. I could not help but conclude they must be sorry that old-fashioned garb could only, at its farthest stretch, take them back that far, and that cut-away tailcoats and neck cloths of white silk would have been out-and-out fancy dress and would have brought the whistle to a constable's lips if he had seen them.

The women were even more extraordinary. To be sure, one was of a sort to be seen in village streets throughout the land, only not often in the lobbies of large hotels. She had stuck with the fashions of her youth throughout the fifty years since its passing and was therefore dressed in skirts which trailed the ground with a lace cap over her white hair. She had on a travelling cape of wool with a red flannel lining and a red-silk-lined hood, and if she had held out an apple and invited me to take a bite of it I might not have run, but I would certainly have broken into a trot in the opposite direction.

The younger companion at her side, most solicitously offering her arm and helping the old woman up the stone steps from the vestibule to the lobby proper, was another sort entirely. Her hair, brownish-grey and wiry with it, was drawn straight back from her forehead and hung down almost to her waist. Her dress, of a greyish-brown one might imagine had been chosen to match her hair, except that no one would look so grimly drab on purpose, hung straight from her shoulders to her calves, like a sack, and the overcoat on top was of a navy serge I had not seen since the last time a troupe of Girl Guides had chosen an inclement day to storm the park at Gilverton and huddle around their campfires until the charabanc returned to fetch them home again.

The final member of the coven was comparatively unremarkable set against the rest: hair of a somewhat suspicious bright brown given the wrinkles which striped her forehead and fanned from the corners of her eyes, and an outfit of military cut, the jacket well served with pockets and the skirt reminiscent of a lady's riding costume with its clever deep pleats and moleskin touches. She took off her hat, threw her gloves into it and looked around for a servant who would take it away. Tot Laidlaw obliged, rushing forward and bowing to them all, but looking at them very hard all the while.

At that interesting moment Hugh arrived, with the boys in tow, just in time to see me gawking at strangers like a guttersnipe. I think I may even have had my mouth open, and he let the spirit of Nanny Palmer live in the glare he gave me.

'We got tired of waiting for you on the terrace,' he said with astounding cheek. 'Thought we'd try here. Good, good. Let's be off then.' As an apology for lateness it failed on every count but I saved my breath, simply rolling my eyes and standing to follow him. He held the door open for me – what manners were drummed in by his own nanny and the subsequent schoolmasters are unshakeable – and I swept out, managing to pick up a mention

77

of 'late booking' and 'lucky cancellation' on my way past the new arrivals.

I had expected to need a long quiet evening to creep my way towards the fact of Alec, his presence in the Hydro, the coincidence of our arrival there and the thorny question of whether I had dragged my loved ones into a case or an assignation, but we were still on the drive heading back to the road when Hugh broached it himself.

'You didn't know Osborne was headed here, did you, Dandy?'

'Oh, yes, that's right, Mummy,' said Teddy. 'We saw him again. I told you he got off the train.'

'I did not,' I said. 'Is he really here then? At the Hydro? What fun.'

'Bit odd,' said Donald. 'Why didn't he tell you?' Hugh was not exactly watching carefully but he was far from looking out of the window.

'He told me about the Hydro,' I said. 'It was his praise of the place that put me in mind to come here. But when he said he was going away, I somehow got the idea that it was London.'

'Hope he doesn't mind you rolling up,' said Hugh. He gave me that same amused look as before.

'I'm sure he doesn't mind any of us "rolling up",' I said. 'Why should he? Unless you think he left Perthshire to escape us.'

At this Teddy snorted. It was an ugly noise, with a good deal of the after-effects of flu about it, and both Hugh and I frowned.

'Sorry,' Teddy said. 'Just, well. Gilver and Osborne. In that order, Mummy. Sort of makes you Mr Osborne's boss. And he's skipped off on a spree and now his boss has come along and caught him.'

'I'm not Mr Osborne's "boss", Teddy,' I said. 'What a nasty, slangy word.'

'What other word *is* there for it?' asked Teddy, with a fair to middling innocent look, not the full-force cherub he sometimes employs, but a lot of round blue eye and round pink mouth nonetheless for a boy of sixteen. 'I'm simply calling a spade a spade.'

'Superior officer,' said Hugh. In Hugh's world, there was only one job his boys could ever conceivably do, and that was how to describe the men under whom they would do it.

'I am glad to say I have never seen a spade,' said Donald in a trilling voice, making us all giggle, except Hugh, naturally.

'What?'

'Oscar Wilde,' I told him. 'Cecily.'

'*Gwendolen*,' said both boys.

Hugh was so disgusted that his children – not to mention his wife – could quote from this oeuvre that he said nothing, just drove the car steadily along the lane and swung it down the hill towards the town.

'He's got a point, mind you,' said Donald, although whether he meant Teddy or Oscar was unclear. 'You have dragged us down, Mother, where Teddy needs words like "boss" to describe the world around him.'

'There is nothing more vulgar than a snob, Donald dear,' I shot back.

'Good grief,' said Hugh. It is almost his strongest epithet and we all quieted on hearing it. 'I wouldn't blame Osborne if his heart *did* sink to see you as large as life at his journey's end. What nonsense you speak, all three of you.'

'Hugh,' I said. 'Alec Osborne is a dear friend who can speak nonsense like a drunken parrot. If he came to the Hydro I am sure it was because he is feeling a little under the weather and needs a pick-me-up – the same as you. I have no more intention of interrupting his treatment than I have yours.'

Hugh raised an eyebrow and one side of his mouth.

'He looked perfectly healthy to me,' he said.

'Perhaps he's here to woo a Moffat maiden,' said Donald. 'Just as you said, Mother.'

'Best not get in the way of that then,' Teddy said.

'I doubt it,' said Hugh. His air of mystery was becoming too irritating to bear. 'It's possible, but I doubt it.'

At that moment, when all three of them were making me want to spank them with a slipper, I spied, out of the motorcar window, distraction and diversion.

'Pull over, please, Hugh,' I said. 'I've just remembered an errand. I'll make my own way back to the house from here.'

'Sure?' said Hugh, chivalry spilling out of him again as it does when he is not concentrating. 'It's no trouble for us to park and wait. Help you carry things.'

'Quite sure,' I said. 'Don't hold tea. If you happen to see Grant—'

'Gosh, yes, Mummy, we'll give her warning,' Teddy said. Donald laughed and even Hugh smiled as they pulled away. I tugged down hard on my hat, hoping to hide as much of the trouble as I could, and made my way to where I had seen the police lamp.

I have no fondness for police stations any more – not since I was required to sit alone in a small room inside one, friendless and anxious, for hours on end while a nasty piece of work of an inspector pretended to suspect me of murder – and although my chin was high and my shoulders back as I marched in, my heart let the side down miserably, thumping away like a trapped rabbit in my chest. I hoped my voice would be steady, but I did not count on it.

'I should like to speak to a sergeant or inspector if there is one,' I asked of the child at the desk. He was surely only just tall enough to make a policeman at all, and was as smooth of cheek as Teddy even this late in the day.

'Certainly, madam,' he said, as meek as a lamb. 'Who can I tell the sergeant it is, please? The inspector is in Dumfries and won't be back round here until Friday.'

'Very well,' I said. 'Mrs Gilver of Perthshire.' I had decided that a private detective might raise hackles and be kept waiting but a woman of my sort, started on the path towards being a dowager, although thankfully far from its end, would elicit exactly this forelock-tugging and prompt service.

It was only minutes later then that I was shown into a shabby but comfortable office, lamps and rugs and cushions in the chairs to soften the municipal green distemper and brown paint, and introduced to a uniformed sergeant who rose from behind the desk and held out a hand to greet me.

'Sergeant Simpson, Mrs Gilver,' he said, sitting down again as I settled myself. 'What can I do for you? I trust you've come to no harm on your visit here, have you?'

'Thank you, Sergeant, no. I am quite well. I have a little matter to discuss with you. A matter of protocol, I suppose you would say. A point of procedure.'

'I'm all ears,' said Sergeant Simpson. I smiled at him and had to work not to do more than smile; this was unfortunately true and the red mark around his head where his cap must sit when he was out patrolling the streets of the town only drew attention to it. He smiled back, in on the joke, and I decided I liked him.

'If there were a death . . .' I said and his smile snapped off. 'I don't know if you'd say a sudden death or a suspicious death, but one where the Fiscal was involved before it was all sorted out and the body returned for burying . . .' I drew breath. 'What I'd like to know is, would the matter pass through the hands of the police on its way?'

'Which case is this you're referring to, madam?' said Sergeant Simpson, seeing through my ruse right away. He even drew out a small notebook and snapped it open on itself with a terrific crack of its India-rubber band.

'In general,' I persisted.

He waited.

'Mrs Addie,' I said, relenting. 'She died at the Hydro a month ago. On the ninth of September. A local doctor signed the death certificate, but it went across the Fiscal's desk and her family are concerned. They are acquaintances of mine and since I was on my way here I promised them I'd have a quiet word.'

Again, he regarded me in silence. Then he closed his little book with a more minor snap and gave me a smile of deep avuncularity – I could not begin to imagine what was coming.

'Are you a detective?' he said.

'Gosh, no,' I replied before I even considered the fact that I was lying to the police, which is surely against the law. 'What on earth makes you think that?'

'My mistake,' said Simpson. 'It was just the very orderly manner in which you put your points across, Mrs Gilver. You struck me that way.'

If I had planned to keep lying my plan was undone by the beaming blush of pleasure which spread across my face. Sergeant Simpson laughed out loud to see it.

'Sorry if I misled you just then,' I said.

'When you answered no to a straight question when the true answer was yes?' he asked and waved a magnanimous hand. 'We policemen are not accustomed to getting our final answer first time out, Mrs Gilver. I daresay it's the same for you.'

I was reeling. I had encountered scorn, hostility and amusement from policemen who heard of my calling and sergeants were always the worst of all. My beloved Inspector Hutchinson, it was true, had grudgingly thawed towards Alec and me over the course of the case we had shared, but this instant chumminess was something else again.

'I am very grateful to find such . . . collegiate spirit in a policeman, Sergeant Simpson,' I said. 'So. Yes. Mrs Addie of Edinburgh died at the Hydro. Heart failure. Dr Ramsay here in town signed the cert., the Fiscal stamped it or whatever the Fiscal does—'

'Enters the record,' supplied Simpson.

'Thank you,' I said. 'The Fiscal entered the record, but the family are troubled. They say she had no history of heart trouble. Said she was as strong as an ox, in fact.'

'Well-chosen phrase,' said Sergeant Simpson. 'I saw the lady in question, you know. She was . . . large-ish.'

'You saw her? About the town?'

'Post-mortem,' he said. 'I saw her after her death. We *were* called in. The lady was away from home and the Hydro – never mind all the white sheets and machines – it's not a hospital. If someone dies away from home or a hospital, we try to look in, you know. Just to see that everything's shipshape.'

He might have been a schoolmaster telling of how he likes to look in on prep to check that boys aren't whispering.

'Who rang you?' I asked.

'Straight to the heart of the thing,' he said. 'You are good at your job, Mrs Gilver.' I might have blushed a little again. 'Yes, it was Dr Laidlaw who rang us up. Shocked to her core, she was, but did the proper thing. She even insisted – well, this was her brother as it happens – they both insisted that Dr Ramsay be called. He came along – he left a party and came right along in his evening suit, there within minutes, late as it was, and he'd no need to – and he examined the body and he didn't hesitate. Heart failure, as you say.'

'And the Fiscal didn't order a full post-mortem exam?' I said.

'He saw no need,' said the sergeant. 'It was a very clear case and properly handled. More than properly, really. Dr Laidlaw could have signed her own name to the thing and never got Dr Ramsay involved at all.'

The good sergeant clearly did not share my view of that particular item of fancy footwork. I paused a moment wondering how best to introduce the point to our little chat. It was sure to reduce the warmth at least a bit. When Sergeant Simpson cleared his throat and resumed speaking, however, I realised that I had paused long enough to make a silence, one which he was moved to fill.

'I'm sorry to hear the family are troubled,' he said and cleared his throat again. 'We had hoped to spare them any pain. Along the lines of what you don't know can't hurt you.' My amazement must have showed on my face. 'Collegiate spirit, you said, wasn't it, Mrs Gilver?' He was teasing me, but very gently. 'In that case between the doctor, the Fiscal and me.'

'Indeed,' I answered. 'I am sure your words appear more mysterious than they really are, Sergeant Simpson, but I'm afraid I don't quite follow.'

'We'd all like to think that our loved ones just slip away in their sleep, don't you agree, Mrs Gilver?' he said. 'Or never knew what hit them. That's another good one. Every boy that didn't come home from the war, eh?' There was a lengthy pause. His gaze slipped away from my face and came to rest on the desktop. 'Instantaneous death, they always said. Never knew what hit him.'

'I am very sorry, Sergeant Simpson,' I said, for that is all there ever is to say.

'It can't possibly be true every time, can it?' He looked up again. 'But I was grateful for it and I try when I can to carry it on.'

'And so what is the truth?' I asked. 'The whole story?'

'She had a shock,' Simpson said. 'A very nasty one. And she didn't die right away. She collapsed. They found her. Dr Laidlaw found her. Got her into her bed, tried to bring her round. Did everything she could but the poor woman's heart gave out in the end. And so it was. Heart failure.'

'What sort of a shock?'

'A fright,' said the sergeant. 'Did you know you can die of fright?'

'I know a loud noise is a danger to a man with heart troubles,' I said. 'I had heard so. But again there was no history of heart troubles at all.'

'Not a loud noise,' he said. 'Oh dear, oh dear.' He took a moment to rearrange some of the small items on his already tidy desk, pushing the pens in the stand until they were all upright, picking up a couple of auditor's tags and dropping them into a little tray. 'Now, tell me, Mrs Gilver,' he went on at last, 'you're not the sort to go upsetting the family for nothing, are you? You seem a lovely lady. I'm sure you wouldn't. But tell me straight so's I know.'

His words about the blunting of bad news had hit home in me and I meant it when I assured him that I would not go making trouble for nothing, not me. He smiled and spoke again, but what he said surprised me.

'There are more things in heaven and earth than are dreamed of in your philosophy,' were his words. Startling ones to hear issuing from a policeman's lips. 'Would you agree with that, Mrs Gilver?'

'Up to a point,' I replied. 'What bearing does it have on this matter, though?'

'Well put, madam,' said the sergeant. 'What a lovely way of

speech you have.' He took a deep breath. 'She had a shock. She got a fright.' I nodded; he had already said this much. Finally he got to the point: 'She saw a ghost.'

'A ghost.' It was not a question. I am not at all sure what it was, beyond an echo.

'Earlier in the day. And she went back at night to see it again. It was too much for a woman of her years, not to mention her size. Her heart gave out. She was fighting for life when they found her.'

'A ghost,' I said again.

'They don't know which one,' said Simpson. 'She never told them.'

'Are there lots?'

'A fair few.'

I was at a loss for words, a deep and enduring loss which went on beyond all the bounds of normal conversational pauses, beyond silences and well into rudeness, and yet I had no expectation of it ending. Sergeant Simpson sat forward, both hands on his desk, and peered at me.

'*I* don't believe in ghosts, Mrs Gilver. I'm not saying any of it was *true.*'

'Oh!' The spell was broken and I could talk again.

'Good heavens above!' said Simpson. 'I'm an elder of the kirk and my father was the session clerk. My wife runs the Sunday school, too. I've no time for nonsense, none at all. But Mrs Addie . . . She saw a shadow, or heard a sound, and she frightened herself out of her precious life. Now. You can see why we wouldn't want to tell her family the poor lady was as daft as all that!'

'When you put it that way, Sergeant,' I said, 'I do begin to.'

And so it was that when I rang up Alec that evening I was able to steal his thunder in the most resounding style. I was in Grant's clutches for a while first, to be sure, as I had expected to be.

'Never,' she had said. 'Never in all my years. I mean, I've seen you in some states after a day's shooting and I've been that busy with the invalids this last while, you've been more tousled than

I'd like. But this! What have you been doing? Where have you *been*?' She was helping me out of my coat and my shirt as she scolded me; clearly I was to have my head stuck under one of the sprays for an actual washing, no matter how recently I had had one and how long she had hoped it would last me.

'I was—' I began, but she was not finished.

'And don't blame the weather,' she said, driving me down onto my knees beside the bath. 'Madam. For Mrs Tilling and Mr Pallister and me have been out in the woods for a nice walk and there's not a hint of drizzle about it. What did you *do*?'

'I had a Turkish bath, Grant,' I said, just as she bent me over the side. 'And it was wonderful. Quite delightful. My skin feels like silk and my—'

'Your skin is under your clothes,' she said. 'Your hair feels like wool, same as it looks. Wild wool. On a fence. In the rain.' She rubbed the hair soap hard between her hands and set to work on me. My teeth were still chattering when I was sitting, head wrapped in a towel, waiting for her to heat her irons.

'I'm glad to hear you had time for a walk, Grant,' I said. 'This is by way of helping Pallister and Mrs Tilling convalesce and you recover from your extra exertions, you know. Coming here, I mean. And if you decide to use the Hydro's facilities, I'm sure we can come to some arrangement.'

'That's very generous of you, madam,' Grant said. 'I'll tell the others. And thank you.'

'I meant as to times, actually,' I said. 'One wouldn't want—' to meet one's cook and maid stark naked in the plunge pool, was what I was thinking.

'Oh, I'm sure,' said Grant. 'But this house runs itself, more or less, the size that it is and all electric with it.' She had misunderstood me, which was probably best, and I let it be.

Alec was most entertained by the notion when I mentioned the delicate matter later over the telephone.

'You don't mind total strangers, but close acquaintance is beyond the pale?'

'Something like that,' I agreed.

'Mind you, Dorothea said she only goes at night when it's empty.'

'Dorothea?' I asked. 'Does her title stick in your throat a little, Alec? I never took you to be so old-fashioned as to baulk at a lady doctor.'

'I'm not,' he said. 'I don't. I just . . . Anyway, Miss Grant and Mrs Tilling would no more take off all their clothes and sit in a cloud of steam than they would—'

'You're probably right,' I said. 'I wonder about Pallister, though. If you meet him in the men's Turkish, be a love and don't tell me.'

'I shan't be in there either,' Alec said. 'I spent one rainy season in Nagpur as a child and the tummy bug I caught there is the stuff of legend amongst the Osborne clan. It put me off heat and humidity for life.'

'Aren't the germs in the drinking water?' I said. 'I don't think they fly through the air.'

'The power of association,' said Alec. 'I don't suppose you've heard of Mr Pavlov and his salivating dogs.'

'Don't you?' I retorted.

'I was talking about that only this afternoon, in fact,' said Alec. 'And you'll never guess to whom.'

'Very likely not,' I said. 'Anyway, let me tell you about my chat with Sergeant Simpson.'

'There's more going on in this here Hydro than meets the eye,' said Alec, talking over me. 'I thought it was all mumbo-jumbo, I have to say, but the psychological angle is—'

'I wonder if that's what Hugh's laughing up his sleeve over,' I said. 'Doesn't seem all that likely.'

'No, no, no,' Alec said. 'That's quite another neck of the woods. Brother Laidlaw – can you believe they call him Tot? – has hit on a bit of a wheeze to keep the place afloat and lessen his boredom. No, I'm talking about *Dr* Laidlaw. She's not that interested in hydropathy per se.'

'I should say not.' I laughed to remember it. 'She seems to be in a world of her own.'

'An ivory tower,' Alec said. 'She called me back for a second examination and we had a very interesting discussion instead. I don't think she got as far as writing my name on the little card. So I'd be surprised if she's even noticed what's going on *now*.'

'Tot's latest wheeze?' I said. 'What is it?'

'No, something else again,' Alec said. 'There are Dr Laidlaw Sr's loyal patients who've been coming for years. Then there's Tot's crowd – rather a fast set, they are. But you will never guess who's started arriving to make a third faction.'

I thought of my eavesdropping in the steam room, and the strange bunch who had turned up in the foyer as I was leaving. I thought of Simpson's revelation too.

'What's the bet?' I asked.

'First pick of the next juicy bit the case offers,' said Alec.

'Does that include shirking the next dull bit?' I said.

'Of course.'

'It's a deal,' I said. 'I am spitting in my palm and holding it to the mouthpiece. I think the wave of new guests coming to the Hydro are . . . mediums.' He was silent. 'Spiritualists.' Still nothing. 'Ghost hunters, darling.'

'Brava,' said Alec, sounding about as pleased as someone who has just dropped his watch down a grating. 'How did you know?'

'And the next irksome task in this case,' I said, 'which I must say is beginning to get interesting, is to go back to Edinburgh to the Addies and delicately try to find out if their mother was the fanciful sort who would see a shadow, call it a ghost and drop dead from the shock of it. A ticklish business to carry it off without offending or alerting them, I must say. I'm glad that it falls to you.'

6

Of course, I had to tell him how I knew, which rather diminished my glory.

'Well, if you will send me off to interview policemen,' I said, 'you can't complain if I turn up treasure.'

'You really are being quite insufferable,' Alec said. He recrossed his legs and took his pipe out of his pocket to stare at it in mourning. We were in the winter gardens, packed with the more solid sort of Hydro guests this morning as the rain fell steadily on the late summer gardens outside, and Alec had come a cropper on that very part of the Hydro's organisation which had so pleased Hugh, namely that all the smoking rooms were gentlemen's rooms and if one wanted to converse with ladies one had to lump it. He was particularly miffed because the ladies were allowed to smoke in the ladies' drawing room, but not so the gentlemen who joined them there.

'What's the point of *that*?' he said. 'Hardly fair.'

'I suppose if all the ladies were puffing away on briars and fat cigars, it would be a nonsense,' I said, 'but until they do, I for one think it's perfectly just. Go and stink up the billiards room by all means and leave us be. Besides, no one's allowed to smoke in *here*.'

I was thankful of it. The winter gardens had soaring glass ceilings and were easily eighty feet from end to end, but even with the little air vents cranked open and the doors propped ajar they had a slightly Turkish feel about them on such a clammy morning. I supposed some of the guests installed in the basket-work armchairs which were dotted in groups around the walls must have braved the weather for some sort of airing before retreating in here, and so their outdoor clothes were gently steaming. Add to that the fact that there were orchids and palms and yet other exotics of unknown name arranged on staging at all the windows and planted in great clumps in the corners, the sort of plants that zealous gardeners will mist with water and even nicotine potions out of a pump spray every day if given their head, and it was hardly surprising that the air in the winter gardens felt like a warm drink, if not a square meal followed by a cigar, as one breathed it. It did not feel at all like the sort of place sickly people should pack into all together, especially after a soaking and the possibility of a chill.

'Anyway,' Alec said. His appetite for squabbling had been diminished by the prospect before him. 'How would you go about asking if Mrs Addie believed in ghosts then?'

'Very carefully,' I replied. 'I agree with the sergeant – no point in upsetting them. On the other hand, if she was fanciful perhaps they knew. Perhaps if they're told that their mother thought she saw a ghost they'll believe in the heart failure after all.'

'Or perhaps they're fanciful too,' Alec said. 'Perhaps they'll think – or her daughter at least – that she *did* see one. We might have done all we need to already.'

'We?' I said. 'What did *you* do? And why, pray, should the daughter be the one to swallow mumbo-jumbo and not the son?' Alec tutted and since I had no wish to sound like a suffragette – all very worthy I am sure, but so dull at parties – I changed the subject back again. 'You might start in by asking them what made her believe in hydropathy? That's the dominant note of mumbo-jumbo around here. Or here's a thought: ask their religion—'

'Church of Scotland,' Alec said. 'You only had to look at them.'

'—under cover of breaking the news that there was no clergyman with her when she died. No time to fetch one and all that. But tell them that another guest, "a very spiritual lady", sat with her and you only hope that brought her comfort. Use the word "spiritual" and make it a woman and see what they say.'

Alec was staring at me with his mouth hanging open.

'Where *do* you get it, Dandy?' he asked.

'You wanted me to help you,' I replied. 'Don't complain that I've managed it.' Then I considered his question. 'I honestly don't know. I never used to be able to think up lies. When I was a child I couldn't do it to save my life. Edward and Mavis concocted the most jaw-dropping tarradiddles and pointed at me and it was always me who got sent to my room with no dinner.'

'Well, I'm glad that your moral standards have deserted you,' Alec said. 'That's exactly the line I shall take. And having them think I went all the way to Edinburgh to broach such a delicate topic face-to-face can't hurt our reputation.'

'You can wheel out your head-undertaker routine again,' I said. 'They'll adore you.'

'What are you going to do in the meantime?' Alec said, ignoring the jibe.

'Attack it from this end,' I said. 'She saw a ghost? Surely she told someone. I shall try to find that someone.'

'Sounds sensible enough,' Alec said. If he meant it as praise he could have done better.

'Not a guest,' I said, musing. 'It's been too long. But I'm sure Dr Laidlaw knows more than she was happy to tell.'

'Might only be that it wasn't her idea to bowdlerise the tale for the Addie relations,' Alec said. 'I'd be surprised if it were, actually. She's a very rational sort. I'd almost say tough-minded, if that didn't sound nasty.'

I noted that he seemed more concerned with tailoring compliments for the good doctor than for me, and not for the first time I considered the way that intimacy of the sort Alec and I shared, now that we had been flung together in perils too many to name, was all very well, but I still missed the courtesy that there used to be.

'If not her,' I said, 'I think I'll go and pester Regina again. She definitely knows something too and might break more easily than the doctor when leaned on.'

I looked around the winter gardens, hoping that if I were very lucky I might see her little round personage bustling about, but there were only a couple of maid-cum-waitresses in black frocks and white caps taking orders, I thought, for coffee. Instead I saw, ambling along, feet dragging on the red clay tiles and making a noise which always grated upon me, Donald and Teddy. As I had suspected, Donald was already pulling at the soft collar of his shirt to loosen his tie, clearly feeling the muggy air too much for him. Again I felt one of my infrequent maternal pangs and was glad all over again to think that the secret of Mrs Addie's death was most likely a white lie of sorts, not a black deed like murder at all. At least, I hoped so. If we uncovered anything much worse, I should really have to winkle my sons out of here and get them home. Perhaps it was even worth concocting a plausible tale I could keep up my sleeve and trot out if need be.

'Mother, you're squinting like a charmed snake,' Donald said. 'Good morning, Mr Osborne.' As the three of them exchanged greetings, I retreated yet further into my own concerns.

Donald and Teddy could not be packed off home. How could I have forgotten? I was supposed to have rung up the factor as soon as we arrived to check that the workmen were set fair to begin their campaign on the draughts and drips of Gilverton first thing this morning. Gilchrist was already greatly troubled by his own treachery, colluding with me unbeknownst to his liege lord, but I had dangled a glittering prospect in front of his eyes and – more to the point – in front of the eyes of his wife who had three daughters under the age of ten and twin baby boys and had been brought up with indoor servants of her own, before marrying and having to make do with a daily maid and part shares in the estate gardeners. In short, I had offered the Gilchrists the chance to put their tin bath out in the yard for horses to drink from, and to turn the old privy into a kennel for their aged and unlovely terrier, and bask instead in an enamelled bath with a basin and lavatory, all installed in the old boxroom a step across the landing from where they slept. I had even agreed to the colour Mrs Gilchrist fancied best, although it made me shudder. Primrose it was called in the catalogue, depicted in a fanciful watercolour complete with bathing nymph. Custard, I called it, and powdered custard out of a tin at that.

There was to be a little gas water-heater above the kitchen sink too, and a larger one above the double sinks of the wash house, so Mrs Gilchrist could throw a cotton cloth over the old wash copper and stand a jug of flowers there. And of course there were to be radiators, all fed by a tank of oil in the yard, and the only coal to be carried would be a decorous brass scuttleful to make a cheery note in the sitting room on those few evening when the family had leisure to sit there. It would make a marked change from the twenty-hour day which began with lighting the kitchen range in the morning and ended with carrying covered shovels into the bedrooms at night, the hours between being filled with stoking and banking like a double shift on a steam engine.

Mrs Gilchrist's eyes had shone as she leafed through the fanciful catalogue and even before she turned them beseechingly upon her husband, I knew she was mine. She was mine, he was hers and therefore he was mine too. He was not happy, but I had promised to draw all of Hugh's inevitable wrath onto myself and had gone so far as to put it in writing that his job was safe. (If the worst came to the worst, he could hide at Benachally and help Donald for a month or two until matters settled again.)

Still, I really should have made sure to ring him. He was not used to having to forge ahead without Hugh. They sometimes reminded me, poring over their maps and plans, of two old women searching for a dropped stitch in their knitting.

Teddy was speaking. I shook all thoughts of Gilverton out of my head and attended to him.

'—could have buttered me both sides and called me a bath bun,' he said. This was a saying he had learned from a sweet nursery maid when he was very small. He took care to reserve it for use out of his father's hearing, but it made me smile. 'Donald too. You'll never guess what the doctor is, Mummy.'

'I shan't take the bet, dear,' I told him. 'I knew.'

'Did you tell Father?' Donald said. He was smirking. 'Because we didn't. He's in there now.' Then the giggles got the better of both of them. I tried and failed not to join in.

'And what did Dr Laidlaw say?' I asked them. 'What regime has she decreed for the pair of you?'

'Rest for me,' said Donald, very gloomy. 'Rest on the terrace with a hot bottle at my feet. Rest in some vibrating electric contraption with bright lamps shining on me – I'm sure to be seasick – and rest while wrapped up like a mummy in hot towels and camphor.'

'Camphor?' I said. 'Are you sure?'

'Might have been menthol,' Donald said. 'Mustard even. Something pretty smelly anyway.' Then he brightened. 'She did say I was to have port wine at lunch and at dinner and red meat too.'

'Interesting,' I said. 'Not a drop of water in any of that anywhere. I'm beginning to wonder how hydropathy got its name.'

'Plenty of water for me,' Teddy said. 'I'm to swim in the bathing pool every morning. Breaststroke, she said. Loosening, whatever that means. And then the hot towels and mothballs, like Don. For expectation.'

'Expectoration,' I said. 'At least, I would have thought so. Well, how gruesome. I hope you're being mummified in a private room.' Of course, what I really hoped was that I would not encounter someone, nicely loosened and now expectorating, in some shared part of the women's accommodations. 'No breaststroke for you then, Donald dear?'

'No, I'm being thrown to the rubbers,' he said. 'Those burly men in blue overalls we saw in the hot rooms yesterday. One of them is supposed to pound me in between the lamps and the menthol.'

I did not much like the sound of that, some thug with big red hands setting about my poor diminished boy, but that was not why my face fell. His words had suggested something far worse to me. If the people dressed in blue in the hot rooms were dedicated, trained 'rubbers' – I supposed that plain term was just about preferable to 'masseur' with its whiff of decadence – then

Regina was most likely to be found all day and every day in one place only, and there was only one way to fall in with her. Grant, I realised, was going to kill me.

In the end, I managed to get away with only the briefest stop in the coolest room before I caught sight of a blue sphere flashing past the opened velvet curtains leading to the rest beds. I shot to my feet, belted my robe firmly and scuttled after her.

'Oh, it's you, Mrs Gilver,' she said, turning as she heard her name. 'Back again, eh? I thought so.' At my look (I hoped it was only puzzled and not actually guilty) she explained. 'I can always tell who's going to take to it and who's not,' she said. 'You might have grumbled a bit when you hit the cold water, madam, but it's nothing to what some of them let out. One lady once said a word I'd never heard in my life, and that's me as used to pull pints in the public bar at the Annandale Arms to help out in the Tup Fair.'

'Well, to be honest, Regina,' I said, 'I was rather hoping to run into you. I've got the most fearful crick in my neck – I think I must have wrenched it in the shock of the plunge, you know – and I wondered if you could help. Unless one has to book an appointment.'

'Depends on the season and how busy we are,' she said. 'But you're in luck this morning, madam. Slab and salt or warm oil?' At my expression, she laughed and explained. One could either lie naked on one of the marble slabs beside the cold sprays and be doused with water and rubbed with rock salt then rinsed off, which sounded more like the beginning of a recipe to cure meat than anything one might visit upon one's own person, or one could be taken to a quiet room, lie down on a couch and be rubbed with warm oil.

'Only that's extra on your bill, madam,' Regina said. 'And a salt rub on the slab down here is included. As many as you feel like.' It was 'first glass sixpence, second glass free' all over again: I was willing to bet that the offer of endless time on the slab with the cold water was not going to ruin the Hydro in the immediate future.

I made my unsurprising choice and Regina steered me up a narrow set of wooden stairs at the side of the changing cubicles and into one of a number of small rooms which led off the upper landing. There was more of the dark wood and red velvet here, and with the couch – even if it was draped in white towels instead of silk shawls – the overall effect was that of a miniature boudoir. I lay down on my front and she expertly shrugged me out of the robe.

'Now then,' she said. 'Crick in your neck, you said? Hmph. I see what you mean.'

I did not need to force rigidity into my muscles, for the novelty of suddenly having someone who was not Grant lay hands upon me and immediately comment on her findings caused an automatic tension to spread through me.

'Wee drop eucalyptus oil,' she said, and then bracing her feet hard, one knee bent and one straight, as I could see perfectly well over the side of the couch, she set about my neck and shoulders like a master baker with a batch of dough.

'Golly,' I said presently. 'Oof. Gosh.'

'This,' she panted. 'Will do you. The world. Of good. Madam.'

'I can see why people come back year after year,' I said, beginning to feel my way.

'They have. So far. Anyway,' Regina said.

This was an opening indeed, if I could just decide how best to use it.

'It must be odd for your old regulars suddenly to have Dr Laidlaw Sr gone and so many changes,' I said. Regina said nothing. She poured on a little more oil, smacked her hands together and set about a different bit of my back, somewhat towards the sides and threatening to be ticklish if I did not try hard to avoid thinking of it in that way.

'Unless you mean something else?' I said. I waited for a while. There was no sound except the unlovely one of oily hands smacking against oily back as she pitched herself with gusto at her task. 'You don't mean that Mrs Addie will cause a scandal, do you?' Her hands lifted off my skin and there was silence except for her fast breathing. I craned round trying to see her and, at the sight of her patient twisting about that way, she was spurred back into action. She laid her hands rather tentatively on my skin, but did not move them.

'I never said that,' she whispered. 'How did you even know about poor Mrs Addie? I never said any such thing.'

'Of course not, my dear,' I said. 'One hears gossip, but not from you. Most commendable.'

'I was fond of her,' Regina said. 'I'd not make tittle-tattle out of her going off that way.' Rather uncertainly, she recommenced her pummelling. 'Anyway it was her heart. It could have happened any time and anywhere. At home, in the pictures.' The rhythm was back to normal, the slaps ringing out again.

'But it happened here,' I said.

I must say, if it could be arranged, it would be splendid to have every interview in every case accompanied by a vigorous back-rub. I could tell from the faltering of her hands again that what I had just said was troubling, could tell it as plain as day before she spoke a sound. And then her words when they came said the same.

'That was the story,' she said. 'But it wasn't true.' I am sure that she must have felt my muscles turning to iron but she made no reference to it. 'She went out, madam. She collapsed away out somewhere. And that right there's enough to stop any nasty talk. She wasn't supposed to be out. She wasn't supposed to go out traipsing for another week. Dr Laidlaw had a full regime all drawn up. If she'd stuck to it, she might be here today, because it was working. You could tell already it was. So as to any scandal sticking to the Hydro, I should say it's the other way on. Vice versa.' As she became more adamant in her words so did she in her rubbing. By the end of this speech I was being thrown about like a cork in the tide and had to grip the couch to hold on.

'She wasn't here?' I said. 'Well, in that case, I agree. Nothing for the Laidlaws to worry about. But why would they say she was at the Hydro if she was out on the town?'

'I don't know,' said Regina. 'I can tell you that, hand on heart. I don't know that I'd say she was in the town, mind you. I thought maybe the woods. The hills, you know.' Privately, I agreed. If she was going to see a ghost and collapse then a lonely spot seemed much more like it. There were only two problems: what had an Edinburgh matron who thought the world of the Hydro been doing in the hills or woods instead of availing herself of the many facilities and diversions for which she had come all this way? That was one. The second problem was even more thorny. If Mrs Addie was out on a wooded hillside in the dark, how exactly had Dr Laidlaw managed to find her there?

I was silent after that, thinking it through without ever being able to frame a question to put to Regina. Before long, she finished me off with a percussive set of blows all up and down my spine from nape to waist and then wiped me with a warm cloth and patted me nicely dry. It was an effort to peel myself up off the couch after the way she had tried to press me into it like a flower after a nature walk, but once I was up I felt quite wonderful and I thought to myself that I really had to try to run into her sometime when I had my bag with me so I could tip her. She did not loiter hopefully, to her credit, but bustled off and left me to wriggle back into my robe and make my own way to the cubicle and my clothes.

I dressed quickly and did not fuss with my hair, eager to get to what I was going to do next. In the dining room – it was comfortably luncheon-time now, although rather early for the bright young things – I scanned the tables for a likely party. Before I spotted one, though, Hugh spotted me and waved me over to make up a fourth with the boys and him. Odd, I thought, waving back and moving towards them. I was not puzzled for long.

'Teddy tells me you've driven poor Osborne off already,' he said, while pushing in my chair. 'Back to Edinburgh on the noon train.'

'Briefly,' I said. 'And nothing to do with me. He had some business or errand of his own to see to. He'll be back tonight, he said, if he can possibly manage it.' Hugh grinned.

'I don't doubt it,' he said. 'And you'll be taking the boys back to the house after tea? You're not staying here for dinner, are you?'

I surveyed the luncheon menu: tomato soup, calf's head brawn, roasted mushrooms, cauliflower cheese, pickled cabbage, loganberry pudding, mint creams.

'I shan't be staying for dinner,' I said firmly. 'In fact, since I'm walking down to the town and the town is so very well served with tea shops and I'm not actually hungry at the moment, I don't think I'll stay for luncheon. Nice to have seen you and said hello, though. Four o'clock in the lobby, boys.'

'I could walk down to the town with you, Mummy,' said Teddy. 'Donald's having his seat in the electric chair.'

'Please don't call it that,' I scolded. 'Not even in jest. I'm going to the lending library, you can certainly come there with me and choose something to read. And then I need to find a hat shop where they do repairs and cleaning, and Mrs Tilling wanted me to track down a florist since the gardens are so bare. You're more than welcome—'

'Never mind,' said Teddy. I had named three of his least favourite establishments. The hat shop alone would have been enough to send him packing. 'There's a little lending library here. I'll see what they can cough up for us.'

'Don't say "cough up",' said Hugh and I almost in perfect unison and we parted on good terms, as always when we agree on something.

On my way out of the dining room I had another scout about for a likely table. Of course Hugh, if he saw me, would withdraw from our shared view of Teddy's vocabulary into his more usual disapproval of me and all my works, but that was not to be helped. Almost at the door, tucked away to the side of the serving table, I saw what I was looking for. Three of the most overdressed, over-coiffed, over-maquillaged women I am sure the Hydro dining room had ever contained: one of them had lace mittens on and yet was spreading brawn onto a cracker. One of the others had a hat perched on her piled-up hair, with so many greenish-black feathers I had to squint to make sure it was not a whole crow.

'Good afternoon,' I said, sidling up to them and standing with my hands on the back of the free chair. 'I've only just found out that you're here. I hope you don't mind me stopping by to say hello.' I was scanning all three of them, and I spotted one preening herself slightly. I stuck my hand out to this one. 'Dandelion Gilver,' I said, thankful for the first time in my life that my parents had given me such a ridiculous name.

'Petrushka Molyneaux,' she said, with a bow which made the feathers catch the light and gleam greener than ever. A likely story, was what I thought. Patsy Miller, probably.

'Of course,' I said. 'How exciting to have you here. And so unexpected. I'm here with my husband and sons who've all been ill with this wretched flu. I had no idea. Does Moffat have lots of ghosts then? I've never heard of any.'

Mrs Molyneaux's face snapped like a rat-trap and her companions recoiled from me.

'A handful,' said the one with brawn in the lace of her mittens. 'The usual number. For the tourists.' She did not say 'such as yourself'. She did not need to.

'That is not why we're here,' said the third of the coven, a young white-faced woman with thin pale hair and enormous pale green eyes like gooseberries. 'And certainly not why Madame Molyneaux has left her consultancy and come all this way.' After a few further pleasantries had been rather stiffly exchanged I left with a flea in my ear (but thinking 'consultancy, indeed'). What charlatans!

Charlatans or no, however, they had given me an idea. If Mrs Addie had conjured a ghost for herself it was more than likely one of the handful laid on for the tourists, and what better way to learn of those than to visit the public library after all.

The rain had let up and although the going was unpleasant, especially as the wind had shaken free the first of the leaves which were now lying sodden underfoot, the air was clear and sparkling and I strode out with a light heart and an empty stomach. This is my favourite internal arrangement if I can manage it, so long as there are pots of tea and buns at my destination; and there were. If Alec could confirm that Mrs Addie believed in ghosties and ghoulies and I could find some witness to place her at one of Moffat's haunted spots, then we could add our voices to the chorus singing 'heart attack' and file the case under jobs well done.

There was no public library in Moffat town, I soon learned, but the reading room in the bath house included, as well as the circulating library, a large reference collection and in one corner, better all the time, a wooden sign hanging on chains and reading 'Local History: please enquire here.' At a desk under this sign, which swung gently in the breeze as I closed the outside door, was the perfect person, just who I wanted to see. She was sixty if a day, high-coloured, dressed with a little more panache than one might look for in a librarian, and she had the round bright eye of one who is interested in all that passes around her. The town gossip, in short, or rather one of the no doubt dense tangle of them; and with those bright gold chains around her neck and that enormous brooch of unlikely blue stones, she did not look the sort of devout little body who would be shocked to speak of the things I was going to ask her.

'Good afternoon,' I said, sitting. Those bright eyes took in everything about me, head to toe, in an instant.

'Good afternoon,' she said. 'How may I help you?'

'I have rather an odd request.' I delivered this with a little wriggle and a titter. Neither of these came naturally to me and so I hoped she believed them. 'I'm interested in the . . . folklore of your delightful town. Folk tales, you know.' From the way she kept peering at me, politely enquiring, no sign of a nod or a smile, it appeared that she did not. I tried again.

'Fascinating, these old superstitions. One wonders how they begin.' She blinked but otherwise her face remained, as before, polite, interested and utterly devoid of any signs of understanding. 'I was in Alloway, recently. Most interesting, the bridge and the kirkyard and all of that . . .'

'Oh, ghosts!' she said in tones one might have expected to be drummed out of a librarian by years of whispering. The very lampshades rang above our heads.

'Ghosts it is,' I said. 'Are there any materials I might consult which would cover—'

'Oh, we're very well off for ghosts!' she exclaimed. I wished she would not keep declaiming the word at full volume. 'That's not an unusual request at all. Why it's only a matter of weeks since I was telling the last reader who wanted to know all about them.'

'Indeed? Are there many?'

'Oh yes, madam. Well there's the Haunted Ram, of course.'

'A public house?' I asked.

'A ram,' she corrected. 'Haunted. And the Devil's Beef Tub is notorious.'

'Haunted cows?'

She sailed on. 'And then, let me see, there's Yellow Mary at the well, although she's not been seen so much since the new wee housie was built there. I always fret that she's trapped underneath it, you know. And not a soul that belongs to Moffat would go up the Gallow Hill at the full moon. Will I write these down for you, madam? I could draw you a wee map too.'

Fifteen minutes later, I came reeling out into the uncertain sunshine with my wee map in my hand and my head swirling with phantasms too many to number; Moffat most certainly was a place where the dead seemed to go about their business unimpeded by their change of state and with no thoughts of lying down quietly and mouldering.

The Devil's Beef Tub was not haunted by cattle after all, but by the spirits of the marauding Johnstone clan – the infamous Border Reivers – and by the spirits of such of their enemies as had tried and failed to besiege them there and grab the stolen herds back again. The problems of the Gallow Hill spoke for themselves. Apparently the earth turned red with the blood of the hanged in the light of the full moon each month (I had forborne to mention to the little librarian that hanging does not cause much bloodshed and that I happened to know that the dark of the moon is the time when nights get really tricky). Even leaving aside Yellow Mary at the well, since she had evidently been squashed, that still left quite a parade of the usual suspects. To wit: a century ago either William Burke or William Hare had stopped the night at the Black Bull Inn, a century before that Bonnie Prince Charlie had watered his horses and left a soldier to die on the banks of the stream. Bloody Mary, of course, had passed a few nights in a nearby castle and her grief and sorrow had seeped into its walls. Reaching back into history, Bruce and Wallace and even Malcolm had paused at Moffat on their travels, watering their horses again (a thirsty lot, the mounts of these Scottish warriors) and imbuing the hills and fields with the sort of vanquished hopes and tragic disappointment which inevitably end up as grey ladies and headless pipers.

I consulted the map and decided to start with the Ram, since it was closest to me. Almost too close, I decided a few minutes later, standing in the middle of the High Street and staring up at it. If Mrs Addie had collapsed here, with scores of houses all around and, even in the evening, plenty of passers-by walking to and from the many inns and public houses, someone would have seen her. Of course, I was hoping that someone *would* have seen her – corroboration of Sergeant Simpson's story was my purpose in this ghost hunt after all – but this spot, halfway up the busiest street in town and only a stone's throw from the water trough where every carter rested his horses like all of his kings before him, was far too unguarded a setting for a death which had been so carefully bowdlerised. If a woman had clutched her heart and dropped to the ground here in front of Moffat's most famous ghost it would surely have been in the papers and the Addies' feelings could not have been spared no matter if the Lord Chief Justice himself joined the Fiscal in wishing them so.

Besides, no one would die of fright from this haunting. The librarian had told me the whole story and there was not enough in it to cause a decent shriek never mind a heart attack. The statue – an impressive bronze of a large full-coated and fully horned ram, standing proudly on a soaring stone base (which might have looked like a mountain crag if the mortar between the stones had not been picked for contrast) – had been commissioned by one William Colvin, a prosperous local farmer, in honour of the town where he had prospered. All was well until, after his death, the statue had been moved from the spot he had so carefully chosen to this one and, displeased, he took up residence inside it and manifested his presence by 'ghostly tapping'. I lifted one side of my hat brim – current fashions worked hard against efficient eavesdropping – edged around one of the four basins set about it and laid my head against the base.

There was silence within. Without, there was laughing. I straightened up and turned to see a pair of housewives, their shawls crossed over their breasts and their full baskets hefted high, giggling at me.

'Colvin's ghaist only comes oot at nicht,' said one.

'Aye, so does mice,' said the other. And I nodded, for I agreed. Tapping noises from inside a hollow stone plinth and the hollow bronze sheep above it would always suggest nesting rodents and not unquiet spirits to me.

I looked once again at the pencilled map the librarian had sketched for me. The Devil's Beef Tub was a fair walk out of town. The well where Yellow Mary lay under the new wee housie was a shorter walk but a stiffer climb, up past the Hydro and around the back of Gallow Hill. Gallow Hill itself I could see looming up to the east and I quite simply was not shod for it. I let my eyes come down the slope to where the Hydro sat, flags flying, windows twinkling, and I was aware of a shift of unease inside me. A house near a church is favoured by villagers, whether for the respectability conferred by such neighbours or for the sanctuary near at hand, should the devil ride, but I always wonder at those cottagers whose gardens abut the graveyard walls, as they often do. Does it ever occur to them as they look with pride at their soaring beans and swelling roots that the rich earth which feeds their crops is fed in its turn? Similarly now, I had to question the placing of a hydro, supposed to offer complete relaxation, in the lee of a gallow hill. Would not exactly those who thought a sulphurous drench would cure their arthritis also believe that the shadow of such a place would disturb their rest? If it came to that, I wondered how many knew that the sulphurous waters themselves came from a well where a Yellow Mary once was found. If she were yellow from the sulphur it suggested she had fallen in and drowned there. If she were yellow from fever then, even if she only lived nearby, it was hardly a testimonial. Or was I getting confused between yellow fever and Typhoid Mary and making more than I should out of nothing? I turned away and surveyed the High Street instead. I was admirably shod for a stroll to a tea shop. Perhaps there was a better way to discover which ghost Mrs Addie had met in the night. Perhaps Regina, who thought it was to the hills and woods that Mrs Addie had gone, would know a little more and could tell me at least which hill or which wood was most likely.

I stopped in my tracks. Of course she knew more, my little round pummelling friend. She must have heard Dr Laidlaw or Dr Ramsay or someone say 'Gallow Hill' or 'the Beef Tub' or something when they brought the invalid back again. How else could she have a view on the matter at all? I abandoned my plans for tea, thinking that there was bound to be a substantial offering at the Hydro very soon, and retraced my steps up the hill.

I should have to find another way of communing with Regina very soon, I thought as I shrugged out of my clothes again. I wondered if I could discover her afternoon free, if Grant could be made to invite her to tea, and if I could gatecrash their party and grill her.

In the meantime, I settled down on the little velvet-covered bench in the changing cubicle with my robe about me, to listen for the squeak of her rubber-soled shoes on the polished boards. I wanted to speak to her but not enough to brave the heat again. I tucked my feet up and made myself very comfortable, except for a faint rumbling in my middle.

The next thing I knew, I started awake at the sound of a cubicle door banging next to me. My neck, its fictitious crick well cured by Regina only that morning, was actually cricked now and made a horrid clicking sound as I stretched it. I was just about to stand and unknot my back and legs too when I became aware of a whispered conversation drifting over the top of the cubicle wall.

'Two women, a mother and daughter, Peggy and Lizzie. That's what she said to me. And that's what brought me.'

'They're common enough names,' came the reply.

'And then what I heard myself, you will not believe when I tell you.'

'Heard from where?'

'Someone who rang up the offices looking for guidance. Rang up after I'd come down here and they passed it along. He didn't know what he was saying at all. Hadn't a clue.'

'And what was it?'

'An old woman and a blind child.' There was a gasp and then a long silence.

'Truly? A blind child?'

'A wee boy. And his grandmother.' This brought another gasp. 'Both very troubled, a lot of turbulence, a lot of excitement.'

'Peggy and Lizzie and an old woman and a blind child.' Her voice had a tone of awe about it now. 'And how many more?'

'Ah,' said the voice. 'That's the question. How many more? Eleven or thirteen? Who's to say?'

'But what I meant was how many more have been contacted.'

'Three more so far.'

'Someone needs to take charge. Someone needs to draw up a list and make sure. We need . . .'

'We most certainly do.' There was a dramatic pause. 'And he is on his way. He is coming from London today and arrives tonight.'

At that thrilling moment – and it was thrilling even to me who did not have the first clue what the thrill might be – a door opened and the unmistakable sound of Regina advancing could be heard all along the cubicle corridor. The two women in the next cubicle opened the door and began to walk away. I opened my own a crack and put my eye to it, watching them.

Of course, it is hard to tell much when everyone is wearing white towelling robes and has her hair twisted up in a turban. One was short and thin and could, I reckoned, be the slip of a girl with the gooseberry eyes I had met at luncheon – she was Mrs Molyneaux's friend after all – and the other was taller and broader, older too by the look of her gait. She might have been one of those I had seen arriving, but from what this pair had just said there were ghost hunters descending upon the Hydro from all around. From London!

I watched them until they disappeared through the velvet curtains and then I opened the door wide. When I did, it was to see Regina, standing with a bundle of wet towels in her arms, regarding me with a look composed of three parts politeness and two parts amusement upon her face.

'Mrs Gilver,' she said. 'Back *again*?'

'Not for more rubbing,' I said. 'And not for more heat.'

'That's all we do in the Russian and Turkish,' she said. Perhaps I imagined that her eyes flared with alarm but I did not think so.

'I simply want to talk to you, my dear,' I said. She looked down at the bundle of towels in her arms and took a step backwards.

'I've to get these to the laundry,' she said.

'I don't want to make any trouble,' I assured her. 'Not for you or for anyone.'

'It's about Mrs Addie, isn't it?'

'I just want to know where she was,' I said. 'Where she went exactly.'

'Why?' said Regina. 'How will that help you?'

'Witnesses,' I replied. 'If someone saw her then there's proof she was there.' She started again to back away. Those two words – 'proof' and 'witnesses' – spoken together had startled her. I left the cubicle and walked beside her, following her right through the staff door and into a bare, distempered corridor.

'You're not supposed to be in here,' she said, miserably.

'Regina, my dear,' I said, relentless (I am not proud of myself sometimes), 'I am sure that Mrs Addie died of a heart attack. I think it was misguided of the Laidlaws to try to spare her relatives' feelings. They should have told them everything. I'd like to tell them everything and then their minds will be at rest. That's all. Nothing to worry you. Now, where exactly did she go when she went out?'

'I don't know,' Regina said. 'I don't even know when it was – except I know it was that Monday – and I don't know how she got there.'

'Walked, I suppose,' I said, and did not miss the glance she gave me. 'Very well, let me try another tack. What made you think she'd been in the country and not in the town?'

'Because of how she was dirty, madam,' she said. 'She was like a bairn that's been playing out.'

'You saw her?' I said. I wished that we were sitting at a tea table where I could ply Regina with buns, instead of standing in this draughty dark corridor with a load of damp towels doing their best to make things dreary. If Regina had witnessed the dying Mrs Addie's return she might well have more to tell me.

'I suppose you could say that,' she said. 'I . . . saw . . . her after the doctor was gone. I laid her out. The undertaker would have done it, but Dr Laidlaw wanted us to take care of her. Nicer that way. And Mrs Cronin was out, with it being Monday, and so it fell to me.'

I was working hard not to let my jaw drop open. This girl had actually washed and clothed the body! If there was a mark of violence upon her, Regina would know.

'And when you laid her out, she was dirty,' I said.

'She was. I remember saying to myself, well to Mrs Addie really, the poor lady. I said, "Where have you been then? What have you been up to?" She looked like she'd been out scrambling up and down hills. Dirt under her nails. Dirty knees. She'd had a bit of a wash, like, off the doctor it must have been, when she got home, but she was still grubby. I made her nice as nice, anyway, when she fell to me. I was always fond of Mrs Addie. I was sorry to see her go.' She broke off at the sound of someone moving in the distance, the squeal of brisk steps in those rubber-soled shoes. I laid a hand on her arm.

'Regina, if you had to guess: where would someone scramble and slip? The Beef Tub, the well or the Gallow Hill? If you've been walking there?'

'Why would she go to one of those places?' she said. She was pulling away from me as the footsteps came closer. I glanced towards the turn in the passageway. I only had a minute.

'To see Yellow Mary or the Reivers or the spirits of the hanged,' I said. To be fair, I must have seemed like a madwoman suddenly to spout these words, gripping her plump little arm like the ancient mariner, hissing at her in the dark that way. She snatched herself free.

'Mrs Addie?' she said. 'Is that what they're saying? That she was one of *them*? She was none of the kind! Is that why they've come then? She was never!' And she turned on her heel and sped off as fast as she could, barrelling along the passageway as though Yellow Mary and the Reivers and the spirits of all the hanged were after her. I hurried back to the staff door, opened it and slipped through, with the merest glance behind me as the foot-steps grew closer still. Idiot! If I had kept my back turned I would have been just another figure in a white robe and turbanned towel. As it was, Mrs Cronin got a good look at me.

7

One thing that can be said for scares and alarums is that they take one's mind off missed meals wonderfully. I had not eaten a bite since my poached egg at breakfast and yet when I climbed back into my clothes again for the third time that day, I did not go straight to the drawing room to wait for tea. I carried on past the doorway, noting that most of the other guests had begun to assemble, and made straight for the telephone in the front hall. It was in a comfortable little kiosk just opposite the door and commanded a moderate amount of privacy. I did not lift the earpiece right away. I needed a moment to marshal my thoughts.

Was Mrs Addie hunting for ghosts? Regina thought not and Alec would soon be able to add her family's views on the matter. Very well then, was she out and about on some other errand and happened simply to see one? Why did she return at night? And where did she return to? Did she bring anything back with her? How did Dr Laidlaw happen to follow her there? Only one of these questions had I the least chance of answering.

'Mrs Bowie,' I said, when the call had been put through and the servant had summoned her. 'I am so pleased to be able to have a word with you, but it is actually Mr Osborne I'm hoping to catch.'

'Oh Mrs Gilver, you missed him!' said Mrs Bowie. There was no outrage in her voice, no disapproval. I guessed that Alec had managed to ascertain Mrs Addie's views on the spirit world without offending her daughter to the point of sulking. 'He was here a good couple of hours but he's away to catch his train now. He'll be back with you before much longer.' I heard her voice grow strained as she twisted her neck, I guessed, to see a clock in the room where she was speaking.

'Oh, dash it,' I said. 'I so much wanted to ask him to raise a few more questions with you than he went away armed with. Our investigation goes on apace, Mrs Bowie, and I have made some pertinent discoveries today.'

'Can you not just ask me yourself?' she said, falling neatly into my plan.

'Well, how very accommodating of you,' I said. 'I should not for the world have asked you to hang on a telephone and be interviewed but if you are sure . . .'

'For my dear mother's rest, anything,' said Mrs Bowie. She would bend over backwards head to heels now that this telephone interview was her own idea. My devious tricks shock me sometimes.

'We are trying to piece together your mother's last day,' I said. 'And I wondered—'

'Oh, but dear Mr Osborne thought of that,' said Mrs Bowie. I noted the adjective with interest. Not only had he not offended the woman; he had made a conquest of her. 'He said it occurred to him coming up on the train.'

'And could you help him with it?' I said.

'Not with much more than we could tell you at our first meeting,' she said. 'She wasn't going to go out for a few days yet. She had treatments planned for all day every day and it was going to be later in the week before she could get down to the town to get some tablet and send a postcard. That's what we told you, if you remember.'

'I certainly do,' I said. 'But did Mr Osborne happen to mention that we think your mother's plans might have changed? We think she did indeed go out that day. The day she died – I'm so sorry to speak baldly, I mean no incivility by it.' This was me trying too late and most likely in vain to match what I am sure had been Alec's Arthurian heights of tender chivalry.

'He did say as much,' said Mrs Bowie, 'but my brother and I are quite in agreement that he – you both, pardon me – are mistaken. If Mother went out she'd have sent me a card, if not a wee parcel, and well . . .'

'Yes?'

'It wouldn't be like her. She always adhered to her treatment diary. It was like a sacred duty to her. She had such regard for old Dr Laidlaw; she'd never have gone against what the Hydro told her to do.'

'I see,' I said. 'I do see, and I daresay you're right, Mrs Bowie. But there's one last thing that Mr Osborne might have neglected to ask. I wonder – I've no desire to upset you – but when your mother's effects came back to you, did you happen to go through them? Did you look through her pockets? Tidy out cloakroom receipts and suchlike. And I wonder – this must seem like awful cheek – but have you sorted through her clothes and shoes and things? Laundered them or sent them for cleaning?'

There was a long silence at the other end. I thought I had horrified the woman, harping on about the clothes and shoes and the very bus tickets of the dead woman. But when eventually she drew breath and spoke again it was not that at all.

'Now, fancy you thinking of that, Mrs Gilver,' she said. 'You really are a pair of wonders, Mr Osborne and you. I've been meaning to write to Dr Laidlaw and ask about Mother's bag and about the clothes she was wearing that day. Her trunk came back right enough on the train, all clean and tidy, and her overnight bag too with her nightgowns. And of course her earthly remains themselves came back. We had the funeral right here in Morningside. But her things from that last day are missing.'

Quietly to myself in the kiosk I mimed whipping a hat off my head and throwing it in the air. *Huzzah!* I was willing to bet they were missing. I was absolutely willing to bet they were. They must have been filthy.

'Not that we're making a fuss over a suit of clothes,' Mrs Bowie was saying now. No Eliza Doolittle she, caring about what had happened to a new straw hat what should have come to her. 'It's just that she always carried her father's watch in her bag.'

'Her *bag's* missing?' I said, astonished that they would accept such a thing.

'Oh, not her proper handbag,' said Mrs Bowie. 'Just her little bag that she kept with her and took out on wee short walks and so on.'

'Ah,' I said. 'I see.'

'It's just that it had a lock of hair from our brother who died, inside the watch-case you see . . . and there were some very precious letters too that she always kept with her. I'd like to have them again if we could find them. Only with all the ill feeling after the police and the Fiscal and all of that, it never did seem like the right time to write and ask and . . .'

'Leave it to me, Mrs Bowie,' I said. 'Put it right out of your mind and leave it to me.' What I really meant was 'For heaven's sake don't write now and go mucking everything up for us' but one cannot talk to clients that way.

'I shall, Mrs Gilver,' she said, 'most thankfully.' With that we made our farewells and I hung up the earpiece and sat back. I had gone panning for silver and found gold.

It was the bag. The Laidlaws and Dr Ramsay and Sergeant Simpson together had decided not to upset the Addies with talk of their mother crashing through undergrowth, chasing ghosts, and tumbling to her death, and so they must have packed her dirty clothes and shoes away, hoping that her son and daughter would never think to ask for them. Perhaps they had even burned them in the boiler if they were really ruined. But they would never have kept or burned a woman's handbag, not even a little indoor bag, surely, with her husband's watch and her cache of letters, presumably tied with a red ribbon and unmistakably precious to the most casual glance. That would have been returned with her trunk and case and her 'proper bag', surely. The only explanation I could come up with was that when she was brought home that night, she had no longer had her bag with her. She had dropped it, lost it somewhere. And if we were lucky and searched very hard it might still be there, lying where it fell.

A shaft of sunlight broke over my head and a choir of angels sang my name in a sweet piping soprano. If one drops a bag somewhere, one returns to search for it. Hallelujah. I might not know why Mrs Addie went out on a spree in the afternoon instead of submitting to her heat lamps and mustard wraps, but I thought I knew why she went back again at night. She was not a ghost hunter hoping to see better against a dark sky than the glimpse she had caught in the daytime. She was a woman with a bundle of precious letters and a lock of precious hair who would venture out to find them even if a ghost was in the offing.

I stood at last – it was my day for huddling in little booths until I was cramped – and as I stretched I heard footsteps and, although there is nothing illicit in making a telephone call from a telephone kiosk, I shrank from emerging but sidled forward and peeped out instead, remaining hidden.

It was two guests, small cases in hand, clearly departing. A couple of Tot's bright young things in their short skirts, high-heels and fox furs.

'Thanks ever so for giving me a lift, ducks,' said one in that infuriating mock-cockney that was all the rage.

'You shouldn't use that accent at the meeting,' said the other. 'They'll think you're teasing. And I'd happily give you a lift all the way to town if you like, not just the station.'

'Oh no, I'm as sick as a kitten in motorcars,' said the first. 'Much better on trains. And of course, I shan't play-act at the meeting. It's serious stuff.'

'What are you going to say? I'd be terrified even to go in the door! They must be monsters.'

'Perfectly respectable men and women, I think,' said her friend. 'I'm going to tell them that Mary Patterson visited me. That she stood by my bed and spoke.'

'What did she say?' The woman's voice was soft, like a child, all the idiot chirping stopped for a moment.

'That she forgave her killers and repented of all her sins.'

'Too absolutely shivery-making for words. How can you?'

'Why not,' said the other. 'After all, that's what happened.'

'Stop it!'

'I opened my eyes and there she was and she looked at me out of her black, black eyes and said, "I am Mary Patterson. I forgive my killers and repent of my sins."'

'Stop, you beast!'

And then both of them shrieked as outside on the drive a motorcar parped its horn. Then they giggled and tripped off down the steps in their silly heels and their silly hats towards the door.

'Ladies,' said a voice. I stuck my head out of the kiosk. Alec Osborne was holding the door open for them, bowing them on their way. 'Hello, Dandy,' he said as he trotted up the steps towards me. 'Have you been there all day since I left? Pining? Well, I'm back now and I have interesting news.'

'Hello, Alec darling,' I said. 'So do I but it's not the sort that can be delivered on the doorstep. It needs a fireside and a glass of something sustaining.'

'Ah, your signature rambling,' said Alec. 'I'm very fond of it, but I warn you it might act as a lullaby after a day like today.'

'Well, deliver your headline then,' I said.

'Mrs Addie didn't believe in ghosts,' he said.

'I know,' I answered. 'In fact, she showed a great deal more courage in the face of one than I could be sure to.'

'You are absolutely infuriating, Dandy,' he said. 'Four bloody hours on a train with no dining carriage it took me to glean that from the Addies. Tinned soup for lunch and no tea.'

'You haven't missed tea,' I said. 'Stop moaning and let's find Hugh and the boys.'

His spirits recovered over Whitstable sandwiches, ginger buns and orange syrup cake and the boys at their most amusing and least annoying. Afterwards, he, I and they set off for Auchenlea leaving Hugh alone, looking like the cat that ate canary in cream sauce. He rippled his eyebrows at me as we were leaving for all the world as though he did not mind Alec and me working, but rather was glad to see me go.

Back at the house, the boys were packed off to their rooms to rest and change for dinner (and were glad to go after a day of the strenuous treatments Dr Laidlaw had decreed for them), Bunty was prised from the kitchen to my side where she belonged, and Alec and I settled in by the drawing-room fire with sherry.

It really was the most pleasant room, deep chairs with high backs and some of the least draughty windows I had ever come across in Scotland. For a moment I wondered if I would have been better to summon a glazier to Gilverton instead of a plumber, then I thought of turning a tap and having a torrent of hot water come gushing out and decided I would put up with a lot of draughts along with that delight. Besides, it is dark twelve hours a day, six months a year and one can close shutters and draw curtains over the rattling windows. I put Gilverton out of my mind and smiled at Alec.

'There is an enormous and unspeakable thing we must discuss,' I said, 'but let's leave it aside as long we can. So instead: how did you manage to broach the question and keep in Mrs Bowie's good books? I'm most impressed.' This was true, but he saw through my ruse in reporting it. He sat up straight and held his hands under his chin, letting his tongue loll out and panting like a puppy.

'Don't patronise me, Dandy,' he said. 'I thought of something else I wanted to ask and managed to slip it in.' Then he sat back again. I cocked my head and waited. 'I told them there was some sort of spiritualists' jamboree going on – a bit of poetic licence as to time and place, you know – and would their mother be likely to duck out of any of her treatments to go and see the fun.'

'I don't follow,' I said.

'Because I'd hate to accuse the Laidlaws of harming the old lady with some electric bath or whatever if she had been out on the town and never gone near the thing.'

'Oh, very twisty,' I said. 'Well done you. And Mrs Bowie said her mother didn't hold with ghosts?'

'She did.'

'Well, it's funny you should have happened to talk of Mrs Addie bunking off,' I said, 'because – here is my news – she *was* outside when she collapsed. Possibly even when she died.'

'Outside?' Alec said. 'In the grounds, you mean? I'm not sure I see why you stopped the presses for that, Dan.'

'Not in the grounds and you will,' I replied and went on to

relate Regina's evidence in the matter of her dirty nails and grimy knees. 'And not only can I explain why she went back out at night, I think we might be able to prove it.' Now Alec cocked *his* head. I sailed on.

'I can't say I'm keen,' he concluded when I was done. 'We could spend a fair old time thrashing about looking for a little handbag with two long paths and a high hill to choose from.'

'But if we found it,' I persisted. 'If we proved that she wasn't here when she died.'

'What if we did?' said Alec. 'The tiniest of white lies to spare her children pain. Why don't we just tell Dr Laidlaw that the Addies are suspicious. Tell her that her discretion has backfired and ask her to write to them and set out the whole story? Why not do that? Aren't we making a lot of bother for ourselves over nothing?'

I shook my head. 'I would love to get her talking, but only if I could do it without showing my hand. I'm sure I could trip her up if I could just get started on it somehow.'

'You're convinced that there's something for her to trip over then?' Alec said.

'Completely convinced,' I said. 'How did Dr Laidlaw manage to find Mrs Addie for one thing? What was *she* doing out in the night where the ghosties are? There's something very wrong with that story somewhere. Not to mention the fact that she wouldn't sign the death certificate and pushed it off onto Ramsay instead.'

'And then also,' said Alec, 'according to you anyway, there's the mystery of the locked room. Didn't you say she gave it fearful looks and went pale?'

I clicked my fingers and tutted. 'Yes. And so did Regina and I meant to ask her about it. After how I scared her today she'll never let me ask her anything ever again.'

'I just find it very hard to believe that Dr Laidlaw is a killer somehow,' Alec said. 'Her brother now . . .'

'I know,' I agreed. 'I found myself thinking that too. It's hardly fair but if something nefarious is going on here I would bet Tot Laidlaw's at the bottom of it. He dropped a couple of very mysterious hints to me, you know. Said I'd have to summon courage to make my trip worthwhile and spoke rather archly of how many hydros we had to drive past to get to this one. Almost as though he knows we're not here as patients.' 'The boys' chests will back it up,' said Alec. 'Hugh's too.'

'And he wasn't twinkling and winking when he said it either. Ugh, I loathe hinters. I can't fathom why Hugh seems to have taken to him.'

Alec laughed and went to pour himself another glass of sherry. 'This is lovely wine,' he said. 'You surely didn't find it in the Moffat licensed victuallers.'

'Pallister brought it with him,' I said. 'Why were you laughing?'

'I'm *not* surprised Hugh has fallen on Tot like a long-lost brother,' he said. 'This whole excursion picked up no end for Hugh when Tot came on the scene.'

'He does seem – Laidlaw, I mean – to have drawn a more glamorous crowd than I was expecting.'

Alec was shaking his head and laughing silently. 'Oh, I know he's beyond the pale, but you have to hand it to him. For years on end Thomas Laidlaw was supposed to be training in hydropathy in the Alps, like his father before him and his sister too, but he bunked off. He went to Monte Carlo and made a fortune there. Then when his father died and left him the Hydro, he came home to sell up, couldn't get Dorothea to agree and found a way to turn it to hand. Now, he's making a fortune *here*. Or was for a while. I rather think he's in deep water now and only just breaking even.'

'How?'

'My dear Dandy, he's running a casino.' My mouth fell open and I had to scramble to stop my cigarette falling into my lap and burning me. 'After midnight,' Alec said, 'when all of Dr Laidlaw's patients are tucked up in their little beds, the winter gardens are transformed. The doors to the terrace are bolted, there's a doorman on the only door to the passageway and the respectable majority know nothing.' He laughed again, but he laughed alone.

'Hugh!' I said. 'All those sly looks and that smirking!' For Hugh loves nothing more on earth than a casino, or rather he loves a casino with a passion equal to his love for grouse, stags, well-managed woodlands and tidy farms running at profit and giving work to his men. I have known him take estate plans to Monaco and spend the days in his room poring over them while the sun shines and the sea sparkles outside, whiling away the hours until darkness falls and the croupiers split their decks for the evening. Finding a casino in a Scottish valley with forests and moors and pheasant outside must have seemed to him like a dream come true.

'It's always been an unaccountable quirk of his to me,' I said. 'I like a game of cards at home with friends, but one meets such dreadful people in public casinos. The sort of people who would give Hugh toothache if he had to share their carriage on a train.'

'But taking their money must be lovely,' Alec said. I had to laugh and nod at that, for while Hugh loves to gamble he does not suffer from the gambler's usual complaint of loss and remorse and threatened penury. He is either lucky or brilliant or has an iron will because he always walks away from the roulette wheel and the rouge-et-noir where chance is all, as well as from the poker table and the vingt-et-un where skill can help one, better off than when he arrived; and what losses he has endured over the years have been of the size which can be met with a shrug and an extra glass of whisky before bedtime. It is intensely irritating to me, not least since on the few occasions when I have joined him I quickly lost my all and wanted nothing more than to keep going and win it back again.

'That certainly explains the bright young things,' I said, shoving thoughts of Hugh aside. 'But why do they have to subject themselves to the salts and waters? If it's supposed to convince the staff and other guests that they are patients, it's not working. You said on the first day that there were two camps.'

Alec shook his head.

'I don't know,' he admitted. 'Something to do with tax, maybe? Tot Laidlaw is what my father used to call a warm man. Onto anything that offers a profit.'

'I wonder if he's charging the ghost hunters a premium for the entertainments,' I said. We gave one another a long and sober look.

'Ah yes,' Alec said. 'The enormous and unspeakable thing. Are you going to say it or shall I?'

'Oh, I don't mind *saying* it. I just don't know what to make of it.'

'Go on then.'

'Very well. The Moffat Hydro is a honey pot which draws not bees but spiritualists, mediums and witchety-woos as though it's Hallowe'en at Alloway Kirk.'

'And our suspicious death was apparently caused by a ghostly visitation.'

'These two things must be related.'

'But not in the most obvious way.'

'Which is?'

'That Mrs Addie saw a ghost and the mediums coming to see it too is no different from archaeologists high-tailing it to Egypt because the Earl has found a new tomb.'

'Poor Porchy,' I said. 'He was a sweet man.' Alec was giving me a very hard look. I sighed and relented. 'No, I can't countenance any of that. It troubles me how detailed things are getting, mind you. Some of the ghosts have names.'

'*Some?*' said Alec. 'How many are there?'

'I overheard someone saying seven had been sighted, or heard tapping or whatever ghosts do. And another dozen were in the offing.'

'Seven?' said Alec. 'With names and everything? That can't be a mistake about a piece of flapping cloth on a lonely fencepost then. Someone must be deliberately making it up. In careful detail, as you say.' I was nodding.

'Extremely careful,' I agreed. 'Because actually it wasn't "another dozen or so". There were four with names or descriptions, and another either eleven or thirteen. As though two schools of thought were having a little academic wrangle. And it seems – again from my overhearings: Nanny Palmer would spank me – that some great personage is coming from London, some panjandrum of the spirit world, to subject the goings-on to serious study. The underlings are all atwitter.'

We sat in silence for a short while, turning it over. It is not a pleasant thing suddenly to have one's solemn and serious work made into a nonsense that way.

'So . . .' said Alec at last, 'do we think then that the Laidlaws believe the Hydro is haunted and they wanted to keep it quiet and that's why they suppressed so many of the facts surrounding Mrs Addie dying?'

'Bad for business?' I said. 'Only it's not, is it? The place is filling up like a pub on market day.'

'And I wish it weren't,' Alec said. 'I don't like those mediums. One of them that passed me in the corridor yesterday had the creepiest eyes I've ever seen outside a fairground. Not that we actually believe . . .'

'Of course not!' I said stoutly.

'So what *do* we think?'

'We think someone is making mischief, Mrs Addie caught wind of it and went to see for herself. That's all. And dropped her bag and went back to find it.'

'And died of fright. But we don't believe there was anything to die of fright of. Does that actually make sense, Dandy, when you get right down to it?'

'Yes,' I said, stouter still. 'She could have got a fright from something she imagined. Easily.' I drained my glass in a most unladylike way. 'Or the whole story of the fright and the heart attack could be covering up murder, it's true. But let's not jump down that hole until we have to.'

'I still think we could just tell Dr Laidlaw that we know her patient went out and collapsed somewhere.'

'I'd rather find the bag and not get Regina into trouble,' I said.

'Because if she was unscrupulous,' Alec persisted, 'she'd have signed that certificate. Why can't we at least just ask her about Mrs Addie and see what she says?'

'We can,' I said. I sat straight up in my chair from where I had been slumping in the aftermath of all our good ideas. Here was the best idea I had had all day. 'Oh, it's delicious, of course we can! Well, you can, anyway.'

'Happy to oblige,' Alec said. 'But how can I?'

'It'll be a bit of a performance – laurels galore if you pull it off. What you do is let on to someone – the doctor herself, Tot, Mrs Cronin—'

'The doctor,' said Alec. 'Mrs Cronin is far too strait-laced to perform to. Do you know she doesn't approve of Sunday bathing? Everyone in the Hydro's supposed to just sit and read the Bible from Saturday teatime through to Monday.'

'Very well, the doctor then. And tell her that an apparition came to you in the night. A Mrs A—. That her spirit is troubled. That she is cold and she needs her clothes. That there is something she wants her dear son and daughter to know.'

'Good God, Dandy.'

'It's perfect!' I insisted. 'One ghost among so many? What better place than a haystack to claim that you've seen a straw of hay?'

'Mother?' We both jumped. Donald and Teddy were standing just inside the doorway, dressed in the dinner jackets that still made me blink: where were the little boys whose shirts buttoned onto their britches?

'Are there ghosts in the Hydro?' said Donald.

'Is that why you didn't want us staying there?'

'But you don't care if Daddy gets haunted?'

I could tell them there were no such things as ghosts. I could tell them that the Hydro was unsuitable on account of the illicit casino and that I did not want them growing up to be gamblers like their father in case they had not inherited his luck and ended by ruining us all. Or I could tell them there might be a murderer at large there and that Daddy could take his chances so long as the three of us were safely miles away. None of it cast me in favourable light.

'There seem to be a fair few ghosts floating around, it's true,' I said.

'Are you and Mr Osborne going to catch them?'

'Can we help you?'

'There are a fair few ghost *stories* floating around,' Alec said, shaking his head at me. 'Your mother and I are going to catch the rascal that's spreading them. And you are forbidden to meddle in any way.'

'Hear, hear,' I said.

'Does Father know?' said Donald.

'Your father doesn't believe in ghosts,' I said, hoping that my sleight of hand would go unnoticed. It did not.

'Does Father know about the rascal spreading stories?' Donald said.

'He doesn't, as it happens,' I replied. 'He has been very ill and needs to rest, like the two of you. Now pour yourselves two small sherries – very small for you, Donald dear, for you're to have more port after dinner.' The prospect of strong drink distracted them as I knew it would, and it took the attention of both, for despite the dinner jackets they were still boys and if one was pouring the other would have to watch and see fair measures.

'Well?' I asked Alec softly. 'What do you think of my idea? Will you ask Dr Laidlaw in the morning?'

'It's your turn, strictly speaking,' he replied. 'Since I went to the Addies.' This was not at all my view of it. He had gone to the Addies as a forfeit and his paying a forfeit conferred no debt upon me.

'I can't say I saw a ghost in the night,' I whispered. 'I'm not sleeping there.'

'Say you saw her in the steam room,' Alec said. 'Say she came floating through the locked door.' The mediums in the Turkish bath had said phantasms did not care for steam but the thought of mentioning the door to Dr Laidlaw was enticing. For that reason and to keep from squabbling like the boys over the sherry glasses I threw up my hands in defeat.

'All right,' I said. 'I give in. But the next two nasty jobs shall fall to you.'

8

To add as much verisimilitude to my tale as any story which treats of a ghost can ever contain, I had at least to go through the motions. I had to be where I had to be to see what I was going to claim to see. In other words, yet again, I was off to the Russian and Turkish. I made a neat job of folding my clothes, getting practised now, and I handed over my things to Regina like an old hand. She eyed me very warily but I smiled and said nothing.

'Will you be wanting a rub-down, madam?' she said.

'Not today, thank you,' I answered. 'I'm sorry I upset you yesterday, Regina. Here.' For once, I had thought of tipping before I was stripped of my worldly possessions. The coins went some way towards Regina's unbending and she managed a bob before she left me.

I made my way into the cool room and subsided. Unfortunately it was not empty today and if I were going to play out this charade with any amount of thoroughness I would have to make sure of at least a moment alone. Besides, the locked door was not in view from here. After five minutes I stood and passed through to the warm room. From the far end, when the curtains were open, one had a view through the hot room to the sprays and if one leaned over and squinted, I thought one could surely catch a glimpse of the door too. Unfortunately, three of the beds were occupied: it was far too early for the bright young naked things with their nail files and picture magazines, but there were three swathed and solid matrons (on closer inspection, perhaps one solid matron and her two solid offspring, but such was the extreme degree of the swathing one could hardly tell) and so again I settled myself to wait out the shortest plausible time before moving on again. Even at that, one of the solid offspring opened an eye and spoke to me as I rose.

'Rather you than me, dear,' she said, and then licked the corners of her lips as a drop of moisture, dislodged by her speaking, ran down each cheek and settled there. I was struck again by the way we were all rendered equal, once I had discarded my tweeds and pearls and good silk stockings and she had sloughed off her serge and lisle (to judge by her vowels anyway). I saw the point all at once of nuns' habits and monks' cowls and thought how restful it must be. Then I smiled to myself, imagining Grant, across the valley, suddenly shivering and not understanding why. I drew the hot-room curtain to one side and slipped through.

There was no one in there, I was pleased to see. Neither, however, was there a view of the locked room. Where exactly had I been when I had got a good clear sight of it? I puzzled and then remembered, with a bit of a groan. Of course, I had been sitting on the edge of the plunging pool, trailing my fingers and learning the lie of the land from the doctor. I sat down on the nearest bed, guessing that the ones by the warm-room doorway might be marginally less blistering than the ones at the top end. How far was I willing to take this rigmarole? Since there was no one here I could surely pass through the marble chamber, past the sprays, along the side of the plunge bath and out again. Who was to know? Regina would think it odd that I managed the whole shebang in twenty minutes but only if she saw me.

I could feel my hair beginning to soften and lie down to die on my head again. If I got out right now and gave it a bit of a blotting with a towel, perhaps I could salvage things. I stood and hurried out and then, in the marble slab room, I stopped. There was Regina, rolling up wet towels from the slab benches, wiping the marble dry and unrolling fresh ones.

'That was quick, Mrs Gilver,' she said. I wondered if I were imagining the arch note in her voice, or if she had come here expressly to see if I were really giving myself over to the heat or if I were up to no good and only faking.

'I far prefer the steam to the dry heat,' I said grandly, and swept open the etched glass door.

Of course, I did not prefer the steam heat at all. I loathed all of the rooms and was fast beginning to detest the feel of marble under my feet and the chafe of towelling on my skin, but there was nothing for it now. If Regina was skulking out there to catch me, I was going to have to jump into that dratted icy pool again, and if I was going to freeze myself half to death then I was jolly well going to boil myself up nicely first, hoping to strike a balance that way. Accordingly, I sat in the steam room – all alone: no gossiping ghouls to help the time pass today – until my blood was thumping and my hair hanging in rat's tails to my chin.

When I emerged, it was to the clearest possible sign that Regina had indeed been watching me. She was gone, but in her place Mrs Cronin, the matron, had come and was busily fiddling with the roses on the spray baths in the most unconvincing way.

'Mrs Gilver,' she said. 'You look rather warm.' Anyone else I should have expected of making fun of me, but Mrs Cronin's face was set like the marble behind her, her mouth a grim line, her eyes cold stones, her voice a monotone.

'Nothing a dip won't see to,' I said. I strode through to the pool, wrenched off my robe and then my courage deserted me. I could not, simply could not, jump in again, not now I knew how bad it would be in there. I walked along to the steps and started down them gingerly. I was out of view of Mrs Cronin but the locked door lay dead ahead of me. Blessing my cowardice, I realised that if a ghost really did come floating through the keyhole, I should see it as plain as day and so I could 'see' one as soon as I cared to, before I was in beyond my knees.

My plan went awry in a way I really should have foreseen. Cringing on the steps, staring at the door, I essayed a little start of surprise, in case Mrs Cronin was peeping at me through one of the Turkish archways. My feet were numb, the steps were slippery, in short, I overbalanced and not only ended up completely submerged in the icy sulphurous depths again but this time I cracked my back on the edge of a stone step too. When I rose spluttering, Mrs Cronin was standing looking down at me, her eyes colder and harder than ever.

'Did you see that?' I said.

'You slipped, madam?'

'I nearly broke my neck!' I said. I was dog-paddling back to the steps.

'There is a handrail,' Mrs Cronin said, just as I reached out for it to haul myself up.

'You didn't see?' I asked again. I was out now and sprinting along the side of the pool to the door.

'Here,' she called after me. 'Where are you going?'

I tried the handle and found it locked as I had expected to. Then I whipped round and scanned the room. 'Does . . . steam escape from in there?' I said. 'I suppose it might have been steam.'

'What do you mean?' said Mrs Cronin.

'I could have sworn I saw someone coming out of there,' I said. 'But the door didn't open.'

'Steam, as you say,' Mrs Cronin said. 'And you were overheated. Your eyes might have misted over.'

'And what about my ears?' I demanded. It was only then when I put my hands on my hips to make my point with more force that I realised I was having this conversation quite without clothes. Mrs Cronin was no doubt used to such things, but not I. I faltered, turned away and snatched up my robe.

'How do you mean, madam?' the matron asked me. 'Did you hear something?'

'She spoke to me,' I said. 'She said she had a message for her daughter and her son. And she said she was cold.' Mrs Cronin's eyes were not hard little pebbles now. They looked enormous in her white face.

'Her daughter and her son?'

'Who was it?' I said. 'You know, don't you?'

'It can't be,' said Mrs Cronin.

'Who?' I said, opening my eyes very wide.

'No one,' she said. 'Regina told me you'd been asking about her. That's what's put it in my mind. Nothing else.'

'Mrs Addie?' I asked.

Mrs Cronin's eyes flashed with panic and her face drained of yet more colour until it was grey and wretched. She turned, slipping a little on the wet floor, and blundered away.

I belted my robe and made my exit calmly. Regina was waiting for me by the cubicles. She held out her hand to give me something and when I caught it I was astonished and, frankly, offended to see that it was my two shillings back again.

'I'll not be bought, madam,' she said. 'I work for Dr Laidlaw and I'm proud to say so.'

'I have no idea what you mean, Regina,' I said. 'I certainly didn't mean to imply anything beyond a tip. But I shall tell Dr Laidlaw what a loyal servant she has in you when I see her. And I shall be seeing her very soon. I have just had an extraordinary experience in the plunging-pool room, one I need to discuss with Dr Laidlaw right away.'

'She's very busy,' Regina said.

'Unless *you* would like to tell me what's behind that locked door.'

'How did you—' she said. 'What locked door?'

'And why Mrs Cronin guessed right first time who might be in there.'

'Is she?' Regina turned as if she could see into the room. 'She sometimes goes in there to cry.' Perhaps it was the after-effects of the cold plunge but to hear this said so matter-of-factly made me shiver.

'Have you seen her?' I asked. This was quite at odds with Regina's robust denials of all ghostliness the day before.

'I told you,' Regina said. 'I work for her, not you.'

It took me a moment to understand what she was saying.

'Wait a minute,' I said. 'You thought I meant Dr Laidlaw was in there?' She frowned, as confused as I was. 'I meant Mrs Addie,' I explained. 'Her ghost, trapped in that room, behind the locked door.'

Regina was made of stern stuff and she did not pale or tremble, but only grew very still while she composed her reply.

'There's no such thing as ghosts,' she said at last.

'You might be in the minority at the Hydro these days,' I said, 'holding hard to that view.'

9

It was not difficult to account for the loyalty of Mrs Cronin and young Regina when I entered the doctor's study moments later in response to her low 'Come in'. She looked like a child who had been sent to sit in a grown-ups' toyless room and wait for its punishment there. Her head shrank down between her shoulders when she saw that it was me.

'Mrs Gilver,' she said, managing a faint smile which did not quite banish the troubled look behind it. 'I've just had a very pleasant talk with one of your neighbours. Did you know he was here? A Mr Osborne of Perthshire.'

A dozen quick thoughts chased one another around my head like little fish. I did not know whether to admit to knowing Alec or to deny it. Had he claimed acquaintance of me? In spite of our agreement, had he gone ahead for some reason and told the tale of the visiting ghost instead of leaving it to me? If he had, then his handling of Mrs Bowie yesterday paled into oblivion beside this, for Dr Laidlaw had a soft look in her eye when she spoke his name. Thankfully, she wanted the pleasure of saying it again and she went on, not noticing that I had not answered.

'Mr Osborne is very interested in my work here. Rather unusual.' She lifted a hand to her throat and moved the locket on a chain which sat there. 'I'm hardly ever lucky enough to have a willing audience these days,' she said. 'Since my dear father died. And even he . . . well, we disagreed. Profoundly. Which made for interesting exchanges but I rarely got the chance simply to air my ideas and see what I thought of them.'

Bravo, Alec, I thought to myself, understanding now what he had been up to. Quite simply, he had softened the doctor up for me.

'Yes, he is a pleasant young chap, isn't he?' I said. 'I've often thought so when we've run into one another at parties.' That was a nicely judged compromise between an implausible lack of acquaintance – Perthshire is not so populous as all that – and the sort of intimate friendship which would have to be explained. 'Well, I hope you don't mind a second interruption of your morning's work, Dr Laidlaw, but I have a matter of great urgency to discuss with you.'

She looked at me for the first time then, I think, and looked as a doctor would, taking in my flushed face and dishevelled hair.

'Are you feeling all right, Mrs Gilver?' she said.

'I don't know,' I replied. 'That is, I would have said so and yet I hope not. It would be much better to put it down to illness really.'

She had risen and approached me at this less-than-certain assurance and now she laid a hand against my forehead, felt gently under my jaw with the tips of her fingers, and finished by cupping my face in her hands and turning it up to hers, looking very intently into my eyes. It was a curiously intimate gesture, and not one that any doctor had subjected me to before. I looked back at her quizzically.

'Perhaps you're tired after your disturbed night,' she said.

'I don't follow you,' I said. My sleep *had* been restless; Bunty, taking her time to get used to the new surroundings, had shifted and snuffled and pawed the counterpane every two hours. I, also still getting used to them, had woken each time and taken much longer than her to settle again.

'The fire drill,' Dr Laidlaw said. 'I have no earthly idea why my brother thinks it's a good idea to have them in the middle of the night. Such confusion, everyone rushing around in their dressing gowns.'

'Have you forgotten, Dr Laidlaw,' I said, 'that I'm not staying in the hotel?' The stricken look she gave me was so far beyond what my mild rebuke deserved that I almost reached out and touched her arm, to try to comfort her.

'I'm so sorry,' she said. 'I did. I forgot. I'm so very sorry.'

I laughed lightly to cover the awkwardness.

'Not at all. Think nothing of it. Am I ill then? Is that what caused the strange experience I just had?' She lifted one of my hands to take my pulse, only realising when she lifted her own arm that she was not wearing a watch. She looked instead at the clock sitting in the middle of the jumble of objects on the crowded chimneypiece. It seemed more likely to topple than ever today, from the pressure of the bills stuffed in behind.

While the doctor was counting, I spoke again.

'That treatment room which leads off from the spray baths?' I said. I felt the pinch of her suddenly tightening her grip on my wrist, but it only lasted a moment and then she continued calmly counting. 'What's in there?'

'Nothing,' she said. She let my hand drop and went back to sit behind her desk, even going so far as to rearrange some papers in front of her as though all her reading and writing could defend her against me. 'Just an unused room. It was never very convenient, what with the chance of someone slipping on the wet floor as she arrived or departed.'

'Did someone slip?' I said. 'Did someone fall?'

'No,' said Dr Laidlaw. A blot of colour was beginning to stain her neck. 'Why would you think so?'

'Well, now,' I said. 'I don't say that I believe it, but I can't account for it exactly. The fact is, I think I might just have seen a ghost there.'

Dr Laidlaw froze and for a long empty moment there was silence between us, then she stood, quite roughly pushing her chair back out of the way, and walked over to the window. She could not see anything through that dingy lace curtain, surely, but still she stayed there facing away from me, her shoulders rising and falling as she fought to bring her breath back under control.

'I know how it sounds,' I said. 'Too silly for words, but there it is. I saw something which might have been wisps of steam, coming from the door. Not from under it or from the keyhole, but just as though the steam were passing right through the glass and wood.'

Dr Laidlaw turned to face me again at last.

'Steam,' she said, with a great rush of breath released so that almost she was laughing.

'At first I thought so,' I said. 'It formed . . . a shape.'

'As steam will,' said Dr Laidlaw, nodding.

'And clouds and inkblots, oh absolutely,' I agreed. 'But the thing is, the shape was quite distinctly a woman.'

'It may well have looked like one.'

'And it spoke to me.'

Still nodding, she came back and took her seat behind the desk, smoothing her skirt and once again touching the locket at her throat.

'You were in the plunging pool?' she said.

'On my way in.'

'You had been in the hot room?'

'The steam room.'

'Ah,' she said, sounding almost relieved.

'I see what you mean,' I agreed again. 'I might have been swooning.'

'It sounds that way.' She was calm again now. She went as far as to sit back in her chair and fold her hands in her lap. 'Perhaps you should move from the warm room to the sprays,' she said. 'I love the cold pool – always have done: it's quite my favourite part of the Hydro – but the sprays are much less taxing.'

'I suppose they would be,' I said. 'Shall I tell you what she said?'

Dr Laidlaw inclined her head and smiled patiently.

'Please do. I'm very interested in the mind, Mrs Gilver. In the things it tells us. What words did your mind put into the mouth of this wraith?'

'What a wonderful word,' I said. 'Although she was hardly wraith-like. Very considerable in outline, actually.' I noted a pucker at her brows as she heard this. 'And what this ample wraith said to me was that she had a message for her son and daughter.' Dr Laidlaw drew breath to speak and then stopped, her eyes darting. 'She also said that she was cold and asked where her clothes were. Isn't that a curious thing?'

'Her clothes?' It was a ragged whisper.

'Yes, she was naked. Or at least she might have had a shift on, it's hard to say.'

Dr Laidlaw was shaking her head, just a little, and very fast.

'Impossible,' she said. 'Impossible.'

'I give you my word,' I told her, making myself look affronted. 'Why on earth would it be impossible for my mind to put those words in the mouth I was imagining? The message for her daughter and son sounds like standard seance fare – we used to have them at school you know: great fun, but the mistresses were very down on it always – and as for saying she was cold and wanted her clothes? Well, I was halfway into a bath of ice-water and wearing nothing myself. No, Dr Laidlaw, you have quite set my worries aside. I shall eschew the hot room and the steam room from now on and I shan't think of it again.' I gazed at her out of innocent eyes. She was still struggling, breathing hard and rather wobbly about the mouth, but she managed a nod and a bit of a smile.

'Indeed,' she said. 'Well, I'm glad I could help.'

'And I'm sorry if I upset you,' I said. 'I know that room is a treasured place for you.'

'Treasured?' she said faintly.

'Regina mentioned it,' I said, trying to sound airy. 'That you go there to mourn your father. Was it his study? Surely not, opening off the ladies' sprays that way.'

'To mourn my *father*?' Dr Laidlaw sounded thunderstruck.

'Actually,' I said, nodding as though the thought were only then occurring to me, 'Regina said merely that you go there to weep. I naturally assumed . . . I mean, what else would you be weeping for?'

I loathed myself for this and was determined to scold myself later, but it was certainly working. Dr Laidlaw was quite undone, slumped back in her chair, jaw fallen, eyes wide.

'I can't imagine what Regina meant by saying such a thing. I shall have to—'

'Oh no, please don't!' I said. 'Perhaps I misheard or misunderstood.'

'Yes.' She seized the lifeline.

'As you say, it was all in my imagination, no doubt.' I summoned my very airiest, breeziest voice. 'It must be coincidence the way it's reminding everyone of Mrs Addie.'

She was, quite simply, turned to stone. I loathed myself even more, but only with a very small part of my attention. With the rest of it, I was watching her. Quite soon the little head-shaking motion began again and her lips started moving. She might have been muttering *impossible, impossible* as before, but this time it was too low for me to catch it. When she finally cleared her throat and spoke up, she said exactly what I had been expecting her to.

'Everyone?'

'Regina and Mrs Cronin,' I said. 'But you mustn't think they've been gossiping. You have a tremendously loyal staff here, Dr Laidlaw. The name just popped out unbidden when I described what I'd heard and seen, you know. It couldn't have been helped.'

I left her then, stricken and stranded amongst her dusty papers, and I had to harden my heart to do so. Indeed, glancing back from the door, I almost crumbled. She looked so very young, sitting round-shouldered, with her hands between her knees, staring down at the desktop. Could I really abandon a child who looked that way? More to the point, could I really pass up the chance further to question a woman who looked so utterly defeated? Surely she would succumb and tell me all sorts of things that I needed to know.

After a long pause, with my hand on the door and my better self tussling with the rest of me, I decided to rest on my laurels awhile. Better to leave her stewing and have her dreading my return than to push her too far right now and have her turn oyster on me.

'Goodbye, Dr Laidlaw,' I said. She did not answer; I do not suppose she even heard me.

Alec was on the terrace, as arranged. So was Hugh, but my wifely duties were discharged with a greeting, the news that he had had no post delivered at Auchenlea, and an undertaking to join him for luncheon.

'I might just slip along and have a word with Alec then,' I said.

'Since you are reading and he is not.' Hugh craned forward in his deckchair, spotted Alec and waved his hat.

'Are you up to anything that should concern me, Dandy?' he said. I thought about the plumbers at Gilverton, the dead Hydro guest and the ghost stories I had been telling and shook my head no.

'Why?' I asked him. 'Are you?' Hugh put on his face a look of such injured innocence that I had to bite my cheeks not to laugh.

'I?' he said. 'Of course not.' In perfect marital harmony, then, each with our secrets, we parted.

There was an empty deckchair next to Alec's, by dint of his having put his hat and a folded newspaper upon it and of his smoking his pipe like a rank beginner so that plumes of blue fugged the air for a yard around him. I waved and coughed and sank down into the cushions.

'Right then,' I said. 'Gosh, this is very comfy. Dr Laidlaw is reduced to a jelly. I was marvellous, even if I do say so. But I've decided to play a long game and leave her to get even more anxious before I give the screws another turn.'

Alec turned and regarded me with rather a stony look on his face.

'You sound more callous every case we get, Dandy,' he said. 'I can't imagine the woman I met eight years ago reporting with such relish that she'd laid another low.'

'Dear, dear,' I said. 'What's got into you? If I wanted to be reproached about how far short I fall from "the woman he met" I'd have stayed up the other end with Hugh.'

'I apologise,' said Alec. 'What reduced her?'

'Only what we agreed,' I said. 'One mention of Mrs Addie's ghost and she was terrified.'

'A patient who died?' Alec said. 'I don't doubt she was. And ghosts? Really, Dandy, who wouldn't be?'

We sat quietly for a while. I looked out over the view when the clouds were across the sun and shut my eyes against the glare when it shone, enjoying the warmth on my face, then I thought I had better start talking again before I slipped into a doze.

'Anyway,' I began. 'If Mrs Addie died outsi—' but Alec had started talking too and was more determined to get to the end.

'She's having a very difficult time of it, you know,' he said. 'Typical story. A daughter and a son. The son's a piece of fluff and the daughter's a born scholar, but the father can't drag himself into the modern age and see it so.'

'She got to medical school, didn't she?' I said. 'Gosh, when I think of my sister and me . . .'

'But it was the will, Dandy,' said Alec. 'Her father's will. He had to leave her the practice – one must leave a medical practice to a doctor – but Tot Laidlaw owns the lion's share of the building and grounds. A controlling interest.'

'Again, I'd say her father was perfectly fair. She got the practice and Tot got extra bricks and mortar instead. Why is she complaining?'

'She's not. She's as sweet-tempered a woman as I've ever met. And at least he can't just sell it out from under her. Much as he might want to.'

'No? Well, again that's a pretty decent arrangement, I'd say.' Alec looked unconvinced and I regarded him closely, wondering from where all this concern for the good doctor was coming. 'Did she just tell you all of this?' I said, not liking to think that he had been taken in by some tale of woe.

'Glad of someone to talk to,' Alec said.

'And I suppose she wants to keep it going and he wants to run it down? And she can't afford to buy him out?'

'Well, she certainly can't afford to buy it,' Alec said. He waved an arm at the terrace, the croquet lawn and the tennis courts beyond. 'I mean, look at it, even if the hotel itself is a bit of a pile. But as to who wants what, it's hard to say. It's Tot who's bending over backwards to keep it ticking over.'

'Up to and including mm-mm.' I hummed through the last bit since a squeakingly respectable family of mother, father and grown-up daughter were strolling by.

'I think he's pretty well using Dorothea as a front,' Alec said.

'Like a speak-easy. What a man he must be – his own sister!'

'And she won't hear a word agai—' Alec began and then stopped and nudged me. 'Look!' he hissed.

I turned to where he was nodding. A perfect parade of individuals was making its stately way along the terrace. The gooseberry-eyed girl was there, the crow-hatted Mrs Molyneaux, our lady of the lace mittens, and many more; and at the centre and slightly in front, the Great Personage. If I had seen him in the street I should have taken him for an actor or perhaps a theatrical impresario, and if anyone had suggested a spirit medium could achieve such grandeur and such a look of prosperity I should have wondered what the world was coming to. He wore a homburg hat as glossy as an otter and an astrakhan coat which reached to his ankles with lapels like those of Beau Brummell. His cane was ebony and had a silver knob of some complicated design, and his tie was yellow satin. As he paced along he surveyed the terrace, the grounds and the sitting guests like a Persian king come among his subjects and greatly pleased by them. It was impossible not to watch, and almost impossible not to giggle.

'What have you—' I waited as the procession passed by. 'What have you managed to find out about him?'

'Nothing except his name,' whispered Alec. 'I insinuated myself into a group of them at breakfast and asked it. But I rather got the impression they thought if I didn't know I wasn't worth telling.'

'And?' I whispered back. 'What *is* his name?'

'Loveday Merrick.'

'If it says that on his birth certificate I'll give you ten sovereigns,' I said. 'Did you get any clues at breakfast as to what he's here for? What any of them are?'

'Not exactly,' Alec said. 'Ghosts, obviously. But most certainly not the Moffat Ram because I floated that and got looks of pity.'

'I thought not. It's one of the outlying ghosts, for sure, not a nice tidy one on a cobbled street in town.'

'One thing one of them did say,' Alec went on. 'One of the young ones – such a waste of a pretty little thing who could get a job in a hat shop if she clicked her fingers—'

'Yes, all right, all right,' I said. 'I understand perfectly. A pretty little thing liked the look of you and dropped hints by way of flirting. You're making conquests all around.'

'Yes, well, never mind all that, but she did say,' Alec resumed, 'that they are trying to calculate an anniversary.'

'An anniversary of what, I wonder. The death of Yellow Mary? Some black day amongst the Johnstone devils? I wonder when they stopped the hangings at Gallow Hill. Hugh would know.'

'Well, a good while ago,' said Alec. 'Surely. Even here. Public hangings had been held decently in town squares in Dorset for years before they finally stopped them.' It is a curious thing, but whereas normally I am the greatest champion of Northamptonshire in particular and England in general, whenever Alec starts on the wonders of Dorset and the sins of Perthshire, I feel my hackles start to rise. It is most disconcerting to think that I am growing a layer of Scotch inside me and so I have never breathed a word of it to him and certainly not to Hugh who would be enchanted. Alec was speaking again.

'Who else have I conquered?' he said.

'Good Lord, the doctor!' I said. 'Didn't you try to? Didn't you know?'

'Really?' he said and then he rose and went to tap out his pipe into the earth around a potted laurel. 'Right then, Dan,' he said upon returning. 'Never mind conquests and for heaven's sake never mind ghosts for a while. What about Mrs Addie? How did the poor woman die?'

'A heart attack, following a fright, following an imagined sighting of a ghost on a country walk. Perfectly simple.'

'Only the Laidlaws didn't tell the police about the walk, the police didn't tell the family about the fright and no one seems to have told Dr Ramsay about the ghost.'

'I understand why anyone with compassion would edit out the ghost and the fright,' I said. 'But I don't at all understand why the same people – the Laidlaws, this is – who drafted in a second doctor to put some distance between themselves and the death, also – at the same time – hid the real distance. She wasn't here. It was nothing to do with them since she didn't die in the Hydro.

Or at least didn't collapse here. It's all very puzzling, I must say.'

'Well, what about this?' Alec said. He was beginning to smoke in that committed way which heralds clear thoughts, and I was ready to welcome them. 'The Hydro is struggling. The Laidlaws are getting desperate. A patient dies, so Tot – it must be Tot – turns the death to account in the cleverest way. The Haunted Hydro, you know. So they don't want any of the mediums to know that she wasn't here *at* the Haunted Hydro when she got the fright that killed her. But if she dropped her bag and went back for it and if we find it then we'll have proved that she was out and about and they'll have to drop all the ghost stories and tell the truth to the Addies.'

'What makes you think it's Tot?' I said. 'He seemed rather horrified by the mediums as far as I could see.'

'All part of the act,' Alec said.

'And anyway, it seems a bit unlikely. A patient dying is far more likely to harm the Hydro with the general public than give it a leg up. How many mediums can there possibly be?'

'You're right,' said Alec with a defeated sigh. 'It would harm the place less if she died of a heart attack out in the open air miles away.'

'Fresh air,' I said.

'Same thing. Don't quibble.'

'I'm not,' I said. 'I'm trying to remember something . . .'

'I say!' Alec said, very loudly. 'I've just thought of this. Someone dropping dead on a lonely hillside has a post-mortem and a full inquiry, doesn't she? So perhaps saying she died here when she didn't is their way of avoiding both. That would make the lie a great big black one and only worthwhile if it was covering something blacker. That makes sense, doesn't it?'

'It certainly does,' I said. 'I wish you hadn't started yelling it at me when I was trying to remember a crucial detail, though.'

'Only . . . where does the locked room come into any of that?'

'I have no idea,' I said. 'Unless I hit on the truth by chance. Perhaps it really was a favoured place of old Dr Laidlaw and young Dr Laidlaw goes there to cry, and since a patient died in her care she's just been crying more.'

Alec gave me a long and uninterpretable look.

'Oh, Dandy,' he said, then he shook himself. 'Those aren't bad shoes. Would you care to join me on a country walk before luncheon?'

'I would not,' I said. 'Have you looked at an ordnance survey of the countryside around here? Contours like thumbprints in every direction. But I wouldn't mind going back to Auchenlea, asking Mrs Tilling for a picnic and setting off in my motorcar.'

'And where shall we try first?' Alec said. 'I'm for the well, because take this Yellow Mary you mentioned. Who's to say that her full name isn't Yellow Mary Patterson? Repenting of her sins and all that?'

I asked a maid to tell Drysdale to bring the motorcar round and then there was just one small matter to see to before we could depart. It had occurred to me as Alec and I were talking that I could drip another cold drop of fear into Dr Laidlaw's ear and so I steered him along the corridor leading to her study en route to the front door. Luck was with me, however, and an even better chance happened along. Not only was the doctor herself outside her study, where I could more easily pretend to run into her, but with her, heads together, shoulders hunched as though against a storm, was her brother. They looked up as they heard our footsteps approach along the passageway. Dr Laidlaw's face fell and Tot missed his usual bumptious good cheer by close to a mile too.

'Mr Osborne,' he said. 'And Mrs Gilver.' He took a breath to deliver a witticism but none came.

'I'm so glad I ran into you again, Dr Laidlaw,' I began. I felt Alec shift away from me and turn a little. 'The coincidence grows and grows. I've just heard from one of the maids that Mrs Addie did indeed have two children. A son and a daughter, exactly as the ghost told me. What do you make of that?'

'I – I cannot account for it,' she said, with her voice breaking.

'What's this?' said Alec, the traitor.

'Oh, no doubt nothing,' I replied, with a careless wave of my hand. 'Perhaps I remembered reading something about it in the newspapers, subliminally, you know. Or whatever.'

'Subconsciously,' the doctor corrected.

'Exactly,' I agreed. 'Was the death *in* the papers?'

Tot Laidlaw rubbed his hands together, a meaningless gesture just then, and laughed with a very dry barking sound.

'Good heavens, I should think not,' he said. 'Good Lord! It was a heart attack that carried the poor woman off, you know. Long history of heart trouble, didn't stick to her treatment diary. Well, one doesn't like to speak ill of the dead . . .'

'In that case, I really *am* puzzled,' I said. 'Although, as you said, Dr Laidlaw, the mind is a wondrous thing. But why on earth should I see the poor woman's ghost floating out of an unused room in the Turkish bath of all places? Where *did* she die, by the way?'

'In—' the doctor began, but her brother cut her off smartly.

'Safely in her bedroom attended by not one but two doctors,' he said. 'We've all got to go sometime.'

'Indeed,' I said.

'And now we must stop bothering you,' said Alec, 'and get along.' He gave a short nod to Tot, a more courtly bow to the doctor and gripped me firmly above my elbow to drag me away.

'They didn't like me asking where she died, did they?' I said, when we were safely out of earshot. Alec finally let go of my arm.

'And Brother Tot told an out-and-out lie,' he said. 'Long history indeed.'

'So no matter what you think, I'm rather proud of that little ruse.' We stepped out of the front door and I carried on down the stone steps and onto the gravel. Alec had stopped at the top of the steps and was staring down at me.

'What do you mean, no matter what I think?' he said. 'I said not a word against it.'

'I assumed you were annoyed with me, grabbing me and marching me off that way,' I told him. He gaped.

'I was worried *for* you,' he said. 'He lied right to our faces, Dandy. It's not a misunderstanding or the Addies' wishful thinking – Tot Laidlaw is lying. And you didn't see his face when you mentioned that the ghost came through that locked door. I don't think his sister had told him that bit.'

'I think we should go to the police station,' I said.

'Anything to avoid tramping through the muddy lanes, eh?' Alec said. This was not entirely fair, but not entirely groundless either and so I said nothing. 'Nothing Tot or Dorothea have said so far suggests more than the cover-up job Sergeant Simpson already admitted to. *We* know that there's something extra up – they're too worried, too anxious – but it's nothing one could explain to a policeman. We need to find the bag, charge them with telling the Addies where their mother died and then flatten them when they admit that they're too scared to risk a PM.'

'Exactly,' I said. 'But before we go sleuthing about in the brambles and nettles for naught, shouldn't we ask at the police station if there has been an unidentified bag handed in in the last month or so? After all, if we think we might find it then why shouldn't someone else have done so already?'

'It wouldn't be unidentified,' Alec said. 'Wasn't it full of letters?'

'The ink might have run in the rain,' I said. 'Oh good, here's the car.' Drysdale rolled very slowly along the gravel and stopped with the back door exactly opposite where I stood; it is a talent of his. Alec opened up, handed me in, and went around to join me.

'Home, please,' I said. And then, because even if we were to make a visit to the police station there was no need to let Drysdale know it, I closed the window between us before picking up where we had left off.

'And unless the watch had a full name engraved on it,' I said, 'there could easily be nothing in the bag at all to say it was Mrs Addie's.'

'Don't you have your names stitched onto the lining?' Alec said. 'Like hats.'

'Good grief, no,' I said. 'Not these days when everyone has latch keys. Imagine what a find it would be for a thief to have a latch key and an address and a diary saying just when the owner was due to be from home.'

'A latch key?' Alec said. 'For Gilverton?'

'Well, not me,' I admitted. 'But one moves with the times.'

'Would Mrs Addie move with them?' Alec asked. He was becoming quite dogged on the point.

'I'm not trying to wriggle out of going looking,' I said. 'By all means, let's search first and ask the police if we turn nothing up, if that's what it takes to convince you!'

Mrs Tilling rose to the occasion of an impromptu packed lunch with her usual mastery. She had been sitting on the lawn outside the dining-room windows with Pallister and Grant as we rolled up the drive, all three in deckchairs and rugs just like the Hydro inmates across the valley. On the grass at their feet, Bunty lay on her back with all four paws waving. It is an attitude I know very well and it speaks of having been fed many titbits and being in hopes of more, even though she is stuffed to bursting. I affected not to notice them; I would not put it past Pallister to ban any further deckchair sitting if he thought it had been marked by a member of the family and met with disapproval. He might even take it out on Bunty and shut her in the boot room for the rest of the day to consider her short-comings. Still, I thought I could discern an extra stiffness to his neck and chin and a slight cast of colour across his cheeks as he padded into the drawing room moments later, with Bunty bounding – arthritically but still just about bounding – behind him.

'Madam,' he said. 'Mr Osborne.'

'Please tell Mrs Tilling to pack luncheon for two, Pallister, and put it in the Cowley,' I said. 'Anything at all. Boiled eggs, bread and jam – I fully appreciate that she is not in her own kitchen. And she needn't trouble herself with drinks because we are going to the well.'

'I shall inform you when the motorcar is ready,' he said. It had taken him a few years to stop asking whether Drysdale was needed. I know it still troubles him to see me racketing about behind a steering wheel, but he is just as good at affecting not to notice things as am I.

Not so Grant, who came in as he was leaving.

'A picnic, madam?' she said. 'Let me see. Yes, I think that can be managed. Shall I wait for you upstairs or will you come now?'

'I'm not changing, Grant,' I said. She frowned deeply and looked at my skirt, which was a very pale dove grey and fashioned in a series of loops, rather like opera house curtains. 'I'll make sure Mr Pallister packs the mackintosh squares,' she said. 'If you can sit on one and keep off the grass that would be lovely.' She started to leave, then turned back again. 'Walls too,' she said. 'Madam. Lichen.'

Alec laughed, but softly so that Grant would not hear him. He is a kind man.

'I know,' I said. 'But we are used to one another and I only have myself to blame. She was twenty when she came to me, you know. I thought she'd be less terrifying than some of the more experienced women my mother interviewed. So all of *that* has happened with me watching. Anyway, I prefer it to Pallister's rectitude sometimes.'

Pallister's rectitude was strained to its limits when he returned.

'All ready to go, madam,' he said and then cleared his throat, lifting a ceremonial hand to his mouth as he did so. 'Mrs Tilling asked me to tell you, madam, that she has packed a small bottle of lime to be used in solution in case you are determined to drink the well water, but also a flask of coffee which she recommends instead.'

'Ah, Mrs Tilling has tasted it then,' I said. 'But I'm hoping that the well water might be less revolting than the stuff at the bath house.'

'It is exactly as unpleasant, madam,' Pallister said. 'And not helped by tin cups.'

'You've been?' I asked. Pallister cranked his back to a pitch of stiff attention that looked likely to break it and then nodded.

'Mrs Tilling, Miss Grant and I took the liberty yesterday,' he said. 'A very pleasant walk, and the well-keeper was most obliging.' It was torturing him to be forced into such intimacy, but I was not done with him.

'There's a well-keeper?' I said. 'I had no idea.'

'Yes, madam,' he said. 'To prevent—' At this his collar appeared to choke him. 'I hope you have an enjoyable outing,' he said. 'Madam. Mr Osborne.'

* * *

'Well, that's good news,' I said, as we drove away. 'If there's a well-keeper we can ask him whether Mrs Addie visited. And about Yellow Mary too.'

Alec was twisted round poking about in the hamper, aided by Bunty who stuck her nose in close and began beating her tail.

'God bless Mrs Tilling,' he said. 'This looks a lot like pigeon pie. And' – there was some rustling as he opened a wrapped package – 'gingerbread. It's hotpot and junket at the Hydro today, I happen to know.'

'And surely if he says she wasn't around then we can save ourselves the searching and go straight to the Beef Tub,' I said. 'Now how would you best describe Mrs Addie to bring her back to the mind of a man who must see strangers every day?'

Thrashing out a description which honoured her memory – one could not simply say that she looked like a piglet in tweeds – and yet served our purpose, took us through the streets of the town, along the broad roads of pleasant villas and out onto a little back way into the hills. 'A well-set-up lady of sixty years with an Edinburgh accent and a fine strong face' was what we settled upon, and I only hoped that there were not so many ladies who visited the well alone that ours could be lost in the crowd.

I should not have thought so, I considered to myself, looking around as we left the last farmhouse behind and bumped onto a rutted track. Moors on both sides rose gradually to form high hills, the Gallow Hill to the west and to the east the beginning of the Eildons which rolled on for many miles, stark and roadless.

'No wonder the pump house does such a roaring trade,' Alec said, craning to look out, 'if this is the other option.' I drew off the track beside a cottage and, following our noses, we crossed a small meadow towards a little three-sided stone bothy, its fourth wall open to the path, no bigger than a dovecote and not nearly so tall. I could see a railing across its open side, presumably guarding the well. Bunty went a short way into the trees to attend to her concerns of her own.

'Reminds me of a crypt,' Alec said. I could see a figure moving in the shadows and I shushed him.

'Good afternoon,' I cried.

'Efternuin,' said a voice. I had expected a well-keeper to be something out of Grimm, bent and ancient and not quite of this world (I have no idea why), but the figure emerging was a youngish man, neatly barbered, neatly dressed and neatly booted. 'Come to tak the watters, have you?' he said. He nodded towards a stone shelf set into the wall. 'Aye well, there's the cups and there's the box for your pennies.' The water at the well was a bargain compared with town prices, it seemed. I was just about to suggest that he might serve us our draughts – for what other purpose had he? – when I noticed that one sleeve of his coat was stitched shut at the elbow and tucked neatly into his pocket. Alec noticed at the same moment as did I and we both rushed forward to help ourselves, becoming a little tangled on the way.

It was not, anyway, a question of letting down a bucket into the depths and hauling it up again, for the well had steps leading down and the water was so high that one could fill a cup just by stooping, or if even that were too much like work one could hold the cup out to a pipe which stuck right out of a fissure in the rock. I tried not to wonder at the nature of the many deposits, black and shining with slime, which grew upon the rock, the pipe, the stopcock and even the steps. I just straightened, held my breath and drank. It was disgusting; not more disgusting than before, but in a different way. On the one hand, it was stronger, more disagreeably eggy, but on the other it was sparkling instead of cloudy and made one think of liver salts.

When I had finished, the well-keeper held out his hand for the cup, took it, held it against his body and wiped it vigorously with a cloth before setting it back on the stone ledge for next time. I dropped my penny in the wooden box which was nailed up by the shelf and then gave him a shilling too.

'What about her?' I asked. Bunty, after rejoining us, had lolloped down the steps and plunged her muzzle into the well to start lapping. 'Stop it, B. Come away!'

'Ocht, she'll no' drink ower much,' said the well-keeper, and right enough Bunty lifted her head almost immediately and shook it, snuffling, trying I assume to drive out the nasty taste. She came back up the steps and sat down beside me, subdued and puzzled.

'Where was that then?' Alec said, as he handed back his own cup in turn. I took this to be a formulation familiar to soldiers for the young man glanced at his empty sleeve.

'Amiens,' he said. 'You, sir?'

'Missed that one, thank God,' Alec said. 'I was at St Quentin when the music stopped.'

'Must have taken you a whiley to get hame fae there,' said the young man. I was pretending to find items of endless interest in the rocky wall of the spring.

'Well, you know,' Alec said. 'It wasn't so bad once the rations started up again.'

'Aye!' said the young man with feeling. I had always rather scorned Alec's deep and serious concern with the menu for every meal and with any opportunity to eat that came along in between them. If he had once been starving, though, I supposed it was a very different thing.

'So will you sign the wee book?' said the well-keeper. Alec caught my eye and I could see the flash even in the dim light of the well house. He seized the book eagerly from its place on the shelf and read down the page, turned back and read again.

'Does everyone sign?' he said, looking up.

'As can,' said the keeper.

'Only . . .' Alec turned to me.

'We're interested in finding out if someone we know came up here while she was visiting the town,' I said. 'She insists she did, but I suspect her of sticking to the pump room and giving herself airs, you know.'

'And her name's no' in there?' asked the young man.

'Can't spot it,' Alec said. 'A Mrs Addie. Lady in her sixties. Edinburgh.'

'When was this?' said the young man.

'A month ago,' said Alec. The well-keeper was shaking his head.

'I'd mind of an old lady all alone, no fae here,' he said. 'Sure and I would.'

'You seem very certain,' I said.

'That's why I'm here,' he replied. 'You'll no ken Yellow Mary, eh no? Not being local.'

'I think I might have heard of her,' I said.

'She was my granny,' he said. 'Fell in the well and drowned. That was when they started paying a well-keeper again.'

'Why was she called Yellow Mary?' I asked him.

'When they drug her oot,' he said. 'Yellow and puffed up like a toadstool she was. I'll never forget the sight of it. Days in this water'll dae that to you.'

'And when was this?' I was calculating furiously. If he was thirty and remembered the day his grandmother died, the longest ago it could be was twenty-five years or so. I felt the cup of water shift inside me. I had assumed a ghost of long ago and to think that I had drunk water a woman had drowned in in my own lifetime was much more disgusting somehow.

'A year past Christmas,' he said. I rather thought even Alec blanched a little at *this* news. Certainly he shot a glance at the black well water and the mossy walls. It was only too easy to believe that some of this depthless vat had been there a year past Christmas, at least a cupful anyway.

'Aye, it was terrible,' the young man went on. 'The Laird was dead against lanterns, up on the hills. Said it feart the birds, stopped them nesting. And so Granny was coming home in the dark and tripped and tumbled and in she went. And the Laird felt so bad, he built this new wee housie and in the summer when the visitors are here I've a job pays me better money as I would get at anything else I could manage.'

'But isn't it terribly dull?' I said.

He smiled at that, a sudden bonny grin that made him look as young as Teddy, and beckoned us around the far end of the well house to where he had set up a little lean-to with an old armchair and a box for a table. There was a spirit lamp and a kettle, just keeping warm. And open on the chair was a volume of – I squinted – Walter Scott.

'Beats workin',' he said, still grinning. 'There's four bairns in the house. I'm better off out here.'

'Good for you, Mr . . . ?' I said.

'Milne,' he supplied.

'And although I'm sorry to hear about Mrs Milne – was she your father's mother?' He nodded. 'At least some good has come of it.' I gave him another shilling, Alec gave a folded note of a denomination I could not see and we made our way back to the motorcar.

'One down, two to go,' I said, throwing it into reversing gear. 'Golly, I never thought about turning when I drove up here.' Bunty, who is always delighted when I am reversing, stuck her snout into the crook of my neck and poured out her love for me, in deep groans.

'Of course, these settled places don't refer to a married woman by her married name,' Alec said. 'Yellow Mary Milne could be Mary Patterson, as easy as anything.'

'Yes, but if she died at Christmas-time then the mediums would hardly be gathering for an anniversary in October, would they? One down. Quite a remarkable young man, wasn't he?'

'Unfortunately not,' said Alec. Then he laughed. 'Except that he's reading Walter Scott and no one's making him,' he said. 'I'd rather brave the house and the four bairns. Fearful stuff. Right, then, Dandy. Where is the Devil's Beef Tub?'

I had reached a gate and I swung back into it thankfully, emerging to drive the rest of the way facing forward. I wiped my neck with my handkerchief, told myself to remember not to dab my mouth with it, for no matter what Hugh says I am not silly when it comes to dogs and their germs.

'Back through the town and out to the north past the Hydro,' I said. 'Keep going until you see the unquiet ghosts of a dozen murderous Reivers. Pity there won't be a tub-keeper to tell us if they did for anyone in the last month or so.'

10

Long before we arrived at the Beef Tub, however, we had both decided it was out of the question. The librarian's map had put it just beyond the northern edge of the town but we trundled along five miles or so, forging into the crease in the hills which would eventually become that blind, deep valley, and we knew there was no way a large lady of sixty who lived in a villa in the city could possibly have come so far.

'And she made her journey down here on a train,' I said, 'so she can't have driven. If she even knows how to. If she had hired a taxi or a dogcart then the driver would have been with her when she collapsed and we'd know it . . . There's no way she could have got here.'

'I agree,' Alec said. 'My God, what a dreary spot. It must get no sun at all from October to May.'

The track was worse with each yard, in fact was now more or less a rocky river bed, and I feared for the underside of my dear little Cowley. Nevertheless I kept driving. Not that Alec was wrong; great lumpen hills bare of trees, bare of gorse, bare even of bracken as far as I could tell, were closing in on us from both sides and all of the light had long disappeared behind the highest of them. As we took a turn to the west the valley narrowed yet further, and I could see what a wonderful spot it must have been for the Reivers, as snug as a key in a keyhole, hiding here.

'I'll turn at the end,' I said. 'Perhaps we can ask at the last farm or cottage, just to make sure.'

'Ask what?' said Alec.

'Well, you might not like it,' I said. 'What I wanted to ask is if they heard a motorcar. Does Dr Laidlaw have a motorcar?'

'I don't know why you keep maligning my impartiality this way,' Alec said. 'Why wouldn't I like it? And I've no idea, by the way.'

'Only, I'm still bothered by the story that she "found" Mrs Addie. What if they saw the ghost together – Dr Laidlaw was very odd to me when I brought up the subject, you know – and what if she brought her back again to look for the lost bag?'

'She would have returned the next day and found it,' Alec said. 'And sent it to the Addies.' I felt myself deflate a bit.

'You're right,' I said. 'There's nothing to ask even if we find someone of whom to ask it. Ah, at last.' Up ahead there was a farmhouse and some buildings, surely the last steading. I reversed into the yard gateway and looked for a place to turn and suddenly it seemed that every door in the place had opened. A woman stood in one wiping her hands on a cloth. An old man came to the large doors of the byre and started towards us, a young man emerged from a shed halfway up the hill behind the steading and numerous children appeared from behind walls and under hedges. Even a sheepdog planted its front paws on the bars of a gate and stared.

'No chance of drivers-by not being noticed here,' I said. 'I give in. Whatever ghost Mrs Addie saw it wasn't one of the Johnstone Reivers.'

'Let's find a spot with a blink of sunshine and start in on that pie,' Alec said. I heard again the echo of his voice, 'not so bad once the rations started up again', and bit my lip on the teasing I might have given him only yesterday, then I waved at the advancing farming folk and gave them a toot of my horn as I drove away.

Our hopes of sunshine – even a blink of it – were folly, but we drew off the road onto a grassy holm just as the valley opened out again and spread the mackintosh squares on a couple of boulders. The grass was nibbled close by sheep, the air was rich with the smell of peat and crushed heather gusting down from the hilltops and a nearby burn chuckled companionably along behind us. In my stout shoes, felt hat, fox fur and driving gloves, and with Bunty settled like a blanket over my feet, it was almost comfortable, but I would not care to have been there any later in the day or when October turned to November either and, although I ventured to remove a glove, I was happy to have a hot beaker of coffee to hold. Alec cut two hearty wedges out of the pigeon pie and handed one to me.

'We should have brought the boys,' I said. 'They love eating like savages. They'd never sit in a dining room again if I didn't make them.'

'You'll have to get to work on Donald,' Alec said.

He was right; we had spared Donald London this last summer, for he was far too callow to enjoy it and far too raw to be any value, but by the coming May he would be nineteen. Still too raw and too callow, of course, but I had been rung up by more than one despairing mother of girls, telling me of the uneven numbers at her daughter's dance and scolding me for keeping a young man like Donald away.

'Lord,' I said, 'it seems ten minutes since Nanny had to check that he'd cleaned his nails and behind his ears before a party. I can't imagine him bringing back a wife to Benachally. Or perhaps he'll be another who refuses to rush into things. Like you.'

'Let's see if he wants to come up the Gallow Hill this afternoon with us to start with,' Alec said, ignoring me. 'Teddy too. Four pairs of eyes and all that. We can say you're looking for something someone dropped this morning and happened to mention to you.'

'He'd never make it,' I said. 'Unless this morning's steam and mustard have had a marked effect on his lungs, anyway.' I ate a bite of pie and drank some coffee, to be sure to get the tremor out of my voice. 'So we're pressing on, are we?' I continued in a brighter tone.

'Absolutely,' Alec said. 'I've been thinking that we should have gone straight for the Gallow Hill at the outset actually.'

'Oh?'

'As I said, Mary Milne could have been Mary Patterson for all we know. But the Johnstone Reivers would be Johnstones, wouldn't they – so where would a Patterson come in to that?'

'The throats they cut could have been Patterson throats,' I said.

'But they'd have been men's throats, wouldn't they? Not women and children and grandmammas. No – a crowd of twenty ghosts all together – a job lot, if you please – must surely be connected to the Gallow Hill. Where else would so many have met their end and hung around haunting?'

'And whatever it was that Mary Patterson repented might well have got her hanged!' I said. I squeezed my handful of pie a little too hard in my enthusiasm and the crust shattered. Mrs Tilling's pastry is always very short; delicious, but dangerous to pale clothing. I heaved Bunty off my feet, stood up and wriggled until all the flakes had fallen off my skirt and onto the ground, where she ran them down and consumed them with snapping teeth and much licking.

'I shan't join you in your dance of joy just yet, Dandy,' Alec said. 'But if we find the bag, just try and stop me.'

'Come on then. If I don't move after Mrs Tilling's pie I get drowsy. Let's walk it off. We might even see the sun if we're quick about it.'

The Gallow Hill was a gentle delight after the stern soaring faces of the Beef Tub fells and if it had been clothed in elms and oaks, and had a few pretty cottages around its base, it might almost have been at home in the Cotswolds. As it was, the cottages were grey and mean-looking and the trees were the spindly larches and lichened beeches which cling onto Scotch hillsides long after they have ceased to have any value in the landscape. Constable himself would have left them out and just painted the sky behind them.

We left the motorcar tucked safely into the side of the lane where it could come to no harm and Alec lifted the latch of the gate to a path and ushered me through. Immediately we were enveloped in silence, none of the noises of life from the town managing to penetrate the high walls of brambles and dog rose which closed around us, darkening and scenting the air with a sweet dampness. Ahead, the path led straight and only slightly upwards for twenty yards and then the hill rose and the path disappeared in a way that reminded me of yew mazes and of being lost and tear-stained as a tiny child.

'I'm glad I don't believe in ghosts,' I said.

'What's the handbag made of?' said Alec. He was already looking studiously at the ground on either side.

'Oh, best brown leather, I have no doubt,' I said. 'Absolutely invisible in this leaf litter. I suppose we must just hope for a glint off the clasp or something. Or Bunty might sniff it out if there are peppermints.'

'Wouldn't any dog in the last month have done the same?' Alec sounded troubled. 'I suppose we *are* hoping for rather a lot, expecting it still to be here, aren't we? Look for signs that Mrs Addie passed along. What size feet would you say?'

'I can never take us seriously when we go all out for snapped twigs and footprints,' I said. 'Have we ever found a footprint, Alec dear?'

He ignored me and so I trained my attention towards the ground at my side of the path and kept walking.

I held out no great hopes; unless Mrs Addie had thrashed her way through the brambles with a stick, it was hard to see how she could have left the path. On the other hand, her bag, if dropped *on* the path, could surely not have lain a night there, never mind a month. And it was the same all the way to the top: a winding track, close growth on either side, a few tree roots underneath, a pleasant smell of earth and the odd wink of light where a branch had broken off and left a chink in the canopy. All in all, if one went in for country walks I could see that this was a charming one, but I could not help but feel that our quest was pointless.

Well, at least it was dry and not too cold and at its end was not a grouse drive and an endless tramp to the next one, but a view, a descent and a cup of tea. We were drawing near the summit now, the beeches and brambles growing sparser and the ground underfoot changing from leaves and dryish mud to blades and then tussocks of grass. At the top we found ourselves in a clearing of sorts, with a view through the treetops to the Hydro chimneys. I made a movement to step forward, but Alec put out an arm to stop me.

'Look,' he said, pointing at the ground.

The grass was long and lush and all around it was flattened by footprints. They circled the clearing and criss-crossed it and appeared to converge on a spot towards the faraway end just before the trees began again. I made my way over.

There was no cairn, no marker of any kind, nothing to say that this was the very place which had given the hill its name. I suppose it was the highest point – at least, looking around, I saw none higher – but if I had had to guess at where the gallows would be, I would have plumped for the middle, not here almost under the lee of the nearest beech.

'Was this the gallows?' I asked. Alec walked over.

'Seems likely,' he said. 'I wonder what all the feet were milling around for? A Sunday school picnic maybe?' I shrugged. 'Well, let's look for the bag, the watch, the lock of hair, the precious letters and the proof that Mrs Addie died here, eh?'

Within minutes I could be sure that the trampling feet were no Sunday school picnic, for there was not a sweet wrapper, a lemonade bottle nor an apple core anywhere in the undergrowth around the clearing. There was nothing. Even Bunty failed to snuffle up so much as a peanut shell.

'Any luck?' I called to Alec. He had gone further than me into the woods, to examine a fallen log about ten yards from the edge of the clearing. He ducked down behind it and I made my way towards him. 'Any luck?' I repeated, looking over. He was bent double scrutinising the bare brown earth, but as far as I could tell there was nothing to see.

'None,' he said. 'I think we're wasting our time, Dandy.' He looked around himself. 'What would she be doing here?'

'If we believe her daughter that she had no time for spooks?' I said. 'An assignation? A widow in her sixties would hardly go to the winter gardens to bat her eyes at some man who took her fancy.'

'Or,' said Alec, taking the baton, 'perhaps Mrs Addie was interested in nature, or local history, or just wanted some—'

'Fresh air and exercise!' I said.

'Quite,' said Alec. 'But why declaim it that way?'

'It's Dr Laidlaw's favourite cure,' I said. 'She told me so. Oh, Alec, this is good. If Mrs Addie was *sent* out – sent as part of her treatment regime – and then she saw a ghost and got her blessed fright and dropped dead, then the doctor who sent her might well not want the family to know!'

Alec was nodding.

'After all,' he said, 'nothing *old* Dr Laidlaw prescribed ever killed her.' We beamed at one another for a bit. Eventually, Alec drew breath to continue but caught it again. I turned slightly towards the clearing and saw him do the same. From the way we had come a murmur of voices had arisen, but they were not speaking words. Instead, the sound was of a whispering, rhythmic chant, very quiet but growing louder. I clicked my tongue to Bunty to follow me, stepped over the log, and joined Alec, crouching. My lips were dry, and as I tried to lick them I found that my tongue was too.

'Guess who!' said Alec. 'Goodness, it sounds like all of them.'

'All twenty?' I whispered.

'Are there twenty?' he whispered back, looking astonished.

'Well, seven already and many more expected,' I said. 'Surely you remember.'

Alec's eyes danced and, although he kept it in, the laughter bubbled through him.

'Dandy, you goose!' he said. 'I meant the mediums. It's the mediums coming chanting up the hill. You thought it was the ghosts? Really?'

'Of course not,' I said, reddening and dipping my head to hide it. 'I misunderstood you. Now, shush, before we're heard.'

We crunched ourselves down even further behind the log, I sending a silent apology to Grant for the fate of my skirt, and waited. The voices grew louder and before too long we caught sight, through the trees, of half a dozen figures, all moving slowly in loops and crosses, passing one another and repassing, gathering – with many feints, but gathering all the same – on the well-trodden spot just at the edge of the trees. In the centre of them all was Loveday Merrick, his bare head thrown back and his hair streaming down. He was muttering under his breath just like the rest of them and as the crescendo swelled, he lifted his silver-topped cane and banged the tip of it hard against the lowest branch of the beech tree. One of the younger mediums uttered a small shriek and then there was silence except for the rattle and rush of a few beech cobs falling through the boughs and dropping to the ground.

'Do you feel anything, Loveday?' said a woman's voice.

'They are not here,' said the great man. It was a pronouncement of some authority and I could see shoulders slumping and faces falling even from my hiding place yards away.

He pounded his stick on the ground.

'But they are close!' A little thrill passed through the group, made up of whispers and darting movements, as the mediums clutched one another. 'They are all together in a warm place very near here.'

'All of them, Loveday?' asked a man. It might have been one of the tall hats with satin piping. 'Can you feel all of them?'

Mr Merrick drew in an enormous breath, all but snorting, and closed his eyes. He began to sway gently. 'Mary and Lizzie and Peggy are here,' he said. 'And the dear old grandmother and the poor blind child. Joseph the Miller is here.' The crowd thrilled to hear it. 'Abigail Simpson, Ann Dougal, Marjorie Docherty too.'

'What about Old Donald?' That was Mrs Molyneaux. 'Is he with them? If we could answer that question, Loveday . . .'

'There is an old man,' said Mr Merrick. He was swaying so far from side to side that the mediums nearest him began to ready themselves to catch him if he fell. 'A Mr Higgins and his Christian name begins with the letter D. Is it Donald? Donald Higgins? Is that you?' He was rocking front to back now too. 'I cannot hear him. Donald Higgins! Come to me! You are with friends. You are safe here. Is it— Is it—'

The cane toppled, the great man crumpled, the companions rushed forward and stopped him from falling. Behind our log Alec and I turned flabbergasted faces to each other. I started to whisper but Alec held a finger to his lips. Out in the clearing, Mr Merrick had recovered. He picked up his cane, swept his hair back into some kind of order and took a flask out of his inside pocket. After a good swig from it, he spoke in what passed for his normal voice again. Still rather grand but not absolutely set to part the clouds and bring God's ear to the opening.

'Now then, my dear friends, what did I say?'

There was a clamour of voices, shouting the names. Loveday Merrick counted them off on his fingers. Hastily scrabbling in my bag for a slip of paper and a stub of pencil, I jotted them down too, as best I could.

'Ten,' he announced at last when he was finished counting. 'Ten of them. This is inarguable evidence, my dear friends. This will set the world on its ears. And those who have laughed will be humbled and those who have scorned will be filled with awe.' He looked around at the upturned faces and clasped hands all about him. 'Now, let's go back to the Hydro for a nice cup of tea.'

Alec spluttered, the inevitable consequence of holding one's breath and then suddenly laughing.

'What was that?' It was the gooseberry-eyed girl. She turned those pale green orbs towards the log where we were hiding and all the others followed, swivelling and craning and making me feel like a hare sitting up in a field. I ducked, waiting for the shot to ring. Loveday Merrick strode to the edge of the trees and, shading his eyes, looked straight towards our hiding place.

'Nothing,' he said. 'A bird turning the litter. Nothing at all.' Then he strode off, his little band of acolytes following after. We waited until we could no longer hear even the echo of their tramping feet before we moved.

'Did he see us?' Alec said.

'I'm not sure,' I answered. 'He certainly made that up about the bird anyway. But why would he not stride over here with his big stick, demanding to know what we were doing?'

'Because it's common land and he wouldn't have the authority?' Alec screwed up his nose even as he said this. 'Not that he's a man who has trouble assuming authority. What on earth *was* all that?'

'Poppycock and tommyrot,' I said. 'I'm ashamed of myself for being rattled earlier. What an old fraud.'

'I agree, naturally,' Alec said. 'But what in particular is it that's riled you?'

'The initial D!' I said. 'It's a music hall trick. Someone here has lost a loved one. Name begins with D. "Oh, that must be old uncle Deuteronomy" pipes up a voice from the second row. "That's right, lovey. Deuteronomy. He's looking for his niece." Sensation all round. I'm just surprised he had the gall to wheel it out amongst his own people. One would think they'd see through it, since they must use exactly the same stuff in music halls of their own.'

'The excitement seemed genuine enough,' Alec said. 'And they seemed to recognise the names he was spouting.'

I read them from my slip of paper, once out loud and once to myself.

'They don't mean anything to me,' I said. 'But one thing does strike me. I don't see how they could be the ghosts of people who were hanged here.'

'Oh?' said Alec.

'Too many women. Not to say that no women were ever executed but they were the unusual cases. If these ghosts were the spirits of the hanged there'd be Williams and Georges and Jameses to spare instead of all these Anns and Lizzies – I mean, you know, not that we actually believe any of it.'

'We really should just take that point as established once and for all,' Alec said. 'And not repeat it ten times a day. Of course, either someone is causing mischief or these mediums are just making it up entirely, but as to what Mrs Addie came in search of and what she thought she saw . . . I don't agree that it couldn't be the spirits of hanged men, just because so many of them are women.'

'But—'

'I think it strengthens the argument if anything. These are the wronged, Dandy. Not the murderers and brigands who deserved their fate, but innocents, wrongly convicted and wrongly hanged. Perhaps that's why Mrs Addie wasn't scared to come back for her bag – which I wish we'd found, by the way. So I should say of course lots of them are women. Perhaps they were wise women hanged for witchcraft.'

'And children,' I reminded him. 'Would a blind child have been hanged with his grandmother?'

'Certainly,' said Alec. 'If it was long enough ago. I'm not going to let you spoil my theory with that.'

I did not need to; its despoliation was waiting for us back at the Hydro.

Mrs Cronin must have been watching for our arrival for she was bearing down on us along the passageway when we climbed the steps into the hall.

'Mrs Gilver, Mr Osborne,' she said. 'I'm glad to have run into you. Look what I've found.' She was carrying some sort of bundle, laid across her arms the way that page boys carry cushions with coronets upon them. This was no velvet and gilt-braided object, though. It was a heap of brown tweed with a chamois leather shoe bag balanced on top. 'Mrs Addie's clothes,' she said. 'After what you told me this morning, I got to thinking.' The colloquial phrase sounded wooden in her mouth, for her tone was very clipped and formal. 'And it occurred to me that Mrs Addie's things must have been sent to the laundry and maybe they'd got forgotten about there. It wasn't the regular day, you see. And so I checked, and there they were! We can send them to her family now.'

'Splendid,' I said. I did not believe a word of it and felt embarrassed for her having to speak the lines.

'I'm just going to tell Dr Laidlaw,' she went on. 'But I have patients waiting, as a matter of fact. So, I wonder if you would be so kind.' With that she held out the bundle. We are brought up to accept whatever is offered – thus gypsies trick us into buying violets at the railway station and climbers we intended to cut manage still to give us their hands – and so, astonished as I was, I held my arms out like a godmother at the altar and accepted the bundle. Mrs Cronin thanked me, turned on her heels and hurried away. Alec and I were left gazing at the pleats and ruffles of her cap until she whisked around the corner and was gone. Alec was first back into the swing.

'Quick, Dandy, before someone sees us!' he said. 'Let's get the swag to my room.'

We hurried along the corridor to the stairs, up two flights and round to the west side, Alec fumbling his key out of his trouser pocket as we went along. Once inside his room I tipped my armful onto the bed and stared at it. Everything was there: shirt, petticoat, stockings, vest, chemise, brassiere and underdrawers – the lot.

'Nonsense,' I said. 'Tweeds, cotton underthings and corsetry go to completely different bits of a laundry, as I well know.' I had spent nine days on a case once pretending to be a lady's maid, and none of the arcane lore I had amassed would ever desert me. 'How could they all be lost together and then found again?'

Alec picked up the coat part of the tweeds and held it against him. It was gargantuan, looking as though it would wrap twice round Alec's frame. He let it drop and lifted the skirt, which was easily a yard wide.

'Everyone kept saying she was a sizeable lady,' he said. 'They were being kind.'

I was unfastening the drawstring of the shoe bag. I drew out one wide leather brogue, turned it up and peered at it.

'Look, Dan,' Alec said. 'A walk up a hill could easily have killed a woman this size.'

'I don't believe it,' I said. I put the shoe down and took the skirt from Alec's hands.

'The woman who fitted these clothes should never have been sent out climbing hills for exercise,' he persisted. 'We've cracked it. Dr Laidlaw prescribed it and it did for her. That's what they're hiding.'

I was examining the skirt, rubbing the material through my fingers. I sniffed the cuffs of the coat too.

'But it's nonsense,' I said.

'They're not hers?' said Alec.

'They might be,' I replied. 'I can telephone to Mrs Bowie and ask her what dress size her mother took. But these clothes weren't worn outside on a muddy hillside. She had dirt under her nails, but her coat cuffs are clean and don't smell of benzene. They smell of lily-of-the-valley cologne.' I put the coat down and sorted through the pile of smaller garments, lifting a stocking. 'She had dirt ground into her knees, Regina said. But look at this stocking. It should be torn, or snagged at least, and it's perfect.'

'Maybe—'.

'No, look at it, Alec.' I held it up and let it dangle. 'It hasn't been washed. Look.'

'It looks clean to me,' Alec said.

'It's still got the shape of the leg in it,' I insisted. 'Clean stockings look like sausage skins, you know. Worn stockings have the ghost of the leg in them.' I had not chosen my words wisely and I let the stocking drop again, unnerved. Alec was rummaging in the coat pockets, or trying to, anyway, but looking for pockets where he would in a coat of his own and not finding any. When he finally plunged his hand into the only two there were in women's suiting, his eyes widened and he drew something out and showed it to me.

'The lack of muck and benzene is a puzzle,' he said, 'but look at this. Proof positive, at least, that she went out that last day.'

In his hand was a striped paper bag, twisted shut at the corners, bearing the name and black-and-white livery of the Moffat Toffee Shop. That, more than the pitiful stocking with the ghost of Mrs Addie's sturdy leg inside it, melted my heart. I picked the bag up and twirled it around to open it.

'Poor thing,' I said, 'she didn't even have one.' For it certainly looked like a full quarter-pound of wrapped toffees in there and the bag had the pristine look that never lasts long after leaving the sweetshop. I glanced up at Alec. He was frowning down at me. He looked to the coat which lay on the bed and back again.

'Doesn't seem all that likely,' he said. 'How do you get to be the size of those tweeds if you don't dip into your toffees as soon as you've bought them?'

'Tablet,' I said. Alec looked into the bag.

'Toffee,' he insisted.

'Yes, it is,' I agreed. 'And it shouldn't be. Mrs Bowie told us when we were there and she said it again on the telephone. Her mother loved the tablet from the Moffat Toffee Shop. Presumably whoever bought these and put them in the pocket of her coat didn't know that.'

'This is very bad,' Alec said. He was trying to refold the skirt and coat into neat squares, hating all of a sudden, I think, to be touching her things.

'That's why Mrs Cronin shoved them at us,' I went on. 'Perhaps we were meant to do what we did or perhaps I was just supposed to witness Dr Laidlaw discovering the bag of sweets. Well, I'm not going to play their game. I shall ring for a maid to deliver them. Someone's laying a false scent, Alec, and I don't want them to know whether or not we've got a sniff of it.'

'A false scent,' Alec said. 'Yes, I see. It wasn't that she went out and they pretended she didn't.' He nodded as he thought his way through the thicket. 'Far from it. She went nowhere and someone is pretending she did.'

'Regina must have been told to say Mrs Addie was a bit grubby and she went much too far.'

'Just as the ghosts are going too far now also,' Alec said. 'All those mediums. It's completely out of hand.'

'Isn't it worrying that there are two stories?' I asked him.

He was nodding faster now. 'The one where she went out and collapsed. And one where she saw a ghost here and died of fright. But there's as much effort going into suppressing the stories as there is to spreading them. Sergeant Simpson, Dr Ramsay, and the Addies all think different things. I don't understand at all.'

'And all of a sudden, I do,' I said. 'They couldn't agree on one. They can't agree on anything much, after all – whether this place is a hospital or a casino, for instance. Whether to sell up or keep going. Even whether these clothes were supposed to have been to the laundry and back or had been put away at day's end with a bag of toffees in the pocket! There are two stories, Alec, because there are two Laidlaws, and they can't agree.'

'And even if it's *not* the two Laidlaws,' Alec said. 'If it's Tot and someone else, or if it's Tot changing his mind. The ghosts are attracting too much attention so he's switched to a new tale. No, don't shake your head at me that way. It makes no difference. Competing stories or successive stories, Dandy – either way when there's so much effort going into covering something up, it rather looks as though that something might be murder.'

I I

The Hydro guests, at least the doctor's devotees and Tot
Laidlaw's bright young things, were making the most of this
afternoon of Indian summer, the way Scots will always do.
Heaven knew in what dark dungeon the mediums were gathered
to stir chickens' entrails and cast knuckle bones in the dust –
or was I mixing up mediums with some other species of ghoul?
– but everyone else was on the terrace, the clock golf course
or the croquet lawn, or could be heard at the tennis courts and
bowling greens, in the swish and whack of gut against sheepskin
or the soft knock of ebony upon ebony and the ripple of
applause.

Alec and I had the winter gardens to ourselves, then, and
thankfully so given the discussion which needed to be had there.

'What in the name of blazes method of murder fools a doctor
and a policeman?' Alec said.

'An untraceable poison?' I suggested. 'Or not even untraceable,
when I come to think of it, since there wasn't a proper post-
mortem. A perfectly traceable poison. Or smothering.'

'Doesn't smothering turn one's face black?' Alec said. 'And
anyway I'd have hated to be the one to overcome Mrs Addie and
hold her down. Unless she was restrained somehow.'

'Strangulation turns the face black, not smothering,' I said.
'But restraints would certainly show – rings of bruises on the
wrists and ankles, mostly likely.'

'And Dr Ramsay and Sergeant Simpson could hardly miss
those.'

'But if Laidlaw was saying she had collapsed and his sister had
seen her do so and if she looked like someone who'd had a heart

attack . . . It doesn't bear thinking about, does it? A little lie from a respectable person who is a good liar?'

'The doctor this would be,' Alec said. 'I'm sure Sergeant Simpson wouldn't have taken Tot's word for anything. The man breaks ten laws every night when the sun goes down.'

'Presumably Simpson doesn't know that,' I said. 'I shall be sure and tell him. He is, after all, my next port of call. Or yours, darling. I shan't fight you for the honour.'

'What we need is an exhumation,' Alec said. 'How does one go about that in these parts? Not the Home Secretary, I don't suppose.'

'I shall ask Simpson that too. Ask about exhumation, tell him we don't trust Tot, tell him about the clothes, ask him about the bag – to be on the safe side.'

'I wish I could believe I'd make a better job of it than you, Dandy,' Alec put a great deal of sincerity into the claim and I did not believe a syllable of it, naturally. 'I'd gladly take it off your hands. But I'd bungle it. Sure to.'

'Let's go together,' I suggested smoothly. 'A united front. I'll start talking – thank you for your kind words – and you can pitch in as and when.'

Alec pushed out his pursed lips and considered my offer from every angle but could see no way of wriggling out of the hole into which he had talked himself.

'Very well,' he said. 'Jolly good. Let's be off then.' It occurred to him no more than it did to me that what we were setting out to do was march into a police station, announce that the bumbling rustics within had plodded down the wrong road once again and then ask them to follow Alec and me to enlightenment.

Sergeant Simpson, on behalf of the Moffat office and perhaps the entirety of the Dumfriesshire Constabulary as far as we knew, declined with some vigour. We re-emerged onto the High Street half an hour later, not exactly with a foot in the seat to send us on our way but certainly we were moving smartly.

'Phew,' Alec said.

'Yes,' I agreed. 'Well, at least we didn't lead with it. We got some good stuff out of him before the portcullis came down.'

Alec was standing with his hat on the back of his head and his hands on his hips, looking up and down the street. He nodded vaguely and gave the rolling wave of the hand he uses to indicate that he wants me to prattle on while he is thinking. It is intensely annoying but prattling while Alec thinks had led to great moments of eureka before and so, through slightly gritted teeth, I obliged him, falling into step as he strode along.

'No handbag, for one,' I said. 'With or without watch and letters. That's worth knowing. Bad news of course that he wouldn't countenance a word with the Fiscal but if I'm not much mistaken, he won't need to. Where are we going?'

'We're here,' Alec said. 'The Moffat Toffee Shop. Just to make doubly trebly sure. Because they're bound to have remembered a woman the size of Mrs Addie, aren't they? What was that about the Fiscal?' He held the door open, and as it dinged with the happy sound of sweetshops everywhere I passed through.

It was enough to rot one's teeth simply to stand and breathe the air. As well as the glittering glass jars of boiled sweets set on shelves behind the counter and the trays of sugar mice and chocolates laid out on waxed paper in the shelves beneath it, there was a sort of shrine to toffee all along one wall. There were bars of toffee wrapped in printed paper, individual toffee morsels done up in coloured twists, tins and boxes of toffee with lurid scenes of Moffat painted upon them – everything from the Ram to the bath house to the municipal gardens complete with bandstand – and a vat of broken toffee pieces into which one could dip a little enamel shovel and fill a bag for tuppence.

I blamed this unwrapped, unfettered heap of toffee pieces for the thick buttery sweetness in the air, almost heavy enough to taste. It was either that, the tray of toffee-apples sitting on top of the counter, plump and shining, or possibly the neat packages of tablet, tied with string, and showing with a slight translucence in their paper that they had been wrapped very recently, while still warm.

'A quarter of your famous Moffat toffee, please,' Alec said to the woman behind the counter. She was dressed in an apron and cap which mirrored the company livery of black and white with bright red trim and looked, therefore, like something from a pantomime. Fifty if a day, she nevertheless dimpled a little at Alec's voice. I decided to hang back and let him have his way.

'Right you are, sir,' she said. 'And is that what brought you here to Moffat?' She must have noticed my arched brow, for she gave me a cold look before turning back to Alec and switching on the twinkle again. 'It wouldn't be the first time,' she confided.

'I'm sure,' Alec said. 'No, I'm at the Hydro for a few days, but a late friend of mine told me to be sure and stop by.' He had let his voice fall and now his head drooped a little too.

'A Moffat man?' asked the shopkeeper, busily trying to think what gentleman had recently been called to his rest, I imagine.

'An Edinburgh lady,' Alec replied. 'And a great devotee of yours. A Mrs Addie. She was often at the Hydro. I wonder if you know who I mean.'

'Mrs Addie?' cried the shopkeeper, pressing a hand to her breast. 'A *late* friend, did you say, sir? Oh mercy, I'm sorry to hear that now!'

'As am I to have broken sad news in such an unfeeling way,' Alec said. The undertaker was back at his post.

'Not at all,' said the shopkeeper. She rummaged under the counter and brought up a doilied plate with a small heap of toffees on it. She took one for herself, her manners all departed with the shock of the news perhaps, and then held it out to Alec the way one would offer a cigarette. He took one and unwrapped it as solemnly as one can.

'It should be tablet, really,' said the shopkeeper with a sad smile. 'Mrs Addie was a one for my mother's tablet. She'd take a toffee if one was offered but it was tablet she bought for herself and tablet she always sent to her daughter.'

'Ah, dear Mrs Bowie,' Alec said. 'She's bearing up well but she feels it.'

'I never met the young lady,' said the shopkeeper. 'Mrs always came in alone.'

'And when was it that you last saw her?' Alec said. The door behind us had tinkled and he spoke rather quickly in case she was about to dismiss him and all his questions and go back to plying her trade.

'Oh, the last time she was here,' came the reply, spoken at a very comfortable pace; there was all the time in the world to discuss poor Mrs Addie, no matter that even now the door tinkled again. 'Last summer. I did wonder if she wasn't coming back again – changed days up there since the old doctor passed – but there! If she wasn't well that'll have been at the bottom of it.'

Here Alec had no choice but to turn to me, even if my insinuation into his tête-à-tête was not to his new friend's liking, for he had not been in Scotland long enough to navigate his way to an understanding of 'last summer' spoken in October. I, in contrast, knew right away that we had scored a crucial point in our game. 'Last summer' to this Moffat worthy could not include the most recent September; it was over a year ago. 'This summer past', 'that summer there' and 'summer just gone' would have answered the case, but 'last summer' was unequivocally nothing to do with Mrs Addie's final trip to the Hydro.

'She *was* back, though,' I said. 'The dear lady.' I should not try that stuff; it does not come naturally and I saw Alec biting his cheeks to hear me. 'Just for a couple of nights, mind you. I wonder that she didn't make it into the shop. I'm sure I would have made a beeline.' I looked around the place and tried to make my eyes shine with greed, or at least to look as though my stomach were not roiling.

The shopkeeper decided to forgive my sin – which was, I expected, chiefly made up of my not being Alec – since I had brought hard news, and she gave a chuckle.

'Oh, Mrs Addie never came to the shop until she'd been a good week with the doctor,' she said. 'She came and did her treatments and as soon as she was able she came down here and undid them all again.'

'I'm not sure I follow,' Alec said.

The woman pulled her face out of its grin and lowered her eyes. 'I meant no disrespect, sir.'

'I shouldn't imagine it for a minute,' he assured her. 'But how could your toffee undo a cured back?' I kicked him gently and he took his cue and changed course like a dressage pony. 'Ah, well. Water under the bridge. Let's just both be thankful we knew her and let's never forget her, eh? Now, to business.' He rubbed his hands together and began a protracted series of negotiations into the differences between toffee, tablet and fudge, the comparative 'nippiness' of pan drops, oddfellows and humbugs and an enquiry into the healthful properties of liquorice sticks which only ended when the queue which had built up behind him reached the door and was letting a draught in.

I bought sugar mice for Donald and Teddy, who would be mystified by my nostalgia, I was sure, and a quarter-pound of comfits for Hugh who is fond of them, and we left at last.

'Well?' said Alec, shifting a large piece of toffee into his cheek and carefully closing the wrapping on the remainder (thus does one try to pretend one is not going to eat the lot and have to sip warm water and baking soda later).

'I think we can take the bad back as a politeness,' I said. 'Mrs Addie came to the Hydro for some "banting".'

'What?'

'A reducing diet. I always think it's a most expressive word.'

'A reducing diet?' said Alec. 'Ah, I see.'

'Which explains why her daughter would be so sure she wasn't off the Hydro grounds within a day of getting there. The Old Doctor must have kept her captive until he had helped her shift a few pounds.'

'It also explains why she was moaning about the food,' Alec said. 'Dorothea – Dr Laidlaw must have had her on a special menu, not the pies and custards the rest of us are wading through.'

'I wonder if knowing that helps us?' I said. 'Let's go back to the house and drop off Bunty. She'll have had enough of the back seat by now.'

'It might do,' Alec said. 'I can see why Dr Laidlaw would be interested in her anyway. I mean to say, standing someone on a set of bathroom scales is pretty black and white, isn't it? There's no way to disguise the fact that something's working. Or not. And I happen to know from our discussions that Doroth— Dr Laidlaw's biggest bugbear is that asking people how they are feeling is a hopeless way of finding out how ill they are.'

'What is the work she does?' I asked. 'Doroth— Dr Laidlaw?' I was not exactly sure why I was teasing him; sometimes I think it has simply become a habit as it was with my brother and sister and me. 'What is it that absorbs her so that she ignores her appointments with her patients?'

'Fascinating stuff,' Alec said. He had coloured a touch at the teasing but let it go by unremarked, which was most unusual. 'And she's an expert in the field. More learned papers than you could shake a stick at and the Hydro is the perfect place to study it.'

'Study what?' I said. We were back at the motorcar and right enough, Bunty was standing up on the back seat with her head out of the side window flap, playing to a crowd of children who were taking turns to pet her. She grew excited enough when she saw me to drive them back a little, just enough to let us through.

'Bonnie doggy, missus,' said a grubby little sort in a tattered dress and a ribbon which only added to the tangles in her hair and did nothing for decoration. 'She looks like a bag ae toffees.' I laughed; it had not struck me before but the black-and-white patterned toffee shop did have a faint air of Dalmatian about it. I decided to spare myself Donald and Teddy's looks of scorn at my sentiment and handed the urchin the bag of sugar mice, calling to her departing back that she should share them.

'Snake oil,' Alec said, once we were in and Bunty had recovered from the joy of reunion. 'Faith healing. Mumbo-jumbo. Only she calls it the Placebo.'

'Sounds like a resort on the Mediterranean,' I said. '"Come to the Placebo – white beaches and dancing every night." And she studies it at the Hydro?'

'She thinks it's the perfect place,' Alec said again. 'Promise you won't tell Hugh.' Light was beginning to dawn upon me. Alec grinned. 'She doesn't believe a bit of it. Not a jot. Not the sitz baths or the sun lamps or anything.'

'Huh!' I said. 'She charges enough for it in that case.'

'Ah yes,' said Alec. 'But she charges because it works. I tell you, Dandy, it's a marvel. The theory is – Do-octor Laidlaw explained it all to me – that Donald and Teddy and Hugh will all get better even though it's complete hocus-pocus. And they'll all get better faster than if they just rested and let nature take its course, and they'll all get better quicker with three different "treatment plans" than if they all did the same. And the more trouble it is the better it works.'

'That must be why the patients who're only there for the casino have to submit to treatments,' I said. 'Only . . . I wonder what she's measuring if they're not ill to start with.'

'Could be any one of a hundred things,' Alec said. 'She's working on an enormous review of it. Thinking about *The Lancet*, no less.'

'She certainly seems to have convinced you,' I said. 'You don't think that maybe if something went wrong – if one of her patients died, for instance – she would cover it up? With *The Lancet* in view?'

'Not patients. Guinea pigs,' Alec said. 'That's what she calls them.'

'Such callousness doesn't exactly speak to—' I began. Then I stopped as a thought struck me. 'Why did she tell you all of this? When she'd only just met you?'

'I'm a control,' Alec said. 'She really does have a first-rate mind, Dan. She tells a select few to see if it still works when we know it's all nonsense.'

'Ah,' I said. We were swinging into Auchenlea's gate now. 'So you're a guinea pig too then, really. I thought for a bit she was taken with you.' I did not turn my head since I was navigating a narrow drive, but I thought I saw him stiffen. 'Won't it muck things up rather – for *The Lancet* – that there's nothing wrong with you? Will you pretend to get better or pretend to stay crocked? Can you even remember what it is that's *supposed* to be wrong with you?'

'Bad back, like Mrs Addie,' Alec said in a distant voice. 'I never thought of that.'

'I wouldn't worry about it,' I said. 'My bright idea about the Fiscal means that you'll have to open your little cage and run away anyway. The experiment is over, at least for you.'

He did not take much convincing. Dr Laidlaw might see Alec as just another dead moth to be pinned but I was becoming ever more sure that he had failed to take a comparably professional view of her. All that choking on her name and letting me rib him. To me she was a suspect, like her brother and Mrs Cronin and even Regina. To Alec she was an innocent, sullied by the coarseness of Tot, and deserving, without question, of all the loyalty Mrs Cronin and Regina could give her. For that reason too I was not as loath as I normally would be to despatch him on an errand.

'I prefer "mission",' he said. I was not going to quibble. Certainly I was not going to fight him for the opportunity to raise the thorny question of exhumation. It would take all of his charm to talk Mrs Bowie into anything of the kind and Mr Addie would not have let me get to the end of the first sentence before he paid his outstanding bill and showed me the door.

'I'm sure I'm right,' I said. 'The family and the Fiscal. Sergeant Simpson repeated that twice or three times, lording it over us who are neither. But what he forgot is that the Fiscal who swallowed the story – the one in Dumfries – is not the Fiscal who'll have to sign the order. He's in Edinburgh. If you can persuade the Addies to ask him – and of course you can; they adore you – then surely . . . Well, I'm not *sure*, to be honest, but I'd wager a modest sum. He probably feels some professional loyalty, but he probably feels some rivalry too and when we get right down to it his first duty is to the citizenry under his care. To wit, Addie and Bowie née. I'll bet you I'm right, Alec.'

'And my job is to go to these respectable people and suggest digging the old girl up and having a poke about to see what we can see,' Alec said. We were standing at the front door of the Hydro. He looked up at it, sighed and consulted his watch. 'I wish there was a bar in there,' he said. 'I hope they'll bring a whisky and soda to the drawing room. Meanwhile what are you going to do?'

'I'm going to get into that locked room if it kills me,' I said. 'I'm half convinced that's where Mrs Addie died. There might still be clues.'

Before that, though, there was a very difficult conversation to be had. I begged Alec to be there and to promise not to leave no matter what happened. Quite simply, now that we thought Mrs Addie *had* been murdered I could no longer countenance Donald and Teddy spending their days at the Hydro. I could not claim to be too keen on the guinea pig end of things either, if it came to that, and it lent me the courage to speak, just not enough to speak without Alec there to protect me.

'Hugh,' I said, joining him at a tea table in the drawing room. *He* had a whisky and soda, I was interested to see, although the boys were tussling with a silver teapot and a three-tiered stand of bread-and-butter, griddle cakes and meringues.

'Boys,' I said. 'Slop out that dishwater and let me pour you a nice hot cup then load up your plates and run along. I need to speak to Daddy.' This was a great treat, for of course they had been trained from the days when their bread was served in soldiers to affect ignorance of the higher, sweeter tiers until the duller fare was gone. I was rather horrified to see them immediately build towers of cake on their tea plates, but I simply poured the tea, told them they could not have sugar in it and waited until they took themselves off to a window seat with a view of the bowling.

'Now then, Hugh,' I said. 'How are you feeling?'

Hugh gave a quick glance towards Alec. It was low of me to force him to speak of his health in front of another man, and a neighbour come to that.

'Perfectly well, Dandy,' he said. 'Thank you for asking.'

I sighed. 'I mean are you feeling the better for having come here?'

'Oh, tremendously so,' he said. 'I've been telling you for years that water treatment is the thing. The boys are vastly improved too.' I smiled and tried not to think about how angry he would be if he ever found out about the snake oil.

'Well, just remember that as you listen to what I'm going to tell you,' I said. 'And remember too that I rented a house. I didn't suggest we stayed here. Remember that, please.'

Hugh took a contemplative sip from his glass. Alec looked away and ordered a drink of his own from a maid who was passing.

'Go on,' Hugh said.

'Yes, now you see, the thing is,' I said. 'What I mean to say is – and you've probably already guessed because not much gets past you and I have seen you laughing once or twice and not sharing the joke.' If I hoped to butter him up with this, I hoped in vain. All I did was make him suspect I knew about the casino. Not much gets past him, as I say. 'The thing is that Alec and I are working.'

'On a case,' Alec said.

'Fraud?' said Hugh, quite loudly. I took it to mean that he had not cashed in his winnings and was trusting Laidlaw with whatever sum he had racked up to date.

'Ah, no,' I said. 'Nor theft – which would be dreadful, nothing worse than a hotel where one's belongings aren't safe. Remember that terrible place in Paris? With the drains?'

'Something less dreadful than theft then?' he said. 'I hope it's going to pay enough to cover the cost of you both rushing down here. Or did it arise after we came?'

'No, no,' I said. 'It was certainly partly responsible for my suggesting decamping to here. But mostly it was you and the boys. And Pallister and Mrs Tilling too.'

'And what is this crime – if it even is a crime – that's not so bad as maids pilfering cufflinks?' he said.

'An odd end to a patient's treatment,' I said. Did he know already? Had he guessed and begun toying with me?

'Seems to me there *are* only two ends,' Hugh said. He had guessed, damn him. 'Recovery or . . . death.'

'Yes,' I said and then hurried on. I judged it best to keep talking and get everything out at once. 'A death. A woman, though, a good bit older than you, and much, much older than the boys, with a very different complaint – bad back and a tendency towards stoutness which she was being treated for with surely completely different treatments from those you'd need if it were your lungs and a long illness like the boys and you. And besides I'm telling you today because I think the boys should leave now that we've decided that it's . . . that is, now that there's a chance that what happened was perhaps that she was . . . murdered. Weeks ago.' I think it was that last point that pushed him over the edge. He set down his glass with a smack that drew attention from several of the other tea tables. I had to calm myself with a few very deep breaths before I dared to look him in the face and when I did it was to see that he was smiling. More than smiling; he was laughing. A silent laugh with shaking shoulders, which I had only ever seen before when he recounted stories from George at the club.

'I actually thought we must be iller than the doctors would tell us,' he said, 'when you suddenly dragged us off down here. It kept me awake one night. But now all is revealed.' All except the hot water and radiators at Gilverton, I thought, giving him a sickly grin. Hugh turned to Alec. 'Are we in any danger, old man?'

Alec shook his head. 'I shouldn't have thought so,' he replied. 'It was one old lady and the place is filled to the rafters with guests. No one else has died recently.'

It was a perfect example of the stiff upper lip and Hugh met it with its cousin, the soaring understatement.

'Ticklish about the boys, mind you,' he said. 'But a little old lady . . .'

'She was rather a large old lady, actually,' I said.

'We could always tell them,' said Alec. 'Put them on their guard.' I was shaking my head before he had finished speaking.

'They'd be out in the shrubbery bent double with magnifying glasses and we'd be completely undone,' I said. 'I really do think they should go.'

'As you wish,' Hugh said. 'Shall we send Mrs Tilling back with them? Shall you eat here with me?'

'Not home to Gilverton,' I said. I was beginning to be aware of a throbbing at my temples. 'I meant they could stay at Auchenlea.'

'I'm for them carrying on with the treatments,' said Hugh. 'Let's tell them to be on their guard – perhaps say that there's been a suspicious stranger lurking about. But I'm for staying on a while anyway.'

'Oh, Hugh, how can you?' I said, losing all patience. 'I know exactly why you're "for staying". I know all about Tot Laidlaw's grubby little enterprise. But how you can throw your own sons to—' I was on thin ice there and so I regrouped. 'How can they be on their guard if they're lying on tables covered with mustard wraps or with electric I don't-know-whats attached to their arms and legs?'

'Nothing grubby about it,' Hugh said, showing me which of my barbs had wounded him. 'Rather disappointingly respectable, in fact. The Moffat bourgeoisie come out to play. Isn't that right, Osborne?'

'We don't get shackled to the couches, Dandy,' Alec said, hurrying past any hint that he had joined Hugh in the casino. 'And there is nothing electric attached to one. Just lamps shining down. Anyone could get up and hop it if he felt he wanted to.'

'I can't believe you're being so cavalier,' I said to Hugh. 'But since you are . . . I will allow them to stay as long as they stay together and don't go into any little treatment rooms on their own. They can play golf and croquet and billiards and rest on the terrace.'

'I can't allow you to suspend the treatments, Dandy,' Hugh said, meeting my glare with that unconcerned look of his. 'Look at Donald! Just look at him and then tell me his baths aren't helping him.' He tapped his pocket where the brochure, now looking very well thumbed, was still folded. 'I'm thinking of going in for a few more. I feel better all the time.'

For two pins I would have told him the whole story, of Dr Laidlaw's swooping in to use the spoils of her father's beloved Hydro for her own cold scientific ends, of her cynical division of hopeful invalids into groups of guinea pigs and controls and of how she only cared about *The Lancet* and was not worthy of the name of doctor at all. For two pins I would but I had forgotten what it was called – that resort on the Mediterranean sea – and so I sat silently fuming instead and let him laugh at me.

Matters were not improved by the arrival in the drawing room at that moment not just of Tot Laidlaw coming out like a famous chef from his kitchen after pudding and walking amongst the tables gathering laurels, but today of his sister too, padding along just behind him like a hand maiden and peering intently at all the faces of the guests for all the world as though she were a proper selfless doctor with the Hippocratic oath on her lips and a black bag in her hand. If it had been rock buns instead of meringues that teatime, I might well have shied one at each of them.

So it was with no great surge of welcome that I agreed they could join us. Several of the other tea-takers scattered around the room looked with envy as dear Dr Laidlaw and good old Tot sat down with Hugh, Alec and me. I found myself thinking, briefly, that they were welcome to them, before reminding myself that this pair were at the very heart of the puzzle of the Hydro and I should be glad of the chance to study them at close quarters. I began with Tot, ready to whisk my eyes away if he caught me looking, but to my surprise he did not. He nodded at Alec and Hugh, gave his sister a glare and ignored me completely. I thought, besides, that there was something rather brittle about his air of jollity today, his winks less languid than usual, his preening more like fidgets than before.

'So,' he said as he settled down, with much plucking at his

trousers and shirt cuffs. He was as dapper as ever in his too-light flannels, cut to flatter a figure in which, the more I saw it, the more I could trace the marks of dissolute living. He was certainly wearing worse than his sister, although I thought he could easily be younger than her. She had the pale cheeks and dark eyes of a dedicated scholar but also the smooth saintly look which they sometimes develop, untouched by the trials of husband, home, servants and children. That was it, I thought, looking at her. Even though thirty if a day and perhaps a good deal more, she looked a girl still. She looked unmarried. It is a look one is well accustomed to these days, when there are still so many of what I cannot bring myself to call 'surplus women'.

'Wonderful fire drill,' Tot was saying. 'Fastest yet. Of course, it helps when not absolutely everyone is upstairs in bed, eh?' He jerked his elbow at Hugh although he was too far away actually to nudge him. Of course! The middle-of-the-night fire drills would not discommode Tot's bright young things, who would still be at the tables and only needed to step outside with their drinks in their hands. I wondered what Dr Laidlaw's patients in their pyjamas made of it all. 'I'm discounting you, Dottie,' he said, giving his sister a penetrating look.

Dr Laidlaw winced but then managed a smile. Alec recrossed his legs and regarded Laidlaw coldly.

'My sister, Mrs Gilver,' Tot went on, turning to me at last. He was grinning his wide grin but I was almost sure I could see a sheen of sweat on his high brow. 'Can you believe she just worked right through the clanging? I had to go and fetch her. If that had been a real fire, Dot, we would both have been in trouble.'

'I'm sorry, Thomas,' she said. 'I've apologised already. I had cotton wool in my ears.'

'Is your study noisy?' Alec asked, with an air of pitching in. 'It's nowhere near— I mean, there's no source of any noise, surely? Foxes? Owls? I haven't heard them.'

'It helps me concentrate,' she said. 'When I'm writing. It gives me the sense of a cocoon, with everything shut out, you know.'

'Oh, yes, we know,' Tot said. He spoke lightly but from the

way his sister shrank from his words he might have been grinding his teeth and glowering at her. 'We know all about your tremendous feats of concentration.' He turned again to take us all in. 'Absent-minded professor. Like our father. Not me! I'm the black sheep that was never going to come to any good, isn't that right, Dottie?'

I turned a little in my chair and looked hard at Hugh. How could he stand this odious person? How could he bear him, airing his family's cruel little sayings that way? I was gratified to see Hugh assume the distant look he affects when trying simply to pretend that what is passing before him is not.

'Still,' Tot said. 'It's all good fun and what else is life for, eh?'

No one managed to summon a reply and so he spoke again.

'Everyone settled? No thoughts of leaving? I'd be sorry to see you take off, old man. And if that business in the steam room is all squared away for your good lady . . . ?'

In other words, I thought, Hugh was having his usual run of luck in the casino and Tot didn't want my encounter with a ghost to cause him to cash his chips before the luck turned and the casino could win it all back again. I caught Alec's eye and a thought passed between us. Had it been Tot who planted the toffees and told Mrs Cronin to make sure we saw them?

'How are your sons, Mrs Gilver?' said Dr Laidlaw, rather blurting it out to change the subject.

'I'm very glad you asked,' I said. I pointed over to where Donald and Teddy were lounging on the window seat. 'Their posture is not what one would hope for, but they seem markedly improved. Thank you.' I took a deep breath and plunged on before my nerve failed me. I had only just remembered an odd little moment Dr Laidlaw and I had shared that very first day and I wondered if alluding to it would shake something loose that might be useful. 'Knowing that you – their doctor – are taking a close interest in their convalescence is most reassuring. We mothers, as I'm sure you know, are rather fierce on the subject of harm coming to our young. I think that almost more than any treatments they might undergo or not undergo it's wonderful to think that they are in safe and caring hands and will not come to any harm here.'

Half of my audience shifted uncomfortably. Hugh was unsettled by this sickly display of sentiment as he would be by any. Alec was trying not to laugh; he knew exactly what the act had cost my dignity. I carried on regardless, for it was the other half I had in my sights and thus far I had only taken aim.

'I blame my own mother, of course,' I said. 'And my nanny too. But I'm sure you won't mind me asking.' I simpered a little here, or tried to, and dared not look at Alec or Hugh. 'I suppose you do drain and clean the plunging pool regularly, don't you? You didn't quite answer when I asked before, Dr Laidlaw, but surely you do.'

And then I watched very closely while trying to appear not to. Dr Laidlaw was doing her scared rabbit routine again, her eyes seeming to take up half her face. Tot Laidlaw, though, was far more interesting. The geniality was gone, the smirk, the crinkling at the eyes, every last twinkle – quite gone. And he *was* sweating, and none too lightly either; droplets gathering into rivulets and coursing down his brow. For the first time I saw that there was more than just the family nose to show that his sister and he were sprung from the same source. With his face pale and his eyes suddenly dark, and with that look of dismay spreading over him like a stain, he might have been her twin. It took him a full minute to shake himself back to life and say something.

'Why, my dear Mrs Gilver, I hardly know what to say. I'm almost flattered, it's almost a compliment. We've really made you so comfortable with all of this' – he broke off and waved around at the drawing room – 'that you've forgotten what Laidlaw's *is*? This Hydropathic Establishment is a hospital, dear lady. A hospital, not a hotel. I could show you the licences and other papers to prove it to you. And cleanliness and hygiene are watchwords here. So fret not, my dear lady, fret not at all.'

'So when was it last cleaned?' said Alec, cutting through all the soft soap.

'As recently as a month ago,' Tot Laidlaw said. He seemed to believe his answer scored a point for him, but Alec and I knew better.

Tot made an excuse shortly afterwards, rose, bowed and walked off, managing to get the swagger back into his stride on his way down the room so that by the time he reached the end of it and passed out into the hall he was quite his old self again.

'I must be running along too,' said Dr Laidlaw. 'I have some work to do.'

'Did that pretty child give you the bundle of clothes, Dr Laidlaw?' I said. 'From Mrs Cronin, via me.'

'Yes,' said Dr Laidlaw miserably. 'Yes, she did.'

'Rather astonishing, eh?' I said. 'What a coincidence!'

'A coincidence?' she said. 'You don't think then that it . . . wraps things up?'

'I suppose if one believed in such things as ghosts one might say she can rest in peace now,' I said. 'But I'm not much of a one for hocus-pocus. Mumbo-jumbo, call it what you like. Are you?'

The doctor muttered something incomprehensible under her breath and not hiding her thankfulness even a bit she hurried away.

'Well,' said Hugh. 'If that's a typical example of the kinds of scenes I'm missing by staying out of your game, Osborne, I can't say I'm sorry.' I rolled my eyes but left Alec to navigate this blatant attempt to sneer.

'Oh, you toughen up over time,' Alec said, masterfully. 'So, Dandy, you were supposed to think the spirit of Mrs Addie wanted her clothes back, got them, and all lived happily ever after.'

'Or mouldered quietly in the grave. Exactly,' I said. 'Unfortunately she won't be allowed to. When are you setting off for town?'

'Tomorrow, first thing,' said Alec. Perhaps he regretted his snub to Hugh for he turned to him now with a rueful smile. 'I must to Edinburgh,' he said, 'to persuade the woman's relations to order an exhumation. We think they'll find poison if they trouble to check, don't we?'

'Poison?' said Hugh, looking sharply down into his glass of whisky. Then he cleared his throat and took a careless swallow of it. 'What about you, Dandy?'

'Interesting as it was to discover that they cleaned the pool after Mrs Addie died,' I said, 'I still need to search for clues in the room where we think the murder was done.' I was over-egging but only a churl could blame me. 'We know which room it is but it's kept under lock and key, as you can imagine.'

'The murder room, eh?' said Hugh. 'You will be careful, won't you?' I could not help but smile.

'I shall,' I said. 'As ever. And thank you.'

'Only, God knows,' Hugh said, 'there are some very strange people about.' He nodded to where a small procession of mediums with Loveday Merrick at its head was making its stately way towards the door. Mr Merrick saw Alec and me, tipped the silver top of his cane to his temple, and moved on.

'Do you know him?' Hugh said.

'Not exactly,' Alec said. 'But I get the impression he knows us.'

'Who is he?' said Hugh. 'Extraordinary-looking chap, even for here.'

I considered briefly telling him that one little murder was not the half of it, that there were ghosts and grandmothers and savage histories piling up behind every door and spirit mediums rushing to greet them.

'He's not connected to the case,' I said firmly. How happy I would be if that were so.

12

Thursday, 24th October 1929

When I took myself off back to the Russian and Turkish it was only to find out what keys there were and who kept them. When I saw Regina's face fall at the sight of me, however, I decided to turn the thumbscrews one last time to see what I could see.

I folded my clothes and handed them over. She took them away and returned. She held out the lead-lined receptacle and in it I dropped my few items of jewellery and my little purse. All of this was done in total silence.

'I shall want a rub-down, Regina,' I said.

'Salt and water on the marble, madam?' she said. 'That's all we're doing today. We're too short-handed to offer oil rubs up in the private rooms.'

I wished I was as intimately acquainted with the Hydro's catalogue as was Hugh. After his hours of browsing he would have known right away whether this restriction was set out in the pages of the brochure – where to be fair, there *were* many detailed exceptions and codicils along the lines of half-hour Nauheim treatments being almost free if one combined them with Schott exercises, but rather pricey if undertaken all on their own – or if Regina had just decided off her own bat that she was not going to let me get her alone in a private treatment room, not even for ready money.

'Short-handed?' I said. 'Is Mrs Cronin having *another* afternoon off?'

'Mrs Cronin is busy,' Regina said. At that unfortunate moment we both heard a door being swept open and the unmistakable sound of Mrs Cronin in her indoor shoes squeaking along the oiled boards to the hot rooms. Regina coloured and bobbed and bore the lead-lined bag away.

'Give me fifteen minutes to get nice and warm,' I said. 'And then come and find me.' I remembered to look as she was departing to see whether there was a ring of keys anywhere about her. There was not.

I had had no intention of venturing into the steam room or plunging pool, but by a chance as I was entering the cool room someone was leaving and in the warm room someone else was moving up again and so, for just a moment, there was a clear view right through the two sets of curtains all the way to the end, where who should be standing and wiping perspiration from her forehead but Mrs Petrushka Molyneaux herself, along with a quorum of underlings. I supposed that she had to come to the Turkish baths to lord it now; everywhere else she was merely one of Loveday Merrick's minions.

Would they go straight to the sprays? I wondered. Or would the whole pack of them venture into the Turkish? It was worth finding out and so I doubled back and sprinted along the side of the pool, past the marble temple and into the steam. I climbed to the top shelf and lay down, trying to breathe silently and become invisible.

It was then that I found out just what a worthy system the cool, warm and hot rooms are, for sprinting straight from the changing cubicle to the steam was a very different matter. Within minutes I was feeling giddy, a few minutes more and I felt as sick as I ever had, Channel crossings included. I told myself to leave, but could not summon the momentum to push myself up and begin moving. I decided instead to have a little snooze and hoped to wake feeling better.

Thankfully, Regina was the sort to face trouble head-on and get it over and she did not give me anything like fifteen minutes before she came to summon me for my rubbing. As a consequence I had not quite slipped into a stupor and I heard her clearly when she opened the door.

'Mrs Gilver?' she said.

186

'Ssh, Regina,' I replied. Through my groggy stupor, it seemed terribly important and absolutely real. 'They'll hear you. And close the door. You're letting the steam out and they'll see you too.' There was a scraping noise as she pulled a heavy iron door-stop forward to prop the steam room open.

'Come out, madam, do!' she said. She came and shook me and then lifted my feet down onto the shelf below and tugged on my arms to sit me up. 'How could you be so silly? How *could* you let yourself get in this state? I told you how to go the baths that first day and don't say I didn't. Don't you dare get me into trouble now.'

We were out into the cool air, or what was left of it with all the steam pouring from the open door. I could see Mrs Molyneaux and the other mediums walking shoulder deep in the plunging pool, but in my mental fog I was sure they were wearing their cloaks and coats and that the hat with the raven feathers was perched on Mrs Molyneaux's head in place of her turban.

Regina sat me down on one of the marble slabs and kicked away the doorstop, closing the steam room off again. She helped me out of my robe and pushed me down until I was lying supine, staring up at the rose of the spray above me.

'Please don't turn the cold water on,' I whimpered.

'I most certainly won't,' Regina said, twisting the lid off a jar of some unknown substance. 'You need to cool down slowly.'

She rubbed her hands together in that powerful way of hers and then began slapping me all over, the rough salt from the jar causing the very last of my torpor to leave me.

'Did Mrs Addie do something silly like that?' I said. Regina's face puckered and I was sure that I could see tears glinting in her eyes. She rubbed the back of one hand roughly across her face and then set it to work on me again.

'I do wish to goodness you would stop about Mrs Addie,' she said. 'It was a very sad day for the Hydro. The first time a patient has ever died and even though it was her own— Well, I won't speak ill of the dead.'

'Her own fault?' I echoed. 'If she went out instead of sticking

187

to her treatment? I suppose if she had stayed in the Hydro and had her heart attack here the doctor would have got to her sooner. But it's rather a harsh judgement.'

'I'd never say anything half so heartless about a dog in the street!' Regina said. 'That's not what I meant at all.'

'So . . . you mean if she had left the spirits alone she wouldn't have been scared out of her wits?' I asked. It was a guess, but a good one. Regina left off slapping me and sank down onto the marble at my side.

'I just don't know what's happening here,' she said. 'First Mrs Addie saw a ghost and then you saw *her* ghost and there's all these funny folk that came to see it too, talking about Old Abigail and Big Effie as if there's spirits and spookies all over the place. I don't like it, madam, and I can't pretend I do.'

'Nor do I, Regina,' I said. 'I wish I could convince you I was on your side. You can talk to me, you know.' She shook her head, but she had already told me more than she knew. For one thing, Big Effie was a new name. As Regina resumed her ministrations with a fretful sigh, I determined to write it on my growing list as soon as I had my notebook near me. For another, it was interesting to know that the ghost Mrs Addie saw was the first and all the others, Big Effie included, came after. Perhaps Alec was right and Tot Laidlaw had made up the first ghost to cover the murder.

'So the strange people—' I said. I lowered my voice, conscious that four or five of them were wading about in the cold pool a few yards from where I lay. '—came to see the same ghost Mrs Addie saw? How did they know it was here?' Regina shook her head. 'Who knew that Mrs Addie had seen one?' She shook her head again. 'The word must have spread from someone.'

'I never told a living soul,' Regina said.

'I believe you,' I said. 'Might I turn over, by the way? This is very refreshing but I'm beginning to feel rather flayed. I trust you, Regina, and I wish you would trust me.' I gave her a piercing look and then turned over onto my front. The marble was unforgiving but the salt on my back felt wonderful.

Regina said nothing, but it was an inviting silence, I thought, instead of a repressing one. I answered the invitation.

'That room over there,' I said. 'The locked one? What's in there?'

'Nothing,' she replied loud enough for it to reverberate around the room.

'What is it used for?' I asked.

'Nothing,' she said. 'It's empty. There's absolutely nothing in there.'

'Since when?' I asked her. She did not answer and her hands fell away from my back. I was aware of a nasty creeping feeling as the wet salt slid off down my sides and dripped onto the marble below me. I raised myself on one elbow and looked over my shoulder. Regina stood with her arms hanging at her sides and more of the salt rub dripping from the ends of her fingers. She was staring at the door and then she raised her hands and stared at them.

'Since Mrs Addie died?' I asked. Regina blinked and the colour which had drained from her came flooding back. 'You've just realised what happened, haven't you? Tell me!' I was speaking in a fierce whisper, but nothing like as fierce as the one she fired back at me.

'No,' she said. 'I'll tell you nothing. It's always been empty. There's never been anything in there. It's never been used for anything.'

'I see,' I said. 'And why would that be?'

She shook her head and, wiping her hands on her apron, she ran away. She did not hurry or trot or bustle: she ran.

I was left cold, covered with salt and lying on a marble slab – all in all much more like an item of stock in a fishmonger's than I ever thought to be – but more determined than ever to get into the locked room and see whatever Regina had just realised was in there. The door was partly glass and so I supposed I could wrap my hand in a scarf and break it, but that would put them all on their guard. I wasted a moment wishing I knew how to pick a lock and wondering where I could learn to do so. Finally, I returned to the more sensible question of who would have a key and how I could lay my hands on it. I had far too much respect for Mrs Cronin even to consider her; she popped up whenever one most needed her not to, even – apparently – taking notes from guests in the middle of her afternoon free. (I wished I knew why the sound of her outdoor shoes, every time I remembered it, bothered me so.) Neither did I much fancy trying to find Tot Laidlaw's private rooms and let myself in there. That left Dr Laidlaw. I was in the changing cubicle by now, dressing and trying to ignore the uncomfortable scrape of salt against my skin, but the thought of searching for anything in that chaotic hovel of an office was enough to make me sink down on the velvet bench with shoulders drooping. Then my head snapped up. There would be no searching. I kicked myself for not thinking of it before. Dr Laidlaw's keys were sitting out for all to see in a Staffordshire sweet dish on her chimneypiece. Now, all I had to do was think of a way to get her out of her room without pausing to lock it.

It would have to wait until evening, naturally, when the Turkish and Russian baths were empty; and so, long after dinner, I left the boys playing cribbage by the fire and Bunty already retired to the middle of my counterpane and drove my little motorcar back over the valley. I wondered how Alec had got on with the Addies and whether Hugh had begun his evening's entertainments. Specifically I wished Alec were here in Moffat to help me and wondered if I could pretend to be joining Hugh if someone saw me – I had overdressed a little for dinner, to Grant's satisfaction, and was just about swanky enough to walk into a casino without attracting attention. (Rather depressing when that is the highest aim of one's toilette, but for this evening anyway I was thankful.)

Hoping to get away without having to make an entrance, though, I parked my motorcar in a passing place halfway along the drive and made the rest of my approach on foot, cursing the shoes Grant had persuaded me into, which had long, pointed toes, slightly turned up too, after the manner of a Turk's slippers, and were very tricky to walk in without kicking gravel up in spouts before one.

It only occurred to me when I had got to the front door and was lurking in the rhododendrons on its far side that I should of course have thought of a different way to enter the Hydro if I wanted to be truly incognito. In my mind's eye I traversed the stone steps, the vestibule, the carpeted steps and the hall beyond. It had to be forty feet without any cover at all until the mouth of the nearest passageway and it did not lead to the Turkish baths by any quick route that I knew. Cursing myself now, I slipped along the front of the building, round the side, down the shallow steps to the terrace level and along past the drawing room to the small smoking room, thinking that with any luck all the smoking gentlemen would be combining their cigars with a game of cards by now and any who were too wholesome for the casino would be tucked up in their blameless beds. I sidled past the window and then put my eye to the gap in the curtain. The room looked empty as far as I could see, but just as I was about to try the handle, I heard a movement from behind me. Someone was coming up the stone steps from the lawn. I darted away into the shadow of a climbing jasmine, hoping that the beads on my dress or the gold buckles on my ridiculous shoes would not catch the light. The figure which appeared at the top of the steps, however, did not so much as glance to either side. He simply strode over the terrace, opened the french window and disappeared inside, drawing it close but not shutting it behind him. I stood for a moment, searching my memory, for I was sure that I recognised him. I had only got a glimpse of his outline, enough to know he was dressed for the evening, but still I had the niggling feeling I knew who he was.

The male members of the bright young set had not resolved themselves into individuals for me; they were still an undifferentiated mass of humanity inside a cloud of laughter and cigarette smoke. It might have been one of the few male mediums, I supposed. Not the unmistakable Loveday Merrick, but one of his lesser fellows. Or perhaps another of our Perthshire neighbours had come to take the waters as had we, far from home and the flu and scarlet fever which were rife there.

Whoever he was, his appearance had told me one thing: I

could be sure there was no one in the smoking room, for I would have heard their manly hellos. So, before I could talk myself out of it, I slipped out of the shadow and in at the door, through the empty room and along the dim corridor beyond. I had my story all ready: Grant collapsed and labouring for breath, me thinking only of Dr Laidlaw and how she had helped Hugh and the boys.

Grant had agreed to let the doctor in when she arrived and to say that she felt much better.

'I'll tell her I coughed out a right big— I mean to say, I'll tell her I enjoyed a productive cough and it cleared things,' she said. I shuddered. 'Like Master Donald that night, remember?'

'How could I forget?' I said. 'But I'm hoping it won't get as far as that.'

'I'm ready to help if it does,' Grant told me.

In preparation for my part in the charade, I made sure my face was troubled and my breath coming in gasps before I knocked on the doctor's door. I was going to say that my little motorcar had run out of petrol and she should go on ahead, that I should get Hugh to ring for his chauffeur. I thought I could be fairly certain of pulling it off, although it did strike me now as tremendously complicated. I missed Alec again. I was sure he would have come up with a way of getting Dr Laidlaw out of her office without my dressing to the nines, roping in Grant and sprinting half a mile in these slippers. I shook the thoughts out of my head and knocked.

There was no answer, but I remembered that this was a woman who ignored fire bells. I knocked again. Still nothing. Feeling very bold, I grasped the handle, turned it and burst in.

'Oh, Dr Laidlaw,' I began, but the room was empty. My eyes darted to the chimneypiece and I saw the jagged shape of the keys in the bon-bon dish. In three strides I was there. I hid the key ring in the folds of my dress, thinking that Grant's taste in flowing robes had its uses, and then I fled to the Turkish and Russian – more Turk than Cossack in my Ali Baba slippers – with luck on my side and not a soul to see me.

It was unsettling in the extreme to be there in the darkness when the place was empty, and none the less so for the sensation being so difficult to explain. Perhaps it was just that the rooms, unheated now, felt dead and much colder than in fact they were. The couches, without their towels, were funeral biers and the marble chamber a mausoleum. Even the pool room was changed by the quiet and dark. The water was a blank, black gleam, bottomless like the well, and the ferns and palms around it, in the dark, were moss and lichen and even reaching hands. I turned away and faced the locked door.

The keyhole was fairly large and so I immediately discounted all the littlest of the keys in my bunch. The first one I tried went in halfway and then stuck. I pulled it out again and picked over the bunch looking for one slightly smaller. Then my fingers froze. I was sure I had heard a scuffling from inside the room. Well, perhaps I had, for an unused room in any house will attract scuffling things. I chose another key and tried again. This one went all the way in but would not turn. Nor when I pulled at it would it come out again. I jiggled it this way and that and felt something give. It was not the key in the lock, though; it was the latch. This door was open.

Using the bunch of keys as a handle I twisted and pushed and the door swung wide. I was ready for anything: a new victim; Tot Laidlaw coming at me with a piece of iron piping; even, I am ashamed to say, the sturdy spectre of Mrs Addie in her robe, hovering three feet above the floor and moaning at me.

What I saw was none of these things. At first I thought the room was absolutely empty, no furniture, no equipment, no fittings of any kind. Nothing more than the marks on the floor where something heavy had been standing and the deep scores across it where the thing had been dragged away. I was staring at these scratches, trying to make sense of them, when I saw a movement from near the far wall.

'Tot?' said a small, broken voice.

I felt beside me on the wall for a light switch and when my fingers met it I did not hesitate but snapped it on.

Dr Laidlaw was huddled on the bare floor of the empty room, hugging her arms about herself and stricken from weeping.

'Shall I fetch him?' I said. She sat up and wiped the tears away with her sleeve.

'No!' she sobbed, and shrank even further into the corner where she was cowering.

'Did he put you in here?' I asked. Nothing Tot did would shock me and I was at a loss as to explain her horror at hearing his name.

'No,' she said again but this time it was a low groan as though she spoke through great exhaustion. 'Please leave us alone, I beg you.'

'As a matter of fact,' I went on, 'how did you get in, since I have your keys?' I did not really believe in the possibility of secret passageways and hidden doors in the panelling, but thought it best to make sure.

Dr Laidlaw roused herself so far as to look at the key ring I waved and then she sank back again. 'Those are spares,' she said. 'Please, please, just leave us alone.'

'But why are you protecting him?' I said. It went against every one of my finer feelings to keep on pestering her while she begged me to stop but I hardened my heart, even as she began crying again. 'I know you want to carry on with your work,' I said. The sobs grew louder. 'But do you need your brother for it? Really and truly, do you?'

'You don't understand,' Dr Laidlaw wailed. 'My brother is very good to me.'

'I *do* understand,' I said. 'He's thought of a way of drawing a crowd of guests for you to work on. But whatever happened to Mrs Addie will come out in the end. This can't go on. And anyway, you refused to sign the death certificate, didn't you? You are blameless. Why not come with me to Sergeant Simpson now and tell him the whole thing.'

'Please,' she begged me, crying harder than ever. 'Please leave me alone. Just leave me.'

Clearly though, she had despaired of my ever relenting, for she sprang up suddenly, rushed past me and was gone.

*   *   *

When I set off to the winter gardens, no doubt well into their night shift as an outpost of Monte Carlo by now, I had no further thought than to see if Tot was there and if I could rattle him again by telling him his sister was sobbing in the locked room. On the way, however, it occurred to me that I could also look around for the tantalising stranger who had entered by the terrace doors. It was bothering me that I could not place him. I turned the corner at the end of the corridor and began to hear the first faint sounds of music and laughter. At the door, a young man dressed like a waiter bowed and ushered me in. I strode ahead with confidence but then faltered at the very oddness of it. That same soaring glass ceiling which filled it with light in the daytime rendered it glamorously dark in the night, the glass gleaming blackly far above the low lamps which lit the tables. Around the tables was the familiar scene: gentlemen in dinner jackets smoking and drinking and concentrating on the dice and cards, and ladies – girls these, mostly – peeping over shoulders and trying to distract them. There were ladies' games going on as well; at least one roulette wheel in the distance and a poker game where a slightly older clutch of females showed every bit as much concentration as the men and smoked, if anything, even harder. I remembered blaming the orchids and their attendants for the fug in here and thinking the ventilation inadequate. In fact, the fans and skylights must work some kind of miracle in the early hours to turn the place back to garden again every day.

The smoke was not the worst of it; over the whole of the room, too, there was that hum of excitement and anxiety which I dislike to the point of loathing, not being hard-hearted enough to view others' losing streaks as entertainments or optimistic enough to view their winning streaks as promises of my own.

I took a glass of champagne from another waiter who was passing with a tray and, sipping at it, I began on a course about the room, looking for Tot or for a familiar outline. The bright young things were like a chorus of starlings.

'—down to my last chip, and it's such a pretty colour I can't bear to bet it.'

'—taken up in a bath chair if I have another cocktail.'

'—give you her address, if you like. She's wonderfully cheap but you have to buy the material yourself and take it in a taxi to Battersea of all places.'

Implausible as it might sound, it was only when I heard my name that I remembered who else I was bound to run into.

'Dandy?' came Hugh's voice. He had half stood but sounded disapproving, of course; that is always where he begins with me. I turned and saw him at one of the card tables. He had a whisky glass and a miniature metropolis of stacks of poker chips in front of him. The men in the other four seats had the familiar half-sick look men get when they play cards with Hugh.

'Hello,' I said.

'Are the boys all right?' he demanded.

'The boys are fine,' I assured him.

'Sir?' said the dealer.

'See you in the morning,' I said and began to edge away. I had seen Tot Laidlaw at last. He was just entering the room from a small doorway set into the inside wall, slapping shoulders and kissing hands, nodding and bowing so much that he hardly had time to stand up straight in between. He stood up straight enough when he saw me, though. He jerked upright as though he had been kicked hard on the bottom and he began to weave between the tables to come and meet me just as I was weaving to get to him. We both noticed Dorothea at the same time. It was the spreading quiet which alerted me, a wave of whispering and nudging as the bright young things pointed her out to one another. She had dried her eyes and smoothed her hair, but in her tweed skirt and knitted jersey she stood out amongst the sequins and silk like a sparrow among peacocks. Tot feinted towards her and then resumed course for me. She reached me long before he did, coming right up and standing in front of me, laying a hand on my arm even.

'How did you know about the death certificate?' she said. 'And about Sergeant Simpson?'

I was momentarily stumped for an answer and when one dawned upon me I almost dared not give it for I knew it would be her undoing. 'Mrs Addie told me.'

Dr Laidlaw gave a shriek of pure anguish.

'Are you one of them?' she said. 'Is she talking to *all* of you?'

'I expect so,' I said. 'And I'm sure in time she'll tell me or someone else how she died too.' Tot was closing in on me but I dodged to the side of his sister and nipped away before he could catch me. There was nothing for him now, if he wanted to avoid a scene, but to take Dorothea by the arm and draw her gently away. The look he aimed at me across the room, meanwhile, would have curdled milk and withered posies, as Nanny Palmer used to say. He kept it up for quite a few moments too, but as Dorothea whispered to him his expression changed until his face was the perfect mirror of his sister's, each with that terrified, wide-eyed gaze.

'Good Lord above,' Alec said, on the telephone the next morning. 'If Mrs Bowie knew the half of it *she'd* drop down dead. I'm trying to make it sound so clean and simple and respectable, as if an exhumation these days is no grubbier than a trip to the dentist or having a horse shod. If she could hear the torrid horrors that her mother's taking part in at your end . . . Still, good work, Dandy.'

'And do you think you'll prevail in the end?' I asked him.

'Oh, I think so,' Alec said. 'Not least because I've had a stroke of great good fortune. Mr Addie is a member of the Royal Burgess Golf Club. No, not a member – a pillar. And guess who else is a member? Unsurprisingly, I must say.'

'Ohhh!' I said. 'The Fiscal.'

'You are a very rewarding audience for snippets of good news, Dan, I must say. Yes, indeed, the Edinburgh Fiscal stands Mr Addie a stiff whisky in the spike bar most Sundays and the odd Thursday evening in the lighter nights too.'

'Joy of joys,' I said. 'That's got to help us.'

'Even so, I think I shall have to stay and do a measure of hand-holding. So you're on your own for a bit yet. What's next?'

'As far as Mrs Addie goes,' I said, 'I'd dearly love to find out what was in that room before they emptied it. There were quite pronounced discoloured dents where something had sat – not one of the ubiquitous couches; it was the wrong shape – and there were scraping marks where it had been moved. Recently too. So I'm looking for something three feet square and extremely heavy. And I'm thinking if it was moved then it must have something to do with her death and if they wanted to keep it under wraps they'd hardly have hoyed it into a cart and paraded it through town, so it must be stashed somewhere. I'm going to search for it.'

'Three feet square?' Alec said. 'Did you get out your tape and measure it while you were chatting to the doctor?'

'I paced it,' I said. 'My feet are nine inches long. And the doctor had rushed off by then. She was rather upset, I'm afraid.' Alec was silent. 'I know you think I'm being hard on her, Alec dear. But the fact is that she's hiding something for that brother of hers.'

'You'll be careful, Dandy, won't you?' Alec said. 'Prowling about searching where you shouldn't be. Be very careful of Tot. And Merrick's lot too.'

'Ah well now,' I said. 'When it comes to the mediums, I've had a brainwave.'

'Oh dear,' Alec said.

'And I shall be quite safe. Like a general, sitting back and sending the troops to the front. I've drafted reinforcements, you see.'

It had taken very little in the way of persuasion. Grant comes from a theatrical background, as is sometimes obvious from the way she paints my face and arranges my hair, and when I had put my plan to her at bedtime the evening before, her face had lit as though all the limelight in the West End had just been shone on it.

'Now, you must think it over very carefully before you agree, Grant,' I said. 'It is far beyond the call of duty.'

'I'm only sorry it's taken so long, madam,' she said. 'I told Becky right from the start that I expected Gilver and Osborne would call on my services. I thought maybe that business with the circus, but this is nearly as good. Spirit mediums? I wonder if there's a sewing machine in the house.' She carried on blithely brushing my hair as I gaped at her in the glass. That circus business, as she called it, had been four years ago and I had thought, back then, that my detecting adventures were a secret all my own.

'I'm slightly feeling my way about what your story's to be,' I told her when she finally stopped planning her costumes, 'but I thought perhaps we could mix a bit of truth in with the lies. We can say that you are here with your employers – as you are – while they're taking the waters – as they are – but that after you arrived you felt a tremendous whatever it is you'd feel.'

'Vibration, madam,' said Grant. She was pinning the side curls into my hair for the night and spoke quite casually.

'I bow to your unexpected greater knowledge,' I said. 'Now, since you are not known in spiritualists' circles . . .' I paused a moment in case she was about to correct me, 'I think you should say that you are a seventh daughter of a seventh daughter or whatever but that you had such upsetting experiences when you first tried to direct your powers, that these days you try to avoid . . .'

'Contact with the other world,' said Grant.

'Quite. Now, as to what was vibrating. I wondered about Mrs Addie, but perhaps you should steer clear of her. So tell me what you make of this instead: the mediums are conversing with – we think, Mr Osborne and I – the spirits of hanged prisoners from the Gallow Hill.' Grant nodded calmly. 'That is to say, they're pretending to. Or are deluded into thinking they are. Just to make it clear that I don't believe any of this.'

'I'll need to see when I get there,' said Grant.

'And the reason we think this,' I said, passing swiftly on, 'is that they're meeting at the hanging place on the hill and also that one of them – actually it wasn't one of them; it was another guest who was going to tell them about it, now that I remember – said that Mary Patterson – when she appeared – was speaking of repenting her sins and forgiving her killers. The judge and the hangman, this would be.'

'That's nice of her,' Grant said. She had finished pinning my hair and was dabbing it with lotion to keep it safe through the night.

'Well, anyway, the mediums seem to know how many they're expecting – either fifteen or seventeen anyway – and they know some of the names but not all. From piecing together old court records, I suppose. They've got some already.' I opened my dressing-table drawer and took out my notebook, leafing through it to the right page. 'Lizzie, Peggy, Marjorie Docherty, Ann Dougal, Big Effie, Mary Patterson, Abigail Simpson, Joseph the Miller and a grandmother with a blind grandson.'

Grant tutted.

'Say what you like about the good old days, madam, but we don't hang blind children any more. No wonder him and his granny are not resting easy.'

'Yes, so what I think you should do is pick a very common name – Rose or Jeannie for a woman, James or William for a man – but best stick to women, since most of them seem to be women so far – and claim to have been . . . contacted.'

'A man,' said Grant, 'because it'll be so much better when I speak in his voice. Listen to this, madam.' She finished stretching my net cap over my hair, then half turned away and cleared her throat. When she spoke again it was in a deep, ragged, rumbling voice which seemed to come straight from the pit of her stomach without her lips moving at all.

'I am William, come down from the hill. Wrongly judged and wrongly hanged, now I seek my revenge.'

'Good God Almighty!' I said. There were shivers running through me from head to toe and Bunty, on the bed, had raised her head and was staring at Grant with her lip drawn back from her remaining upper teeth in the closest thing she could ever make to a snarl.

'It's really nothing, madam,' Grant said. 'Just a question of breath control. I could teach you.'

'I am glad to say I don't foresee needing to know,' I told her. 'But William it is – wrongly judged and wrongly hanged. Excellent, Grant. You can start in the morning.'

13

Friday, 25th October 1929

I was lucky enough to witness her arrival too. Mrs Scott, Mrs Davies and the gooseberry-eyed girl, who I had discovered was called Olivia, were taking morning coffee in the ladies' drawing room, no sign of Mr Merrick, and I was waiting there to see Donald and Teddy safely out of their respective Faradaic heat bath and ten lengths of breaststroke, install them on the terrace with hot bottles and then begin my search for the missing yard-square object. As I sat there I saw a mousy figure enter at the double doors, hesitate and then come creeping towards the party of ladies who were just one table away from me, reading luridly coloured picture papers which I did not recognise – *Spiritualists' Weekly*, perhaps. Grant was wearing something close to a novice's habit, a plain grey pinafore dress and white neckpiece underneath it, and had straightened her hair and scraped it to either side of her head. Her hands were clasped in front of her and she made only darting glances up to see where she was going, keeping her head for the most part decently bowed.

'Excuse me,' she said, bobbing a curtsy when Mrs Scott deigned to notice her. 'Are you the . . . Someone told me I should speak to you. I'm in need of counsel. I just don't know what to do.' Before any of the women could answer, Grant seemed to buckle at the knees and she sank into a chair, raising a shaking hand to her brow. 'I feel sick,' she said. 'Oh my, I feel so very sick. Such great evil. I don't think I can bear it.' She went so far as to make a couple of rather convincing noises which caused Mrs Scott to edge away as far as she could without leaving her chair. The gooseberry-eyed girl, Olivia, put a hand out and touched Grant's arm. Grant immediately raised her head and smiled. I would have said that roses bloomed in her cheeks but no one, even from a theatrical background, even a Barrymore, could change colour at will.

'Thank you,' Grant said. Then she frowned a little and looked at the girl's hand on her arm. 'What did you do?'

'I am at peace with my gift,' said Olivia. 'I simply shared my peace with you.'

'Gift!' said Grant. 'It's a curse! I pray and pray for it to be taken away and I pray for forgiveness for whatever I did to bring it down upon my wicked head.'

'My dear girl,' said Mrs Scott. I was surprised to hear Grant addressed this way. She is slightly older than me and it has been a while since I was a 'girl', dear or otherwise. But something about the white collar and meekly parted hair had taken years off her. 'My dear girl, you have not been among friends. You are among them now. Please, tell us what's troubling you.'

'I'm staying in the town with my lady – I'm a maid, you see – and oh, there's such great evil. I can't sleep! That voice! I wish I could believe I'm dreaming, but it's real. And the look of him. I asked for help at the church but the minister scorned me. Then – I'm ashamed to admit it – but I stepped into the Crown for a glass of port, just to help me sleep; because we're right next door and the sound of the men in the bar put the notion in my head, and someone there was saying that up at the Hydro there was a convention of spiritualists. I thought maybe you could help me.'

'I'm sure we can,' said Mrs Davies. 'This voice, what does it say? And what is it that you see?'

'Oh, a terrible sight,' said Grant. 'A rough, low beast of a man and . . . harmed. Not right at all. His neck!' All three mediums were sitting on the edges of their seats now and no one could blame them. It was a bravura performance.

'And what does he say?' said Olivia Gooseberry. I hoped that Grant would not unleash the dreadful rumbling sound of her ghost. Not here in the ladies' drawing room. I felt my shoulders rise as I braced myself for it, but I should have trusted her.

'He says . . .' Grant hesitated. 'It doesn't come through my ears, you know. It's as though I'm speaking it, only not in my voice – oh, it's too hard to explain.'

'A channel!' said Mrs Scott. 'Don't fret, my dear. We understand completely. What does he say?'

'He says . . .' She stopped again. 'It's such wickedness, I hardly want to tell you.' All three were wound like springs now. If Grant did not tell them at her next approach, one of them would pinch her.

'He says, "I am William." He never says a surname. "I was wrongly judged and wrongly hanged. I am come to wreak my revenge." And some other things I can never make out and something about his mother but he's always crying by then.'

The three mediums were dumbfounded, a tableau of rapt stupefaction which lasted so long that Grant raised her head and took a surreptitious peek at them.

Mrs Scott was the first to find her voice.

'No surname?' she asked weakly. 'Not even an initial?' I thought I could see Grant considering the initial. 'M' was always a good bet in Scotland as were 'O' in Ireland and 'T' in Cornwall, but very sensibly she shook her head no.

'What does it mean, Mrs Scott?' asked Olivia.

'Something stupendous,' Mrs Scott replied. 'Something unhoped-for and almost undreamed-of. We must find Mrs Molyneaux, ladies. Or perhaps . . . dare we . . . Yes! We must take this straight to Mr Merrick himself.' She rose. 'Stay here, my dear. Help yourself to a cup of coffee. Ring for a fresh pot. Tell them to put it on Mrs Scott's bill if it's extra. We shall return.'

They stood and sailed out of the room with the wind behind them and the harbour in view, leaving Grant and me gazing at one another over the empty chairs.

'That seems to have gone down rather well then,' I said softly.

'I wonder which part of what I said convinced them,' said Grant. 'I hope they tell me. I can suddenly make out the mumbled words if they let me in on what I'm supposed to be hearing, can't I?'

'Practise some restraint for now,' I answered. 'That would be my advice anyway. You seem to have done plenty to get their attention.'

It was with the greatest reluctance that I managed to drag myself away, for I wanted nothing more than to skulk in my chair and overhear what happened when Mr Merrick appeared on the scene. But generals do not skulk about the front line once the orders are given and I had tasks of my own.

Attics or basement, I wondered as I made my way across the hall to the servants' door. If the missing object was as heavy as all that I imagined it would be no small matter to lug it up to the attics, even using the invalid lift by which the frailer Hydro guests made their way between bedroom and baths. I would start in the basement, and it seemed sensible to start in the very corridor where Regina, Mrs Cronin and I had all converged that day. There had been doors on either side of it and what could they be except boxrooms? Or possibly boiler rooms, for all that steam had to have its source somewhere.

Finding the place was not going to be easy, though. I could go to the Turkish baths and start from there, but if anyone saw me I could not claim to be lost. If I started at the other end I could, with a little more plausibility, say that I was taking a short cut and had misplaced myself.

I skirted the kitchens, the sculleries and laundry, a boot room, the wine cellar and a boxroom where the casino tables stood waiting for nightfall under their baize covers. What is more, I did it without a single servant seeing me. I even found time to congratulate myself on how much improved in stealth I was these days. When I reached the less populous and well-utilised areas of below stairs, I began to pay close attention to the floor, looking for scraping marks, and I began to try the handles of the doors. Most were locked and I regretted the impulsive way I had thrust Dr Laidlaw's keys into her hands as she rushed past me the evening before. Those few doors which were unlocked opened to show me guests' luggage, old deckchairs with their canvas faded and fraying, a collection of toboggans awaiting the winter, a heap of rusting bicycles from early in the century, and any number of moth-eaten tennis nets rolled up and stuffed into tea chests.

At the end of a short corridor leading off the main one, outside yet another locked door, I thought I saw some scratch marks but could not be sure. I put my eye to the keyhole and saw nothing except grey light with strings of cobweb floating in it. I straightened and sneezed, deadening the sound with my finger and thumb pinched around my nose, the way that Nanny Palmer always told me would burst my ear drums, then I lit a match and took a closer look at the scratch marks on the floor. I was almost sure they were about as far apart as the marks on the tiled floor of the empty room last night. Did I dare go back to Dr Laidlaw's office and re-steal her keys to get through this door? I did not; and besides, she would surely not have returned the keys to the dish from which they had been taken. I was at a loss as to how else I could gain entry to a locked windowless basement, short of hacking the door down with an axe, when I stopped short. It was *not* windowless, there was grey light and cobwebs in there. If I could work out where on the outside of the building that room lay then I could peer in at the window.

I sighed. My accomplishments were over for the day then: I am pitifully incapable of finding my way around strange houses. Outside, if the sun is shining and it is not noon at the equator, I can navigate as well as anyone else who was taught geography along with her letters and numbers as a child. It is not much help in Perthshire, where the admittedly long hours of daylight in the short months of summer are usually filled with driving rain, but at least the capacity is there if the conditions allow. Inside houses it is another matter and I have been given lewd winks more than once before now because I was wandering a corridor at a house party where I had no reason to be.

I did not even try to form a plan in my head of the Hydro interior today. Instead, I used a mental version of the unravelling jersey method. Back on the main corridor I went along muttering 'left, left, left' to myself until I found a staircase. I went up to the ground floor and walked along the corridor I found there saying 'right, right, right'. At the end I emerged into a corner of the dining room. I crossed it and the hall and emerged from the front door, walked round to the dining-room window, kept walking saying 'left, left, left' which took me to the corner of the lawn and then, still saying 'right, right, right', I fought my way through the dense shrubbery which screened off the servants' area from the lawns below the terrace where, for the first time in my life, I was pleased to have to brush cobwebs from my face.

Here there were dusty windows a plenty. I peered in at them, seeing the same tennis nets, bicycles and toboggans I had seen before. I passed a garden door, moved on, and saw deckchairs and luggage. I had seen all of these things from the corridor. Where was the room behind the locked one at the end of the offshoot?

And then it struck me. That short offshoot of corridor led to the outside wall. That door didn't open onto a room. It opened onto this path and the grey light I had seen was filtering through these rhododendrons. I had just brushed away the very strings of cobweb I had seen through the keyhole. I went back and looked at the mossy bricks and, right enough, there were faint but unmistakable scratches there. Darkened now after a few weeks in the weather, but still clear. And the moss had been ripped out too and lay shrivelling.

I followed the path, navigating by the scraped bricks, until I came to a break in the shrubs. The path carried on but led only to the laundry yard and back into the house again. Through the gap in the rhododendrons, however, was the side lawn, rather neglected – no clock golf or croquet here – and shaded by spreading cedars. Was it my imagination, I wondered, or were there faint depressions in the grass? It was not the gardeners' pride, this unused patch of lawn, being rather spongy with more of the moss and rather sparse under the cedars where the long needles had fallen and never been raked away, and I was almost sure that I could see the traces of two wheels – a sack barrow, perhaps – which had crossed it recently. I set off in pursuit of them.

Halfway over I began to fear that the traces were my imagination, nothing more. They disappeared completely for yards at a time and when I fancied I saw them again they were fainter than ever. I had almost given up when, under the massiest of the cedars in the densest shade, I saw a patch about six feet long where the brittle needles had snapped and sprung up at either end: a clear and undeniable imprint of two wheels, not my imagination at all. I skirted them carefully and then stood beyond them gazing ahead at where they could have been going.

I was near the edge of the grounds now and could see portions of the high grey garden wall between the trees and bushes which bordered them. Then, behind some sort of apple or cherry tree, its leaves just beginning to yellow, I saw what I had not realised I was looking for but realised now that I must have been: the smooth, rounded shape of a ridge tile. There was a roof over there, and where there is a roof there is a building below it and where there is a building there is somewhere to wheel a heavy object and try to hide it. I glanced about me but this was a desolate spot, away from the terrace and the sunshine, so I picked up my pace and made for the shadows.

It must have been an apple house at some time, I thought as I drew near. A tiny little place – a howf, as they call them in Perthshire – windowless but with slatted openings near the top, built against the wall. I rattled the door handle but of course it was locked. Even if it was not usually kept locked it would have been locked for the last month or so. For the signs were unmistakable here. There were snapped twigs and turned earth and a smear of mud on the lintel of the little door, and I rather thought the object had been badly handled in because the door paint was scraped too and the wood showed fresh and white underneath it. The flakes of paint were still scattered on the slab of sandstone set into the ground for a doorstep.

If only Alec were here. He could grab onto that branch and pull himself up. He could put a foot on the lintel and step over, holding onto the roof, and from there he could squint down through those slats and see what was in there.

I imagined the whole climb in my head, seeing Alec shinning up and shouting down. I imagined asking Hugh to do it for me.

Would he be spurred to a second boyhood by the thought that Osborne was not beyond such antics, or would this be more of my silliness at which he would simply lift an eyebrow and turn away? Donald was far too frail still but what about Teddy? Thus finally, I shamed myself into action. My poor sickly sons were not to go climbing trees just because their mother was a ninny. I took off my gloves and laid my hands purposefully against the strongest-looking joint between the trunk and a branch.

'Heave-ho!' I said and set my foot against the bark to start scrambling.

I weighed considerably more than I did the last time I climbed a tree and my shoulders were aching when I had got myself up high enough to step over and stand on the door lintel. It looked much further away than it had when viewed from below, but I knew from jumping over burns that distances are deceptive when there is a six-foot drop or rushing cold water and probably I would step over the gap between branch and lintel without a thought if it was a gap between carpet and hearthrug, avoiding nothing more than a cold stone floor. I let go with one hand and stretched one leg over, feeling for a toehold. Something shifted, my foot slipped. For a minute I was hanging by one hand from the tree and then I got both feet back onto the crook of the branch, wrapped both arms tightly round the trunk and stayed there with my heart hammering. I looked down at what had fallen from above the door. Not a stone, not mortar, as I had first thought. I would have laughed if I had not been still so close to crying. It was a key.

When I retell the story of my discovery in the apple house, it is hard to decide what to suppress and what report. On the one hand, I am rather proud of the way I rubbed my hands together and climbed a tree – I do not judge the moments when I contemplated asking my son to take a deep breath through his pleurisy and do it for me as worth sharing – but on the other hand I wish I had thought to feel above the door for a key before I tore my stocking and scraped my cheek on the bark.

Besides, the end of the incident does overshadow whatever one would choose to tell of its beginning.

I found the courage to slither down from my perch in not many more minutes, with a locked door and a key to tempt me. The lock was stiff and the key rusty – I rather thought that whoever had recently opened the door had brought a second key with him and did not know about this one; certainly there had been no oiling for some time. I had to use both hands to get it to turn but, at length, turn it did and I opened the apple-house door with held breath and thumping blood.

It was there! Three feet square by four feet tall, made of wood like a barrel and just sitting there. Not at all, I saw, the new-fangled and dangerous equipment I had counted on finding. I breathed out and it was when I breathed in again, the first time with the door open, that the smell got to me. I retched and stumbled backwards with my hands over my face. That smell! It is conventional to say that an unpleasant odour hits one, but this did so much more. It entered me, it filled my nose and my lungs and my mouth, it made my eyes water, it got among the strands of my hair and the fibres of my clothes and I knew immediately that it would be many days before it left me, if it ever did. I feared immediately that I would dream of this smell as long as I lived.

I could not have entered the little apple house if my life hung from my doing so, but I stayed there with my arm over my face, breathing the smell through the wool of my coat, and tried to look again at what I had found instead of some harmful – fatal! – machinery. It was a crate, a container. I had been looking for clues about what had killed Mrs Addie. I had not found them. Instead – I could not deny it – I had found Mrs Addie herself.

I scrabbled at the door, got it closed, got it locked and put the key back where I had found it. Then I tottered away to rest against another of the gnarled old trees and stood staring.

No one had smelled it because of the slats. Designed to draw all humidity away from the apples and stop them rotting, they had carried the stink of putrefaction up into the air and let it drift away. It was the perfect place to hide a body.

All I now had to decide was whether to telephone to the police right away or speak to Alec, and ask him what he thought the Addies would want to do. I stood up from where I had been slumping against the tree as though my sergeant-major had summoned me to attention. Alec was in Edinburgh engineering the exhumation of Mrs Addie's body from its Morningside grave. It made no sense at all for me to think that I had found her body in that odd square barrel here in Moffat. If the woman really had been laid out by Regina and carried by an undertaker to her funeral at home then how could she be mouldering so revoltingly in there?

She could not. But then what was it in there?

I have had the experience, not often but each time has been memorable, of vertigo washing over me like a wave. In the early months when the babies were coming I came close to swooning many times. I have been assailed by tidal waves of nausea once or twice too. And recently, since I started detecting, I have undergone great sweeping storms of dread when something I knew deep down was clamouring to be brought into the front of my mind and dealt with there. This was the first time, however, I had ever felt what I was feeling now. An enormous, unstoppable rush of absolute terror, engulfing me entirely and leaving me weak and helpless as it passed.

And all of a sudden, the ghosts were not a nonsense, the mediums not a joke, Loveday Merrick not a charlatan, and Mrs Addie not just a well-loved and much-missed old lady who might have been wronged.

All of a sudden, standing there, everything seemed to skew just a little from what I thought I knew about the world around me and I could feel them all: Effie and Lizzie and Mary and their sins and killers, the ghosts and echoes and whispers, the other world reaching out, pleading, to this one.

Mrs Addie was in her grave in Edinburgh, or near it anyway in mid-exhumation, possibly. In that little apple house, not frail and wispy, not floating in a shift, not a wraith at all, but hulking, stinking and evil, was her ghost.

I stumbled out from the shrubs onto the lawn and made

my shaking way around to the terrace steps, desperate to be safely with other people and far away from that crawling madness that threatened to worm its way through me if I stayed there. Hugh hailed me as I passed. He was in his deck-chair again.

'You all right, Dandy?' he said. 'You look peaky.'

There was no one in the world who could have done more to bring me back to earth. 'I found something rather unpleasant in the shrubbery,' I managed to say. 'A dead thing. I almost stumbled over it and it's sickened me.' Hugh was torn between disappointment at this poor showing and that smugness which even the best of men sometimes display in the face of feminine weakness. 'Smell,' I said, holding out my sleeve. He took a deep sniff at the wool of my coat to show what stern stuff he was made of and then wrinkled his nose.

'Faint hint of something,' he said. 'Nothing like that stag that time.' It was true; the smell of the crate in the apple house had been quite different from the stag which had ruined a delightful picnic one day when the boys were tiny (although only because they had to be spanked and taken home when they would not stop poking it).

'I'll see you for tea,' I said faintly and made my way to the telephone kiosk to speak to Alec who I hoped would have more sympathy for me than to cap my horrors with memories of his own.

I had quite forgotten what story Alec would have to tell me or I would not have rung him at all.

Mrs Bowie was not at her brother's house and Mr Addie was lying down. I looked at my watch – half past twelve: a very odd time for a nap and my first indication that matters had moved swiftly. Mr Osborne was still here, the maid said, and she would fetch him.

'Hello, Dandy,' Alec said, sounding rather flattened. 'I'm coming back to Moffat on the 2.40. Do you really want to hear this now?'

'I really do,' I said. 'And the first thing I want to hear is this:

did either Mr Addie or Mrs Bowie see their mother's body when it was brought home for the funeral?'

'Not only then,' said Alec. 'But poor Mr Addie had to see it this morning too. When they dug it up again. He managed to hold on to his insides, which is more than can be said for the whole of the party, but he's taken himself off to bed now and I'd be surprised if he's seen again today.'

'Poor man,' I said. 'It was definitely her then?'

'Apparently so,' Alec said. 'I wouldn't have liked to be on oath that what we saw in that coffin was the woman in the picture—'

'You were *there*?'

'I was there,' Alec said. 'I thought it was the least I could do to stand beside poor Addie since it was me egging him on. I was one of the ones who couldn't contain himself, I'm afraid. A very poor show.'

'And is it too soon to know anything?'

'It's too soon to know some things,' Alec said, 'but did you know that the doctor doing the exhuming just starts in on it right there? He started looking for poisons right away.'

'And?'

'Nothing doing,' Alec said. 'Because of the stomach contents.' He swallowed audibly. 'If you can get a good jugful of stomach contents, then graveside poison tests are easy.'

'And what was wrong with them?'

'There were none,' Alec said. 'She was empty. Nothing in her stomach, nothing in her bladder or . . . other areas with similar function nearby. So he's had to go back to his laboratory to look in her liver and kidneys for arsenic and at her blood for strychnine. Cyanide turns one bright pink – did you know? – so it wasn't that anyway.'

'And no other obvious sign of something that could have killed her?' I asked.

'None,' Alec said. 'No marks of violence. The only thing he ventured – and it's not much I can tell you – is that she was dehydrated.'

'What does that mean?' I asked.

'She hadn't drunk anything. It sounds as if this grated carrot diet Dorothea had her on was a pretty tough regime.' I was interested to note that having to look at a month-old corpse had put Alec into an acerbic mood which did not even sweeten for Dr Laidlaw.

'Well, I shall be very glad to see you back here again,' I said. 'I desperately need to talk to you but only if you promise not to laugh at me.'

'I'm not finished with *my* report yet,' he said. 'I saved the best bit.'

'Go on.'

'Whatever the doctor turns up in his laboratory, he knows already it wasn't a heart attack,' said Alec. 'He had a good look at Mrs Addie's heart this morning as he removed it – so did I, as a matter of fact. It didn't reveal much to me but the pathologist said there was nothing wrong with it.'

'Good grief,' I said. 'So . . . did he telephone to the police? Are they coming to arrest the Laidlaws? And Dr Ramsay?'

'Not a bit of it,' Alec said. 'Apparently it's not unusual. And Dr Ramsay's certificate said "heart failure following suspected heart attack". There's nothing so far to say that wasn't a perfectly fair conclusion.'

'That's right,' I said. 'That's what he said to me. Everyone dies of heart failure in the end.'

'I came close to it myself this morning when I looked at Mrs Addie's face,' Alec said. At least he was almost laughing. 'Now your turn, Dan. God, I've only just stopped feeling sick, you know. You're a tonic, dearie.'

'Thank you,' I said, and then hesitated. How could I add my morning's nightmares to his own? And besides, now that I had got away from the place I was beginning to doubt the truth of it, hoping that if I hugged the horrid facts to myself they might go away. 'And look – never mind my stuff just now. You catch your train and we can discuss it later.'

'All right,' Alec said. 'Was it Grant who turned it up for you?'

I laughed. 'Oh, Grant!' I said. 'Grant was wonderful. She

thought up the perfect thing to say to be taken right into the mediums' bosom. She's having a whale of a time. All news later, darling, hm? Safe journey.'

I went back to Auchenlea then, missing the Hydro luncheon and looking forward to pot luck from Mrs Tilling. She was beginning to settle into this novelty of a 'holiday' but even taking things very easy she is still rather marvellous and there were no such horrors as shop bread or tinned soup coming into the dining room. She had dispensed with savouries and it was true that she had asked me only that morning if I would prefer salmon or lamb for dinner when, at Gilverton with Hugh of course, there would be the one and then the other. Besides, I could not possibly stay for the Hydro's midday feast because I was crawling all over with an itch to be rid of the clothes which had soaked up the smell and I needed to rub my hair with a lavender cloth at least, if not stand under the spray bath and wash it.

The chances of that ending well were greatly increased by my coming upon Grant on the road out of town, clearly heading back to the house herself despite being told she could have the day for her spiritualist venture.

'I needed a rest from it, madam,' she said, when she had climbed in and we were under way again. 'They're very tiring people to spend your time with, those mediums. And that Loveday one . . . *Loveday!*'

'My thoughts exactly, Grant,' I said, hoping that I sounded convincing. They had been my thoughts, my whole life through, up until that morning. 'What has he been up to?'

'He sat me in a chair and chanted at me until my eyes were crossed. It didn't do any good, because I was reciting poetry in my head all the time and he'd no chance of mesmerising me.'

'Just as well. Did you pretend?'

'Of course,' said Grant. 'What was William's surname, he wanted to know. And where did he die and what was his message for his mother?'

'What did you tell him?'

'I didn't venture so much as an initial for the surname,' she said. 'I said he'd died in Scotland and that he wanted to tell his mother he was sorry.'

'They can't have liked the "Scotland" bit,' I said, chuckling.

'Not much. Anyway, madam, I've managed to find out a wee bit more than I've given away, if you'd like me to tell you.'

We were at Auchenlea now and I urged her to accompany me to my bedroom and discuss things as I changed.

'Why's that then?' she asked with a touch of the old Grant. 'Madam.' She had chosen my clothes that morning.

'Smell,' I said, shrugging out of my coat and handing it to her. She sniffed very gingerly.

'Just smells like the well, but worse,' she said. I sniffed at it again. Was she right? The morning's sudden rush of terror had receded even further and I was almost ready to dismiss it as pure fancy. Still, the smell was real. I shuddered and set a good pace upstairs to get rid of it.

'Here's what I've found out,' Grant said, as I was undressing. 'All the while saying I don't want to know and it's wickedness and why won't the good Lord take this curse off of my head.'

'Which I did think was jolly clever, I must say. You seemed absolutely not one bit as though you were trying to find things out from them.'

'And so I found out all the more,' Grant said. 'And here it is. It started about a month ago.' That was no surprise. 'And it started in a very small way too. The usual thing; a snippet in *Spiritualists' Weekly*' – it appeared that such was indeed the name of the coloured paper Mrs Scott had been reading – 'saying that a lady had died of fright at the Moffat Hydro after seeing a ghost. It was just a report, a letter from a respectable person, a professional man, and they get them all the time. Who would have thought it, eh?'

'Not I.' I picked up a tea dress but at Grant's frown and small shake of the head I put it back again.

'So one medium came to the Hydro to see what she could see. Very discreetly.'

'Not discreetly enough though, I'll bet. Do you think if I rub my hair with lavender it will do?' Grant sniffed my head and stood up sharply.

'I see what you mean, actually, madam,' she said. 'That's really quite nasty. Anyway, to go on with my report, it was when this first medium was here that one of the other guests mentioned a second ghost, and this one by name, and it was a name the medium knew. So she ups and writes to that Mrs Scott who is a very big noise in Glasgow and by sheer chance Mrs Scott has had a letter of her own, quoting the name of a third ghost, and she was just on the point of trying to decide whether to pack her traps and come to investigate it.'

'Ah yes, I think I heard a veiled mention of that,' I said.

'And by the time she got here, there was another of her acquaintances just arriving – it's a small world I daresay – because she had actually been rung up on the telephone all the way in Carlisle by someone who had been staying here and had left early because Lizzie Haldane was in her bedroom and wouldn't go away even when she – the guest this is – shook a Bible at her.'

'How did you get all of this out of them, Grant?'

'Och, they're trying to convince me to stay and be part of it,' she said. 'They're talking about the centennial and how it's the biggest thing there's been in spiritualists' circles since that automatic writing in America that got them all birling.'

'Now that is very interesting,' I said. 'A centennial, eh? I think I had only heard the word anniversary up until now. A centennial of what, I wonder.'

'Not the last hanging at the Gallow Hill anyway,' Grant said. 'I made sure and asked about that on account of what "William" is saying. They stopped hanging in Moffat a lot of years ago. It's all down in Dumfries now. I'll run you a bath, madam, and tell Mrs Tilling to hold back luncheon.'

I dropped Grant at the end of the Hydro drive in the afternoon and watched with wonder as she assumed the character of the devout little mouse who was cursed with a gift of seeing. She put her head down, clasped her hands in front of her and managed to shrink her shoulders until they were almost gone completely. She turned her toes inwards from their usual confident ten-to-two and began to creep towards the hotel.

I was there to try to decide my next step. If Alec had been around, perhaps I could have summoned the courage to return to the apple house and face whatever was waiting for me. As it was I ended up back on the terrace again, sitting with Hugh.

'Feeling better, Dandy?' he asked. 'You look it.'

'Mrs Tilling has cured me,' I said. 'With clear soup and cold chicken.'

'Ah,' said Hugh. 'Yes, it was mutton stew and batter pudding here. It wouldn't have been good for you.' We sat a while. 'So,' he continued at last, 'how's it all going?'

'It's very hard to say,' I told him. 'The family exhumed the body and tested it for poison but thus far there's nothing doing.' He looked somewhere between startled and flabbergasted at this news. I am sure he put my detecting down under 'dabbles' for the most part and so hearing that doctors and Fiscals and pathologists jumped when Alec and I clicked our fingers – or so it might have seemed – was an arresting idea. 'And I thought I had tracked down a missing piece of equipment which might have gone wrong and caused the death even if the body didn't show signs of violence. But it turned out to be . . . something else.' I could not possibly tell him, but if I did not tell someone I would burst with it.

Hugh was nodding in that way of his when he is only half listening to me. Then, still not paying full attention, he turned and spoke.

'Can't you use the brochure?' he said.

'What's that?' I looked at his breast pocket, from where as ever the folded catalogue of delights was peeping out. He removed it and handed it over.

'If you went through the brochure and cross-checked it with the typed sheet they hand out to the day-guests to say what's on offer, wouldn't that tell you what they've ditched?'

I was aware of the flush rising up through my neck and settling in two spots on my face.

'Didn't you think of that?' Hugh said. 'I hope you've not been chasing around on needless adventures, Dandy, when the answer was right here in my breast pocket.' I said nothing. He looked more closely at me. 'You've got a little blemish on your cheek,' he said. 'I can see it quite clearly now that you've – ahem – got your colour back.'

Ah yes, I thought. A blemish on my cheek. Or rather a graze from hugging a tree when I almost fell out of it because I did not think to look in the usual place for a key to open a door. 'As I say, though,' I told him, with an attempt at dignity, 'it wasn't equipment gone wrong at all.'

'Still,' said Hugh. 'Worth it, perhaps. Just to be thorough.'

'Oh, I suppose so,' I said, with little grace. At least if I stayed there humouring Hugh I would be far away from the apple house.

'I shall go and fetch today's sheet for you right now,' Hugh said, unwinding his blanket and standing. 'Glad to help when I can.'

I had started in on the easy ones before he returned. The Turkish and Russian baths were available, as I knew only too well. Salt rubs, oil rubs and mustard wraps too.

'Here we go then,' he said, striding along the terrace towards me. He looked in peak form again, although whether from rest and hydropathy or from besting his wife at her own business it was hard to say. 'You read them off, Dandy, and I'll see if they're on here.'

'Electric heat baths,' I began. 'Faradaic, galvanic, diathermic, ultraviolet and ionised.'

'All present and correct,' said Hugh. 'Speak up though, won't you?'

'No, dear, I won't,' I said. 'We are trying to catch a possible murderer, remember? Nauheim, including nascent carbonic and Schott exercises, plombiers, pine bath – at last something one can understand: although how one bathes in pine . . . ? – Aix douche and Vichy douche.'

'All here,' said Hugh. 'And the pine bath is quite lovely, I can tell you.'

'Hydropathic baths then,' I said, turning the page. 'Or what you and I would call water at home. Needle, spray, sitz, long. Is a long bath just a bath?'

'In the waters,' said Hugh.

'Head, eye, ear and nose sprays, ugh. Ascending sprays.' Hugh cleared his throat and frowned. 'Wave baths, Turkish baths, steam baths, plunging pool, swimming baths – we knew about all of these – and that's just about it.' I turned another page.

'And that's it here too,' Hugh said. 'Now, at least you can discount the theory of a treatment gone wrong. I still say this was well worthwhile, don't you? Dandy?' He turned to look at me. 'Dandy?'

'There's one more,' I said. I had let the brochure fall open on my lap.

'You've gone pale again,' said Hugh. 'Shall I fetch you a glass of water?'

'Not Moffat water,' I said. 'That smell.'

'What have you read that's upset you so?' Hugh said. He went as far as to reach out a hand towards me.

'Mud,' I said. 'A mud bath. Not . . . what I imagined at all.'

'Ah, I asked about the mud bath,' said Hugh, taking the brochure and flipping through its pages. 'They've only got one in the ladies' side, since it's mostly good for shedding weight, I believe. And even the ladies' one is—' He broke off.

'Yes,' I said. 'It's a little barrel sort of thing about three feet square and four feet tall, and one sits in it, up to one's neck in sulphurous mud. And I would imagine one comes out really quite filthy so that even if one washes and washes one would still have dirt under one's nails and so on.'

'Hmph. Sounds nasty,' said Hugh, 'but I don't quite see why it's upsetting you so. Not really.'

'It's the *smell*,' I said again. 'Imagine sitting in a stinking vat of sulphurous mud, and dying there.' Hugh looked up sharply and his face, as mine had, turned pale. 'What could anyone ever have done to deserve to die in a place like that?'

'I can't imagine,' Hugh said. He remained pale but he stood up very decisively and looked around him, like an officer surveying a battlefield, or a matron a ward. 'Will you be all right for a bit, Dandy my dear?' I nodded. 'I'm going to find the boys and take them away,' he said. 'I don't think I really believed it until now.'

'Shall I just come too?' I said. 'If we're leaving.' He wheeled round and fixed me with a look which would have done either matron or officer proud.

'We're *not* leaving,' he said. 'You and Alec are staying to solve this outrage and I shall help you. But it's no place for the boys. Only I don't like leaving you alone when you look absol—' He stopped, with his mouth open, staring into the open french window of the drawing room. 'Is that Grant?' he said. 'What on earth is *she* doing here? And what on earth is she wearing? She looks as though she's joined a nunnery.'

'She'll be very pleased to hear that you think so,' I said. 'It's exactly the impression she was hoping to give. Fetch her, would you, if you can do it discreetly, not if she's with the mediums. She can sit with me while you get the boys to Auchenlea. We can always pretend just to have started chatting.'

'Did you say "mediums"?' asked Hugh. 'What on earth do you mean?'

'Oh, that's quite another part of the forest,' I said. 'Or possibly another forest entirely. At least I think so.'

'Spirit mediums?' said Hugh. 'Oh, she's seen us. She's coming over.'

'Madam, sir,' said Grant. She would say no more until she knew for sure whether Hugh was to be trusted with whatever she had to tell me.

'I know what's going on, Grant,' Hugh said. 'Or at least I know that something is.'

'Mr Merrick has offered up a sprat to catch a mackerel, madam,' she said. 'He wants me to ask if there's a James here. Someone almost said the full name but he shushed her. I think they're testing me.'

220

'Grant,' said Hugh, 'please sit down and tell me what is going on. You are here disguised as a nun' – Grant beamed – 'to be tested by spirit mediums? I'm not sure I follow you.'

'Oh,' I said. I was exhausted by it all suddenly. 'There's some kind of ghost hunters' gathering going on. There's a centennial anniversary of . . . something bad and the ghosts are amassing.' Grant had sat down on the edge of Hugh's deckchair so he had no choice but to sink down beside me on mine. 'Various people have reported being contacted by an assortment of ghosts but they're still short of the number they're expecting which is either fifteen or seventeen depending how you count them. Don't look at me like that, Hugh. I'm only reporting what I've been told. Or what I've overhead, mostly.'

'Now, some of the ghosts have names, sir,' Grant chipped in. 'And some of them don't. So Madam's idea was that I would think up a common name and say I'd been contacted and they'd believe it was one of the nameless ones introducing himself at last.'

'I see,' said Hugh. 'Fifteen ghosts with names.'

'Seventeen possibly,' I said. 'Big Effie, Marjorie Docherty, Old Abigail Simpson. I've got them written down but I can't remember them all. Mary Patterson who repents of her sins. Lizzie and Peggy.'

'Haldane,' said Hugh. 'Elizabeth and Peggy Haldane.'

'That's right, madam,' said Grant, boggling at him. 'That's what Mrs Scott said this morning. Haldane.'

'How in the blazes do you know that, Hugh?' I said. 'Good God, don't tell me they've appeared to *you*.'

'Merciful heavens,' said Grant.

Hugh shook his head at both of us. 'I know the name because I study my Scottish history,' he said. 'Or rather in this case because I listened to the ghost stories at my nurse's knee. Those people you mentioned and several more were killed in Edinburgh by Burke and Hare. Almost exactly a hundred years ago.'

14

'Why . . .' I began, but I had to take another run at it. 'Why on earth would the ghosts of the victims of Burke and Hare be haunting the Moffat Hydro?'

'Actually in the Hydro?' said Hugh.

'They think they're up at the Gallow Hill, really, sir,' Grant put in. 'But they come to the Hydro to contact the living.'

'Very well then,' I said. 'Why would the ghosts of the victims of Burke and Hare be up a hill in Moffat then?'

'Well,' said Hugh. 'The story goes—' He was interrupted by a gasp from Grant.

'The name we picked, madam!' she said. 'William! No wonder they're tied in knots trying to make me say William who?'

'I don't understand,' I said.

'It was William Burke and William Hare,' said Hugh. 'My word, Grant, that must have set the cat among the pigeons.'

'I said I'd been "wrongly judged and wrongly hanged" and was come down the hill to wreak revenge.'

'Must be William Burke then,' I said. 'He was hanged, wasn't he? And Hare turned King's evidence on him and got away?'

'Yes, but the story goes,' said Hugh again, 'that William Hare was pursued wherever he went by the ghosts of his victims – all fifteen of his murder victims or seventeen if you count those who died of natural causes but who he kept out of their decent Christian graves. The legend is that the ghosts – if they caught him – would bring him to justice. That's why he kept on the move. Down to London, home to Ireland, back again.'

'I suppose Moffat would be on his way,' I said. 'Did he stop here? I looked into all the local ghosts at the library and *someone* dreadful stopped at the Black Bull. I remember that much. It might have been Deacon Brodie, mind you, or Sawney Bean. They do run in together after a while: Mary in every castle and Wallace in every cave.'

'It was King Robert in the cave,' Hugh said, mildly for him when he takes me to task about ancient Scotch history. 'And Bloody Mary did move about quite a bit, you know.'

'Whether she did or not,' I said, 'I shall go and check, but I'm becoming surer and surer that William Hare stopped at the inn.'

'Fleeing the ghosts of his victims, but they caught up with him and took him up the Gallow Hill and hanged him there as he should have been hanged with his pal in Edinburgh,' said Grant. Then she blushed. 'Or so the mediums believe, madam. Sir.'

'And a hundred years later, they're all getting together again to talk about old times,' I said. Both Grant and Hugh gave me looks of one sort or another. They do not have the long experience of talking about cases that Alec and I do.

'And now I've brought one of the resurrection men to the party when no one asked him,' said Grant, catching on. 'And who's this James, sir, that Mr Merrick was asking me to name?'

Hugh shook his head. 'That was the saddest one of all,' he said. 'Daft Jamie.'

'I think I've heard of him,' I put in.

'He was a simpleton,' Hugh said, 'but well known and well liked in the streets of the old town. One of the students in the dissecting room recognised him. He was Burke and Hare's undoing.'

We all sat in silence for a moment or two, thinking of poor daft Jamie and the rest of them.

'What sins did Mary Patterson have to repent of?' I asked presently.

'She was a woman of ill-repute,' Hugh said. 'Some of the medical students recognised her too, but they were ashamed to say so.'

'Dearie me,' said Grant, which was as good a way to sum it all up as any. 'So will I say to the mediums that I can hear Jamie then?' She put on a dull, idiotic-sounding voice. '"I'm Jamie, I am. Jamie Daff." They often get the name a wee bit wrong, you know. It helps folk believe they're trying to hear it over all the miles between this world and the next. "Help poor Jamie. Help me. Don't let that bad man find me."' Hugh looked the way I had when she had first turned her talents on me.

'I suppose you might as well,' I said. 'But all of these revelations don't help at all with the question of why Mrs Addie died. Even now we suspect she died in a mud bath.'

'Depends where they got the mud,' said Grant. 'Sir. Madam.' She stood, bobbed and left us.

'I don't think I'm cut out for this game,' said Hugh, staring after her.

'It's not always like this,' I said. 'And I can't let you say that when you've just solved two of the things that were puzzling Alec and me for days on end. Without even trying.'

'I can't see how you can call it a solution,' said Hugh. 'If where we've ended up is that a woman sat in a vat of Gallow Hill mud, and out of the mud came fifteen ghosts and she died of fright.'

'It really *isn't* always like this,' I said again. 'I assure you.'

'I'm going to fetch the boys,' said Hugh, standing. He looked in through the french windows. 'Grant is holding court in there like Charlotte of Mecklenburg. I'm off.' I watched him all the way to the end of the terrace, striding along, furious with the silliness and frightfulness of it all, and annoyed with himself that he could not resist taking his sons out of harm's way, even though the harm was nonsense, as it must be.

'That's a very soupy look you've got on your face, Dan.' I turned and saw Alec standing at my other side, smiling down at me. He sat on the chair where Hugh had so recently been, swung his legs up and grinned at me.

'So. Have I missed anything?' he said.

When I had finished my report all he could do was give a long, low whistle.

'The first thing I need to do is go and check that what I remember from the library is right enough,' I said.

'Do you?' Alec said.

I laughed. 'No, not really, but it's something I *can* do and I can't think of anything else. What about you?'

'I'm going to wait for the PM report,' Alec said. 'Mr Addie said he'll telephone to me. Probably tomorrow. Mrs Bowie's still on about her grandfather's watch, by the way. Good grief, to think of us all over the well path and the Beef Tub and the Gallow Hill like a pair of bloodhounds that day!'

'I don't suppose it could be something as silly as theft that got Mrs Addie killed, could it?' I said. 'This watch isn't diamond-encrusted or anything? Only I wonder why they didn't send her bag back to the family with her clothes. I wonder why they didn't send *those* back until I prompted them, come to that.'

'A plain gold watch, I think,' said Alec. 'And one doesn't poison someone and set her to die in a vat of mud to achieve a burglary. A knock on the head with a cosh is more what you'd look for if it was theft at the bottom of it.'

'And no marks of violence at all,' I said. 'It's hard to believe they can still tell after a month. I mean, what does . . .? Did she still . . .?'

'Believe me, Dandy,' said Alec. 'You don't want to know.'

We went our separate ways after that, I to the library and Alec to the men's baths for a salt rub which he richly deserved after all his horrors. I had only got halfway across the drawing room though when Grant waylaid me.

'They want me to stay, madam,' she said. Her eyes were as round as beads. 'They're going to pay for my room so I can stay and go to their seance. It was Mr Merrick's idea.'

'You don't have to do it,' I said. I had misunderstood the round eyes.

'But may I?' she said.

'Certainly, you may,' I replied. 'But you must promise me that you will not put yourself in any danger, Grant. Remember that Mr Osborne and the master are both here. I shall give you the numbers of their rooms and you are not to hesitate to go there.'

I fished in my bag for a slip of paper. Grant was fishing too.

'I think it'll be just one day, madam,' she said. 'So here's what to lay out for yourself for tomorrow and if you decide to change for dinner, wear the peacock blue, and your Turkish slippers are in the airing cupboard. I steamed them after your game of rugby football the other night.'

'I was working on the case, Grant,' I said. 'I did mention that they weren't a suitable choice, if you remember.'

We swapped slips of paper and I went on my way. The voice from the depths of an armchair in a dark corner by the door surprised me.

'She said she was a maid, right enough.' A great leonine head of silver hair bent forward around the wing of the armchair. It was Loveday Merrick. 'To a woman staying in town. I never put her together with you, Mrs Gilver.'

'It's Mr . . . Merrick, isn't it?' I said. 'That's not my maid. My maid's name is Palmer and she's at home sewing. That girl promised to give me the recipe for a hair lotion she uses. I overheard her talking about it in the steam baths one day.'

'Ah, the steam baths are indeed a wonderful place for overhearing,' he said. 'Good day, Mrs Gilver.'

'Good day, Mr Merrick,' I said. It was not until I was halfway to town that I thought to wonder how he knew me.

The librarian was closing up for the day when I pulled in at the kerb and hopped down.

'Tch,' I said. 'I'm so sorry to have missed you, but if you don't mind answering questions while you lock the door, you could help me out a little.'

'Happy to oblige, madam,' she said. There was no sign that she remembered me.

'I suppose I could ask in the Black Bull but a library is much more to my taste,' I went on, buttering her up for no reason except that I had planned to. When I rehearse a conversation ahead of execution I very often cannot amend as I go. 'It's about the Black Bull as a matter of fact,' I said. 'My husband and I are having one of these little disagreements. I

226

say that William Hare stayed there and he thinks it was Deacon Brodie.'

'Oh, no, no, no,' said the librarian. She had finished with her locks and bolts now and she stowed her bunch of keys away safely in a large bag with a stout clasp, snapping it tightly and checking it twice before she put the handle over her arm. I could not drag my eyes away from it although I had no idea why. 'Deacon Brodie was never in Moffat, madam, I'm glad to say. But William Hare was and no two ways about it. And you're the third one to ask about him this last weather, you know.'

'Really?' I said.

'A lady was in the other day asking about ghosts and ne'er-do-wells and I told her. Drew her a map and everything. And then a gentleman was here too about a month ago. Almost the same thing. All the ghosts of Moffat. He didn't need a map though.'

'I see,' I said. It did not seem worth telling her that the lady from last time was me.

'Now, ordinarily,' I said to Alec on the telephone that evening, 'I'd think it couldn't have been Tot Laidlaw because she said she didn't know him, but if she'd forgotten me after three days then it certainly could be.'

'Ordinarily I'd think it wasn't Tot because she said "gentleman",' Alec replied.

'Ah yes, but to the librarian "a gentleman" is anyone who isn't wearing boots,' I said. 'And what it made me think about was the letter to *Spooks' Monthly* that Grant heard about. That was a "gentleman" too – a respectable sort, a professional man I think she said. And someone else at some time during this case has spoken of a respectable man . . . I wish I could think who it was and what we were speaking about.'

'And you're sure it must have been Tot?' Alec said. 'Because I was wondering about Loveday Merrick. If he's a fraud – and he must be, mustn't he? – then wouldn't he have to mug up in advance?'

'But this gentleman didn't need a map,' I said. 'I'm sure it was Tot. His latest wheeze, you know. Give the place the reputation for being haunted and get some extra business that way. I mean to say, any man who's running a casino . . . he can't hope to get away with *that* indefinitely.'

'Far from it,' Alec said. 'Two young oafs were talking in the hot room—'

'Aha!' I said.

'And one of them happened to say to the other that he would miss it when it was gone. That it was such a fag having to drag himself all the way through France for the same terms.'

'Well, there you are then,' I said. 'Tot's been whispering stories into just the right ears to get the Hydro started on its career as a haunted house. Or writing letters to the right magazines anyway.'

'You don't mean to say that he killed Mrs Addie to get the ball rolling?' said Alec.

'I don't know. I hope the PM turns up something. Or Grant does. Oh, by the way, don't jump out of your skin if there's a knock at your door tonight, will you? Grant's staying to do a seance and I've told her to come to you if she gets in any difficulties. I don't trust that Merrick at all. And I'd hate anything to befall her.'

'I saw her in the dining room,' Alec said. 'She had them all eating out of her hand. I think she'll be fine.'

Saturday, 26th October 1929

But when I next saw her she was not fine at all.

I had decided to have one last crack at Regina or Mrs Cronin, whichever one I ran into first. They both knew more than they were telling, and for some reason I could not get Regina, especially, out of my mind. She had been in my thoughts since my conversation with the librarian the afternoon before and she had walked through my dreams too. I had been in one of the little cubicles, sitting on the velvet bench, quite naked, waiting for her to come to me. My pose must have been, I imagine, similar to the way Grant held herself when I caught sight of her in the resting room the next morning. She was perched on the edge of one of the couches, still dressed in her grey pinafore and outdoor coat and still with her hat on and her bag clutched on her knees.

'I'm waiting for Dr Laidlaw,' she said. 'She was supposed to be assessing me for the galvanic baths. I'm sure she said it was here I was to wait.'

'The Turkish and Russian resting room?' I said. 'How long have you been here?'

'An hour, madam, and it's very hot.' I did not alarm her with news of how hot it got once one started through the velvet curtains.

'Is that all that's troubling you, Grant?' I said. 'You seem rather forlorn.'

'I'd have liked to press that shirt before you wore it, madam,' she said. 'That's not the one that was on the list I gave you. And I'm tired too. It was gone three before they let up last night, with their moaning and swaying.'

I bit my cheeks so as not to smile. The mediums would be mortified if they could hear this depth of scorn.

'I could do with just sitting in the drawing room with a weekly paper and a pot of tea, madam, I can tell you,' Grant went on, 'but if you're staying here you have to have treatments. It's the rules.'

'Yes, it is,' I said. 'And it's always puzzled me. I mean, some of the treatments are free and so you'd think it would make sound business sense to restrict them, not shove them down everyone's throats this way.' Grant looked uninterested in the profits and losses of the Laidlaws' Hydro and so I changed the subject to one where I expected she would shine. 'How did you acquit yourself last night?' I asked her. 'Could you tell what they made of you?'

'Oh, they'd like to bottle me and keep me,' Grant said. 'They're not safe to be out alone. That Loveday one tried to trick me again, right enough. He asked me if there was a Mrs A "amongst their number". That's how he put it.'

'Gosh,' I said. 'What did you say?'

'I put their eyes out on organ stops, I can tell you,' said Grant, brightening at the memory. 'I asked if they meant the large lady who was here but didn't belong with the others.'

'Oh, bravo,' I said. 'Grant, I was thinking in terms of a tip but I am beginning to wonder if you shouldn't be on the payroll this time. Pro-rata.'

'Not that I've found out anything much,' said Grant. She and Hugh were both far too scrupulous about claiming their honours, compared with Alec and me. I said nothing about it, though, because I could hear someone approaching from the hot rooms.

Then the velvet curtains were opening and Mrs Cronin was by my side.

'Mrs Gilver,' she said. 'What can I do for you this morning?' She said it in the tone which would usually go better with the words 'What do you want from me now?' I decided to try to put her on her back foot.

'It's not me you need to think of,' I said. 'It's this poor girl here. Do you know she's been waiting for Dr Laidlaw for an hour to see to her treatment? She had a very bad night and now she's just hanging around. People are supposed to come here to be made better, Mrs Cronin, not to be worn out from endless waiting.'

Mrs Cronin's face was like a hatchet.

'I'm here,' she said. 'I'm here, aren't I? The lady has come to no harm.'

'The lady,' I said, and I did not miss Grant's look of intense amusement to hear the word coming out of my mouth about her, 'can surely expect more for her money than to come to no harm. Good grief, if the Hydro is setting the jumps as low as that now!' I changed tack, hoping to shake something out of her. 'What's keeping Dr Laidlaw, anyway? Where is she?' I turned my eyes slowly and very deliberately toward the spray bath room and the locked door beyond it. Mrs Cronin flushed.

'She's in her study,' she said.

'Well, I think I shall go there,' I retorted. 'And see what exactly it is that's so much more important than her patients *today*.' Mrs

Cronin made a move as though to follow me, but I turned and barred her way. 'Oh no, my dear matron,' I said. 'You are here instead, as you say. You must take care of this' – I turned to indicate Grant and, since Mrs Cronin could not see my face, I dropped a wink at her – 'lady.'

I found it hard to account for myself, thinking it over as I stalked the halls and passageways en route to Dr Laidlaw's study once more. I did not usually forget myself so far as to antagonise those who were either suspects or useful witnesses. Perhaps it was the unfamiliar demands placed upon me by Hugh, or perhaps it was Grant of all people, being part of the case this time. Perhaps it was a cocktail of guilt over dragging Donald and Teddy into it and guilt over then banishing them to the paltry entertainments of Auchenlea until we were done, although that was Hugh's doing, to be fair. Or perhaps it was just understandable frustration that every time one question was answered in this puzzle the answer only led to seven more questions and Mrs Addie was still there right in the middle as dead as ever and with no one nearer knowing why.

Then I turned the corner to the passageway leading to Dr Laidlaw's study door and smiled, for all the clouds were gone and the sun was bright again. There was Alec, standing like a totem pole in the middle of the passageway, staring with ferocious nonchalance in the opposite direction from the door. When he saw it was me, he stood at ease and then crept softly back and put his ear against the wood again. Setting all thought of Hugh, the boys and Grant far from my mind – they would have been horrified, and Nanny Palmer would have wept – I tiptoed over and joined him.

'I don't know what that means,' Dr Laidlaw was saying. She sounded as though she had been weeping. 'I'm not interested in your money!'

'*Your* money, Dottie,' her brother replied.

I put my mouth very close to Alec's ear and breathed my words rather than whispered them.

'What are they talking about?'

Alec turned back to me and placed a finger on his lips.

'What money?' wailed Dorothea. 'What have you done now?'

'I?' said Tot. 'I, sister mine? Not I. You should really look at the pieces of paper shoved under your nose before you sign them.'

'But I can't carry on with this . . . charade,' she said. 'I'm frightened. That dreadful woman knows something about Mrs Addie, I'm sure.' I stiffened and Alec waggled his eyebrows at me.

'She's been listening to fairy stories. It's the smooth young man you need to watch out for,' said Tot. 'I've met his type before.' I waggled mine back. 'Anyway, it's not long now.'

'Until what?' said Dr Laidlaw, her voice rising.

'Don't you trouble your pretty little head about it, Dottie,' said Tot. 'Just make sure you keep your books up to date, eh? And don't say I'm not good to you.'

'I don't say that,' said Dorothea. 'I know very well how good you have been, but you don't understand my work and what I need. This can't go on.'

'And it won't, Dot,' her brother said. 'It's nearly over.'

'But it's getting worse,' she said. 'All those people. The London people were bad enough, but these new people, more and more every day. Who *are* they?'

'Don't trouble yourself about them,' Laidlaw said. 'They'll get what's coming to them. They all will.'

'What do you mean when you talk that way?' said Dorothea. 'You sound dreadful. You're frightening me.'

This outburst was greeted with silence. I drew away a little to ease the crick that was developing in my neck, but Alec stayed glued to the panelling. Then, all of a sudden, his eyes flared. He mouthed, 'Tot!', grabbed my arm and dragged me around the nearest corner, less than a second, it seemed, before the door opened and closed.

We waited with breath held and hearts hammering. If he came this way we would be undone.

'Phew,' I said at last, as the sound of his jaunty footsteps faded away in the other direction.

'If people would only say "lovely chatting to you, see you at luncheon, goodbye, goodbye" at the ends of their conversations,' Alec said, 'listening at doors would be much less nerve-racking.'

'So what was all that about?' I asked.

'Search me,' Alec said. 'I thought *she* wanted to keep going and *he* wanted to sell up and cut loose. In fact I know she did because she told me and then one of the rubbers told me too. But from what they were saying just now it sounds as though she's for packing it in and he won't hear of it.'

'Yet,' I said. 'If he's ready to sell what's he waiting for? What bits of paper do you think he's had her signing?'

'He *is* a gambler,' said Alec. 'Perhaps he's got the place mortgaged and he's waiting to cash in his chips.'

'Waiting for what?' I said.

'Well, the market to peak, I suppose,' Alec said. 'It's tremendously exciting what's happening in New York, Dandy. Did you read the newspaper yesterday? The busiest day on the stock exchange since its beginning. Hugh is going to kill you, you know.'

'But then why would it matter whether the books were up to date?' I said, ignoring the sideswipe. 'For a mortgage. And why do you suppose Tot insists that every guest has treatments?'

'Isn't that Dr Laidlaw?' Alec said.

'No, I'm sure it's Tot. One of the bright young things that's really here for the casino was moaning about it. They've even got Grant signed up for galvanic baths, whatever they are.'

'That can't be related,' Alec said.

'And what do you suppose he meant by that nasty vague threat about the mediums?' I asked.

'I've no idea, but I think we should get Grant safely away before it happens. Terrace or winter gardens?' Alec said. 'I need to speak to you.'

'Depends if we need privacy,' I said. 'It's such a lovely day the winter gardens will be deserted.'

'Winter gardens it is,' he agreed. 'I've got the post-mortem report and I rather think privacy would be a good thing.'

I would have preferred fresh air, not to say a stiff breeze, if I was to be the audience for a report on livers and kidneys and such-like, but the terrace was at capacity, muffled figures rolled in blankets on every deckchair, making the most of the brightness even though there was precious little warmth to the sunshine this late in the year. We settled ourselves under one of the open roof-vents, but since the gardeners had been misting the orchids very recently it was a stuffy spot nonetheless, not to mention the faint residue of alcohol and tobacco smoke which I could not miss, now that I had seen all the drinking and carousing which went on in here.

'Well?' I said. 'Poison?'

'Not a one,' Alec replied. 'Not a trace, not a wisp of anything in any of her organs. Nothing.'

'And her heart was healthy.'

'Her heart was fine.'

'So what did she die of?'

'Dieting?' said Alec. 'I'm only half joking. The doctor said again in the report what he said at the graveside. She had nothing in her stomach at all. Or anywhere. She was empty.'

'Well, those bladders and adjacent systems you spoke about often . . . empty out at the last,' I said. 'It never happens in the beautiful death scenes in plays but I learned as much in the conva-lescent home.'

'As did I in the trenches,' Alec said. He sat forward and stared at the floor. 'I feel wretched for the Addies, you know. I persuaded them to dig the poor old girl up and there's nothing to show for it except a hint that her last few days were a misery for a woman who so much enjoyed her food. I can't even lay hands on her jewellery and send it back to them.'

'Jewellery?'

'Well, the watch.'

'Jewellery,' I said again.

He looked up at me. 'What is it, Dan?'

'I've got it,' I breathed.

'Oh, at last,' said Alec. 'Go on then.'

'It was something Regina said,' I told him. 'And I couldn't

remember what it was. I've been kicking myself that every time I talk to Regina I'm in a robe and turban without any of my things – my notebook and pencil – and I couldn't write it down. But it's not just that, you see. And then watching the librarian locking up yesterday made it even worse. I dreamed about it last night. And then I saw Grant sitting there this morning and she looked so out of place in her outdoor clothes.'

'Well, what is it? Tell me,' Alec said.

'I know where Mrs Addie's bag is,' I said. 'I never have my things when I speak to Regina because she takes away one's clothes and folds them and she takes away one's bag and jewellery and puts them in a sort of . . . it's hard to describe but the clasp is very like the one I saw the librarian closing . . . then into a locked cupboard in return for a ribbon, with a key, which you wear round your wrist.'

'And if Mrs Addie died – of untraceable poison? – in the mud room by the Turkish baths . . .' Alec said.

'Her clothes were folded in a neat bundle and could be produced a month later when someone thought of them,' I said. 'But her bag must have been locked away in a little pouch in a cupboard. Regina said guests sometimes leave things in there for weeks together, because it's so secure. I'll bet you anything you like it's still there.'

'But why didn't they think of it?' Alec said. 'Whoever it was who killed her. Mrs Cronin, or Regina, or one of the Laidlaws.'

'Definitely not Regina,' I said.

'Why not?'

'Because,' I said, 'I think Regina probably noticed the clothes. She gave them to . . . Mrs Cronin, who gave them to Dr Laidlaw or Tot. But they couldn't explain to the Addies why they weren't with the rest of their mother's things so they just hung on to them. Until we came along and they cut their losses. But if Regina had killed her she'd have remembered about the bag too.'

'And why didn't the real killer remember?'

'Because no one else apart from Regina is as bound up with the question of keys and lockers and so it didn't occur to them.'

'But why didn't anyone see the key? On the ribbon? On the corpse?' Alec asked me, but even as he spoke the answer occurred to him and he groaned.

'The ribbon came off the corpse when they heaved it out of the mud bath,' I said. 'If we really want Mrs Addie's father's watch back again we need to go to the apple house and start digging.'

Clearly, it was my turn for a task such as this one, after Alec's graveside duty the day before, and so it is testament to his character as nothing else could be that he insisted we both go. We took stout waxed gloves and scarves to tie over our faces and we made a silent agreement to forget the emptiness of poor Mrs Addie's various bodily systems, or not to discuss it anyway.

Besides, now that I knew that the smell was only more of the Moffat brimstone, along with a few traces of nothing worse than I had encountered during the war, it did not seem to smell quite as bad as it had before.

'Shall we just shovel it out then?' Alec said. As well as the opening in the top of the bath where one stepped in, there was a trapdoor in the back closed with a pin and sealed with some kind of putty and it looked as though most of the contents might run out quite readily if we got it open.

'You shovel and I'll go through the shovellings,' I said, claiming the worst of the job for myself. Alec wrenched up the pin and removed it and immediately there was a cracking noise as the putty seal around the little door began to bulge.

'I think you fit the pin in there to act as a handle,' I said, pointing. Alec nodded and did so. Then he looked at me, pulled the scarf a little higher over his nose and yanked the door open.

I stepped back, but it was not the volcanic flow of reeking slime I was expecting. Instead, inside the trapdoor was a wall of dried grey clay which hardly moved except for a few flakes falling off and crumbling as they hit the floor. Alec raised his shovel to strike at the block of clay, but I stopped him.

'Wait!' He froze with his hands above his head. 'Look!' I said.

I bent in close to the opening, pointing at a crack in the mud. I took my glove off for this was careful work. I picked away at the crack for a minute and then rubbed hard with the pads of my finger and thumb. Where I had rubbed one could see the faint pink colour of a scrap of fabric, less than a quarter-inch across. It was the needle in our particular haystack: the end of the ribbon. I took the scarf away from my face and grinned up at him.

'I declare this key found,' I said, and pinching the fraying end hard between my nails I pulled, it gave, I pulled some more, I had three inches of it out now and I took a better hold. A firm tug and it was six inches. I wrapped it around my hand.

'Stop!' Alec cried.

He was too late. I sat back with the whole length of unknotted ribbon in my hand and looked at the wall of mud somewhere inside of which the tiny key was still hiding.

'Sorry,' I said.

'Don't mention it,' said Alec. 'I always preferred knocking down sandcastles to building them.' He raised the shovel high over his head again and brought it down cleanly into the middle of the clay.

Never in all his childhood years of laying waste to castles on the Dorset beaches can he have wielded a shovel to such spectacular ends. The clay shattered and sent a cascade of dust and small cobbles, as hard as rock, all over the apple house, Alec and me. I did not even have a chance to shut my mouth in time and the taste of that eggy, murky powder, coating my teeth and lips and then turning slick as I tried to spit it out again will be with me always. Alec fared rather better. He was still wearing the scarf around his face, for one thing, and he was above the worst of it so that only dust, puffing up, reached his hair and clothes. I, on the other hand, had little flakes and lumps of clay in all the creases of my clothing. I stood up and shook myself like a dog. Alec started laughing.

'Funny now,' I said. 'Until we both go down with cholera.' At least, though, there was no point in daintily picking through the mess, since we could not get any filthier if we tried, so I pulled my gloves back on, shuddering at the way they scraped over the silt on my skin, and plunged both hands into the middle of the cascade, roughly where I thought the key must be.

In retrospect, given that the key was about the size of a sixpence, knowing how long it can take to find a sixpence in a plum pudding, and allowing that the plum pudding in this case was larger than a whisky barrel, I should have been prepared for how long it took to find it. After another twenty minutes I was looking back ruefully at the moment I had believed we could not get filthier and was rehearsing a theory to put to Alec that the key was taken off the ribbon as the corpse broke the surface of the mud and that we were wasting our time, when suddenly I felt a hard little nub under my fingers. I grasped it and pressed it, expecting it to crumble like the many other little nubs which had fooled me as we crouched there. This time, my fingers felt something more unyielding than clay and I drew my hands out, noting the dust filling my turned-back cuffs, and held it up.

'Oh thank God,' Alec said. 'Now where exactly are these lockers, Dan? Let's go.'

'In the ladies' Turkish baths,' I said. 'We need to wait until night-time at least, if you actually come along at all. But that's all right, because it will take us until then to get clean again.'

Before we left we covered our tracks. We scraped most of the clay back inside the barrel and tried to fashion it into the shape it might have assumed if the pin had spontaneously snapped, the door burst open and the contents spilled all on their own. It was not, one had to say, very convincing, especially as we forgot to drop the pin on the floor underneath the spill.

'We could dig a hole and bury it,' I said, but Alec picked it up and threw it across the room instead.

'I'm not digging another inch in that stuff,' he said. 'It shot clear when the thing burst open.'

'Which it wouldn't do as the mud dried, would it?' I said. This thought had been troubling me. 'It would get smaller and shrink.'

'It settled against the door, Dandy,' Alec said very darkly. 'And that's the end of it. Now how are we getting home?'

The only possible thing, of course, was to go in my beloved little Cowley and we could not even ask for newspapers to cover the seats. Alec spread his handkerchief and I tried to hover as much as possible, hanging onto the steering wheel and not settling my whole weight onto the upholstery. I drove right around to the kitchen door at Auchenlea and Mrs Tilling and Pallister both came to see who it was.

Mrs Tilling stepped back and put her apron over her nose, but Pallister, to his credit, closed the motorcar door behind me and took the whole disgusting spectacle in his stride.

'I shall fetch a blanket for you to wrap around yourself, madam, while you proceed to your bathroom and then you can lay it down on the floor. If you would care to step into the scullery, Mr Osborne' – Mrs Tilling rumbled – 'that is to say, if you would care to step over to the stables, Mr Osborne, we can take a first pass at you there. I shall look out some of Master's things for you.'

When the blanket arrived, Mrs Tilling held it out to me at arm's length as Pallister ushered Alec across the yard, putting his arm behind him without touching, the way a shepherd herds flighty sheep with an outstretched crook.

'My goodness, madam,' Mrs Tilling said. 'What is it?'

'Just mud,' I said. 'Almost entirely mud.'

'Miss Grant's not here, you know.' It might have been a warning that I would have to manage on my own, but I did not think so.

'Thank heaven for small mercies,' I said. 'I haven't been put over someone's knee and spanked with a brush for years.'

Mrs Tilling laughed and then buried her face in her apron again. 'Don't make me laugh, madam,' she said. 'It's worse when you breathe it in deeply. Now, I'll go and make a nice light luncheon for Mr Osborne and you, shall I?'

'Anything but eggs,' I said, then I kicked off my shoes, wound myself up in the blanket like a mummy and waddled off to my bathroom and the bliss of the hot water spray.

15

Apart from the oddness of Alec in Hugh's clothes in Hugh's seat at the table, luncheon was heaven. Simply to be clean and sweet-smelling was rather fine, but to feel for once that we were ahead of ourselves in this case, that we did not need to puzzle and wonder, but could wait for whatever the bag would tell us and talk in the meantime of other things, was a treat indeed. Donald and Teddy were better than I could have hoped for and since it had been their father who had plucked them away from the Hydro they were not, thankfully, complaining much to me. We were almost done before they mentioned it.

'I must say,' Donald announced, 'that it's always nice to know why. If it was the casino why not just say it was the casino and besides, we were always back here by the time it got going.'

'Might have been the type it attracted,' Teddy said. 'Flappers and suchlike. What?' he asked me, for I was staring at him.

'I'm not sure,' I said. 'Something about what you just . . . what was it?'

'I don't think it was that anyway,' Donald said. 'I think it was the mediums, actually.' I had just swallowed a mouthful of cheese and was safe. Alec on the other hand inhaled an oatcake crumb and began coughing determinedly.

'Ugh,' he said. 'I can still taste it when I cough, Dan. You know about the mediums then, you two?'

'You can hardly miss them,' Teddy said. 'And there's something about lying in rows of deckchairs all staring the same way that makes people very careless about whispering. We heard about the Big Seance even though it was supposed to be the most tremendous secret.'

'Well, the Big Seance passed off last night without a murmur,' I said. 'Grant was there. She stayed at the Hydro to attend it.'

'I don't think so, Mother,' Donald said. 'I mean, I'm sure there was a seance last night – was Miss Grant really there? Why? – because they have one every time the sun goes down instead of cocktails. But the Big Seance is something else again. And it's not going to be at the Hydro, is it, Ted?'

'Up the hill,' said Teddy. He was spreading butter on an oatcake and then crumbling cheese on top of the butter.

'Teddy, for heaven's sake,' I said. He sighed and scraped the whole mess off again.

'Are you going to be in for lunch every day?' he asked me. 'Because I think I'm well enough for picnics as long as the weather holds.'

So we had something to mull over after all during the afternoon, waiting for the time when we could slip into the ladies' Turkish and search for the locker which matched the key.

'I wonder if Grant will consent to attending the Big Seance Up the Hill,' I said, lighting a cigarette. I could not help sniffing my fingers as I lifted the cigarette holder to my lips.

'Do you?' Alec said. 'Not I. She's a game girl, your Grant. She'll be there.'

'I wonder if they'll check behind fallen logs for spies,' I said. Bunty was standing in the doorway peering at me from under her brows with her head down. She had taken great offence to the smell I had brought home with me and had abandoned me for Mrs Tilling and the hope of pastry scraps in the kitchens but she looked almost ready to forgive me now.

'What would you do if the ghosts really came?' Alec said. 'What if a spectral gallows appeared and the ghost of William Hare materialised hanging from it?'

'I'd be glad to have something to tell the Addies,' I said. 'Even if I had to forfeit our fee to excuse the nonsense.' I clicked my fingers and Bunty took another couple of steps towards me. Rather a nerve to be so princess and pea-ish when one considered what she rolled in on walks if I did not manage to stop her. 'That's a thought though, Alec, isn't it? How exactly were fifteen – or even seventeen – ghosts supposed to lay their hands on enough good timber and nails to make a gallows? How would they hold the hammer? That seems rather a weak point in the argument, if you ask me.'

'Oh, *that* seems weak,' Alec said, laughing. 'If they persuaded a living carpenter to take the job you'd think all questions were answered then?'

'I suppose they could have *scared* William Hare to death the way they're supposed to have scared Mrs Addie. But how would they have buried the body? I'm doing it again.'

'Speaking of bending workmen to your will,' Alec said, 'how goes Gilverton?'

I shook my head. The last time I had spoken to Gilchrist he had talked vaguely of one of the houses being finished and looking very good but when I asked if it was Gilverton or Benachally which was ready he had somehow managed not to answer.

'And Hugh hasn't been in touch with his American broker?'

'I don't think he's given it a thought,' I answered. 'I'm not sure he's even looking at the newspaper now. Why?'

'Oh, rumblings,' Alec said. 'I've sold this and that actually.'

'At last!' I said as Bunty crossed the final few feet of carpet and put her head on my lap. 'Good girl. I'm sorry about that nasty smell. Who's a good old girl then?'

'I miss Millie,' Alec said. 'I'd have brought her and left her here if I'd thought Hugh would be in on it. I really do hope we get this thing solved and off our hands soon, Dandy.'

'A rough draft of a blackmail letter in Mrs Addie's handbag would be good,' I said. 'And then the police would have the trouble of finding out how it was done.'

'Or an empty poison phial marked "untraceable",' Alec said. 'And then the police could try to find out why.'

'Fingers crossed,' I said. 'We'll know soon enough.'

He waited for me in his room, in the end, judging it too risky to be found in the ladies' Turkish after hours, so it was I alone who slipped in and, with an ear cocked for anyone else who might be skulking where she had no business to be, flitted along the cubicle corridor to the little square room at the end where the lockers were. The clothes shelves were open – Mrs Addie's things could never have languished a month there – but there were two rows of little cubby holes with doors and locks running along above them. My key, Mrs Addie's key, was number twenty-three and I struck a match and peered at the brass numbers on the little doors. It was only a minute before I had the door open and was reaching for the familiar lead-and-velvet boxing glove. I grabbed it, locked the door, dropped the key in my pocket and fled to Alec's room, praying that none of the Hydro staff would see me.

None did. I was only seen by one person the whole of the way. He was standing at a landing window on the second floor looking out into the night. It was Loveday Merrick, without his entourage for once, just standing there staring out at the Gallow Hill, all alone.

'Mrs Gilver,' he said, touching his temple with his finger. 'We meet again. I in the calm before my storm, you in the thick of yours.'

'Good evening, Mr Merrick,' I said and scuttled past him. I repeated it word for word to Alec but he was just as stumped as me.

'Never mind him, anyway,' he said. 'Did you get it?' He locked the door behind me as I opened my coat and let the lead-lined bag fall onto his bed.

'Of course I did,' I said. 'I don't generally walk around clutching my middle like that. Now, since you missed out on fetching it, you are to open it up. I insist. You have had the short end of every stick so far. Time for a lollipop instead.'

Alec gladly took the key from me and opened the clasp. He wrenched the hinge open and peered inside.

'One very small brown bag, good quality but mended in the handles,' he said. 'At last. And inside . . .' He fumbled a little with the fastening, being unused to opening women's handbags, I presume, but got there in the end. 'Inside, for example but without prejudice to the generality: Father's watch.' He sprang the casing and tipped the watch itself forward. 'Complete with lock of hair.' He delved back into the bag again. 'And a bundle of precious letters, tied up as you prophesied, Dandy, with ribbon.'

'I think I prophesied red ribbon though,' I said, 'and this is blue.'

'Sherlock Holmes would be ashamed of you,' Alec said. 'Now, let's see. What else is in here? Oh, my word! Is it? It is. This might be something useful.'

He held up a small, narrow black book, with gilt edges to its pages and a pencil with a tassel fitted down its spine. It was a diary.

'In which I very much hope Mrs Enid Addie wrote down all her suspicions about the individual who had threatened to do her harm,' Alec said.

'Oh, you're in favour of women scribbling lots of silly notes now, are you?' I said. Alec was riffling through it, squinting. 'Can't you read her writing?' I guessed. 'Oh well then. I suppose you'd better give it to me.'

It was not the prize for which I had been hoping. Mrs Addie was a woman of orderly mind who used her diary to record appointments and anniversaries and to remind herself to pay bills. The only longer items than these were Bible passages, entered each Monday as she turned over a new page, anything from 'A faithful friend is the medicine of life' to 'Better a dinner of herbs' which was hard to take from a woman of her size.

'Hmph, nothing on the last day,' said Alec, looking over my shoulder. I had gone quickly, of course, to September and the clues I hoped to find there and it was troubling indeed to see the blank pages after all the luncheons and dinners and meetings at clubs. She had jotted down her daughter's birthday in December. 'Lace?' she had written, and had marked the day of her Ladies' Circle Christmas entertainment in good time too. 'King's Theatre!' she had written, but nothing could have spoken more eloquently of a life snuffed out than the way the pencilled notes got to September the eighth and then all but stopped.

'I wonder why she didn't put in the Bible passage on the last Monday,' I said.

'Maybe she did it in the evening,' Alec said. 'And she was dead by then.'

'I don't think so,' I said. 'If you're going to write something in your diary every week when you turn over the fresh page, you'd do it on Monday morning when you sat down at your writing table to prepare for what was coming.'

'Well, perhaps it was because she was away from home,' Alec said.

'Perhaps,' I said. I continued turning the pages. 'Look here though. In June she was at a friend's in Inverness. Look, all week. But she still filled in her passage. "The eternal God is thy refuge and underneath are the everlasting arms." Doesn't seem as though she expected to enjoy the visit much if she needed that to comfort her. And look again in February. She was in the sleeper train coming back from London. "And the Lord went before them by day in a pillar of cloud to lead them the way" etc, etc. Oh Alec, look at this one! "Gather up the fragments that remain, that nothing be lost." For the week of the church jumble sale. It's priceless. I like Mrs Addie more and more.'

Alec was nodding. 'You're right, Dan. She'd have loved to have thought up a good passage to go along with a spell in the Hydro. Something with a bit of anointing, perhaps. Or even "Physician, heal thyself" at a pinch.'

'So why didn't she do it?'

'Maybe . . . if she died of natural causes,' Alec said. 'If we're wrong about murder and misadventure and it was all perfectly innocent . . . maybe she was already feeling rotten on Monday morning, which is why she didn't eat or drink anything, and she felt too bad to pore over a Bible. They've always got such tiny print. If it was a sick headache . . .'

I had already had one beam of sunshine and choir of angels in this case. As Alec spoke, the beam of sunshine returned and threatened to blind me. The choir thundered and bellowed until I was deafened too.

'I know how she died,' I said. 'I know what killed her. And, Alec, it's beastly.'

Alec started up with a jolt. 'I got some brandy sent up,' he said. 'Only I forgot to offer you one with all the excitement of the bag. Have one now, Dan. You've gone an awfully funny colour.' When he had given me a large glassful and I had taken two sips I felt rather better again and I laid out my revelation.

'She didn't write in the diary on Monday morning because she was in the mud bath,' I said. 'She went in the mud bath on Sunday. She even said it to Mrs Bowie on the telephone. She was ringing off because she was going for her bath. And I thought she meant a bath with ducks and bubbles. But everything is a bath here. Hot lamps and salt is bath. Faradaic rays is a bath. She went in her bath on Sunday evening. And by Monday evening she was dead. Dehydrated, empty, starved and thirsty, and finally dead.

'And the point of planting toffees in her bag wasn't to make us think she'd been out – not particularly – it was to make us think she had been around at all on the Monday when the shops are open and had some sort of ordinary day.'

'Dear God, Dandy,' Alec said. 'I'm very sorry to say I think you're right.'

'What a horrible, wicked way to kill someone. What a wicked, wicked thing to do. And to this woman.' I waved the diary at him. 'A woman who helps out at jumble sales and buys lace for her daughter. A woman who makes daring little jests with Bible passages that no one except herself will ever see. How could anyone have done that to her?' Alec refilled my glass even though it was hardly started. I think he had to do something.

'We will avenge her,' he said. 'At least whoever it was isn't going to get away with it, eh?'

I took another swallow – one really could not call it a sip – and nodded.

'Sorry,' I said. 'Just all of a sudden . . .'

'I know,' said Alec. 'So. Who was it?'

'We agree that it wasn't Regina?' I said. 'She'd never have left the bag in the locker if she had known Mrs Addie died in the mud room.'

'Agreed,' said Alec. 'And not the doctor. Apart from the fact that she is a doctor, she's too upset about it. Horrified. I mean if you murder someone you don't go and weep in the room where you did it, do you?'

'One might want to,' I said, 'but one would probably resist, it's true. But why would Tot kill a blameless Edinburgh matron like Mrs Addie? I can imagine him doing someone down for monetary gain. I can imagine him shoving a girl off a cliff if she had got her hooks into him. But why would he pick one of the Hydro guests and kill her?'

'I have no idea,' said Alec. 'Mrs Cronin?'

'Yes,' I said, nodding slowly. 'There's something about Mrs Cronin. Something about whether it was Sunday or Monday or . . .'

'She doesn't approve of treatments on Sunday,' Alec said. 'Is that it?'

'So it couldn't have been her, you mean? But could someone plan a murder but not want to do it on the Sabbath day? That's an odd conjunction of sin and piety, surely.'

'And besides,' Alec said, 'Mrs Addie had been coming to the Hydro for years. Why would Mrs Cronin suddenly kill her now?'

'Tot, then,' I said.

'Maybe. Mrs Addie could have found out about the casino and threatened him.'

'But how could Tot get a woman like Mrs Addie – any woman really – into a mud bath? She'd shriek the place down.'

'Well, it had to be someone who could get in and out of that mud room,' said Alec. 'Someone with a key.'

'Only if she died in the bath before it left the mud room,' I said. 'What if she was waylaid in the grounds and dragged off to the apple house and killed there? What if the bath had already been moved by the time Mrs Addie died in it? It could have been anyone in that case. It could have been a wandering maniac.'

'But the Laidlaws covered it up and got Regina to wash her and got Dr Ramsay to sign a certificate,' Alec said. 'Why would they do that if she had been murdered by a wandering lunatic?'

'To save the reputation of the Hydro while continuing to run a casino that destroys it? I don't understand their feelings about the Hydro at all. Dot wants to run it and Tot wants to sell. Then

Tot wants to keep it and Dot wants to sell. What changed? And now they seem to be in agreement that their time here is almost done, but they're still arguing as much as ever.'

'I think the moment has arrived,' Alec said, 'to hand all of this over to the police. We've got plenty of evidence now. If I telephone to the Edinburgh pathologist tomorrow and tell him about the mud bath he'll be on to the Fiscal like a bullet. He hated having to conclude "natural causes", you know, but there was nothing else he could do.'

'All right then,' I said. 'Tomorrow we hand it all over. To the Edinburgh Fiscal, via the pathologist. Agreed. Just one thing I want to do tonight, though. I've got a padlock on my spare wheel. I'd like to go and padlock up the apple house. Just in case. Just to be on the safe side.'

Alec stood and held out a hand to me, smiling with great affection – perhaps I still looked ghastly – and then jumped clear into the air at the sound of a knock on his door.

'Who is it?' Alec said, opening the door just a little.

'Ah, Mr Osborne,' said the oily, chuckling voice. 'Good, good. We're missing you downstairs, you know. The poker table's not the same without you and I knew you weren't away on another of your mysterious jaunts tonight again. Just wanted to make sure you weren't asleep. Make sure you were coming.'

'I'm not sure, Laidlaw,' Alec said. 'I'm rather tired this evening.'

I saw a quick movement as Laidlaw darted to the side to see past Alec into the room. I do not think he saw me; it was just a flash of the side of his head that *I* caught before Alec pulled the door to.

'Not going to bed, are you?' Laidlaw said, with another burbling chuckle in his voice. 'What a waste of an evening that is! Come on down, old chap, and I'll stand you a round. I shan't be there myself tonight – well, off and on, you know – but I just wanted to see that everything's shipshape. Come on down, eh?'

'I'll see,' Alec said. 'I'll sit and read awhile and then I'll see.'

'Ha-ha-ha,' said Laidlaw. 'Yes, nothing like a spot of "reading".'

Even able to see only a slice of his shoulder, still I knew he was winking. Alec was flushed dark when he closed the door and turned to me.

'Odious creature,' he said.

'Have you been losing lots of money?' I said. 'Why is he so desperate for you to be there?'

'No idea,' said Alec. 'And there's something up with him tonight. He was doing his act, but the strain was showi—' He was interrupted by a second knock at the door, this one very different from the first: timid and soft.

'And now Dorothea!' I said. But I was wrong. When Alec opened the door a crack this time he said a startled hello, then swung it wide and pulled Grant inside.

'Oh, sir!' she said. 'I'm so sorry to—' Then she saw me. 'Oh, thank goodness you're here, madam. I don't know what to do.'

'What is it, Grant?' I said. 'Alec, give her a brandy.' Grant took the glass and swallowed a goodly measure without so much as blinking.

'It's tonight, madam,' she said. 'The anniversary. The centennial. That Loveday Merrick has decided it's tonight and it's all my fault!'

'The Big Seance?' I said. 'How is it *your* fault? They've been talking about it since before you got here. Donald and Teddy overheard about it days ago.'

'But I gave them the last name,' Grant said. 'Mr Gilver told me another one – Mrs Ostler – and I said she'd come to me and that's it. Fifteen of them. Joseph the Miller, Old Abigail Simpson, Mary Patterson, Big Effie, the grandmother, the blind child, Ann Dougal, the Haldane sisters, Marjorie Docherty, Daft Jamie, one man nobody knows, two nameless women and now Mrs Ostler and that's the lot.'

'You've been doing your homework,' I said.

'It was the master,' said Grant. 'He told me all about it and made me learn the names.' I could believe it too. 'And now they want me to go up the Gallow Hill with them and be the channel!'

'You could always say that a sixteenth has been in touch,' Alec said. 'And then wait around for the seventeenth who never shows up.'

'Mr Merrick doesn't think the last two are coming,' Grant said. 'He reckons if corpses who'd never been buried right made ghosts . . .' She flushed, darted a glance at Alec and then looked away again. I did not follow her but he seemed to.

'Ah,' he said. 'No one would get a night's sleep in Flanders, eh?'

'That makes sense,' I said. 'It's the first sensible thing I've heard out of any of them. How would you feel about going if you knew Mr Osborne and I were nearby, Grant?'

'Nearby where?' she said.

'In the trees, in earshot,' Alec said. 'Hiding behind a fallen log on the far side of the clearing. And if you start to worry then just say a word . . . pick a word, Dandy.'

'Resurrection,' I said.

'A word that wouldn't happen to come up any other way,' Alec said patiently.

'Oh. Yes, I see. Mohair.'

'Perfect,' said Alec. 'If you feel frightened, Grant, or just want to stop, say "mohair", loud and clear, and we'll swoop in and get you.'

'Thank you,' Grant said. 'That's a great comfort, sir. Can we make it cashmere, please?'

The Big Seance, as I could not help calling it to myself, was set for midnight – of course – and so Alec and I had plenty of time to unfasten the padlock from my spare wheel and make our careful way over the dark lawns to the apple house. The key was where we had left it above the lintel and I had remembered correctly that there was a hasp set into the edge of the door.

'It doesn't smell nearly as bad,' I said. 'I wonder why.'

'Familiarity breeding the contempt out of us,' Alec said.

'I do know I'm probably being silly,' I went on. 'It's sat there for over a month. There's no reason to suppose it won't sit there overnight until the police can come.'

Alec nodded absently but he also reached the key down and turned it in the lock. He opened the door. I held my breath for a wave of stink which never came.

'Your instincts are sound, Dandy,' he said. 'But your timing is terrible. It's gone.'

He struck a match and held it up and we looked together at the inside of the little room, empty except for an elderly apple crate or two. The floor was rather dusty, but for all ordinary purposes quite bare.

'Someone's onto us,' I said. 'Did Tot Laidlaw drum up that silly excuse to come to your room just so he could sniff you?'

'Possibly, possibly,' Alec said. 'I wonder where they took it, whoever spirited it away.'

'Back to the place it came from,' I said. 'To make us look like idiots when the police come.'

'But who knew that we were getting close?' Alec said.

'Well, I was fairly outspoken to Mrs Cronin this morning. Good God, Alec, I said I was going to Dr Laidlaw to complain that patients were not taken care of. Was that it?'

'Whatever it was, we can't do any more here tonight,' Alec said. 'We can confirm one another's stories if it comes to that anyway. Why on earth would we lie? And unless Mrs Tilling or Mr Pallister has been feeling very assiduous . . .'

'Oh wonder of wonders! Of course. All the dust. No, I'm pretty sure they're leaving our clothes tied up in sacks in the stables until Grant can cast her expert eye. And we have the ribbon and the key.'

'So let's get up the hill and behind our log before the crowd starts to gather,' Alec said. 'I suppose we had better walk all the way. Hugh's Rolls-Royce pulled onto the verge would attract comment.'

'And nothing would persuade me back into my poor little motorcar until Drysdale has had a go at it,' I said. 'We're walking.'

One would have thought we would be talking nineteen to the dozen as we tramped along the lanes and onto the dark path through the trees, but the prospect facing us had perhaps begun to needle Alec as it certainly had me. I do not believe in ghosts, not even a little, that one lurid episode under the trees notwithstanding, and I knew that the portents leading to this seance of seances were all dropped in by Grant at Hugh's prompting and were counterfeit to their core. Except that the mediums and the murder had to be connected. It was simply too much of a coincidence for the Laidlaws to cover the tracks of a murder with talk of a ghost and then for mediums to gather from all the four corners with talk of more. No, it was perfectly clear: a man – a gentleman or professional man, a respectable sort anyway – had sent a letter to the mediums' magazine right at the beginning and a gentleman had asked at the library for all the grisly details of Burke and Hare. It was Tot Laidlaw, it must be. Starting rumours and planting clues. To shore up the story of Mrs Addie's death? But he had suppressed that story, got the doctor to all but lie on the death certificate, told her family nothing. Why would he hush it up and then turn around and start to shout it from the rooftops? Embellish it, even?

'You're blowing like a whale, Dandy,' said Alec softly. 'Shall I slow down?'

'I'm thinking,' I said. 'I hope Tot Laidlaw has something planned for this jamboree and we catch him at it.'

'You're still sure it's him then?' Alec said.

'More and more. But don't ask me why. Or why he killed Mrs Addie.'

'What sort of thing do you see him planning?' Alec said.

'Ghostly lights?' I said. 'Blowing in bottle tops to make spooky noises, I don't know. But he did say he wouldn't be at the casino much tonight. Maybe he's up the hill already.'

'We should stop speaking then, and tread very softly,' Alec said.

Accordingly, we crept up the rising path as quiet as two ghosts ourselves. It was possible that Tot Laidlaw was hiding behind one of the trees, I supposed, but the darkness was so complete and the silence so deep that I felt sure we were here alone. We reached the clearing and crossed it, picked our way through the trees and settled down behind the fallen trunk. No mackintosh squares today, but if Grant found the heart to complain about some earth on the knees of my stockings considering what was waiting bundled up for her in the stables I should take my scolding in honour of her dedication.

'Have you ever been to a seance?' Alec said, presently. I heard the familiar sound of him taking out his pipe and settling it in his mouth, even though he could not light it.

'Not really,' I said. 'I was present at one, if one wants to be precise about it, but only because it was held in my night nursery while I was sleeping there. My mother sacked the nurses, as you can well imagine.'

'I can't believe Nanny Whats-her-name would put up with such a thing,' said Alec.

'Palmer,' I said. 'She was at her sister's in Norwich for a confinement. I slept through the whole thing – not least because the nurses put rum in my milk at bedtime. Ssh!'

Very faintly in the distance we could hear the rustling of leaves and a sound like far-off bees humming. It was the same murmuring as before, only this time there were more of them; the tramp of feet sounded like an army battalion and the bees were an angry swarm long before we saw the first of the torches. They were proper flaming torches, soaked rags wound round long sticks, and my heart flipped and leapt like a fish at the sight of them. For flaming torches turn a crowd into a mob, and I was astonished to see what a crowd of mediums there was now. There had to be twenty of them, young and old, male and female, all walking in step and murmuring in time. And at the head of them was Grant in her grey dress and white neckpiece, her face a mask of pure terror in the light of the burning torch she carried wavering in her hands.

'Oh Alec,' I breathed. 'She's petrified. Let's just go and stop this nonsense right now.'

'She's acting, Dan,' said Alec. 'Look at her now.'

Grant had surged ahead of the rest of the procession so that none of the mediums could see her face, which had split into a grin. With the torch held under her chin it was quite the scariest thing I had ever seen. It was, however, swiftly outrun by what was to follow.

16

My detecting career has put me in the way of several experiences – scenes witnessed, persons met, tasks undertaken – which my parents, Nanny Palmer, Mademoiselle Toulemonde, and the staff of my finishing school never foresaw and for which they failed to equip me. None of it, not the bodies plummeting from heights with firm hands at their backs, not the circus midgets in their caravans, not the digging of graves in the moonlight, rattled me as thoroughly, sent as many goose pimples marching over my flesh like an army of ants and left me as waxen and trembling as the night of the Big Seance.

It started quietly enough. The mediums stood in a circle all around the edge of the clearing, muttering their endless chant. Between the bodies of the two standing closest to Alec and me I could see that Grant was in the middle, with Loveday Merrick at her side. He thumped his cane on the ground and the muttering stopped.

'Extinguish the torches,' he commanded in that booming voice of his and the mediums clustered around a fire bucket someone must have brought up the hill. One by one they dipped the torches, setting off a sizzling loud enough in the quiet night to sound like the devil's own firebrand, and sending a cloud of smoke up into the air. When the dowsed torches emerged from the water, however, they were still alight and within moments were burning as bright as ever again.

'They've used sulphur and lime instead of tar,' Alec whispered. 'They'll never get them out that way.'

There was silence in the clearing except for sounds of blowing as some of the mediums tried and failed to puff out the flaming rags as one would a birthday candle. I could feel a surge of laughter bubbling up inside me and I concentrated on containing it. After an awkward moment, one of the mediums piped up.

'How do we do it, Loveday?' Alec's shoulders were shaking now too.

'Roll them on the ground,' he said. 'And stamp on them.'

The few men in the crowd did just that but most of the women dabbed uselessly at the grass with theirs and made little darting movements with their feet, and all in all it took a full five minutes before every last one of the torches was out. Even at that there was some ominous glowing and when a gust of wind swept across the clearing several of them reignited for a second time and had to be rolled and stamped on again.

At last, though, there was darkness and silence and, with a few deep breaths, we quenched our threatened giggles. I could just about make out the white gleam of Grant's neckpiece although my eyes watered and ached from the strain of looking. There came a muffled sound which I took to be Loveday's cane again and then some movement I could not clearly see.

'We are gathered here,' said Merrick, sounding exactly like a minister at the start of a wedding, 'on this twenty-sixth night of October in the year nineteen hundred and twenty-nine, one hundred years to the night since the black devil himself, William Hare, was sent to his eternal punishment. We come to honour the souls of his victims who became his avengers, to seek intercourse with them, to be the bearers of their messages from the world beyond to the world of the living. Most humbly we offer ourselves in service to them.'

It was all I could do not to whisper 'Amen'.

Nothing happened for perhaps a minute. An owl hooted. Down in the town a door slammed, but up here on the hill all was quiet and still until the cane thumped again.

'Be not afraid, gentle spirits,' said Loveday's voice. 'We call upon you in peace and friendship to make yourselves known. We offer you this channel, pure and clean, and we beg you to come to us. Come down through the higher planes to our lowly sphere.'

He paused. 'Speak!' I am sure I was not the only one who jumped at the sudden bellow. 'Speak, Jamie! We shall not mock you here. Speak, Mary! Your sins are forgiven here! Speak, thou poor blind child! You will be given an audience here with us tonight.'

'What a load of complete tommyrot,' Alec breathed in my ear.

There was a low moaning out in the clearing.

'I feel them, Loveday,' said a voice. It was perhaps Mrs Molyneaux's, but it was set so sepulchrally low and was so bursting with portent it was hard to say. 'They are close, but they are frightened to appear.'

'He's here!' The voice was a pure peal of sound, pitched as high as the cry of a newborn. It was Grant. There was a ripple of interest all around the ring of mediums then Grant spoke again in her everyday voice. 'They're scared, Mr Merrick, because the bad man's here.'

'William?' said Merrick.

'Aye, that's me,' said Grant, low and guttural now and completely terrifying.

'Evil, evil, evil creature,' said a female's voice from somewhere to our left. 'I can feel him. My skin's crawling, my stomach's heaving.' She made a few half-hearted sick-noises but she did not have Grant's talent for it and sounded more as though she were trying to keep from swallowing a fly.

'Get away fro—' said a voice which had not spoken before.

'No!' said Merrick. 'William, if you can hear me. What is your full name?'

Grant rumbled and groaned a bit and then spoke in the low voice again. This time we could all hear the rather chewed-up vowels of a strong Irish brogue about the words.

'I am the ghost of William Burke, wrongly judged and wrongly hanged, I come to wreak revenge on them as left me.'

Whispers of 'Burke!', 'It's Burke!' went around the ring. Even Alec leaned in close to me and whispered: 'Why did she go for Burke?' I shrugged and shushed him. Grant was speaking again.

'Twas him, twas all him and yet I hanged and not he. And her with her nagging and goading me on and I hanged and not she.

And so I shall be with him always and I'll haunt him and harry his soul to the end of days.'

'William!' said Merrick. His voice was set for a parade ground, a bark of sound. 'William, you were wronged. Four of you did the deed and one of you paid the price. You were wronged. But the others . . .'

'Give not thy soul unto a woman,' said Burke's voice. 'Faithless and treacherous creatures, tricking us and blinding us to goodness with their wiles.'

'Typical,' I muttered.

'Mr Merrick?' Grant was speaking for herself now. 'Why don't I take William away? If he's gone perhaps the others will come.'

Sensation! The mediums broke into such a storm of chatter that I could not hear a single word. At length, however, Mrs Scott's voice rose clear of the others.

'Are you telling us that you are a drawer as well as a channel?' she said.

'I don't know what you'd call it,' said Grant, faltering very convincingly. 'This curse of mine . . . I try not to think of it and *never* speak of it. But I . . . There was this room in a house in the village when I was a child. No one would go in and so I went and found out what the trouble was and I took the poor spirit out and down to the river and . . .'

'And what, girl?' said Merrick. He sounded as though he were smiling.

'I sent her away,' said Grant.

Sensation upon sensation! This time I did pick out a word from the crowd, because they were all repeating the same one. It appeared that Grant was not only a medium, a channel and a drawer. She was a quencher too.

'If you're sure, Miss Grant,' said Mr Merrick.

'He doesn't belong here,' Grant said. She raised her voice. 'William Burke, William Burke, I command you to follow me.' The white of her neckpiece disappeared as she turned around and I could not see or hear her walk away.

'Where will she go?' Alec said.

257

'Home for a bath and cocoa if she's got any sense,' I answered. 'At least I hope so. Because we can't follow her to make sure she's all right, can we?'

It took a moment for the seance to get under way again after Grant's spectacular exit, but in time muttering resumed and swaying too. The mediums, holding hands around the circle like a giant game of ring-a-roses, began to get into the swing of things.

'I see a child,' said a piping voice. Olivia Gooseberry, I thought. 'Come, child. Oh, oh, he's leading an old woman by the hand. And he's not blind! He can see. Let me listen.' There was a long silence. 'Yes, yes, he can see!'

'I hear him,' said a nearby voice. 'Oh, there he is. Oh bonny, beautiful boy! So happy.' Beside me, Alec groaned quietly. I turned and smiled at the look of disgust on his face. Then I frowned.

'Is it my imagination or is it getting lighter?' I breathed. I turned back to the circle. It was definitely lighter now. I could see their linked hands and I could see light reflected on the pink faces of the ones at the far side.

'The clouds must be lifting,' Alec said. But to me it looked like the light of dawn. How long had we been here? It must surely not even be two o'clock in the morning yet and while Scotland in June is a great trial one can at least be sure of a good night's sleep in the darkness by the end of October. I shrank down further behind the log, feeling my shoes sinking into the earth but not caring. If I could see the mediums, then they could see me.

'Mary, Mary,' one of them was saying. 'Oh, how beautiful you look. See how her hair shines and see the cross around her neck!'

'I'll bet,' Alec muttered.

'I see her,' said another. 'And Lizzie and Peggy too.'

'Ahhhhhh,' said Loveday Merrick. There was instant silence. 'Davey Riley. And Josephine Riley too. How wonderful to meet you both at last. And who is that with you? Mrs Ritchie! Welcome, dear lady.'

'It's the last three with no names,' someone said. 'Oh Loveday, you are wonderful. Mr and Mrs Riley and Mrs Ritchie, we welcome your spirits and offer ourselves to serve you.'

'There they are!' said Mrs Molyneaux. 'Oh, there they are, holding hands. Oh welcome, welcome, dear friends.'

'You're very quiet,' said Mr Merrick, suddenly turning and directing his gaze to a woman and man at the right side of the clearing. They had not joined in the greeting. I could see them – it was lighter than ever – shuffle their feet and look at the ground.

'I haven't heard a thing, Mr Merrick,' said the female half of the pair. 'I haven't been chosen.'

'Me neither,' said the man. 'I've not pleased the spirits tonight.'

'Mrs Riley has a message for her grandchild,' came a cry from opposite. Mr Merrick swung round.

'Ah, well done,' he said. 'You are a true and faithful servant . . . ?'

'Anne Tasker,' said the woman, sounding thrilled.

'And what is the message, Anne Tasker?' he said. Then he turned our way, looking past us towards the Hydro. 'What . . . ?'

'That light's beginning to get quite—' Alec said. He turned and at the same moment so did I and together, in the warm glow of the sky to the west of us, we saw a tiny orange fleck rise up from behind the trees of the Hydro grounds and wisp off into the dark. A second later, before we could move, footsteps came pounding back into the clearing. It was Grant.

'Fire,' she shouted, rushing back into the middle of the clearing and pointing. 'There's a fire! Look behind yourselves! Can't you see?'

'It's the Hydro!' I shouted, standing up and scrambling through the trees for a better view, all thoughts of secrecy gone. Alec was at my side and I could hear footsteps as some of the mediums came behind us. Ahead, glowing between the tree trunks, the light grew brighter and now we could smell it too, the sweet pleasant smell of smoke on a chilly night. I plunged onward and at last could feel the slope steepening under my feet. I crashed on, down another few feet, through the brambles, snagged my coat on a branch, struggled and then shrugged out of it. Alec caught my arm.

'You'll break your neck, Dan,' he said. 'Let's go back and come round by the path. There will be others there already. Listen!' Now we could hear faint shouts and then a sudden scream.

'Hugh is in there,' I said. Still he hesitated. 'And Dorothea.' I did not wait to see how he might react, but just turned away and went back to breaking through the undergrowth with my arm in front of my face against the thorns.

'Let me through, my dear lady,' came the booming voice of Loveday Merrick. He was right behind me. 'Let me through. I have a cane.'

He pushed past me and began whacking a path through the bracken and brambles. I was at his heels. Someone bumped into me from behind and fell heavily. I did not even turn to see who it might be.

The flames were growing; I was sure of it. It was not just that we were getting closer. And I could hear the fire itself now, over the sound of shouts and screams. A roaring and rushing and then a great creak and crash and the sky was filled with a shower of sparks. The roof was falling.

Then all at once we were down out of the woods, Merrick, Alec, Grant, the gooseberry girl and I, and the garden wall of the Hydro was before us. We raced along the dark lane and in at the back gate to the servants' area and stable yard. The place looked fine from here, locked up for the night, dark and quiet, but suddenly there was a squeak and a groan and then one of the windows by the back door blew out and shattered over the cobbles of the yard. Grant shrieked and pulled me back. Merrick had opened the gate to the lawns and we all rushed through, blundering in the dark under the cedars, heading for the light ahead of us, and when we got there we could see that it was the fire reflected on the pale clothes and white faces of the crowd who stood helpless, watching, on the lawns.

Every window on the west side was alive with leaping flames and the slivers of glass on the ground reflected the light and sparkled like rubies. I caught the arm of a woman in dressing gown and bedroom slippers.

'Is everyone out?' I said. 'Is everyone safe?'

But she was too shocked to speak to me. Her lip trembled and she shook her head, turning back to look at the blaze. I began frantically darting through the crowd, calling Hugh's name. At the other end of the house a Dennis engine was parked on the grass and I could see the gleaming helmets and the glittering buckles and buttons of the firemen as they scurried around with their ladders and hoses. One hose was spouting water already, straight into one of the dining-room windows, but it only served to increase the smoke while doing nothing to lessen the force of the flames. I turned away and kept calling. I was beginning to whimper when I heard someone answer me. I wheeled round. Alec and he were walking calmly towards me.

'Good heavens, Dandy,' Hugh said. 'Yes, yes, I'm fine. I was playing cards and heard the alarm. I strolled out of the nearest door and didn't even have to hurry. There, there, my dear. Now please, pull yourself together, or you'll upset the servants.'

What he really meant was that I would delight the servants and the other guests and be one of the highlights of the evening which everyone told and retold if I did not stop clutching him and weeping.

'But you're filthy with soot,' I said. 'How did that happen if you strolled out?'

'Naturally when one found out it wasn't a drill one went back in to help the women,' said Hugh. 'Now, I'm off to get the car if I can.' He gave me a tight smile and left. I stared after him.

'Don't believe a word of it,' Alec said. 'I heard him bellowing *your* name. That's how I found him.'

'He went back in?' I said and I knew that my voice shook as I spoke. Alec rolled his eyes. 'Well, next time he lectures me about taking on dangerous cases when I have sons to think of I shall take great pleasure in reminding him. Is everyone out?'

'They seem to be,' Alec said.

'Mr Osborne!' It was Dorothea Laidlaw, white and shaking, standing like a ghost at our side. She had eyes only for Alec, not so much as a nod to me.

'My dear Dr Laidlaw,' Alec said. He took off his coat and put it around her shoulders.

'I can't believe this is happening,' she said. 'Everything my father . . . his whole life. And all of my work.' She turned and blundered off. She did not console any of the huddled groups of guests in their dressing gowns who stood around hugging one another and watching in helpless horror as another enormous section of the roof fell in with a sigh and a cascade of embers. She did not look twice at the groups of bright young things shivering in their beaded dresses or the young bloods who ignored them and stood smoking, watching the Hydro burn.

'Drat,' said Alec. 'She's gone off with my pipe in the pocket.'

Slowly, the scene was changing. Some young men from the casino crowd were setting benches together in the quiet dimness just beyond the heat of the flames and I saw Regina and Mrs Cronin help an elderly lady over to one and lie her down with a blanket under her head and a robe to cover her. Another of the maids was ripping towels into strips and dipping them in the fountain, then passing them out to be laid on people's blistering faces for relief. Before long, I was sure someone would find a way to make tea and the world would begin to turn on its axis again. I was just beginning to calculate how many we could fit into Hugh's Rolls-Royce and how many we could give comfortable lodgings to at Auchenlea, when I felt someone seize my arm.

'The doctor's in the mud bath room.' It was Loveday Merrick. His great, handsome face was drawn up in horror and his sonorous voice was cracking. 'Someone saw. Someone just told me!'

'Alec,' I cried. 'Dr Laidlaw's gone back in. To the mud room!'

'Damn it, Dandy,' he said, rushing up. 'We should have known she'd do something like this. I'll tell the firemen. Perhaps they can get to her.'

But I was furiously thinking. The whole of the Turkish and Russian baths was made of marble and the corridor which led to it was stone.

'Come with me,' I said, grabbing his arm and leading him to the garden door where the mud bath had been brought outside.

'Madam,' said Grant. 'What are you doing?'

'Dr Laidlaw went back in,' I said.

'I know,' said Grant. 'I saw her.' She pointed to the gap in the wall which led to the servants' yard and the garden door. 'I was just . . .' She held out her hand to show me the dripping wet handkerchief she held there. I snatched it up and tied it over my face.

'I'll do it,' I said. 'I know where she's gone. Tell Mrs Cronin and Regina to have wet towels ready.' Then, before I could change my mind, I dashed to where the garden door stood open, with Alec behind me.

'Sorry there's only one hanky,' I said as we darted inside. I turned the corner from the offshoot to the passageway proper and sprinted for the stairs.

'Not too bad in here, anyway,' Alec said.

There was a faintly acrid smell in the air and I thought I could see a light haze of drifting smoke, but it wasn't until we got to the top of the stairs that my eyes began smarting and I heard Alec start to cough, but we were heading away from where the smoke was thickest and with a great rush of thankfulness I saw that the door to the Turkish and Russian was closed. I tested the handle – not hot – wrenched it open and hustled myself and Alec through. In here the air was clear and all was as ever. It was warm, but not any warmer than when the baths were open. I took Alec's hand and pulled him along the cubicle corridor, through the resting room, up the side of the plunging pool and through the round room where the spray baths were. The mud room door was closed and I prayed that she had not locked it behind her.

Alec grabbed the handle and pulled it open and I did not have time to think what he meant by his yelp of pain before we were in the room, choking on smoke and looking up through the hole in the ceiling at the flames raging and crackling above us.

'Dr Laidlaw,' I shouted, retching at the smoke.

'Help me!' came a man's voice. I stumbled forward, came up hard against the solid wooden side of mud bath and screamed

263

to see Dr Ramsay's head, shining with sweat and twisted with terror.

'Help me!' he screamed again. Alec was struggling with the fastening and when the top trapdoor burst open he hauled the doctor out by his armpits then together we dragged him clear.

'Thank God it's empty,' Alec said, grimly, 'or we'd never have shifted him.'

The doctor was dressed, dinner jacket and black tie, and his patent shoes scraped on the tiles as we lugged him outside and closed the door. Back in the marble spray-bath room everything had changed, even in the moments we had been away. The walls were running with condensation as the temperature rose and the plaster ceiling was bulging and darkening even as we looked at it. We dragged the doctor into the plunge pool room, but things were worse there. A brown bloom was spreading over the ceiling and a few wisps of black smoke were beginning to curl away from the surface of the plaster. Suddenly, at the far end, the door to the corridor blew open and we could hear the fire crackling and roaring beyond it.

'Oh God,' Alec said. Dr Ramsay was unconscious, hanging from our shoulders, slack and helpless.

I looked around desperately. There was no other way out. Just the solid marble walls and the long empty pool of cold water. A thought struck me and I dropped down and stuck my hand into the water. It really was still cold.

'Quick!' I said. 'Into the pool.' We dragged the doctor over and let him drop into the water. He came up spluttering and choking but wide awake again. I stepped up on the edge and jumped in beside him, feeling the same sharp slap and then the ache of the cold. I put my arm across Dr Ramsay's back and held him up. 'Come on, Alec,' I said. 'Jump in!'

'I need to see if she's there,' he said and ran back towards the mud room. As I watched, a long thin section of plaster with a burning beam behind it arched gently down and closed off my view of him with a sheet of flames.

'Now, Dr Ramsay,' I said. 'When the ceiling goes, take a big breath and go under. Stay under as long as you can. Do you understand me? Alec!' I shouted over my shoulder. 'Alec, hurry!'

'He left me there to die,' said Dr Ramsay. I was watching the ceiling. The edge of the hole where the long thin strip had collapsed was licking and curling with tongues of flame and the brown bloom above us was darkening to black and blistering all over. 'I thought it was one of his jokes. I actually climbed in and let him close the thing!'

'Well, you're out now,' I said, wishing he would shut up and let me listen for Alec.

'It started as a tease! He's such a joker himself. I was only teasing.'

'I know,' I said. 'Alec!' I turned back to the doctor. 'Get ready to breathe in and duck. It wasn't seemly behaviour for a professional man, though, was it, Dr Ramsay?' For I had worked it out as soon as I saw him there. The gentleman who wrote to say a woman died of fright at the Moffat Hydro. It was Dr Ramsay. 'You thought if he had the nerve to dream up a story like that he deserved a bit of ribbing, eh?' I said. 'So you wrote to the magazine. And then when the mediums began to arrive you went to the library, didn't you, and asked what ghosts you could tell tales of in Moffat and have them believed. You let some of Tot's friends in on the joke, didn't you? And persuaded them to spread your stories for you.'

'It was only a tease,' he said again. 'And he was ready to kill me!'

'I think, my dear doctor,' I said, 'that he was going to kill you because the story of Mrs Addie was crumbling and he didn't want you to tell the police that he . . . what shall we say? . . . bribed you to sign the certificate?'

'Not bribery,' said the doctor. 'He was going to write off my losings.'

At last, I remembered the other mention of a respectable man. Hugh had said that Tot's casino attracted them. *That* was who I had seen slipping into the Hydro by the smoking-room door. He was on his way to the poker table or roulette wheel, where he would not have to pay his debts, at least not at twenty shillings to the pound.

'And I wouldn't have done it if there was a mark of violence on her,' the doctor said. 'She died of natural causes. She must have. Heart failure was the truth after all.'

'She died as you were going to,' I said. 'Only without the fire to make it quick for her. Now, duck under! Alec, please! Alec, *hurry*!'

There was a huge creak and as I took in an enormous breath and let myself sink, I saw the ceiling above us give way and let a ball of yellow fire, ragged with grey and orange fringes all around, come rolling down towards us and then I was under the cold water and the silence filled my ears. I had lost Dr Ramsay. I felt for where he should be, but there was only the swish of empty water there and I knew that I would be able to hold my breath much longer if I kept from moving. So I crouched down as low as I could with my eyes shut and prayed and prayed, until my chest was searing with pain and my head was pounding.

When I could not hold on another second, I pushed off the bottom and came up through the warming water, letting my lungs empty and then filling them again as soon as my mouth broke the surface. It was hot and bright, filled with the sound of breaking timber and shattering glass, a nightmare place. I dragged in another breath, looking all around for Alec or Dr Ramsay, but the surface of the water was blocked with sizzling debris and I could see nothing. I closed my eyes, gulped as much air as I could and went under again.

I counted to two hundred before I felt myself begin to swoon and pushed upwards the second time. Up in the air, the nightmare was worse than ever. The ceiling was gone and a black chasm with fire at its edges rose above me. All around, pyres of broken timber and plaster were crackling like bonfires and belching smoke up into the air. Someone was screaming with pain nearby.

'Alec!' I tried to call out, but my voice was no more than a ragged whisper. 'Oh, Alec.' I looked up and saw a shard of floor beam coming straight down towards me like a burning arrow. I dragged in a breath and sank again.

It was warm all the way to the bottom this time, and I felt sluggish and heavy in my clothes and shoes. Odd objects bumped against me, but when I reached out my hand it was pieces of plaster, turning to mud in the wet, and I pushed them away.

I knew that my lungs gave in more quickly this third time. It seemed hardly a moment before I was rising again and when I got to the surface I lay back weak and panting, before I dared open my eyes.

The fire in the resting room was still crackling and leaping, but in here the flames were mere flickers and the smoke had cleared. I lifted my arms and let them float on the surface of the water, then shrieked as someone clutched my hand.

'Dan!' I turned and there was Alec, surging towards me through the debris in the pool. His face was shining red, his lips blistered, but he was alive and he was smiling at me. 'She wasn't there,' he said. 'I couldn't get to you for all the burning rubbish but I've been shouting and shouting.'

'I was under the water,' I said. 'Holding my breath.'

'What a good idea,' Alec said, touching his lips and wincing. 'I'm going to look like a toffee apple tomorrow.'

'Where's Dr Ramsay?' I said. Alec nodded to a spot behind me but then tightened his grip on my arm.

'Don't look,' he said. 'He tried to get out and a piece of the ceiling fell on him.'

'I told him to hold his breath and duck!' I said. 'Is he dead?'

Alec raised his eyebrows and then winced again as his wrinkling forehead stung.

'He's very very dead,' he said. 'Please don't look, darling. Now, I reckon since we're soaking wet, if we go the way we came we've got a fair chance of getting out of here. What do you say? We can always come back if it gets sticky.'

I shook my head, feeling the rat's tails of my hair lashing back and forth. With every gulping breath I was taking in more of the sulphurous burning stink.

'I'm never coming back to this bloody place ever again,' I said and began wading to the edge of the pool to haul myself out. 'I understand now why fire and brimstone are such an effective threat, I can tell you.'

We sizzled a bit in some of the corridors on our way to the outside and the floor felt hot through my shoes now and then, but we met no serious harm and when we emerged and came reeling out onto the lawns, we might not have looked as beleaguered as we felt for the crowd gathered there ignored us absolutely. They were all looking upwards to exactly the same spot on the first floor, some with their hands clasped over their mouths and some with their hands clasped for praying. I cast my gaze to where they were facing and saw Alec, from the corner of my eye, do the same.

Framed in one of the windows, a figure stood with a bundle of papers in its arms. The papers were on fire but she – it was a woman; it was Dr Laidlaw – threw them out anyway.

'Stamp on them!' she said. 'Don't use the hose. My work! My life's work!'

'Never mind your life's work,' shouted one of the firemen. 'Save your *life*, you silly lassie. Jump and I'll catch you.'

She bent and picked up another armful of paper folders and notebooks, casting them out of the window and then screaming as she saw them start to burn while they fell. Her hair was on fire now and one sleeve of her dress too, and yet no one turned away. We simply stood there, horrified, watching.

'Jump and I'll catch you!' called the fireman again. Three of his colleagues came, running heavily in their boots and helmets, and the four of them stretched a tarpaulin sheet under the window.

'Jump, Dr Laidlaw,' someone else cried.

'Do what your father would tell you!' It was Mrs Cronin, standing wringing her hands, gazing up in horror.

'Dorothea, for God's sake!' It was Alec's anguished voice beside me.

She seemed to look at him for a long still moment in the midst of all that chaos and confusion and then slowly she turned away, walked into the fire and was gone.

Then from all around came shrieks of disbelief and sounds of weeping as though, with that one last horror, this dreadful night had undone everyone.

'All for nothing,' said Mrs Cronin, beside me, still staring. 'All for nothing after all.' Then there came a cry of 'Nurse!' from over by the benches and Mrs Cronin gathered herself and turned away.

'I was going to propose,' Alec said, once she had gone. He spoke quite calmly, as though of some small matter which had slipped his mind. I turned and regarded him, realising only now how many little signs I had missed and how unknowingly cruel I had been, teasing him. Now it was time to be kind.

'I don't think you would have if you had really known her,' I said. He did not turn. He was still looking up at the window, but he cocked his head a little my way. 'Not tonight,' I said. 'I'll tell you tomorrow. Right now we need to get you some ointment for your face. I can't believe you didn't think to go under.' I turned away, hoping to see an ambulance man who might help with some first aid, but what I saw was Grant, barrelling towards me with tears pouring down her face. She stopped dead three feet short and curtsied.

'I'm very glad you're all right,' she said. 'Madam.'

I felt my lip begin to wobble and held out my open arms. She stepped into them and hugged me so hard that drips of plunge-pool water were squeezed out of my clothes and fell into my shoes. Over her shoulder I saw Hugh, whose face was a battle-ground of at least four different emotions: shock at Grant, disgust with me, and horrified interest as to what had happened to Alec's face; what was filling his eyes and making him sniff, though, was something it made me smile to see. He nodded and then turned and walked away. I would never allude to the fact that I saw his shoulders shaking as he wept out his feelings quietly for no one to witness.

'I'm so glad to see you safe and well, my dear Mrs Gilver,' said Loveday Merrick. He took off the magnificent astrakhan overcoat and gave it to me. 'I can't imagine why that woman told me the doctor was in the mud room. I would never have forgiven myself if you had come to harm because of me.'

'Who *are* you, Mr Merrick?' I said. 'I know you're not who everyone believes you to be. And how did you know what that little room *was*?'

But he saw me swaying on my feet and made the same decision I had for Alec moments before.

'I shall call upon you tomorrow, if I may,' he replied, 'and tell you the whole story.'

'You can come tonight and sleep in an armchair, if you like,' I said. 'I've been trying to think how many refugees we could take in.'

He bowed his acceptance. 'More than I deserve after I put you in danger.'

'But a doctor *was* in the mud room,' I said. 'Just not Dr Laidlaw. One of the local men. He didn't escape, I'm very sorry to say.'

'Ah!' he said. 'Right enough, she didn't say a name. Just "the doctor".'

'Who was it who told you?' I asked him.

'I didn't catch her name either,' Merrick said. 'A stout lady in a robe and turban. I haven't seen her again since she spoke to me.'

17

The police, in the persons of Sergeant Simpson and the same smooth-cheeked boy I had met before, were on the scene now and, although all I wanted to do in the world was peel off my soaking, stinking clothes and fall into my bed with my arms around Bunty, I veered over to the sergeant on my way to the drive and Hugh's motorcar and stood squarely in front of him.

'This fire wasn't an accident,' I said.

'No need to convince me, madam,' said Sergeant Simpson. 'A great white elephant like this going up just as business is going down. I wasn't born yesterday.'

'And two people at least have lost their lives in it,' I said. 'One was deliberately shut up so he couldn't escape. Dr Ramsay from Well Street.' The sergeant's eyebrows rose and he swept off his cap.

'Right enough?' he said. 'Well, that puts a very different face on things. By all accounts the Laidlaw woman was a suicide but what you've just told me is murder, plain and simple. If you'll come down to the station and make a statement, madam.' I could feel my face fall.

'*Could* I do it tomorrow, Sergeant Simpson?' I pleaded. 'I'm dead on my feet. Couldn't you just put Tot Laidlaw in jail tonight anyway?' The sergeant was shaking his head. 'Where is he?' Simpson nodded over my shoulder and I turned. Across at the fountain, where the benches were set in rows with blanketed figures resting on them, Tot Laidlaw was very much in evidence, walking to and fro with towels and mugs of tea – I was right; someone somehow had got a kettle going – and stopping to lay his hand on shoulders and once even a brow.

'Would you have a man to spare to send over to Auchenlea?' I asked. Sergeant Simpson thought a moment and then nodded. I crossed to Laidlaw and took him by the arm.

'My dear Mr Laidlaw,' I said. 'I am so very sorry about your poor sister.' Tot switched his expression from cod sympathy to cod anguish as though he had turned a dial. 'Now, you must get some rest tonight somehow,' I said. 'Whenever you feel you can leave, I insist you come to Auchenlea and spend a few hours at ease. Tomorrow will be a trial and you need to prepare for it.'

'Mrs Gilver, I couldn't possibly,' he began. 'I have no means of getting there. My motorcar has taken some of the wounded to Dumfries to the infirmary already.'

'I've thought of that,' I said. 'One of Sergeant Simpson's men is going to drive you.' His eyes flashed but he could hardly show his hand by refusing. Instead he gave me one of his sweeping bows.

'If I can,' he said. 'And thank you.'

Then I saw Hugh standing waving at me from the rhododendrons which bordered the drive and, gratefully, I left it all behind me.

Hugh's face was thunderous and what with the soot and the sheen of heat he looked like the very devil. Normal service had evidently been resumed.

'Why are all those people in my Rolls?' he said.

'We're taking them home and giving them succour,' I told him. 'It's the least we can do.'

Somehow the word had got to Pallister and Mrs Tilling in advance of our arrival and, when we entered the hall at almost half past three, the fire was burning there and blankets were set ready in the armchairs. The drawing-room fire was just as high and there beds had been made on the sofas and footstools drawn up to the chairs to fashion more. In the dining room soup was keeping warm in an electric contraption and as soon as she heard us coming Mrs Tilling appeared with two tall jugs of cocoa.

Mr Loveday and the four elderly ladies we had brought along

sank down into chairs and let Mrs Tilling and Grant begin to fuss over them.

'How many guests, sir?' said Pallister.

'Five,' said Hugh.

'We're ready for eleven,' Pallister replied. 'I took the liberty of asking Master Teddy to move into Master Donald's room an hour or so ago. I've vacated my own quarters – I shan't be retiring tonight, of course – and the female servants have managed to make room for three women in their quarters. So perhaps I could ask Drysdale to return for another carload?'

'Very good, Pallister,' said Hugh. He stalked off to the stairs and, I suspected, the bathroom, but not before Mrs Tilling called out.

'I've put sacks for sooty clothes in all three of the bathrooms and laid out dressing gowns. It would help a great deal if you just used the sprays and don't fill the bath itself and put the boiler under strain.'

Hugh stopped as though he had been shot in the back and when he began again climbing the stairs he was a broken man. To be forbidden a proper bath, and urged instead into one of these new-fangled operations so that a load of strangers could use his hot water was the final straw on this dreadful night.

'Poor old Hugh,' Alec said. 'He didn't cash his chips, you know.'

'I know,' I said. 'Or at least I'm not surprised. A gentleman doesn't cash his chips until he's leaving. But money won and lost isn't really money lost, is it? He's finished no worse than he started, I daresay.' I made a move towards the nearest armchair and then stopped myself. 'Where can we sit when we're so filthy?' I said. 'I feel as though I shall fall over if I try to stay standing.'

'Let's nab the bathrooms first while the guests are drinking their soup,' Alec said. And dreadful hostess though it made me, I agreed.

Half an hour later, clean and warm, although oddly attired for a social gathering, Alec, Loveday Merrick and I had found a quiet spot and sat down at last to make sense of the puzzle as best we might. I was sitting on my bed with Bunty at my back like a pillow. Alec was on the dressing-table stool and Mr Merrick, the oldest among us, and the most undone by the night's exertions, was in the little upholstered chair by the window, telling all and making Alec's jaw and mine drop to our laps in wonder.

'So I suppose the best sort of way to describe what I am,' he said, 'is a professional sceptic. I keep my reputation with the snake oil peddlers by dint of very cautious balancing. Someone has to be most egregious – most egregious indeed – before I'll go all out and expose them. And even then I don't do it myself. None of the debunking is ever traced back to me. On the other hand, if it's just the usual comforting nonsense I have a quiet word and they respect me all the more for it. I couldn't resist this Burke and Hare caper when it met my ears. Never thought it would end like this, I can tell you.'

'I don't actually think the ghosts and the fire are connected,' I said. 'Not closely anyway. The fire wasn't started to kill Dr Ramsay, it was just a convenient way for him to go since it was planned.'

'So Dr Laidlaw started the fire to kill herself?' Mr Merrick said. 'Such wickedness! She could have taken twenty souls with her.'

'No, no, no,' I said. 'Dorothea Laidlaw would never have done such a thing. She didn't start the fire at all.'

'But you said something to me, Dandy,' said Alec, 'suggesting there was something about her I wouldn't care to know.'

I submitted him to very close attention, trying to decide what to say. Unfortunately he caught me at it.

'You're not about to break my heart,' he said. 'Didn't you listen to a thing I told you. I admired her, but that's all.'

I was not half so sure as he seemed to be, but I took his words at face value.

'Mrs Addie,' I said. 'It was Dr Laidlaw who killed her. She put the poor woman in the mud bath on Sunday evening and then went back to her study to ıer precious work.'

'Oh dear God,' said Alec. 'She forgot?'

'Not the sort of woman you'd want in charge of your children, eh?'

Alec took a mighty breath in, held it for a long moment during which Merrick and I watched him anxiously, and then let it go in a great rush which left him slumped against the dressing table behind him.

'The prospect of marriage doesn't seem to agree with me,' he said. He was beyond being embarrassed by Merrick's presence. 'She seemed ideal. A rational, educated woman happy to pursue her own . . . I took to her at once. And it was hard to resist the prospect of slaying the dragon, of course. Or at least getting her away from that brother of hers. Ah, well.' He grinned at us. 'Onward and upward. Third time lucky maybe.'

'It wasn't the first time or the last that she'd forgotten a patient,' I said. 'Usually, Mrs Cronin checked and double-checked. But Monday was Mrs Cronin's day off. I *knew* it was. I should have paid attention to the way her coat and outdoor shoes kept bothering me. So on a Monday the baths were very quiet. This was before Tot started the new regime of insisting everyone had treatments, you see.'

'So she just sat there until Monday night,' Alec said. 'Forgotten.'

'And I think somehow it was Tot who found her,' I said. 'Perhaps he went looking for Dorothea – she loved the plunging pool and only ever went in it when the baths were closed and empty. At any rate, it was Tot who thought up the cover story of the ghost and the fright and it was he who got Dr Ramsay to sign the certificate in return for forgiving the gambling debts. He washed the body. Perhaps he tipped it into the plunging pool and that's why they had to clean it out all of a sudden. And he either told Dorothea, or she found out somehow. Perhaps she caught him at it even.'

'I don't suppose we shall ever know,' Alec said.

'Anyway,' I went on, 'he gave the body to Regina to lay out and talked that fool of a sergeant round and the only way for Dorothea to have stopped it all would be for her to admit to something which would have her struck off and disgraced and prevent her from doing the one thing she cared about. Her damned precious working. That's the main thing to remember. She was taking care of her own interests all the way.'

'That's not quite fair, Dandy,' Alec said. 'That *was* when she started asking Tot to close the Hydro. She must have been terrified she'd forget again.'

'Oh, Tot's the real villain of the piece, I'll grant you,' I said.

'Because the forms he made her sign were insurance forms, weren't they? He insured the hotel to the hilt and started planning the fire. Planned it for the middle of the night when all his chums would be in the casino too and if some poor invalid slept through it and died – too bad!'

'Why did he insist on all the treatments, I wonder?' asked Merrick.

'Same reason he blew a gasket if one called the Hydro an hotel,' I said. 'Presumably the insurance for hotels isn't as good as for hospitals. He needed all of his chums to say with their hands on their hearts that they had been undergoing treatments at the time of the fire. They knew the names and everything – heat lamps and sitz baths. I mean, even Sergeant Simpson knew that a huge hotel going up in flames must be an insurance job, didn't he?'

'Why did Laidlaw start the rumours about Burke and Hare?' Alec said. 'You'd think he'd want the death of Mrs Addie to die down, not to become notorious.'

'Ah yes,' I said. 'You didn't hear that bit. He didn't start them. That was Dr Ramsay's big tease. He was giving Tot Laidlaw a taste of his own medicine. At least, partly that and partly sucking up in a strange way. I think he always very much wanted to be one of Tot's set, you know. And Tot was such a joker: the story of Mrs Addie dying of fright had at least a *bit* of a tease in it. But not only was Tot unwilling to take what he dished out, very soon it got completely out of hand. Especially after your entrance, Mr Merrick. Not to mention Grant's.'

Merrick chuckled. 'She was very good,' he said. 'For a minute, she almost convinced me. I mean, she wasn't known in the trade and I couldn't see what her angle was at all.'

'You really don't believe a scrap of it then?' I said.

'Good grief, of course not,' Merrick replied. And because there could have been any number of women of any size milling about the grounds of the Hydro in robes and turbans after the fire, I did not tell him.

'That sounds like a car,' said Alec, cocking his ear. 'It might be Laidlaw now.' I stood and crossed to the window.

'It's Drysdale with the next batch,' I said. 'I should go down and see to them.'

'Go to bed,' Alec said. 'Mrs Tilling is in her element down there. You'd only get in the way.'

I took no more than that rather graceless persuasion. I climbed under the covers, and I think I had fallen asleep before the door had softly closed behind them.

Sunday, 27th October 1929

It was Hugh who woke me, at daybreak, the blank grey light of steady rain falling from thick cloud, just the weather one would want to put out the last smoking ember of a fire.

'Damn dog,' Hugh was saying. I felt a tug on the covers as he tried and failed to make Bunty shift.

'Good morning, dear,' I said, sitting up. 'Thank you for not waking me when you came up.'

'A bomb wouldn't have woken you,' Hugh said. 'I waited up until Laidlaw arrived, about five, but by then everyone was settled in their billets. It looks like a field hospital downstairs, Dandy. If we can't get shot of them today, I'm for taking the boys and going home.'

'I'll go and see what's what now,' I said, carefully not responding to the suggestion.

The blankets were rolled and the furniture put back in the drawing room, but I could hear low voices in the dining room and so I made my way there with Bunty padding in her stiff morning way beside me.

Ten people were sitting at the dining table, eating porridge, while Pallister stood like a formal footman on one side of the door and the constable stood like a bad copy of him at the other.

Some of the guests looked perfectly at home – the bright young things – but a few of the Hydro's long-time patients were turning huge eyes on Pallister as though he was their headmaster and might at any moment decide to cane them. One could hardly blame them; even after all these years he sometimes produces just those feelings in me.

Alec was there, Donald and Teddy too, and Merrick, and at the head of the table was Tot Laidlaw, slightly weary about the eyes and blue about the chin, but holding his audience in the palm of his hand with all his usual brio.

'My poor sister,' he said, 'my poor dear sister. Well, I hardly have to tell all of you who loved her too. She was just so very absent-minded. I'm sure when the firemen look through the wreckage they'll find it started in her study. That paraffin heater of hers, probably. Poor Dot. But what she did to Dr Ramsay . . . Well, she must have lost her mind.'

'I can't believe it,' one of the older women was saying. 'A terrible shocking thing.' But her eyes were wide with delight.

'She loved him,' Laidlaw said. 'And he just didn't love her back. Any excuse to get him up there and talk to him, you know. She even dragged him out of bed one time to sign a death certificate she could have signed herself. Poor Dottie. And poor Dr Ramsay. She must have tricked him into a windowless room and locked him there. She must have lost her mind.'

'I think she possibly did lose her mind at the end, Mr Laidlaw,' I said. 'But she didn't kill Dr Ramsay.'

Tot Laidlaw raised his head and stared at me.

'Aren't you wondering why my face looks this way?' said Alec. He was indeed a dreadful sight this morning, shining with ointment and blistered where he wasn't raw. 'I tried to get to Dr Ramsay.'

'But you failed,' said Laidlaw. The relief in his voice was unmistakable.

'He did,' I said. I drew out the last remaining chair at the foot of the table and sat down. 'But I didn't. I had a very interesting talk with him before he died.'

There was a moment of perfect stillness and then Tot Laidlaw leapt to his feet and raced for the door. The young constable was after him like a dog at the track, but it was Loveday Merrick who foiled his plan. He stuck out his silver-topped cane and when Laidlaw sprawled on the carpet, Merrick planted one of his enormous feet squarely in the middle of his back and leaned enough of his weight on it to start Laidlaw squealing.

'Ladies,' I said, 'coffee will be served in the other room.' The women stood – I have always been excellent at drawing off the ladies, even inexperienced ones such as some of these – and began to shuffle around the far side of the table to avoid the squirming Laidlaw and the young constable who was advancing with his handcuffs open.

'I'm stopping here, though,' Donald said.

'Yes, me too,' said Teddy.

I threw them a glance. Perhaps it was because the rest of us were wan from exhaustion and adventures but they really did look a lot better than they had a week ago, rosy and bright-eyed, the Moffat Hydro's last two satisfied customers.

In the drawing room, Hugh was sitting behind a newspaper with a cigarette in his mouth. This was very odd, for he normally does not smoke until at least luncheon-time. He took one glance at the party of women and raised the newspaper higher than ever.

The women began to twitter like a flock of little birds.

'Old Dr Laidlaw must be turning in his grave!'

'—been coming here for twenty-three years. I'll have to go to Peebles now.'

'—never have dreamed Tot could be such a sewer.'

'—sister was dull but she didn't deserve *that*, darling.'

'And why did he do it?'

'Yes, why would you burn down your own hotel and destroy your livelihood?'

'For the insurance, of course. Now that doesn't surprise me about dear old Tot at all.'

Hugh cleared his throat and spoke from behind his newspaper barricade.

'He'd better get onto his insurance broker quickly then, because if they've been buying common stocks like the rest of us he'll be lucky to see a farthing.'

I walked across and peered over the top of the newspaper.

'Hugh?' I said. 'Is something wrong?'

'Just reading the news from America, Dandy,' he said. 'I'd like a quiet word, please.'

I left the guests as Mrs Tilling advanced with a laden coffee tray and followed Hugh upstairs to our bedroom again. He shut the door and rubbed his face hard with his hands. I had not seen him indulge in such a gesture since the night when Teddy was small and his temperature from measles went higher than Nanny's thermometer would show.

'Hugh, what is it?' I said.

'While we've been here in a little world of our own,' he said, 'the American stock market has crashed, Dandy. Through the floor. I'm very sorry to tell you this, my dear, but we've taken heavy losses.'

'Oh,' I said. 'Well, money won and lost isn't really lost at all, is it?'

'Did you read any of those papers I asked you to sign and post to the broker?' Hugh said.

'No,' I replied. 'Should I have?'

He did not answer. He turned and looked at the room, surprised I think to see that it was a strange one.

'If we leave Mrs Tilling and Pallister here to hold the fort,' he said, 'and Drysdale to bring them home whenever these walking wounded are off our hands, can we just go home this morning, please? You and me? Home to Gilverton, while we can.'

'Well, actually, Hugh, I said, 'there's some good news and some bad news. About those papers. I didn't want to release the funds from the stuff you sold because I had plans for them, you see. But I didn't have time to look those particular ones out from that enormous bundle. I was nursing all of you and half the servants, remember. And so I didn't post them. The papers. To the broker. They're in my desk in my sitting room at home.'

'You didn't post any of them?' Hugh said.

'Not a one.'

He strode over and took a firm hold of my upper arms as though he were about to shake me. Instead, he made an announcement.

'I'm going to buy you a sable coat, Dandy,' he said. 'And a mink one too.'

'You might not want to,' I answered. 'That was the good news. The bad news is that we might not be able to go home just now.'

'Oh?' he said. 'Why not?' I wriggled out of his grasp before continuing. Hugh had never shaken me like a rag doll until my teeth rattled, of course, and never would. Still.

'Well,' I said, 'the plumbers are in. I've spent that money on central heating radiators and new bathrooms for Gilverton and Benachally.'

'Pipes and taps and radiators?' said Hugh. 'At Gilverton?'

'And Benachally, yes. And Gilchrist said they'd finished with one house but not started on the next yet. So depending on which one it is we might not be able to go home. Just yet. Until they're done. But I must say for them to have done one in a week is a miracle so it shouldn't be long.'

He had, I realised, stopped listening a while ago. I think he stopped listening when I said 'Gilchrist'.

'My factor,' he said and his voice was shaking. '*My* factor knew about this and never told me?'

'You were ill, Hugh,' I said. He marched across the room to the little desk where there was a telephone and fumed and swore until the call had been connected and Gilchrist – I assumed – was on the line. There were a few sharp exchanges and then the earpiece was banged into the cradle.

'Well, at least we can go home,' he said.

'They did Gilverton first?' I said. I hated it when he was this angry, but the thought of my new bathroom and the delicious warmth in my bedroom lifted my spirits anyway.

'In a week, Dandy? Don't be ridiculous,' said Hugh. 'They started with Woods Cottage. The factor's house. Well, that's all to the good in a way. When we advertise for a new man we can say the house is modern, can't we?'

'You're not sacking him!' I said. 'Hugh, it was my fault. And you stopped it in time. And think if we'd crashed with the stock exchange. How can you be angry with anyone today?'

There was a soft knock at the door and we both composed our faces.

'Come in,' I called.

It was Grant.

'I'm sorry I'm so late,' she said. 'Madam. Only every stitch you had on last night is ruined and Mrs Tilling tells me your pale grey is in a bad way too. And I can't even *find* your good coat.' It was snagged on a bush on the Gallow Hill, so one could hardly blame her. 'So I've been down to the town to Irene's, which is not a bad little dress shop for a place of this size, and I've bought you something new.' She turned in the doorway, picked up three enormous parcels done up with pale yellow paper and tied with dark brown ribbon. 'Now, they're quite daring for you, madam,' she said, heaping them on the bed beside Bunty, 'but they don't carry a wide stock. You'll need to stop in and pay the bill, by the way, and just remember when you do that these are London modes. She goes down on buying trips three times a year.'

I turned to see what Hugh was making of all this.

'I shall have Gilchrist and you shall have Grant,' he said softly and left the room. I was delighted to note that he was whistling.

Postscript

I would greatly have preferred it had the Addies been willing to send a cheque through the post, for the thought of facing them once the endless grisly details came out was not an easy one. As Sergeant Simpson had said, all we ever want to hear is that death was instantaneous and our loved one did not suffer a moment's pain, but that soothing tale was never going to do in this instance.

Unfortunately Mr Addie was immovable on the point. Alec and I were summoned back to Fairways to give our report and receive our dues and as we stood on the doorstep one bright, crisp November day, the grin he gave me was as sickly as the one I returned. When the door opened, however, our reception was not at all what we had been dreading.

Mrs Bowie née Addie had beaten the housemaid to the tape. She surged across the doorstep, pressed me to her bosom and then threw out an arm to haul Alec into an uncomfortable and somewhat excruciating three-way hug. Over her shoulder I saw the housemaid boggle, shrug and turn back to the baize door, leaving us to it.

'How will we ever thank you?' said Mrs Bowie, almost shrieking but muffled quite a bit against Alec's coat and my fox fur. She stood back at last, just holding on to one hand of each, and beamed. Never had an Edinburgh matron acted more like a West End starlet on an opening night.

Now Mr Addie joined us too, coming halfway along the hall from the drawing-room door and shifting from foot to foot, saying:

'Hear, hear. Yes, indeed. I quite agree. Now away and let our guests in the door, Margaret. We've many things to say.'

Mrs Bowie gave us both one last squeeze of the hand and then switched to ushering us inside, taking coats, offering coffee and fussing about the fire, the sunlight coming through the blinds and the comfort of the chairs. Anyone would think we had brought her mother back to her and Alec and I shared more than one puzzled glance, before the coffee and plain biscuits were served and the four of us were settled.

'I'd a letter from the Dumfries Fiscal you wouldn't believe,' said Mr Addie. 'Grovel? What? He tied himself in a sailor's knot apologising. And another from the Chief Constable. A telegram, no less, from the Edinburgh pathologist and, ahem—' He broke off and smoothed his moustache before continuing. 'An invitation to dine with the Fiscal here in Edinburgh.'

'Both of us,' said Mrs Bowie. 'To dine with him and his wife.'

'Of course, I know him from the golf club,' said her brother, playing it down, but I could see what a leap it was from two men drinking in a clubhouse to Mrs Bowie putting her pearls on and climbing into a taxi for dinner at eight. The Addies, it would appear, were being wooed out of plans to write to *The Scotsman* or instruct a lawyer.

'And all because of you,' said Mrs Bowie. 'If it weren't for you two dear people, the story of Mother's death would have stood forever quite quite wrong, and her troubled spirit would never have found its rest.'

'And for that we are most grateful of all,' Mr Addie said. 'It's a new world to me, I must say, and I'm a plain man for the most part, but your associate has opened my eyes as well as calmed my mind.'

'Ah,' I said. I could think of nothing more, but threw a frantic glance at Alec for aid.

'I'll just fetch him in,' said Mrs Bowie. 'He stepped out to take a turn in the fresh air. It's that draining, you know.' And she bustled off through the double doors to the adjoining room and then out of the french windows into the garden. Alec and I both sipped coffee the better to cover our total bewilderment and within a minute Mrs Bowie was back, skipping up the stone steps like a girl and holding the french window wide. I only just began to realise who was about to step through it as he appeared: leonine and magnificent, the sunlight giving him a kind of halo in his full regalia of astrakhan coat, silk scarf and silver-topped cane, Loveday Merrick strode into the room.

'Mrs Gilver, Mr Osborne,' he said.

'Mr Merrick. What are— What a pleasant surprise.' Alec had found his voice first.

'I had to come,' said the great man. 'Mrs Addie would not be denied.'

'Marvellous,' said Mrs Bowie. 'I always believed there was something, but I never dreamed to have it proven to me.'

'Proven?' I said, unable to help myself.

'Beyond all doubt,' said Mr Addie. 'Mr Merrick seems to know my mother better nearly than I do myself. And it's not at all a case of – ahem – crossing the palm with silver, for he has refused to take a penny piece and has told us from Mother in the strongest terms that she's going to her rest now and if anyone else comes around saying they've a message we've not to listen.'

'Marvellous indeed,' said Alec. 'It's good to hear that she's . . . in such good . . . after her ordeal.'

'Oh, but that's what she was so very determined to tell us,' Mrs Bowie said. 'There was no ordeal.'

'Really?' I said.

'She was warm and comfortable and she drifted off to sleep,' Mr Addie said.

'And when she awoke she was surrounded by soft white light and she was floating, quite weightless, above the ground, looking down but feeling nothing but calm.'

'Remarkable,' I said. 'She wasn't at all distressed by what she saw whilst "looking down"?' Both Addies looked puzzled and Loveday swept in.

'There was indeed great wickedness,' he said. 'Thomas Laidlaw was a man lost to all goodness. But none of his capers had the power to touch Mrs Addie by then. And good may come of evil, you know.'

'This is the most wonderful bit of all,' Mrs Bowie said. 'And there's no way Mr Merrick could have known of it unless Mother told him. So we know we can trust him.'

'I see,' I said and waited. If Loveday Merrick had found good in any of what had happened at the Hydro I was more than keen to hear.

'Mother's sore back,' Mrs Bowie said. 'It wasn't the old trouble after all. It was something else.'

'And if she hadn't passed when she did,' said Mr Addie, 'how she did, drifting off that way, she would have been in for a very unpleasant time of it.'

'What was it?' Alec asked, rather baldly. I had already guessed; their very reluctance to say it screamed its name.

'A growth,' said Mrs Bowie in hushed tones. 'Of the spine. Advanced and unstoppable. Mr Merrick told us.'

'After Mrs Addie told *you*?' I asked Loveday, turning a face I was keeping carefully blank towards him.

'And so good came of evil, you see,' Loveday Merrick repeated. 'A calm, easeful death instead of the suffering that was coming.'

'But wouldn't the post-mort—' Alec began, but he caught himself just in time.

'And no,' Loveday said later when he, Alec and I were walking back down through the city towards the railway station together, 'the post-mortem wouldn't. If it had been an organ, then certainly, but a growth in the muscle tissue around the spine? It could easily be missed. There are no holes in my story for the Addies to fall through. I've been doing this for a long time and I'm rather good at it now.'

He had tucked my hand under his arm in an avuncular way, shepherding me safely through the drifts of fallen leaves and over the cobbles slick with the last of the morning's frost, and now he gave me a squeeze with his elbow as well as a slight wink. I was instantly his ally and found myself speaking up.

'Where's the harm, Alec, really? If Mr Merrick has brought comfort to the poor Addies and proofed them against being picked off by music-hall mediums in future, where's the harm?'

'Gilver and Osborne, servants of truth,' muttered Alec. I could see what he meant and when he shot rather a poisonous look at the way my gloved hand was nestled in the crook of Merrick's arm I could see what he meant there too.

'Ah, yes,' said Merrick. 'Truth. I'm glad you mentioned it and I'm very glad we have this chance to speak plainly away from the family and their sensitivities. Now, I don't know how much you've been told about what Tot's been coming out with.'

'Nothing,' I said, astonished. 'Told by whom?'

'Oh, I've found Sergeant Simpson pretty forthcoming,' Merrick said. In other words, he had the police eating out of his hand as well as the family. Thank goodness, I thought to myself, that his intentions were pure, for Svengali had nothing on him. Under cover of getting a handkerchief out of my pocket to dab at a smut on my cheek, I got my hand away and moved to walk a little closer to Alec, who was persuasive at times, but never actually mesmerising.

'And I think,' Merrick went on, 'that Laidlaw simply can't resist showing off, telling how clever he's been.'

'How *clever*?' I said. 'The man's in jail, his sister dead, his hotel burned down and his reputation in shreds.'

'But for a while there,' said Merrick, 'oh, for a while there it looked so promising. It was high stakes, but Tot Laidlaw's nothing if not a player. The insurance was all stoked up, although it took his last pennies to stoke it, it seems. The guests were taking treatments to keep the books square – Dorothea would have got a tidy sum for the loss of such a successful clinic, you know. The casino was only open to the kind of hard-bitten gambler who'd keep his mouth shut so long as the cards were dealt.' Alec caught my eye a little at that, but we said nothing, although I tucked the phrase away to use on Hugh sometime when I needed to.

'What about Dr Ramsay?' Alec said.

'Yes, using Dr Ramsay was a mistake,' said Merrick, 'but one that Laidlaw almost managed to put right – dragging that infernal mud bath back to the Turkish, tricking the poor fool into it.'

'Was he counting on it burning to ash and hiding his crime?' I asked.

'I don't think he could have been thinking very clearly at all by then,' said Merrick. 'But he was certainly planning a hero's death for Ramsay: a doctor going in to save souls with no thought for his own neck.'

'And what of Laidlaw's neck?' Alec asked. 'Will he hang?'

Merrick shook his head. 'I don't think so,' he said. 'He didn't kill Mrs Addie and he didn't kill his sister.'

'But he threw that poor woman's body in the water and hid what killed her – it *was* him, wasn't it?'

Alec and I had spent long hours discussing exactly what happened after Mrs Addie entered her mud bath that Sunday night in September. One thing we had agreed on was that Regina and Mrs Cronin were innocents in the matter, or at least guilty of no more than an abundance of loyalty. Regina was horrified when the truth finally dawned upon her, and Mrs Cronin had spent the last month at the Hydro trying to be everywhere at once in case Dorothea forgot someone again. No good would come of pointing the police in their direction, besmirching their good names and thrilling the newspapers.

When it came to the Laidlaws, however, we found it harder to see eye to eye. I blamed Tot for just about everything; Dorothea forgot her patient and failed to tell the truth about it, swept up in her brother's schemes. But I was sure it was Tot who found the body, washed it, handed it to Regina, signed up Dr Ramsay and lied to the police about the outing and the ghost. At some point in the grisly process, Dorothea found out what he was doing, certainly, but whether she happened upon him at the pool, actually dousing the poor dead Mrs Addie in cold water, or answered the door to Dr Ramsay and wondered what he was doing there, Tot was the engineer of it all.

Alec did not agree. He made the admittedly compelling point that Tot's usual round would not suddenly take him into the ladies' baths one evening and that Dorothea must at least have found the body and turned to him for help in dealing with it. I argued him down: he might well have gone there looking for his sister; knowing the kind of man he was, he might have gone looking for someone who was not his sister. But, in the end, Dorothea Laidlaw was too sensitive a topic for Alec and me to argue for long.

I returned my attention to Merrick, who had got on to Ramsay himself by this time.

'Although Laidlaw's at least partly responsible for what happened to Ramsay in the end,' he was saying.

'Wholly responsible,' said Alec fiercely. 'Tot killed Ramsay plain and simple.' He suspected me of blaming myself for Dr Ramsay's death and was always most vociferous about Laidlaw's guilt any time the matter arose between us.

'Ah, but Ramsay's never going to melt a jury's hearts,' Merrick said. 'He put his name to the death certificate of a murder victim to escape his gambling debts. And he spun ghost stories. Some of my "colleagues" are easily angry enough to give Laidlaw's lawyers chapter and verse on that one. And then Ramsay isn't a local man and the Laidlaws are Moffat from generations back. I can't see fifteen good Dumfries men letting him swing.'

'But he's a fiend,' I said. 'He's brought nothing but shame on the town and the county.'

'It would be shame to you, Mrs Gilver, and to me,' Merrick said. 'But others have a taste for notoriety we don't share. He's brought high drama, filled all the inns with newspapermen, he's rid the place of a white elephant and made space to build some neat wee houses instead, and it'll be a long while again before Moffat sees its next casino.'

'You really think Laidlaw will have the gall to play his lovable scamp act again after all of this?' I said. 'To a jury?'

'I've no doubt,' said Merrick. 'Of course he'll never see the outside of a prison cell but he'll not be short of visitors either.'

We had arrived at Morningside Road, bustling with motorcars, carriages, carts and trams, bicycles, pedestrians and omnibuses, all surging up from the city or pressing down there. Mr Merrick stopped outside a small tearoom and consulted his watch.

'I believe I shall rest a while here and take refreshment,' he said. 'I've time before my train and the Addies, with their grief, were rather trying.' He took his leave, then ducked inside the tearoom door and left Alec and me to carry on alone.

'I'm almost glad our acquaintance with Loveday Merrick is drawing to a close,' I said presently. 'I find him more than a little unnerving.'

'Yes, I know what you mean,' Alec said. 'That sensation of having one's strings pulled and not quite being able to resist him. For all he said about Tot Laidlaw winning over juries I think Merrick is the real snake-charmer of this case, don't you?'

'I certainly never found *Tot* irresistible,' I said, shuddering.

'Ah, but your senses are honed from years of sniffing out tricksters,' Alec said. 'I say, Dandy?'

'Hm?' I said. We were passing one of those little hat shops one finds in places like Morningside. Just one rather dashing evening cap on a stand in a chiffon-draped window.

'You don't suppose there's anything in it after all, do you? Merrick's peculiar talent, I mean. I mean, who's to say what Mrs Addie's sore back was? I would never have believed her son and daughter could be taken in before I saw it this morning. So maybe they weren't taken in after all. Maybe Merrick isn't just an uncoverer of charlatans. Maybe he's the one nugget of gold amongst the dross. And maybe that's why he dedicates his life to showing the dross for what it is.'

This was quite a long speech for Alec and an even more remarkably candid one. I said nothing for a while. He had seen more death than I ever would if I lived to be ninety and kept detecting until I dropped. If he could bring himself to believe in a soft white light and kindly spirits looking down he might be able to lay who knew what old worries to rest and face the future. He might even be able to contemplate a wife who was more than a sensible girl who wanted a family. He would give his heart, newly minted, to his own true love and not mind the silly nonsense for a minute.

On the other hand, he had just muttered about servants of

truth and he had made a clear distinction between dross and gold. And so it was my turn to risk ridicule.

'There's good news and bad on that score, darling,' I said, and I tucked my hand into his arm where it fitted very well indeed. 'I'm sorry to say that Loveday Merrick wouldn't know an actual ghost if it walked up and spoke to him. That's the bad news. On the other hand . . .' I took a deep breath and told him how it was I came to know.

Facts and Fictions

The ghosts of Moffat do include the Haunted Ram but although the Johnstone Reivers must have spoiled the Beef Tub as a picnic spot during their lives, they are long gone. The well is real but, thankfully, Yellow Mary is not. And while there is a story that William Hare spent a night in The Black Bull we have no information about where he went the next morning or where, in the end, he died.

The Moffat Hydro was real enough until it burned down in 1921. I have merely given it a few extra years and made them eventful ones.

Notes from Mr Pallister's Pantry

Butlering while from home.

A removal to a Highland shooting lodge or a
London house has long been amongst the greatest
challenges to a butler's smooth running of the
household. These modern days, however, even
the best of families, living quietly, in an
ordered fashion, might suddenly present him
with much more.

If a master, or more usually a mistress,
suddenly decides to take off across the country
to rented lodgings, an up-to-date butler,
moving with the times, must be ready, as a
general is ready for a desert campaign.

Provisions are the key. Proper provisioning
is essential to survive any manner of exile. A
household can withstand whatever surroundings,
staffing and equipage a hasty decision might
entail so long as a few small essentials are
packed and brought along. Below are the basic
provisions for breakfast, comprising the barest
essentials to cover an overnight stop. From
this list a skilled butler, housekeeper or
cook can extrapolate luncheon, tea and dinner
requirements accordingly.

Coffee roasted to the master's taste

Tea – breakfast for the mistress

Tea - breakfast for the staff

Cocoa for the nursery

Good dry loaf sugar

Porridge oats ground to the master's taste

Powdered milk in case of disputes with
unsatisfactory local dairies

Butter packed in sealed cold crocks: ditto

Strong flour in case of disputes with
unsatisfactory local bakers

Yeast: ditto

Fine flour: ditto

Jam, marmalade, jelly and honey

Bacon well wrapped in waxed cloth

Eggs, four per person per day of proposed
stay in case of unsatisfactory local farms

One large jug of water per person per day
of proposed stay in case of sour well-water,
hard public water or drought

If a butler making these reasonable requests
should meet with opposition and assurances
that any or even all of his requirements can
be met by unknown merchants and suppliers in an
unknown place, then the responsibility passes
to the opposer and assurer. On his head be it,
come what may.

From Mrs Tilling's Recipes

TABLET

Scottish tablet is easier on the teeth than toffee and many times more delicious than southern fudge. While fudge sticks to the mouth and can be sickly, tablet – with its silky but crumbly texture and its rich and creamy flavour – is always welcome. Mind you, hand on heart, it is fairly sweet.

2lbs of sugar	*A knob of butter*
1 tin of Carnation condensed milk	*1 gill of fresh milk*

Place all the ingredients in a large, heavy-bottomed pan and bring slowly to the boil. Keep boiling, stirring all the time, until the sugar has dissolved. This will take a few minutes. Boiling sugar is very hot – beware.

Remove the smooth mixture from the heat and, beat it very vigorously with a wooden spoon. It will thicken as it cools and, slowly, it will become harder and harder to beat effectively. You must persevere. When the mixture is thick but before it gets stiff, pour it into a buttered shortbread tin and leave it in a cold larder overnight to harden. Then cut it into squares, wrap it in greaseproof paper and tie the little parcels with string.

Nothing is a surer seller at a sale of work, fête or jumble and nothing makes a more thoughtful gift to take when invited for tea.